THE
CIVIL WAR

GREAT AMERICAN WRITERS

THE

CIVIL WAR

THE RED BADGE OF COURAGE
BY STEPHEN CRANE

TALES OF SOLDIERS AND CIVILIANS
BY AMBROSE BIERCE

UNCLE TOM'S CABIN
(*an extract*)
BY HARRIET BEECHER STOWE

GALLERY BOOKS

An Imprint of W. H. Smith Publishers Inc.
112 Madison Avenue
New York City 10016

The Red Badge of Courage by Stephen Crane was first published in 1895
Tales of Soldiers and Civilians by Ambrose Bierce was first published in 1891,
revised in 1898
Uncle Tom's Cabin by Harriet Beecher Stowe was first published in 1852

This volume first published in 1989 by
The Octopus Group Limited
Michelin House, 81 Fulham Road, London SW3 6RB

This edition published in 1989 by Gallery Books
An imprint of W. H. Smith Publishers Inc.
112 Madison Avenue, New York, New York 10016

© 1989 The Octopus Group Limited
ISBN 0 8317 1323 2
Printed at The Bath Press, Avon

CONTENTS

THE
RED BADGE
OF
COURAGE

AN EPISODE OF
THE AMERICAN CIVIL WAR

BY

STEPHEN CRANE

Chapter One

THE COLD PASSED RELUCTANTLY from the earth, and the retiring fogs revealed an army stretched out on the hills, resting. As the landscape changed from brown to green, the army awakened, and began to tremble with eagerness at the noise of rumours. It cast its eyes upon the roads, which were growing from long troughs of liquid mud to proper thoroughfares. A river, amber-tinted in the shadow of its banks, purled at the army's feet; and at night, when the stream had become of a sorrowful blackness, one could see across it the red, eyelike gleam of hostile camp-fires set in the low brows of distant hills.

Once a certain tall soldier developed virtues and went resolutely to wash a shirt. He came flying back from a brook waving his garment bannerlike. He was swelled with a tale he had heard from a reliable friend, who had heard it from a truthful cavalryman, who had heard it from his trustworthy brother, one of the orderlies at division headquarters. He adopted the important air of a herald in red and gold.

'We're goin' t'move t'morrah – sure,' he said pompously to a group in the company street. 'We're goin' way up the river, cut across, an' come around in behint 'em.'

To his attentive audience he drew a loud and elaborate plan of a very brilliant campaign. When he had finished, the blue-clothed men scattered into small arguing groups between the rows of squat brown huts. A negro teamster who had been dancing upon a cracker box with the hilarious encouragement of twoscore soldiers was deserted. He sat mournfully down. Smoke drifted lazily from a multitude of quaint chimneys.

It's a lie that's all it is – a thunderin' lie!' said another private loudly. His smooth face was flushed, and his hands were thrust sulkily into his trousers' pockets. He took the matter as an affront to him. 'I don't believe the derned old army's ever going to move. We're set. I've got ready to move eight times in the last two weeks, and we ain't moved yet.'

The tall soldier felt called upon to defend the truth of a rumour he himself had introduced. He and the loud one came near to fighting over it.

A corporal began to swear before the assemblage. He had just put a costly board floor in his house, he said. During the early spring he had refrained from adding extensively to the comfort of his environment because he had felt that the army might start on the march at any moment. Of late, however, he had been impressed that they were in a sort of eternal camp.

Many of the men engaged in a spirited debate. One outlined in a peculiarly lucid manner all the plans of the commanding general. He was opposed by men who advocated that there were other plans of campaign. They clamored at each other, numbers making futile bids for the popular attention. Meanwhile, the soldier who had fetched the rumor bustled about with much importance. He was continually assailed by questions.

'What's up, Jim?'

'Th' army's goin' t'move.'

'Ah, what yeh talkin' about? How yeh know it is?'

'Well, yeh kin b'lieve me er not, jest as yeh like. I don't care a hang.'

There was much food for thought in the manner in which he replied. He came near to convincing them by disdaining to produce proofs. They grew much excited over it.

There was a youthful private who listened with eager ears to the words of the tall soldier and to the varied comments of his comrades. After receiving a fill of discussions concerning marches and attacks, he went to his hut and crawled through an intricate hole that served it as a door. He wished to be alone with some new thoughts that had lately come to him.

He lay down on a wide bunk that stretched across the end of the room. In the other end, cracker boxes were made to serve as furniture. They were grouped about the fireplace. A picture from an illustrated weekly was upon the log walls, and three rifles were paralleled on pegs. Equipments hung on handy projections, and some tin dishes lay upon a small pile of firewood. A folded tent was serving as a roof. The sunlight, without, beating upon it, made it glow a light yellow shade. A small window shot an oblique square of whiter light upon the cluttered floor. The smoke from the fire at times neglected the clay chimney and wreathed into the room, and this flimsy chimney of clay and sticks made endless threats to set ablaze the whole establishment.

The youth was in a little trance of astonishment. So they were at last going to fight. On the morrow, perhaps, there would be a battle, and he would be in it. For a time he was obliged to labor to make himself believe. He could not accept with assurance an omen that he was about to mingle in one of those great affairs of the earth.

He had, of course, dreamed of battles all his life – of vague and bloody conflicts that had thrilled him with their sweep and fire. In visions he had seen himself in many struggles. He had imagined peoples secure in the shadow of his eagle-eyed prowess. But awake he had regarded battles as crimson blotches on the pages of the past. He had put them as things of the bygone with his thought-images of heavy crowns and high castles. There was a portion of the world's history which he had regarded as the time of wars, but it, he thought, had been long gone over the horizon and had disappeared forever.

From his home his youthful eyes had looked upon the war in his own country with distrust. It must be some sort of play affair. He had long despaired of witnessing a Greeklike struggle. Such would be no more, he had said. Men were better, or more timid. Secular and religious education had effaced the throat-grappling instinct, or else firm finance held in check the passions.

He had burned several times to enlist. Tales of great movements shook the land. They might not be distinctly Homeric, but there seemed to be much glory in them. He had read of marches, sieges, conflicts, and he had longed to see it all. His busy mind had drawn for him large pictures extravagant in color, lurid with breathless deeds.

But his mother had discouraged him. She had affected to look with some contempt upon the quality of his war ardor and patriotism. She could calmly seat herself and with no apparent difficulty give him many hundreds of reasons why he was of vastly more importance on the farm than on the field of battle. She had had certain ways of expression that told him that her statements on the subject came from a deep conviction. Moreover, on her side, was his belief that her ethical motive in the argument was impregnable.

At last, however, he had made firm rebellion against this yellow light thrown upon the color of his ambitions. The newspapers, the gossip of the village, his own picturings, had aroused him to an uncheckable degree. They were in truth fighting down there. Almost every day the newspapers printed accounts of a decisive victory.

One night, as he lay in bed, the winds had carried to him the clangoring of the church bell as some enthusiast jerked the rope frantically to tell the twisted news of a great battle. This voice of the people rejoicing in the night had made him shiver in a prolonged ecstasy of excitement. Later, he had gone down to his mother's room and had spoken thus: 'Ma, I'm going to enlist.'

'Henry, don't you be a fool,' his mother had replied. She had then covered her face with the quilt. There was an end to the matter for that night.

Nevertheless, the next morning he had gone to a town that was near his mother's farm and had enlisted in a company that was forming there. When he had returned home his mother was milking the brindle cow. Four others stood waiting. 'Ma, I've enlisted,' he had said to her diffidently. There was a short silence. 'The Lord's will be done, Henry,' she had finally replied, and had then continued to milk the brindle cow.

When he had stood in the doorway with his soldier's clothes on his back, and with the light of excitement and expectancy in his eyes almost defeating the glow of regret for the home bonds, he had seen two tears leaving their trails on his mother's scarred cheeks.

Still, she had disappointed him by saying nothing whatever about returning with his shield or on it. He had privately primed himself for a beautiful scene. He had prepared certain sentences which he thought could be used with touching effect. But her words destroyed his plans. She had doggedly peeled potatoes and addressed him as follows: 'You watch out, Henry, an' take good care of yerself in this here fighting business – you watch out, an' take good care of yerself. Don't go a-thinkin' you can lick the hull rebel army at the start, because yeh can't. Yer jest one little feller amongst a hull lot of others, and yeh've got to keep quiet an' do what they tell yeh. I know how you are, Henry.

'I've knet yeh eight pair of socks, Henry, and I've put in all yer best shirts, because I want my boy to be jest as warm and comf'able as anybody in the army. Whenever they get holes in 'em, I want yeh to send 'em right-away back to me, so's I kin dern 'em.

'An' allus be careful an' choose yer comp'ny. There's lots of bad men in the army, Henry. The army makes 'em wild, and they like nothing better than the job of leading off a young feller like you, as ain't never been away from home much and has allus had a mother, an' a-learning 'em to drink and swear. Keep clear of them folks, Henry. I don't want yeh to ever do anything, Henry, that yeh would be 'shamed to let me know about. Jest think as if I was a-watchin' yeh. If yeh keep that in yer mind allus, I guess yeh'll come out about right.

'Yeh must allus remember yer father, too, child, an' remember he never drunk a drop of licker in his life, and seldom swore a cross oath.

'I don't know what else to tell yeh, Henry, excepting that yeh must never do no shirking, child, on my account. If so be a time comes when yeh have to be kilt or do a mean thing, why, Henry, don't think of anything 'cept what's right, because there's many a woman has to bear up 'ginst sech things these times, and the Lord'll take keer of us all.

'Don't forgit about the socks and the shirts, child; and I've put a cup of blackberry jam with yer bundle, because I know yeh like it above all things. Good-by, Henry. Watch out, and be a good boy.'

He had, of course, been impatient under the ordeal of this speech. It had not been quite what he expected, and he had borne it with an air or irritation. He departed feeling vague relief.

Still, when he had looked back from the gate, he had seen his mother kneeling among the potato parings. Her brown face, upraised, was stained with tears, and her spare form was quivering. He bowed his head and went on, feeling suddenly ashamed of his purposes.

From his home he had gone to the seminary to bid adieu to many schoolmates. They had thronged about him with wonder and admiration. He had felt the gulf now between them and had swelled with calm pride. He and some of his fellows who had donned blue were quite overwhelmed with privileges for all of one afternoon, and it had been a very delicious thing. They had strutted.

A certain light-haired girl had made vivacious fun at his martial spirit, but there was another and darker girl whom he had gazed at steadfastly, and he thought she grew demure and sad at the sight of his blue and brass. As he had walked down the path between the rows of oaks, he had turned his head and detected her at a window watching his departure. As he perceived her, she had immediately begun to stare up through the high tree branches at the sky. He had seen a good deal of flurry and haste in her movement as she changed her attitude. He often thought of it.

On the way to Washington his spirit had soared. The regiment was fed and caressed at station after station until the youth had believed that he must be a hero. There was a lavish expenditure of bread and cold meats, coffee, and pickles and cheese. As he basked in the smiles of the girls and was patted and complimented by the old men, he had felt growing within him the strength to do mighty deeds of arms.

After the complicated journeyings with many pauses, there had come months of monotonous life in a camp. He had had the belief that real war was a series of death struggles with small time in between for sleep and meals; but since his regiment had come to the field the army had done little but sit still and try to keep warm.

He was brought then gradually back to his old ideas. Greeklike struggles would be no more. Men were better, or more timid. Secular and religious education had effaced the throat-grappling instinct, or else firm finance held in check the passions.

He had grown to regard himself merely as a part of a vast blue demonstration. His province was to look out, as far as he could, for his personal comfort. For recreation he could twiddle his thumbs and speculate on the thoughts which must agitate the minds of the generals. Also, he was drilled and drilled and reviewed, and drilled and drilled and reviewed.

The only foes he had seen were some pickets along the river bank. They were a sun-tanned, philosophical lot, who sometimes shot reflectively at the blue pickets. When reproached for this afterward, they usually expressed sorrow, and swore by their gods that the guns had exploded without their permission. The youth, on guard duty one night, conversed across the stream with one of them. He was a slightly ragged man, who spat skillfully between his shoes and possessed a great fund of bland and infantile assurance. The youth liked him personally.

'Yank,' the other had informed him, 'yer a right dum good feller.' This sentiment, floating to him upon the still air, had made him temporarily regret war.

Various veterans had told him tales. Some talked of gray, bewhiskered hordes who were advancing with relentless curses and chewing tobacco with unspeakable valor; tremendous bodies of fierce soldiery who were sweeping along like the Huns. Others spoke of tattered and eternally hungry men who fired despondent powders. 'They'll charge through hell's fire an' brimstone t'git a holt on a haversack, an'sech stomachs ain't a-lastin' long,' he was told. From the stories, the youth imagined the red, live bones sticking out through slits in the faded uniforms.

Still, he could not put a whole faith in veterans' tales, for recruits were their prey. They talked much of smoke, fire, and blood, but he could not tell how much might be lies. They persistently yelled 'Fresh fish!' at him, and were in no wise to be trusted.

However, he perceived now that it did not greatly matter what kind of soldiers he was going to fight, so long as they fought, which fact no one disputed. There was a more serious problem. He lay in his bunk pondering upon it. He tried to mathematically prove to himself that he would not run from a battle.

Previously he had never felt obliged to wrestle too seriously with this question. In his life he had taken certain things for granted, never challenging his belief in ultimate success, and bothering little about means and roads. But here he was confronted with a thing of moment. It had suddenly appeared to him that perhaps in a battle he might run. He was forced to admit that as far as war was concerned he knew nothing of himself.

A sufficient time before he would have allowed the problem to kick its heels at the outer portals of his mind, but now he felt compelled to give serious attention to it.

A little panic-fear grew in his mind. As his imagination went forward to a fight, he saw hideous possibilities. He contemplated the lurking menaces of the future, and failed in an effort to see himself standing stoutly in the midst of them. He recalled his visions of broken-bladed glory, but in the shadow of the impending tumult he suspected them to be impossible pictures.

He sprang from the bunk and began to pace nervously to and fro. Good Lord, what's th'matter with me?' he said aloud.

He felt that in this crisis his laws of life were useless. Whatever he had learned of himself was here of no avail. He was an unknown quantity. He saw that he would again be obliged to experiment as he had in early youth. He must accumulate information of himself, and meanwhile he resolved to remain close upon his guard lest those qualities of which he knew nothing should everlastingly disgrace him. 'Good Lord!' he repeated in dismay.

After a time the tall soldier slid dexterously through the hole. The loud private followed. They were wrangling.

'That's all right,' said the tall soldier as he entered. He waved his hand expressively. 'You can believe me or not, jest as you like. All you got to do is sit down and wait as quiet as you can. Then pretty soon you'll find out I was right.'

His comrade grunted stubbornly. For a moment he seemed to be searching for a formidable reply. Finally he said: 'Well, you don't know everything in the world do you?'

'Didn't say I knew everything in the world,' retorted the other sharply. He began to stow various articles snugly into his knapsack.

The youth, pausing in his nervous walk, looked down at the busy figure. 'Going to be a battle, sure, is there, Jim?' he asked.

'Of course there is,' replied the tall soldier. 'Of course there is. You jest wait 'til to-morrow, and you'll see one of the biggest battles that ever was. You jest wait.'

'Thunder!' said the youth.

'Oh, you'll see fighting this time, my boy, what'll be regular out-and-out fighting,' added the tall soldier, with the air of a man who is about to exhibit a battle for the benefit of his friends.

'Huh!' said the loud one from a corner.

'Well,' remarked the youth, 'like as not this story'll turn out jest like them others did.'

'Not much it won't,' replied the tall soldier, exasperated. 'Not much it won't. Didn't the cavalry all start this morning?' He glared about him. No one denied his statement. 'The cavalry started this morning,' he continued. 'They say there ain't hardly any cavalry left in camp. They're going to Richmond, or some place, while we fight all the Johnnies. It's some dodge like that. The regiment's got orders, too. A feller what seen 'em go to headquarters told me a little while ago. And they're raising blazes all over camp – anybody can see that.'

'Shucks!' said the loud one.

The youth remained silent for a time. At last he spoke to the tall soldier. 'Jim!'

'What?'

'How do you think the reg'ment 'll do?'

'Oh, they'll fight all right, I guess, after they once get into it,' said the other with cold judgment. He made a fine use of the third person. 'There's been heaps of fun poked at 'em because they're new, of course, and all that; but they'll fight all right, I guess.'

'Think any of the boys 'll run?' persisted the youth.

'Oh, there may be a few of 'em run, but there's them kind in every regiment, 'specially when they first goes under fire,' said the other in a tolerant way. 'Of course it might happen that the hull kit-and-boodle might start and run, if some big fighting came first-off, and then again they might stay and fight like fun. But you can't bet on nothing. Of course they ain't never been under fire yet, and it ain't likely they'll lick the hull rebel army all-to-oncet the first time; but I think they'll fight better than some, if worse than others. That's the way I figger. They call the reg'ment "Fresh fish" and everything; but the boys come of good stock, and most of 'em 'll fight like sin after they oncet git shootin',' he added, with a mighty emphasis on the last four words.

'Oh you think you know –' began the loud soldier with scorn.

The other turned savagely upon him. They had a rapid altercation, in which they fastened upon each other various strange epithets.

The youth at last interrupted them. 'Did you ever think you might run yourself, Jim?' he asked. On concluding the sentence he laughed as if he had meant to aim a joke. The loud soldier also giggled.

The tall private waved his hand. 'Well,' said he profoundly, 'I've thought it might get too hot for Jim Conklin in some of them scrimmages, and if a whole lot of boys started and run, why, I s'pose I'd start and run. And if I once started to run, I'd run like the devil, and no mistake. But if everybody was a-standing and a-fighting, why, I'd stand and fight. Be jiminey, I would. I'll bet on it.'

'Huh!' said the loud one.

The youth of this tale felt gratitude for these words of his comrade. He had feared that all of the untried men possessed a great and correct confidence. He now was in a measure reassured.

Chapter Two

THE NEXT MORNING THE YOUTH discovered that his tall comrade had been the fast-flying messenger of a mistake. There was much scoffing at the latter by those who had yesterday been firm adherents of his views, and there was even a little sneering by men who had never believed the rumor. The tall one fought with a man from Chatfield Corners and beat him severely.

The youth felt, however, that his problem was in no wise lifted from him. There was, on the contrary, an irritating prolongation. The tale had created in him a great concern for himself. Now, with the newborn question in his mind, he was compelled to sink back into his old place as part of a blue demonstration.

For days he made ceaseless calculations, but they were all wondrously unsatisfactory. He found that he could establish nothing. He finally concluded that the only way to prove himself was to go into the blaze, and then figuratively to watch his legs to discover their merits and faults. He reluctantly admitted that he could not sit still and with a mental slate and pencil derive an answer. To gain it, he must have blaze, blood, and danger, even as a chemist requires this, that, and the other. So he fretted for an opportunity.

Meanwhile he continually tried to measure himself by his comrades. The tall soldier, for one, gave him some assurance. This man's serene unconcern dealt him a measure of confidence, for he had known him since childhood, and from his intimate knowledge he did not see how he could be capable of anything that was beyond him, the youth. Still, he thought that his comrade might be mistaken about himself. Or, on the other hand, he might be a man heretofore doomed to peace and obscurity, but, in reality, made to shine in war.

The youth would have liked to have discovered another who suspected himself. A sympathetic comparison of mental notes would have been a joy to him.

He occasionally tried to fathom a comrade with seductive sentences. He looked about to find men in the proper mood. All attempts failed to bring forth any statement which looked in any way like a confession to those doubts which he privately acknowledged in himself. He was afraid to make an open declaration of his concern, because he dreaded to place some unscrupulous confidant upon the high plane of the unconfessed from which elevation he could be derided.

In regard to his companions his mind wavered between two opinions, according to his mood. Sometimes he inclined to believing them all heroes. In fact, he usually admitted in secret the superior development of the higher qualities in others. He could conceive of men going very insignificantly about the world bearing a load of courage unseen, and although he had known many of his comrades through boyhood, he began to fear that his judgment of them had been blind. Then, in other moments, he flouted these theories, and assured himself that his fellows were all privately wondering and quaking.

His emotions made him feel strange in the presence of men who talked excitedly of a prospective battle as of a drama they were about to witness, with nothing but eagerness and curiosity apparent in their faces. It was often that he suspected them to be liars.

He did not pass such thoughts without severe condemnation of himself. He dinned reproaches at times. He was convicted by himself of many shameful crimes against the gods of traditions.

In his great anxiety his heart was continually clamoring at what he considered the intolerable slowness of the generals. They seemed content to perch tranquilly on the river bank, and leave him bowed down by the weight of a great problem. He wanted it settled forthwith. He could not long bear such a load, he said. Sometimes his anger at the commanders reached an acute stage, and he grumbled about the camp like a veteran.

One morning, however, he found himself in the ranks of his prepared regiment. The men were whispering speculations and recounting the old rumors. In the gloom before the break of the day their uniforms glowed a deep purple hue. From across the river the red eyes were still peering. In the eastern sky there was a yellow patch like a rug laid for the feet of the coming sun; and against it, black and patternlike, loomed the gigantic figure of the colonel on a gigantic horse.

From off in the darkness came the trampling of feet. The youth could occasionally see dark shadows that moved like monsters. The regiment stood at rest for what seemed a long time. The youth grew impatient. It was unendurable the way these affairs were managed. He wondered how long they were to be kept waiting.

As he looked all about him and pondered upon the mystic gloom, he began to believe that at any moment the ominous distance might be aflare, and the rolling crashes of an engagement come to his ears. Staring once at the red eyes across the river, he conceived them to be growing larger, as the orbs of a row of dragons approaching. He turned toward the colonel and saw him lift his gigantic arm and calmly stroke his mustache.

At last he heard from along the road at the foot of the hill the clatter of a horse's galloping hoofs. It must be the coming of orders. He bent forward, scarce breathing. The exciting clickety-click, as it grew louder and louder, seemed to be beating upon his soul. Presently a horseman with jangling equipment drew rein before the colonel of the regiment. The two held a short, sharp-worded conversation. The men in the foremost ranks craned their necks.

As the horseman wheeled his animal and galloped away he turned to shout over his shoulder, 'Don't forget that box of cigars!' The colonel mumbled in reply. The youth wondered what a box of cigars had to do with the war.

A moment later the regiment went swinging off into the darkness. It was now like one of those moving monsters wending with many feet. The air was heavy, and cold with dew. A mass of wet grass, marched upon, rustled like silk.

There was an occasional flash and glimmer of steel from the backs of all these huge crawling reptiles. From the road came creakings and grumblings as some surly guns were dragged away.

The men stumbled along still muttering speculations. There was a subdued debate. Once a man fell down, and as he reached for his rifle a comrade, unseeing, trod upon his hand. He of the injured fingers swore bitterly and aloud. A low, tittering laugh went among his fellows.

Presently they passed into a roadway and marched forward with easy strides. A dark regiment moved before them, and from behind also came the tinkle of equipments on the bodies of marching men.

The rushing yellow of the developing day went on behind their backs. When the sunrays at last struck full and mellowingly upon the earth, the youth saw that the landscape was streaked with two long, thin, black columns which disappeared on the brow of a hill in front and rearward vanished in a wood. They were like two serpents crawling from the cavern of the night.

The river was not in view. The tall soldier burst into praises of what he thought to be his powers of perception.

Some of the tall one's companions cried with emphasis that they, too, had evolved the same thing, and they congratulated themselves upon it. But there were others who said that the tall one's plan was not the true one at all. They persisted with other theories. There was a vigorous discussion.

The youth took no part in them. As he walked along in careless line he was engaged with his own eternal debate. He could not hinder himself from dwelling upon it. He was despondent and sullen, and threw shifting glances about him. He looked ahead, often expecting to hear from the advance the rattle of firing.

But the long serpents crawled slowly from hill to hill without bluster of smoke. A dun-colored cloud of dust floated away to the right. The sky overhead was of a fairy blue.

The youth studied the faces of his companions, ever on the watch to detect kindred emotions. He suffered disappointment. Some ardor of the air which was causing the veteran commands to move with glee – almost with song – had infected the new regiment. The men began to speak of victory as of a thing they knew. Also, the tall soldier received his vindication. They were certainly going to come around in behind the enemy. They expressed commiseration for that part of the army which had been left upon the river bank, felicitating themselves upon being a part of a blasting host.

The youth, considering himself as separated from the others, was saddened by the blithe and merry speeches that went from rank to rank. The company wags all made their best endeavours. The regiment tramped to the tune of laughter.

The blatant soldier often convulsed whole files by his biting sarcasms aimed at the tall one.

And it was not long before all the men seemed to forget their mission. Whole brigades grinned in unison, and regiments laughed.

A rather fat soldier attempted to pilfer a horse from a dooryard. He planned to load his knapsack upon it. He was escaping with his prize when a young girl rushed from the house and grabbed the animal's mane. There followed a wrangle. The young girl, with pink cheeks and shining eyes, stood like a dauntless statue.

The observant regiment, standing at rest in the roadway, whooped at once, and entered whole-souled upon the side of the maiden. The men became so engrossed in this affair that they entirely ceased to remember their own large war. They jeered the piratical private, and called attention to various defects in his personal appearance; and they were wildly enthusiastic in support of the young girl.

To her, from some distance, came bold advice. 'Hit him with a stick.'

There were crows and catcalls showered upon him when he retreated without the horse. The regiment rejoiced at his downfall. Loud and vociferous congratulations were showered upon the maiden, who stood panting and regarding the troops with defiance.

At nightfall the column broke into regimental pieces, and the fragments went into the fields to camp. Tents sprang up like strange plants. Camp fires, like red, peculiar blossoms, dotted the night.

The youth kept from intercourse with his companions as much as circumstances would allow him. In the evening he wandered a few paces into the gloom. From this little distance the many fires, with the black forms of men passing to and fro before the crimson rays, made weird and satanic effects.

He lay down in the grass. The blades pressed tenderly against his cheek. The moon had been lighted and was hung in a treetop. The liquid stillness of the night enveloping him made him feel vast pity for himself. There was a caress in the soft winds; and the whole mood of the darkness, he thought, was one of sympathy for himself in his distress.

He wished, without reserve, that he was at home again making the endless rounds from the house to the barn, from the barn to the fields, from the fields to the barn, from the barn to the house. He remembered he had often cursed the brindle cow and her mates, and had sometimes flung milking stools. But, from his present point of view, there was a halo of happiness about each of their heads, and he would have sacrificed all the brass buttons on the continent to have been enabled to return to them. He told himself that he was not formed for a soldier. And he mused seriously upon the radical differences between himself and those men who were dodging implike around the fires.

As he mused thus he heard the rustle of grass, and, upon turning his head, discovered the loud soldier. He called out, 'Oh, Wilson!'

The latter approached and looked down. 'Why, hello, Henry; is it you? What you doing here?'

'Oh, thinking,' said the youth.

The other sat down and carefully lighted his pipe. 'You're getting blue, my boy. You're looking thundering peeked. What the dickens is wrong with you?'

'Oh, nothing,' said the youth.

The loud soldier launched then into the subject of the anticipated fight. 'Oh, we've got 'em now!' As he spoke his boyish face was wreathed in a gleeful smile, and his voice had an exultant ring. 'We've got 'em now. At last, by the eternal thunders, we'll lick 'em good!

'If the truth was known,' he added more soberly, 'they've licked us about every clip up to now; but this time – this time – we'll lick 'em good!'

'I thought you was objecting to this march a little while ago,' said the youth coldly.

'Oh, it wasn't that,' explained the other. 'I don't mind marching, if there's going to be fighting at the end of it. What I hate is this getting moved here and moved there, with no good coming of it, as far as I can see, excepting sore feet and damned short rations.'

'Well, Jim Conklin says we'll get a plenty of fighting this time.'

'He's right for once, I guess, though I can't see how it come. This time we're in for a big battle, and we've got the best end of it, certain sure. Gee rod! how we will thump 'em!'

He arose and began to pace to a fro excitedly. The thrill of his enthusiasm made him walk with an elastic step. He was sprightly, vigorous, fiery in his belief in success. He looked into the future with clear, proud eye, and he swore with the air of an old soldier.

The youth watched him for a moment in silence. When he finally spoke his voice was as bitter as dregs. 'Oh, you're going to do great things, I s'pose!'

The loud soldier blew a thoughtful cloud of smoke from his pipe. 'Oh, I don't know,' he remarked with dignity; 'I don't know. I s'pose I'll do as well as the rest. I'm going to try like thunder.' He evidently complimented himself upon the modesty of this statement.

'How do you know you won't run when the time comes?' asked the youth.

'Run?' said the loud one; 'run? – of course not!' he laughed.

'Well,' continued the youth, 'lots of good-a-'nough men have thought they was going to do great things before the fight, but when the time come they skedaddled.'

'Oh, that's all true, I s'pose,' replied the other; 'but I'm not going to skedaddle. The man that bets on my running will lose his money, that's all.' He nodded confidently.

'Oh, shucks!' said the youth. 'You ain't the bravest man in the world, are you?'

'No, I ain't,' exclaimed the loud soldier indignantly; 'and I didn't say I was the bravest man in the world, neither. I said I was going to do my share of fighting – that's what I said. And I am, too. Who are you, anyhow? You talk as if you thought you was Napoleon Bonaparte.' He glared at the youth for a moment, and then strode away.

The youth called in a savage voice after his comrade: 'Well, you needn't git mad about it!' But the other continued on his way and made no reply.

He felt alone in space when his injured comrade had disappeared. His failure to discover any mite of resemblance in their view points made him more miserable than before. No one seemed to be wrestling with such a terrific personal problem. He was a mental outcast.

He went slowly to his tent and stretched himself on a blanket by the side of the snoring tall soldier. In the darkness he saw visions of a thousand-tongued fear that would babble at his back and cause him to flee, while others were going coolly about their country's business. He admitted that he would not be able to cope with this monster. He felt that every nerve in his body would be an ear to hear the voices, while other men would remain stolid and deaf.

And as he sweated with the pain of these thoughts, he could hear low, serene sentences. 'I'll bid five.' 'Make it six.' 'Seven.' 'Seven goes.'

He stared at the red, shivering reflection of a fire on the white wall of his tent until, exhausted and ill from the monotony of his suffering, he fell asleep.

Chapter Three

WHEN ANOTHER NIGHT CAME the columns, changed to purple streaks, filed across two pontoon bridges. A glaring fire wine-tinted the waters of the river. Its rays, shining upon the moving masses of troops, brought forth here and there sudden gleams of silver or gold. Upon the other shore a dark and mysterious range of hills was curved against the sky. The insect voices of the night sang solemnly.

After this crossing the youth assured himself that at any moment they might be suddenly and fearfully assaulted from the caves of the lowering woods. He kept his eyes watchfully upon the darkness.

But his regiment went unmolested to a camping place, and its soldiers slept the brave sleep of wearied men. In the morning they were routed out with early energy, and hustled along a narrow road that led deep into the forest.

It was during this rapid march that the regiment lost many of the marks of a new command.

The men had begun to count the miles upon their fingers, and they grew tired. 'Sore feet an' damned short rations, that's all,' said the loud soldier. There was perspiration and grumblings. After a time they began to shed their knapsacks. Some tossed them unconcernedly down; others hid them carefully, asserting their plans to return for them at some convenient time. Men extricated themselves from thick shirts. Presently few carried anything but their necessary clothing, blankets, haversacks, canteens, and arms and ammunition. 'You can now eat and shoot,' said the tall soldier to the youth. 'That's all you want to do.'

There was sudden change from the ponderous infantry of theory to the light and speedy infantry of practice. The regiment, relieved of a burden, received a new impetus. But there was much loss of valuable knapsacks, and, on the whole, very good shirts.

But the regiment was not yet veteranlike in appearance. Veteran regiments in the army were likely to be very small aggregations of men. Once, when the command had first come to the field, some perambulating veterans, noting the length of their column, had accosted them thus: 'Hey, fellers, what brigade is that?' And when the men had replied that they formed a regiment and not a brigade, the older soldiers had laughed, and said, 'O Gawd!'

Also, there was too great a similarity in the hats. The hats of a regiment should properly represent the history of headgear for a period of years. And, moreover, there were no letters of faded gold speaking from the colors. They were new and beautiful, and the color bearer habitually oiled the pole.

Presently the army again sat down to think. The odor of the peaceful pines was in the men's nostrils. The sound of monotonous axe blows ran through the forest, and the insects, nodding upon their perches, crooned like old women. The youth returned to his theory of a blue demonstration.

One gray dawn, however, he was kicked in the leg by the tall soldier, and then, before he was entirely awake, he found himself running down a wood road in the midst of men who were panting from the first effects of speed. His canteen banged rhythmically upon his thigh, and his haversack bobbed softly. His musket bounced a trifle from his shoulder at each stride and made his cap feel uncertain upon his head.

He could hear the men whisper in jerky sentences: 'Say – what's all this – about?' 'What th' thunder – we – skedaddlin' this way fer?' 'Billie – keep off m' feet. Yeh run – like a cow.' And the loud soldier's shrill voice could be heard: 'What th' devil they in sich a hurry for?'

The youth thought the damp fog of early morning moved from the rush of a great body of troops. From the distance came a sudden spattering of firing.

He was bewildered. As he ran with his comrades he strenuously tried to think, but all he knew was that if he fell down those coming behind would tread upon him. All his faculties seemed to be needed to guide him over and past obstructions. He felt carried along by a mob.

The sun spread disclosing rays, and, one by one, regiments burst into view like armed men just born of the earth. The youth perceived that the time had come. He was about to be measured. For a moment he felt in the face of his great trial like a babe, and the flesh over his heart seemed very thin. He seized time to look about him calculatingly.

But he instantly saw that it would be impossible for him to escape from the regiment. It inclosed him. And there were iron laws of tradition and law on four sides. He was in a moving box.

As he perceived this fact it occurred to him that he had never wished to come to the war. He had not enlisted of his free will. He had been dragged by the merciless government. And now they were taking him out to be slaughtered.

The regiment slid down a bank and wallowed across a little stream. The mournful current moved slowly on, and from the water, shaded black, some white bubble eyes looked at the men.

As they climbed the hill on the farther side artillery began to boom. Here the youth forgot many things as he felt a sudden impulse of curiosity. He scrambled up the bank with a speed that could not be exceeded by a bloodthirsty man.

He expected a battle scene.

There were some little fields girted and squeezed by a forest. Spread over the grass and in among the tree trunks, he could see knots and waving lines of skirmishers who were running hither and thither and firing at the landscape. A dark battle line lay upon a sunstruck clearing that gleamed orange color. A flag fluttered.

Other regiments floundered up the bank. The brigade was formed in line of battle, and after a pause started slowly through the woods in the rear of the receding skirmishers, who were continually melting into the scene to appear again farther on. They were always busy as bees, deeply absorbed in their little combats.

The youth tried to observe everything. He did not use care to avoid trees and branches, and his forgotten feet were constantly knocking against stones or getting entangled in briers. He was aware that these battalions with their commotions were woven red and startling into the gentle fabric of softened greens and browns. It looked to be a wrong place for a battlefield.

The skirmishers in advance fascinated him. Their shots into thickets and at distant and prominent trees spoke to him of tragedies – hidden, mysterious, solemn.

Once the line encountered the body of a dead soldier. He lay upon his back staring at the sky. He was dressed in an awkward suit of yellowish brown. The youth could see the soles of his shoes had been worn to the thinness of writing paper, and from a great rent in one the dead foot projected piteously. And it was as if fate had betrayed the soldier. In death, it exposed to his enemies that poverty which in life he had perhaps concealed from his friends.

The ranks opened covertly to avoid the corpse. The invulnerable dead man forced a way for himself. The youth looked keenly at the ashen face. The wind raised the tawny beard. It moved as if a hand were stroking it. He vaguely desired to walk around and around the body and stare; the impulse of the living to try to read in dead eyes the answer to the Question.

During the march the ardor the youth had acquired when out of view rapidly faded to nothing. His curiosity was quite easily satisfied. If an intense scene had caught him with its wild swing as he came to the top of the bank, he might have gone roaring on. This advance upon Nature was too calm. He had opportunity to reflect. He had time in which to wonder about himself and to attempt to probe his sensations.

Absurd ideas took hold upon him. He thought that he did not relish the landscape. It threatened him. A coldness swept over his back, and it is true that his trousers felt to him that they were no fit for his legs at all.

A house standing placidly in distant fields had to him an ominous look. The shadows of the wood were formidable. He was certain that in this vista there lurked fierce-eyed hosts. The swift thought came to him that the generals did not know what they were about. It was all a trap. Suddenly those close forests would bristle with rifle barrels. Ironlike brigades would appear in the rear. They were all going to be sacrificed. The generals were stupids. The enemy would presently swallow the whole command. He glared about him, expecting to see the stealthy approach of his death.

He thought that he must break from the ranks and harangue his comrades. They must not all be killed like pigs; and he was sure it would come to pass unless they were informed of these dangers. The generals were idiots to send them marching into a regular pen. There was but one pair of eyes in the corps. He would step forth and make a speech. Shrill and passionate words came to his lips.

The line, broken into moving fragments by the ground, went calmly on through fields and woods. The youth looked at the men nearest him, and saw, for the most part, expressions of deep interest, as if they were investigating something that had fascinated them. One or two stepped with overvaliant airs as if they were already plunged into war. Others walked as upon thin ice. The greater part of the untested men appeared quiet and absorbed. They were going to look at war, the red animal – war, the blood-swollen god. And they were deeply engrossed in this march.

As he looked the youth gripped his outcry at his throat. He saw that even if the men were tottering with fear they would laugh at his warning. They would jeer him, and, if practicable, pelt him with missiles. Admitting that he might be wrong, a frenzied declamation of the kind would turn him into a worm.

He assumed, then, the demeanor of one who knows that he is doomed alone to unwritten responsibilities. He lagged, with tragic glances at the sky.

He was surprised presently by the young lieutenant of his company, who began heartily to beat him with a sword, calling out in a loud and insolent voice: 'Come, young man, get up into the ranks there. No skulking 'll do here.' He mended his pace with suitable haste. And he hated the lieutenant, who had no appreciation of fine minds. He was a mere brute.

After a time the brigade was halted in the cathedral light of a forest. The busy skirmishers were still popping. Through the aisles of the wood could be seen the floating smoke from their rifles. Sometimes it went up in little balls, white and compact.

During this halt many men in the regiment began erecting tiny hills in front of them. They used stones, sticks, earth, and anything they thought might turn a bullet. Some built comparatively large ones, while others seemed content with little ones.

This procedure caused a discussion among the men. Some wished to fight like duelists, believing it to be correct to stand erect and be, from their feet to their foreheads, a mark. They said they scorned the devices of the cautious. But the others scoffed in reply, and pointed to the veterans on the flanks who were digging at the ground like terriers. In a short time there was quite a barricade along the regimental fronts. Directly, however, they were ordered to withdraw from that place.

This astounded the youth. He forgot his stewing over the advance movement. 'Well, then, what did they march us out here for?' he demanded of the tall soldier. The latter with calm faith began a heavy explanation, although he had been compelled to leave a little protection of stones and dirt to which he had devoted much care and skill.

When the regiment was aligned in another position each man's regard for his safety caused another line of small intrenchments. They ate their noon meal behind a third one. They were moved from this one also. They were marched from place to place with apparent aimlessness.

The youth had been taught that a man became another thing in a battle. He saw his salvation in such a change. Hence this waiting was an ordeal to him. He was in a fever of impatience. He considered that there was denoted a lack of purpose on the part of the generals. He began to complain to the tall soldier. 'I can't stand this much longer,' he cried. 'I don't see what good it does to make us wear out our legs for nothin'.' He wished to return to camp, knowing that this affair was a blue demonstration; or else to go into a battle and discover that he had been a fool in his doubts, and was, in truth, a man of traditional courage. The strain of present circumstances he felt to be intolerable.

The philosophical tall soldier measured a sandwich of cracker and pork and swallowed it in a nonchalant manner. 'Oh, I suppose we must go reconnoitering around the country jest to keep 'em from getting too close, or to develop 'em or something.'

'Huh!' said the loud soldier.

'Well,' cried the youth, still fidgeting, 'I'd rather do anything 'most than go tramping 'round the country all day long doing no good to nobody and jest tiring ourselves out.'

'So would I,' said the loud soldier. 'It ain't right. I tell you if anybody with any sense was a-runnin' this army it –'

'Oh, shut up!' roared the tall private. 'You little fool. You little damn' cuss. You ain't had that there coat and them pants for six months, and yet you talk as if –'

'Well, I wanta do some fighting anyway,' interrupted the other. 'I didn't come here to walk. I could 'ave walked to home – 'round an' 'round the barn, if I jest wanted to walk.'

The tall one, red-faced, swallowed another sandwich as if taking poison in despair.

But gradually, as he chewed, his face became again quiet and contented. He could not rage in fierce argument in the presence of such sandwiches. During his meals he always wore an air of blissful contemplation of the food he had swallowed. His spirit seemed then to be communing with the viands.

He accepted new environment and circumstance with great coolness, eating from his haversack at every opportunity. On the march he went along with the stride of a hunter, objecting to neither gait nor distance. And he had not raised his voice when he had been ordered away from three little protective piles of earth and stone, each of which had been an engineering feat worthy of being made sacred to the name of his grandmother.

In the afternoon the regiment went out over the same ground it had taken in the morning. The landscape then ceased to threaten the youth. He had been close to it and become familiar with it.

When, however, they began to pass into a new region, his old fears of stupidity and incompetence reassailed him, but this time he doggedly let them babble. He was occupied with his problem, and in his desperation he concluded that the stupidity did not greatly matter.

Once he thought he had concluded that it would be better to get killed directly and end his troubles. Regarding death thus out of the corner of his eye, he conceived it to be nothing but rest, and he was filled with a momentary astonishment that he should have made an extraordinary commotion over the mere matter of getting killed. He would die; he would go to some place where he would be understood. It was useless to expect appreciation of his profound and fine senses from such men as the lieutenant. He must look to the grave for comprehension.

The skirmish fire increased to a long clattering sound. With it was mingled far-away cheering. A battery spoke.

Directly the youth would see the skirmishers running. They were pursued by the sound of musketry fire. After a time the hot, dangerous flashes of the rifles were visible. Smoke clouds went slowly and insolently across the fields like observant phantoms. The din became crescendo, like the roar of an oncoming train.

A brigade ahead of them and on the right went into action with a rending roar. It was as if it had exploded. And thereafter it lay stretched in the distance behind a long gray wall, that one was obliged to look twice at to make sure that it was smoke.

The youth, forgetting his neat plan of getting killed, gazed spellbound. His eyes grew wide and busy with the action of the scene. His mouth was a little ways open.

Of a sudden he felt a heavy and sad hand laid upon his shoulder. Awakening from his trance of observation he turned and beheld the loud soldier.

'It's my first and last battle, old boy,' said the latter, with intense gloom. He was quite pale and his girlish lip was trembling.

'Eh?' murmured the youth in great astonishment.

'It's my first and last battle, old boy,' continued the loud soldier. 'Something tells me —'

'What?'

'I'm a gone coon this first time and — and I w-want you to take these here things — to — my — folks.' He ended in a quavering sob of pity for himself. He handed the youth a little packet done up in a yellow envelope.

'Why, what the devil —' began the youth again.

But the other gave him a glance as from the depths of a tomb, and raised his limp hand in a prophetic manner and turned away.

Chapter Four

THE BRIGADE WAS HALTED IN the fringe of a grove. The men crouched among the trees and pointed their restless guns out at the fields. They tried to look beyond the smoke.

Out of this they could see running men. Some shouted information and gestured as they hurried.

The men of the new regiment watched and listened eagerly, while their tongues ran on in gossip of the battle. They mouthed rumors that had flown like birds out of the unknown.

'They say Perry has been driven in with big loss.'

'Yes, Carrott went t' th' hospital. He said he was sick. That smart lieutenant is commanding 'G' Company. Th' boys say they won't be under Carrott no more if they all have t' desert. They allus knew he was a —'

'Hannises' batt'ry is took.'

'It ain't either. I saw Hannises' batt'ry off on th' left not more than fifteen minutes ago.'

'Well —'

'Th' general, he ses he is goin' t' take th' hull cammand of th' 304th when we go inteh action, an' then he ses we'll do sech fightin' as never another one reg'ment done.'

'They say we're catchin' it over on th' left. They say th' enemy driv' our line inteh a devil of a swamp an' took Hannises' batt'ry.'

'No sech thing. Hannises' batt'ry was 'long here 'bout a minute ago.'

'That young Hasbrouck, he makes a good off'cer. He ain't afraid 'a nothin'.'

'I met one of th' 148th Maine boys an' he ses his brigade fit th' hull rebel army fer four hours over on th' turnpike road an' killed about five thousand of 'em. He ses one more sech fight as that an' th' war 'll be over.'

'Bill wasn't scared either. No, sir! It wasn't that. Bill ain't a-gittin' scared easy. He was jest mad, that's what he was. When that feller trod on his hand, he up an' sed that he was willin' t' give his hand t' his country, but he be dumbed if he was goin' t' have every dumb bushwhacker in th' kentry walkin' 'round on it. So he went t' th' hospital disregardless of th' fight. Three fingers was crunched. Th' dern doctor wanted t' amputate 'm, an' Bill, he raised a heluva row, I hear. He's a funny feller.'

The din in front swelled to a tremendous chorus. The youth and his fellows were frozen to silence. They could see a flag that tossed in the smoke angrily. Near it were the blurred and agitated forms of troops. There came a turbulent stream of men across the fields. A battery changing position at a frantic gallop scattered the stragglers right and left.

A shell screaming like a storm banshee went over the huddled heads of the reserves. It landed in the grove, and exploding redly flung the brown earth. There was a little shower of pine needles.

Bullets began to whistle among the branches and nip at the trees. Twigs and leaves came sailing down. It was as if a thousand axes, wee and invisible, were being wielded. Many of the men were constantly dodging and ducking their heads.

The lieutenant of the youth's company was shot in the hand. He began to swear so wondrously that a nervous laugh went along the regimental line. The officer's profanity sounded conventional. It relieved the tightened senses of the new men. It was as if he had hit his fingers with a tack hammer at home.

He held the wounded member carefully away from his side so that the blood would not drip upon his trousers.

The captain of the company, tucking his sword under his arm, produced a handkerchief and began to bind with it the lieutenant's wound. And they disputed as to how the binding should be done.

The battle flag in the distance jerked about madly. It seemed to be struggling to free itself from an agony. The billowing smoke was filled with horizontal flashes.

Men running swiftly emerged from it. They grew in numbers until it was seen that the whole command was fleeing. The flag suddenly sank down as if dying. Its motion as it fell was a gesture of despair.

Wild yells came from behind the walls of smoke. A sketch in gray and red dissolved into a moblike body of men who galloped like wild horses.

The veteran regiments on the right and left of the 304th immediately began to jeer. With the passionate song of the bullets and the banshee shrieks of shells were mingled loud catcalls and bits of facetious advice concerning places of safety.

But the new regiment was breathless with horror. 'Gawd! Saunders's got crushed!' whispered the man at the youth's elbow. They shrank back and crouched as if compelled to await a flood.

The youth shot a swift glance along the blue ranks of the regiment. The profiles were motionless, carven; and afterward he remembered that the color sergeant was standing with his legs apart, as if he expected to be pushed to the ground.

The following throng went whirling around the flank. Here and there were officers carried along on the stream like exasperated chips. They were striking about them with their swords and with their left fists, punching every head they could reach. They cursed like highwaymen.

A mounted officer displayed the furious anger of a spoiled child. He raged with his head, his arms, and his legs.

Another, the commander of the brigade, was galloping about bawling. His hat was gone and his clothes were awry. He resembled a man who has come from bed to go to a fire. The hoofs of his horse often threatened the heads of the running men, but they scampered with singular fortune. In this rush they were apparently all deaf and blind. They heeded not the largest and longest of the oaths that were thrown at them from all directions.

Frequently over this tumult could be heard the grim jokes of the critical veterans; but the retreating men apparently were not even conscious of the presence of an audience.

The battle reflection that shone for an instant in the faces on the mad current made the youth feel that forceful hands from heaven would not have been able to have held him in place if he could have got intelligent control of his legs.

There was an appalling imprint upon these faces. The struggle in the smoke had pictured an exaggeration of itself on the bleached cheeks and in the eyes wild with one desire.

The sight of this stampede exerted a floodlike force that seemed able to drag sticks and stones and men from the ground. They of the reserves had to hold on. They grew pale and firm, and red and quaking.

The youth achieved one little thought in the midst of this chaos. The composite monster which had caused the other troops to flee had not then appeared. He resolved to get a view of it, and then, he thought he might very likely run better than the rest of them.

Chapter Five

THERE WERE MOMENTS OF WAITING. The youth thought of the village street at home before the arrival of the circus parade on a day in the spring. He remembered how he had stood, a small, thrillful boy, prepared to follow the dingy lady upon the white horse, or the band in its faded chariot. He saw the yellow road, the lines of expectant people, and the sober houses. He particularly remembered an old fellow who used to sit upon a cracker box in front of the store and feign to despise such exhibitions. A thousand details of color and form surged in his mind. The old fellow upon the cracker box appeared in middle prominence.

Some one cried, 'Here they come!'

There was rustling and muttering among the men. They displayed a feverish desire to have every possible cartridge ready to their hands. The boxes were pulled around into various positions, and adjusted with great care. It was as if seven hundred new bonnets were being tried on.

The tall soldier, having prepared his rifle, produced a red handkerchief of some kind. He was engaged in knitting it about his throat with exquisite attention to its position, when the cry was repeated up and down the line in a muffled roar of sound.

'Here they come! Here they come!' Gun locks clicked.

Across the smoke-infested fields came a brown swarm of running men who were giving shrill yells. They came on, stooping and swinging their rifles at all angles. A flag, tilted forward, sped near the front.

As he caught sight of them the youth was momentarily startled by a thought that perhaps his gun was not loaded. He stood trying to rally his faltering intellect so that he might recollect the moment when he had loaded, but he could not.

A hatless general pulled his dripping horse to a stand near the colonel of the 304th. He shook his fist in the other's face. 'You've got to hold 'em back!' he shouted, savagely; 'you've got to hold 'em back!'

In his agitation the colonel began to stammer. 'A-all r-right, General, all right, by Gawd! We-we'll do our – we-we'll d-d-do – do our best, General.' The general made a passionate gesture and galloped away. The colonel, perchance to relieve his feelings, began to scold like a wet parrot. The youth, turning swiftly to make sure that the rear was unmolested, saw the commander regarding his men in a highly resentful manner, as if he regretted above everything his association with them.

The man at the youth's elbow was mumbling, as if to himself: 'Oh, we're in for it now! oh, we're in for it now!'

The captain of the company had been pacing excitedly to and fro in the rear. He coaxed in schoolmistress fashion, as to a congregation of boys with primers. His talk was an endless repetition. 'Reserve your fire, boys – don't shoot till I tell you – save your fire – wait till they get close up – don't be damned fools –'

Perspiration streamed down the youth's face, which was soiled like that of a weeping urchin. He frequently, with a nervous movement, wiped his eyes with his coat sleeve. His mouth was still a little ways open.

He got the one glance at the foe-swarming field in front of him, and instantly ceased to debate the question of his piece being loaded. Before he was ready to begin – before he had announced to himself that he was about to fight – he threw the obedient, well-balanced rifle into position and fired a first wild shot. Directly he was working at his weapon like an automatic affair.

He suddenly lost concern for himself, and forgot to look at a menacing fate. He became not a man but a member. He felt that something of which he was a part – a regiment, an army, a cause, or a country – was in a crisis. He was welded into a common personality which was dominated by a single desire. For some moments he could not flee no more than a little finger can commit a revolution from a hand.

If he had thought the regiment was about to be annihilated perhaps he could have amputated himself from it. But its noise gave him assurance. The regiment was like a firework that, once ignited, proceeds superior to circumstances until its blazing vitality fades. It wheezed and banged with a mighty power. He pictured the ground before it as strewn with the discomfited.

There was a consciousness always of the presence of his comrades about him. He felt the subtle battle brotherhood more potent even than the cause for which they were fighting. It was a mysterious fraternity born of the smoke and danger of death.

He was at a task. He was like a carpenter who has made many boxes, making still another box, only there was furious haste in his movements. He, in this thought, was careering off in other places, even as the carpenter who as he works whistles and thinks of his friend or his enemy, his home or a saloon. And these jolted dreams were never perfect to him afterwards, but remained a mass of blurred shapes.

Presently he began to feel the effects of the war atmosphere – a blistering sweat, a sensation that his eyeballs were about to crack like hot stones. A burning roar filled his ears.

Following this came a red rage. He developed the acute exasperation of a pestered animal, a well-meaning cow worried by dogs. He had a mad feeling against his rifle, which could only be used against one life at a time. He wished to rush forward and strangle with his fingers. He craved a power that would enable him to make a world-sweeping gesture and brush all back. His impotency appeared to him, and made his rage into that of a driven beast.

Buried in the smoke of many rifles his anger was directed not so much against the men whom he knew were rushing toward him as against the swirling battle phantoms which were choking him, stuffing their smoke robes down his parched throat. He fought frantically for respite for his senses, for air, as a babe being smothered attacks the deadly blankets.

There was a blare of heated rage mingled with a certain expression of intentness on all faces. Many of the men were making low-toned noises with their mouths, and these subdued cheers, snarls, imprecations, prayers, made a wild, barbaric song that went as an undercurrent of sound, strange and chantlike with the resounding chords of the war march. The man at the youth's elbow was babbling. In it there was something soft and tender like the monologue of a babe. The tall soldier was swearing in a loud voice. From his lips came a black procession of curious oaths. Of a sudden another broke out in a querulous way like a man who had mislaid his hat. 'Well, why don't they support us? Why don't they send supports? Do they think –'

The youth in his battle sleep heard this as one who dozes hears.

There was a singular absence of heroic poses. The men bending and surging in their haste and rage were in every impossible attitude. The steel ramrods clanked and clanged with incessant din as the men pounded them furiously into the hot rifle barrels. The flaps of the cartridge boxes were all unfastened, and bobbed idiotically with each movement. The rifles, once loaded, were jerked to the shoulder and fired without apparent aim into the smoke or at one of the blurred and shifting forms which upon the field before the regiment had been growing larger and larger like puppets under a magician's hand.

The officers, at their intervals, rearward, neglected to stand in picturesque attitudes. They were bobbing to and fro roaring directions and encourage-ments. The dimensions of their howls were extraordinary. They expended their lungs with prodigal wills. And often they nearly stood upon their heads in their anxiety to observe the enemy on the other side of the tumbling smoke.

The lieutenant of the youth's company had encountered a soldier who had fled screaming at the first volley of his comrades. Behind the lines these two were acting out a little isolated scene. The man was blubbering and staring with sheeplike eyes at the lieutenant, who had seized him by the collar and was pommeling him. He drove him back into the ranks with many blows. The soldier went mechanically, dully, with his animal-like eyes upon the officer. Perhaps there was to him a divinity expressed in the voice of the other – stern, hard, with no reflection of fear in it. He tried to reload his gun, but his shaking hands prevented. The lieutenant was obliged to assist him.

The men dropped here and there like bundles. The captain of the youth's company had been killed in an early part of the action. His body lay stretched out in the position of a tired man resting, but upon his face there was an astonished and sorrowful look, as if he thought some friend had done him an ill turn. The babbling man was grazed by a shot that made the blood stream widely down his face. He clapped both hands to his head. 'Oh!' he said, and ran. Another grunted suddenly as if he had been struck by a club in the stomach. He sat down and gazed ruefully. In his eyes there was mute, indefinite reproach. Farther up the line a man, standing by a tree, had had his knee joint splintered by a ball. Immediately he had dropped his rifle and gripped the tree with both arms. And there he remained, clinging desperately and crying for assistance that he might withdraw his hold upon the tree.

At last an exultant yell went along the quivering line. The firing dwindled from an uproar to a last vindictive popping. As the smoke slowly eddied away, the youth saw that the charge had been repulsed. The enemy were scattered into reluctant groups. He saw a man climb to the top of the fence, straddle the rail, and fire a parting shot. The waves had receded, leaving bits of dark *débris* upon the ground.

Some in the regiment began to whoop frenziedly. Many were silent. Apparently they were trying to contemplate themselves.

After the fever had left his veins, the youth thought that at last he was going to suffocate. He became aware of the foul atmosphere in which he had been struggling. He was grimy and dripping like a laborer in a foundry. He grasped his canteen and took a long swallow of the warmed water.

A sentence with variations went up and down the line. 'Well, we've helt 'em, back. We've helt 'em back; derned if we haven't.' The men said it blissfully, leering at each other with dirty smiles.

The youth turned to look behind him and off to the right and off to the left. He experienced the joy of a man who at last finds leisure in which to look about him.

Under foot there were a few ghastly forms motionless. They lay twisted in fantastic contortions. Arms were bent and heads were turned in incredible ways. It seemed that the dead men must have fallen from some great height to get into such positions. They looked to be dumped upon the ground from the sky.

From a position in the rear of the grove a battery was throwing shells over it. The flash of the guns startled the youth at first. He thought they were aimed directly at him. Through the trees he watched the black figures of the gunners as they worked swiftly and intently. Their labor seemed a complicated thing. He wondered how they could remember its formula in the midst of confusion.

The guns squatted in a row like savage chiefs. They argued with abrupt violence. It was a grim pow-wow. Their busy servants ran hither and thither.

A small procession of wounded men were going drearily toward the rear. It was a flow of blood from the torn body of the brigade.

To the right and to the left were the dark lines of other troops. Far in front he thought he could see lighter masses protruding in points from the forest. They were suggestive of unnumbered thousands.

Once he saw a tiny battery go dashing along the line of the horizon. The tiny riders were beating the tiny horses.

From a sloping hill came the sound of cheerings and clashes. Smoke welled slowly through the leaves.

Batteries were speaking with thunderous oratorical effort. Here and there were flags, the red in the stripes dominating. They splashed bits of warm color upon the dark lines of troops.

The youth felt the old thrill at the sight of the emblem. They were like beautiful birds strangely undaunted in a storm.

As he listened to the din from the hillside, to a deep pulsating thunder that came from afar to the left, and to the lesser clamors which came from many directions, it occurred to him that they were fighting, too, over there, and over there, and over there. Heretofore he had supposed that all the battle was directly under his nose.

As he gazed around him the youth felt a flash of astonishment at the blue, pure sky and the sun gleamings on the trees and fields. It was surprising that Nature had gone tranquilly on with her golden process in the midst of so much devilment.

Chapter Six

THE YOUTH AWAKENED SLOWLY. He came gradually back to a position from which he could regard himself. For moments he had been scrutinizing his person in a dazed way as if he had never before seen himself. Then he picked up his cap from the ground. He wriggled in his jacket to make a more comfortable fit, and kneeling relaced his shoe. He thoughtfully mopped his reeking features.

So it was all over at last! The supreme trial had been passed. The red, formidable difficulties of war had been vanquished.

He went into an ecstasy of self-satisfaction. He had the most delightful sensations of his life. Standing as if apart from himself, he viewed that last scene. He perceived that the man who had fought thus was magnificent.

He felt that he was a fine fellow. He saw himself even with those ideals which he had considered as far beyond him. He smiled in deep gratification.

Upon his fellows he beamed tenderness and good will. 'Gee! ain't it hot, hey?' he said affably to a man who was polishing his streaming face with his coat sleeves.

'You bet!' said the other, grinning sociably. 'I never seen sech dumb hotness.' He sprawled out luxuriously on the ground. 'Gee, yes! An' I hope we don't have no more fightin' till a week from Monday.'

There were some handshakings and deep speeches with men whose features were familiar, but with whom the youth now felt the bonds of tied hearts. He helped a cursing comrade to bind up a wound of the shin.

But, of a sudden, cries of amazement broke out along the ranks of the new regiment. 'Here they come ag'in! Here they come ag'in!' The man who had sprawled upon the ground started and said, 'Gosh!'

The youth turned quick eyes upon the field. He discerned forms begin to swell in masses out of a distant wood. He again saw the tilted flag speeding forwards.

The shells, which had ceased to trouble the regiment for a time, came swirling again, and exploded in the grass or among the leaves of the trees. They looked to be strange war flowers bursting into fierce bloom.

The men groaned. The luster faded from their eyes. Their smudged countenances now expressed a profound dejection. They moved their stiffened bodies slowly, and watched in sullen mood the frantic approach of the enemy. The slaves toiling in the temple of this god began to feel rebellion at his harsh tasks.

They fretted and complained each to each. 'Oh, say, this is too much of a good thing! Why can't somebody send us supports?'

'We ain't never going to stand this second banging. I didn't come here to fight the hull damn' rebel army.'

There was one who raised a doleful cry. 'I wish Bill Smithers had trod on my hand, insteader me treddin' on his'n.' The sore joints of the regiment creaked as it painfully floundered into position to repulse.

The youth stared. Surely, he thought, this impossible thing was not about to happen. He waited as if he expected the enemy to suddenly stop, apologize, and retire bowing. It was all a mistake.

But the firing began somewhere on the regimental line and ripped along in both directions. The level sheets of flame developed great clouds of smoke that tumbled and tossed in the mild wind near the ground for a moment, and then rolled through the ranks as through a gate. The clouds were tinged an earthlike yellow in the sunrays and in the shadow were a sorry blue. The flag was sometimes eaten and lost in this mass of vapor, but more often it projected, sun-touched, resplendent.

In the youth's eyes there came a look that one can see in the orbs of a jaded horse. His neck was quivering with nervous weakness and the muscles of his arms felt numb and bloodless. His hands, too, seemed large and awkward as if he was wearing invisible mittens. And there was a great uncertainty about his knee joints.

The words that comrades had uttered previous to the firing began to recur to him. 'Oh, say, this is too much of a good thing! What do they take us for – why don't they send supports? I didn't come here to fight the hull damned rebel army.'

He began to exaggerate the endurance, the skill, and the valor of those who were coming. Himself reeling from exhaustion, he was astonished beyond measure at such persistency. They must be machines of steel. It was very gloomy struggling against such affairs, wound up perhaps to fight until sundown.

He slowly lifted up his rifle and catching a glimpse of the thickspread field he blazed at a cantering cluster. He stopped then and began to peer as best he could through the smoke. He caught changing views of the ground covered with men who were all running like pursued imps, and yelling.

To the youth it was an onslaught of redoubtable dragons. He became like the man who lost his legs at the approach of the red and green monster. He waited in a sort of a horrified, listening attitude. He seemed to shut his eyes and wait to be gobbled.

A man near to him who up to this time had been working feverishly at his rifle suddenly stopped and ran with howls. A lad whose face had borne an expression of exalted courage, the majesty of he who dares give his life, was, at an instant, smitten abject. He blanched like one who has come to the edge of a cliff at midnight and is suddenly made aware. There was a revelation. He, too, threw down his gun and fled. There was no shame in his face. He ran like a rabbit.

Others began to scamper away through the smoke. The youth turned his head, shaken from his trance by this movement as if the regiment was leaving him behind. He saw the few fleeting forms.

He yelled then with fright and swung about. For a moment, in the great clamor, he was like a proverbial chicken. He lost the direction of safety. Destruction threatened him from all points.

Directly he began to speed toward the rear in great leaps. His rifle and cap were gone. His unbuttoned coat bulged in the wind. The flap of his cartridge box bobbed wildly, and his canteen, by its slender cord, swung out behind. On his face was all the horror of those things which he imagined.

The lieutenant sprang forward bawling. The youth saw his features wrathfully red, and saw him make a dab with his sword. His one thought of the incident was that the lieutenant was a peculiar creature to feel interested in such matters upon this occasion.

He ran like a blind man. Two or three times he fell down. Once he knocked his shoulders so heavily against a tree that he went headlong.

Since he had turned his back upon the fight his fears had been wondrously magnified. Death about to thrust him between the shoulder blades was far more dreadful than death about to smite him between the eyes. When he thought of it later, he conceived the impression that it is better to view the appalling than to be merely within hearing. The noises of the battle were like stones; he believed himself liable to be crushed.

As he ran on he mingled with others. He dimly saw men on his right and on his left, and he heard footsteps behind him. He thought that all the regiment was fleeing, pursued by these ominous crashes.

In his flight the sound of these following footsteps gave him his one meager relief. He felt vaguely that death must make a first choice of the men who were nearest; the initial morsels for the dragons would be then those who were following him. So he displayed the zeal of an insane sprinter in his purpose to keep them in the rear. There was a race.

As he, leading, went across a little field, he found himself in a region of shells. They hurtled over his head with long wild screams. As he listened he imagined them to have rows of cruel teeth that grinned at him. Once one lit before him and the livid lightning of the explosion effectually barred the way in his chosen direction. He groveled on the ground and then springing up went careering off through some bushes.

He experienced a thrill of amazement when he came within view of a battery in action. The men there seemed to be in conventional moods, altogether unaware of the impending annihilation. The battery was disputing with a distant antagonist and the gunners were wrapped in admiration of their shooting. They were continually bending in coaxing postures over the guns. They seemed to be patting them on the back and encouraging them with words. The guns, stolid and undaunted, spoke with dogged valor.

The precise gunners were coolly enthusiastic. They lifted their eyes every chance to the smoke-wreathed hillock from whence the hostile battery addressed them. The youth pitied them as he ran. Methodical idiots! Machine-like fools! The refined joy of planting shells in the midst of the other battery's formation would appear a little thing when the infantry came swooping out of the woods.

The face of a youthful rider, who was jerking his frantic horse with an abandon of temper he might display in a placid barnyard, was impressed deeply upon his mind. He knew that he looked upon a man who would presently be dead.

Too, he felt a pity for the guns, standing, six good comrades, in a bold row.

He saw a brigade going to the relief of its pestered fellows. He scrambled upon a wee hill and watched it sweeping finely, keeping formation in difficult places. The blue of the line was crusted with steel color, and brilliant flags projected. Officers were shouting.

The sight also filled him with wonder. The brigade was hurrying briskly to be gulped into the infernal mouths of the war god. What manner of men were they, anyhow? Ah, it was some wondrous breed! Or else they didn't comprehend – the fools.

A furious order caused commotion in the artillery. An officer on a bounding horse made maniacal motions with his arms. The teams went swinging up from the rear, the guns were whirled about, and the battery scampered away. The cannon with their noses poked slantingly at the ground grunted and grumbled like stout men, brave but with objections to hurry.

The youth went on, moderating his pace since he had left the place of noises.

Later he came upon a general of division seated upon a horse that pricked its ears in an interested way at the battle. There was a great gleaming of yellow and patent leather about the saddle and bridle. The quiet man astride looked mouse-colored upon such a splendid charger.

A jingling staff was galloping hither and thither. Sometimes the general was surrounded by horsemen and at other times he was quite alone. He looked to be much harassed. He had the appearance of a business man whose market is swinging up and down.

The youth went slinking around this spot. He went as near as he dared trying to overhear words. Perhaps the general, unable to comprehend the chaos, might call upon him for information. And he could tell him. He knew all concerning it. Of a surety the force was in a fix, and any fool could see that if they did not retreat while they had opportunity – why –

He felt that he would like to thrash the general, or at least approach and tell him in plain words exactly what he thought him to be. It was criminal to stay calmly in one spot and make no effort to stay destruction. He loitered in a fever of eagerness for the division commander to apply to him.

As he warily moved about, he heard the general call out irritably: 'Tompkins, go over an' see Taylor, an' tell him not t' be in such an all-fired hurry; tell him t' halt his brigade in th' edge of th' woods; tell him t' detach a reg'ment – say I think th' center 'll break if we don't help it out some; tell him t' hurry up.'

A slim youth on a fine chestnut horse caught these swift words from the mouth of his superior. He made his horse bound into a gallop almost from a walk in his haste to go upon his mission. There was a cloud of dust.

A moment later the youth saw the general bounce excitedly in his saddle.

'Yes, by heavens, they have!' The officer leaned forward. His face was aflame with excitement. 'Yes, by heavens, they've held 'im! They've held 'im!'

He began to blithely roar at his staff: 'We'll wallop 'im now. We'll wallop 'im now. We've got 'em sure.' He turned suddenly upon an aide: 'Here – you – Jones – quick – ride after Tompkins – see Taylor – tell him t' go in – everlastingly – like blazes – anything.'

As another officer sped his horse after the first messenger, the general beamed upon the earth like a sun. In his eyes was a desire to chant a pæan. He kept repeating, 'They've held 'em, by heavens!'

His excitement made his horse plunge, and he merrily kicked and swore at it. He held a little carnival of joy on horseback.

Chapter Seven

THE YOUTH CRINGED AS IF discovered in a crime. By heavens, they had won after all! The imbecile line had remained and become victors. He could hear cheering.

He lifted himself up on his toes and looked in the direction of the fight. A yellow fog lay wallowing on the treetops. From beneath it came the clatter of musketry. Hoarse cries told of an advance.

He turned away amazed and angry. He felt that he had been wronged.

He had fled, he told himself, because annihilation approached. He had done a good part in saving himself, who was a little piece of the army. He had considered the time, he said, to be one in which it was the duty of every little piece to rescue itself if possible. Later the officers could fit the little pieces together again, and make a battle front. If none of the little pieces were wise enough to save themselves from the flurry of death at such a time, why, then, where would be the army? It was all plain that he had proceeded according to very correct and commendable rules. His actions had been sagacious things.

They had been full of strategy. They were the work of a master's legs.

Thoughts of his comrades came to him. The brittle blue line had withstood the blows and won. He grew bitter over it. It seemed that the blind ignorance and stupidity of those little pieces had betrayed him. He had been overturned and crushed by their lack of sense in holding the position, when intelligent deliberation would have convinced them that it was impossible. He, the enlightened man who looks afar in the dark, had fled because of his superior perceptions and knowledge. He felt a great anger against his comrades. He knew it could be proved that they had been fools.

He wondered what they would remark when later he appeared in camp. His mind heard howls of derision. Their density would not enable them to understand his sharper point of view.

He began to pity himself acutely. He was ill used. He was trodden beneath the feet of an iron injustice. He had proceeded with wisdom and from the most righteous motives under heaven's blue only to be frustrated by hateful circumstances.

A dull, animal-like rebellion against his fellows, war in the abstract, and fate grew within him. He shambled along with bowed head, his brain in a tumult of agony and despair. When he looked loweringly up, quivering at each sound, his eyes had the expression of those of a criminal who thinks his guilt and his punishment great, and knows that he can find no words.

He went from the fields into a thick woods, as if resolved to bury himself. He wished to get out of hearing of the crackling shots which were to him like voices.

The ground was cluttered with vines and bushes, and the trees grew close and spread out like bouquets. He was obliged to force his way with much noise. The creepers, catching against his legs, cried out harshly as their sprays were torn from the barks of trees. The swishing saplings tried to make known his presence to the world. He could not conciliate the forest. As he made his way, it was always calling out protestations. When he separated embraces of trees and vines the disturbed foliages waved their arms and turned their face leaves toward him. He dreaded lest these noisy motions and cries should bring men to look at him. So he went far, seeking dark and intricate places.

After a time the sound of musketry grew faint and the cannon boomed in the distance. The sun, suddenly apparent, blazed among the trees. The insects were making rhythmical noises. They seemed to be grinding their teeth in unison. A woodpecker stuck his impudent head around the side of a tree. A bird flew on lighthearted wing.

Off was the rumble of death. It seemed now that Nature had no ears.

This landscape gave him assurance. A fair field holding life. It was the religion of peace. It would die if its timid eyes were compelled to see blood. He conceived Nature to be a woman with a deep aversion to tragedy.

He threw a pine cone at a jovial squirrel, and he ran with chattering fear. High in a treetop he stopped, and, poking his head cautiously from behind a branch, looked down with an air of trepidation.

The youth felt triumphant at this exhibition. There was the law, he said. Nature had given him a sign. The squirrel, immediately upon recognizing danger, had taken to his legs without ado. He did not stand stolidly bearing his furry belly to the missile, and die with an upward glance at the sympathetic heavens. On the contrary, he had fled as fast as his legs could carry him; and he was but an ordinary squirrel, too – doubtless no philosopher of his race. The youth wended, feeling that Nature was of his mind. She re-enforced his argument with proofs that lived where the sun shone.

Once he found himself almost into a swamp. He was obliged to walk upon bog tufts and watch his feet to keep from the oily mire. Pausing at one time to look about him he saw, out at some black water, a small animal pounce in and emerge directly with a gleaming fish.

The youth went again into the deep thickets. The brushed branches made a noise that drowned the sounds of cannon. He walked on, going from obscurity into promises of a greater obscurity.

At length he reached a place where the high, arching boughs made a chapel. He softly pushed the green doors aside and entered. Pine needles were a gentle brown carpet. There was a religious half light.

Near the threshold he stopped, horror-stricken at the sight of a thing.

He was being looked at by a dead man who was seated with his back against a columnlike tree. The corpse was dressed in a uniform that once had been blue, but was now faded to a melancholy shade of green. The eyes, staring at the youth, had changed to the dull hue to be seen on the side of a dead fish. The mouth was open. Its red had changed to an appalling yellow. Over the gray skin of the face ran little ants. One was trundling some sort of a bundle along the upper lip.

The youth gave a shriek as he confronted the thing. He was for moments turned to stone before it. He remained staring into the liquid-looking eyes. The dead man and the living man exchanged a long look. Then the youth cautiously put one hand behind him and brought it against a tree. Leaning upon this he retreated, step by step, with his face still toward the thing. He feared that if he turned his back the body might spring up and steathily pursue him.

The branches, pushing against him, threatened to throw him over upon it. His unguided feet, too, caught aggravatingly in brambles; and with it all he received a subtle suggestion to touch the corpse. As he thought of his hand upon it he shuddered profoundly.

At last he burst the bonds which had fastened him to the spot and fled, unheeding the underbrush. He was pursued by a sight of the black ants swarming greedily upon the gray face and venturing horribly near to the eyes.

After a time he paused, and, breathless and panting, listened. He imagined some strange voice would come from the dead throat and squawk after him in horrible menaces.

The trees about the portal of the chapel moved soughingly in a soft wind. A sad silence was upon the little guarding edifice.

Chapter Eight

THE TREES BEGAN SOFTLY TO SING a hymn of twilight. The sun sank until slanted bronze rays struck the forest. There was a lull in the noises of insects as if they had bowed their beaks and were making a devotional pause. There was silence save for the chanted chorus of the trees.

Then, upon this stillness, there suddenly broke a tremendous clangor of sounds. A crimson roar came from the distance.

The youth stopped. He was transfixed by this terrific medley of all noises. It was as if worlds were being rended. There was the ripping sound of musketry and the breaking crash of the artillery.

His mind flew in all directions. He conceived the two armies to be at each other panther fashion. He listened for a time. Then he began to run in the direction of the battle. He saw that it was an ironical thing for him to be running thus toward that which he had been at such pains to avoid. But he said, in substance, to himself that if the earth and the moon were about to clash, many persons would doubtless plan to get upon the roofs to witness the collision.

As he ran, he became aware that the forest had stopped its music, as if at last becoming capable of hearing the foreign sounds. The trees hushed and stood motionless. Everything seemed to be listening to the crackle and clatter and earshaking thunder. The chorus pealed over the still earth.

It suddenly occurred to the youth that the fight in which he had been was, after all, but perfunctory popping. In the hearing of this present din he was doubtful if he had seen real battle scenes. This uproar explained a celestial battle; it was tumbling hordes a-struggle in the air.

Reflecting, he saw a sort of humor in the point of view of himself and his fellows during the late encounter. They had taken themselves and the enemy very seriously and had imagined that they were deciding the war. Individuals must have supposed that they were cutting the letters of their names deep into everlasting tablets of brass, or enshrining their reputations forever in the hearts of their countrymen, while, as to fact, the affair would appear in printed reports under a meek and immaterial title. But he saw that it was good, else, he said, in battle everyone would surely run save forlorn hopes and their ilk.

He went rapidly on. He wished to come to the edge of the forest that he might peer out.

As he hastened, there passed through his mind pictures of stupendous conflicts. His accumulated thought upon such subjects was used to form scenes. The noise was as the voice of an eloquent being, describing.

Sometimes the brambles formed chains and tried to hold him back. Trees, confronting him, stretched out their arms and forbade him to pass. After its previous hostility this new resistance of the forest filled him with a fine bitterness. It seemed that Nature could not be quite ready to kill him.

But he obstinately took roundabout ways, and presently he was where he could see long gray walls of vapor where lay battle lines. The voices of cannon shook him. The musketry sounded in long irregular surges that played havoc with his ears. He stood regardant for a moment. His eyes had an awestruck expression. He gawked in the direction of the fight.

Presently he proceeded again on his forward way. The battle was like the grinding of an immense and terrible machine to him. Its complexities and powers, its grim processes, fascinated him. He must go close and see it produce corpses.

He came to a fence and clambered over it. On the far side, the ground was littered with clothes and guns. A newspaper, folded up, lay in the dirt. A dead soldier was stretched with his face hidden in his arm. Farther off there was a group of four or five corpses keeping mournful company. A hot sun had blazed upon the spot.

In this place the youth felt that he was an invader. This forgotten part of the battle ground was owned by the dead men, and he hurried, in the vague apprehension that one of the swollen forms would rise and tell him to begone.

He came finally to a road from which he could see in the distance dark and agitated bodies of troops, smoke-fringed. In the lane was a blood-stained crowd streaming to the rear. The wounded men were cursing, groaning, and wailing. In the air, always, was a mighty swell of sound that it seemed could sway the earth. With the courageous words of the artillery and the spiteful sentences of the musketry mingled red cheers. And from this region of noises came the steady current of the maimed.

One of the wounded men had a shoeful of blood. He hopped like a schoolboy in a game. He was laughing hysterically.

One was swearing that he had been shot in the arm through the commanding general's mismanagement of the army. One was marching with an air imitative of some sublime drum major. Upon his features was an unholy mixture of merriment and agony. As he marched he sang a bit of doggerel in a high and quavering voice:

> 'Sing a song 'a vic'try,
> A pocketful 'a bullets,
> Five an' twenty dead men
> Baked in a – pie.'

Parts of the procession limped and staggered to this tune.

Another had the gray seal of death already upon his face. His lips were curled in hard lines and his teeth were clinched. His hands were bloody from where he had pressed them upon his wound. He seemed to be awaiting the moment when he should pitch headlong. He stalked like the specter of a soldier, his eyes burning with the power of a stare into the unknown.

There were some who proceeded sullenly, full of anger at their wounds, and ready to turn upon anything as an obscure cause.

An officer was carried along by two privates. He was peevish. 'Don't joggle so, Johnson, yeh fool,' he cried. 'Think m' leg is made of iron? If yeh can't carry me decent, put me down an' let some one else do it.'

He bellowed at the tottering crowd who blocked the quick march of his bearers. 'Say, make way there, can't yeh? Make way, dickens take it all.'

They sulkily parted and went to the roadsides. As he was carried past they made pert remarks to him. When he raged in reply and threatened them, they told him to be damned.

The shoulder of one of the tramping bearers knocked heavily against the spectral soldier who was staring into the unknown.

The youth joined this crowd and marched along with it. The torn bodies expressed the awful machinery in which the men had been entangled.

Orderlies and couriers occasionally broke through the throng in the roadway, scattering wounded men right and left, galloping on followed by howls. The melancholy march was continually disturbed by the messengers, and sometimes by bustling batteries that came swinging and thumping down upon them, the officers shouting orders to clear the way.

There was a tattered man, fouled with dust, blood and powder stain from hair to shoes, who trudged quietly at the youth's side. He was listening with eagerness and much humility to the lurid descriptions of a bearded sergeant. His lean features wore an expression of awe and admiration. He was like a listener in a country store to wondrous tales told among the sugar barrels. He eyed the story-teller with unspeakable wonder. His mouth was agape in yokel fashion.

The sergeant, taking note of this, gave pause to his elaborate history, while he administered a sardonic comment. 'Be keerful, honey, you'll be a-ketchin' flies,' he said.

The tattered man shrank back abashed.

After a time he began to sidle near to the youth, and in a different way try to make him a friend. His voice was gentle as a girl's voice and his eyes were pleading. The youth saw with surprise that the soldier had two wounds, one in the head, bound with a blood-soaked rag, and the other in the arm, making that member dangle like a broken bough.

After they had walked together for some time the tattered man mustered sufficient courage to speak. 'Was pretty good fight, wa'n't it?' he timidly said. The youth, deep in thought, glanced up at the bloody and grim figure with its lamblike eyes. 'What?'

'Was pretty good fight, wa'n't it?'

'Yes,' said the youth shortly. He quickened his pace.

But the other hobbled industriously after him. There was an air of apology in his manner, but he evidently thought that he needed only to talk for a time, and the youth would perceive that he was a good fellow.

'Was pretty good fight, wa'n't it?' he began in a small voice, and then he achieved the fortitude to continue. 'Dern me if I ever see fellers fight so. Laws, how they did fight! I knowed th' boys'd like when they onct got square at it. Th' boys ain't had no fair chanct up t' now, but this time they showed what they was. I knowed it'd turn out this way. Yeh can't lick them boys. No, sir! They're fighters, they be.'

He breathed a deep breath of humble admiration. He had looked at the youth for encouragement several times. He received none, but gradually he seemed to get absorbed in his subject.

'I was talkin' 'cross pickets with a boy from Georgie, onct, an' that boy, he ses, "Your fellers'll all run like hell when they onct hearn a gun," he ses. "Mebbe they will," I ses, "but I don't b'lieve none of it," I ses; "an' b'jiminey," I ses back t' 'um, "mebbe your fellers'll all run like hell when they onct hearn a gun," I ses. He larfed. Well, they didn't run today, did they, hey? No, sir! They fit, an' fit, an' fit.'

His homely face was suffused with a light of love for the army which was to him all things beautiful and powerful.

After a time he turned to the youth. 'Where yeh hit, ol' boy?' he asked in a brotherly tone.

The youth felt instant panic at this question, although its first full import was not borne in upon him.

'What?' he asked.

'Where yeh hit?' repeated the tattered man.

'Why,' began the youth, 'I – I – that is – why – I–'

He turned away suddenly and slid through the crowd. His brow was heavily flushed, and his fingers were picking nervously at one of his buttons. He bent his head and fastened his eyes studiously upon the button as if it were a little problem.

The tattered man looked after him in astonishment.

Chapter Nine

THE YOUTH FELL BACK IN THE procession until the tattered soldier was not in sight. Then he started to walk on with the others.

But he was amid wounds. The mob of men was bleeding. Because of the tattered soldier's question he now felt that his shame could be viewed. He was continually casting sidelong glances to see if the men were contemplating the letters of guilt he felt burned into his brow.

At times he regarded the wounded soldiers in an envious way. He conceived persons with torn bodies to be peculiarly happy. He wished that he, too, had a wound, a red badge of courage.

The spectral soldier was at his side like a stalking reproach. The man's eyes were still fixed in a stare into the unknown. His gray, appalling face had attracted attention in the crowd, and men, slowing to his dreary pace, were walking with him. They were discussing his plight, questioning him and giving him advice. In a dogged way he repelled them, signing to them to go on and leave him alone. The shadows of his face were deepening and his tight lips seemed holding in check the moan of great despair. There could be seen a certain stiffness in the movements of his body, as if he were taking infinite care not to arouse the passion of his wounds. As he went on, he seemed always looking for a place, like one who goes to choose a grave.

Something in the gesture of the man as he waved the bloody and pitying soldiers away made the youth start as if bitten. He yelled in horror. Tottering forward he laid a quivering hand upon the man's arm. As the latter slowly turned his waxlike features toward him, the youth screamed:

'Gawd!' Jim Conklin!'

The tall soldier made a little commonplace smile. 'Hello, Henry,' he said.

The youth swayed on his legs and glared strangely. He stuttered and stammered. 'Oh, Jim – oh, Jim – oh, Jim –'

The tall soldier held out his gory hand. There was a curious red and black combination of new blood and old blood upon it. 'Where yeh been, Henry?' he asked. He continued in a monotonous voice, 'I thought mebbe yeh got

keeled over. There's been thunder t' pay t'-day. I was worryin' about it a good
deal.'

The youth still lamented. 'Oh, Jim – oh, Jim – oh, Jim –'

'Yeh know,' said the tall soldier, 'I was out there.' He made a careful gesture.
'An', Lord, what a circus! An', b'jiminey, I got shot – I got shot. Yes,
b'jiminey, I got shot.' He reiterated this fact in a bewildered way, as if he did
not know how it came about.

The youth put forth anxious arms to assist him, but the tall soldier went
firmly on as if propelled. Since the youth's arrival as a guardian for his friend,
the other wounded men had ceased to display much interest. They occupied
themselves again in dragging their own tragedies toward the rear.

Suddenly, as the two friends marched on, the tall soldier seemed to be
overcome by a terror. His face turned to a semblance of gray paste. He
clutched the youth's arm and looked all about him, as if dreading to be
overheard. Then he began to speak in a shaking whisper:

'I tell yeh what I'm 'fraid of, Henry – I'll tell yeh what I'm 'fraid of. I'm 'fraid
I'll fall down – an' then yeh know – them damned artillery wagons – they like as
not 'll run over me. That's what I'm 'fraid of –'

The youth cried out to him hysterically: 'I'll take care of yeh, Jim! I'll take
care of yeh! I swear t'Gawd I will!'

'Sure – will yeh, Henry?' the tall soldier beseeched.

'Yes – yes – I tell yeh – I'll take care of yeh, Jim!' protested the youth. He
could not speak accurately because of the gulpings in his throat.

But the tall soldier continued to beg in a lowly way. He now hung babelike to
the youth's arm. His eyes rolled in the wildness of his terror. 'I was allus a good
friend t' yeh, wa'n't I, Henry? I've allus been a pretty good feller, ain't I? An' it
ain't much t' ask, is it? Jest t' pull me along outer th' road? I'd do it fer you,
wouldn't I, Henry?'

He paused in piteous anxiety to await his friend's reply.

The youth had reached an anguish where the sobs scorched him. He strove
to express his loyalty, but he could only make fantastic gestures.

However, the tall soldier seemed suddenly to forget all those fears. He
became again the grim, stalking specter of a soldier. He went stonily forward.
The youth wished his friend to lean upon him, but the other always shook his
head and strangely protested. 'No – no – no – leave me be – leave me be –'

His look was fixed again upon the unknown. He moved with mysterious
purpose, and all of the youth's offers he brushed aside. 'No – no – leave me be –
leave me be –'

The youth had to follow.

Presently the latter heard a voice talking softly near his shoulders. Turning
he saw that it belonged to the tattered soldier. 'Ye'd better take 'im outa th'
road, pardner. There's a batt'ry comin' helitywhoop down th' road an' he'll git
runned over. He's a goner anyhow in about five minutes – yeh kin see that.
Ye'd better take 'im outa th' road. Where th' blazes does he git his stren'th
from?'

'Lord knows!' cried the youth. He was shaking his hands helplessly.

He ran forward presently and grasped the tall soldier by the arm. 'Jim! Jim!'
he coaxed, 'come with me.'

The tall soldier weakly tried to wrench himself free. 'Huh,' he said vacantly.
He stared at the youth for a moment. At last he spoke as if dimly

comprehending. 'Oh! Inteh th' fields? Oh!'

He started blindly through the grass.

The youth turned once to look at the lashing riders and jouncing guns of the battery. He was startled from this view by a shrill outcry from the tattered man.

'Gawd! He's runnin'!'

Turning his head swiftly, the youth saw his friend running in a staggering and stumbling way toward a little clump of bushes. His heart seemed to wrench itself almost free from his body at this sight. He made a noise of pain. He and the tattered man began a pursuit. There was a singular race.

When he overtook the tall soldier he began to plead with all the words he could find. 'Jim – Jim – what are you doing – what makes you do this way – you'll hurt yerself.'

The same purpose was in the tall soldier's face. He protested in a dulled way, keeping his eyes fastened on the mystic place of his intentions. 'No – no – don't tech me – leave me be – leave me be –'

The youth, aghast and filled with wonder at the tall soldier, began quaveringly to question him. 'Where yeh goin', Jim? What you thinking about? Where you going? Tell me, won't you, Jim?'

The tall soldier faced about as upon relentless pursuers. In his eyes there was great appeal. 'Leave me be, can't yeh? Leave me be fer a minnit.'

The youth recoiled. 'Why, Jim,' he said, in a dazed way, 'what's the matter with you?'

The tall soldier turned and, lurching dangerously, went on. The youth and the tattered soldier followed, sneaking as if whipped, feeling unable to face the stricken man if he should again confront them. They began to have thoughts of a solemn ceremony. There was something ritelike in these movements of the doomed soldier. And there was a resemblance in him to a devotee of a mad religion, blood-sucking, muscle-wrenching, bone-crushing. They were awed and afraid. They hung back lest he have at command a dreadful weapon.

At last, they saw him stop and stand motionless. Hastening up, they perceived that his face wore an expression telling that he had at last found the place for which he had struggled. His spare figure was erect; his bloody hands were quietly at his side. He was waiting with patience for something that he had come to meet. He was at the rendezvous. They paused and stood, expectant.

There was silence.

Finally, the chest of the doomed soldier began to heave with a strained motion. It increased in violence until it was as if an animal was within and was kicking and tumbling furiously to be free.

This spectacle of gradual strangulation made the youth writhe, and once as his friend rolled his eyes, he saw something in them that made him sink wailing to the ground. He raised his voice in a last supreme call.

'Jim – Jim – Jim –'

The tall soldier opened his lips and spoke. He made a gesture. 'Leave me be – don't tech me – leave me be –'

There was another silence while he waited.

Suddenly, his formed stiffened and straightened. Then it was shaken by a prolonged ague. He stared into space. To the two watchers there was a curious and profound dignity in the firm lines of his awful face.

He was invaded by a creeping strangeness that slowly enveloped him. For a moment the tremor of his legs caused him to dance a sort of hideous hornpipe. His arms bent wildly about his head in expression of implike enthusiasm.

His tall figure stretched itself to its full height. There was a slight rending sound. Then it began to swing forward, slow and straight, in the manner of a falling tree. A swift muscular contortion made the left shoulder strike the ground first.

The body seemed to bounce a little way from the earth. 'God!' said the tattered soldier.

The youth had watched, spellbound, this ceremony at the place of meeting. His face had been twisted into an expression of every agony he had imagined for his friend.

He now sprang to his feet and, going closer, gazed upon the pastlike face. The mouth was open and the teeth showed in a laugh.

As the flap of the blue jacket fell away from the body, he could see that the side looked as if it had been chewed by wolves.

The youth turned, with sudden, livid rage, toward the battlefield. He shook his fist. He seemed about to deliver a philippic.

'Hell –'

The red sun was pasted in the sky like a wafer.

Chapter Ten

THE TATTERED MAN STOOD MUSING.

'Well, he was reg'lar jim-dandy fer nerve, wa'n't he,' said he finally in a little awestruck voice. 'A reg'lar jim-dandy.' He thoughtfully poked one of the docile hands with his foot. 'I wonner where he got 'is stren'th from? I never seen a man do that before. It was a funny thing. Well, he was a reg'lar jim-dandy.'

The youth desired to screech out his grief. He was stabbed, but his tongue lay dead in the tomb of his mouth. He threw himself again upon the ground and began to brood.

The tattered man stood musing.

'Look-a-here, pardner,' he said, after a time. He regarded the corpse as he spoke. 'He's up an' gone, ain't 'e, an' we might as well begin t' look out fer ol' number one. This here thing is all over. He's up an' gone, ain't he? An' he's all right here. Nobody won't bother 'im. An' I must say I ain't enjoying any great health m'self these days.'

The youth, awakened by the tattered soldier's tone, looked quickly up. He saw that he was swinging uncertainly on his legs and that his face had turned to a shade of blue.

'Good Lord!' he cried, 'you ain't goin' t' – not you, too.'

The tattered man waved his hand. 'Nary die,' he said. 'All I want is some pea soup an' a good bed. Some pea soup,' he repeated dreamfully.

The youth arose from the ground. 'I wonder where he came from. I left him over there.' He pointed. 'And now I find 'im here.' He indicated a new direction. They both turned toward the body as if to ask of it a question.

'Well,' at length spoke the tattered man, 'there ain't no use in our stayin' here an' tryin' t' ask him anything.'

The youth nodded an assent wearily. They both turned to gaze for a moment at the corpse.

The youth murmured something.

'Well, he was a jim-dandy, wa'n't 'e?' said the tattered man as if in response.

They turned their backs upon it and started away. For a time they stole softly, treading with their toes. It remained laughing there in the grass.

'I'm commencin' t' feel pretty bad,' said the tattered man, suddenly breaking one of his little silences. 'I'm commencin' t' feel pretty damn' bad.'

The youth groaned. 'O Lord!' He wondered if he was to be the tortured witness of another grim encounter.

But his companion waved his hand reassuringly. 'Oh, I'm not goin' t' die yit. There too much dependin' on me fer me t' die yit. No, sir! Nary die! I *can't*! Ye'd oughta see th' swad a' chil'ren I've got, an' all like that.'

The youth glancing at his companion could see by the shadow of a smile that he was making some kind of fun.

As they plodded on the tattered soldier continued to talk. 'Besides, if I died, I wouldn't die th' way that feller did. That was th' funniest thing. I'd jest flop down, I would. I never seen a feller die th' way that feller did.

'Yeh know Tom Jamison, he lives next door t' me up home. He's a nice feller, he is, an' we was allus good friends. Smart, too. Smart as a steel trap. Well, when we was a-fightin' this atternoon, all-of-a-sudden he begin t' rip up an' cuss an' beller at me. "Yer shot, yeh blamed infernal!" – he swear horrible – he ses t' me. I put up m' hand t' m' head an' when I looked at m' fingers, I seen, sure 'nough, I was shot. I give a holler an' begin t' run, but b'fore I could git away another one hit me in th' arm an' whirl' me clean 'round. I got skeared when they was all a-shootin' b'hind me an' I run t' beat all, but I cotch it pretty bad. I've an idee I'd a' been fightin' yit, if t'wasn't fer Tom Jamison.'

Then he made a calm announcement: 'There's two of 'em – little ones – but they're beginnin' t' have fun with me now. I don't b'lieve I kin walk much furder.'

They went slowly on in silence. 'Yeh look pretty peek-ed yerself,' said the tattered man at last. 'I bet yeh've got a worser one than yeh think. Ye'd better take keer of yer hurt. It don't do t' let sech things go. It might be inside mostly, an' them plays thunder. Where is it located?' But he continued his harangue without waiting for a reply. 'I see 'a feller git hit plum in th' head when my reg'ment was a-standin' at ease onct. An' everybody yelled out to 'im: Hurt, John? Are yeh hurt much? "No," ses he. He looked kinder surprised, an' he went on tellin' 'em how he felt. He sed he didn't feel nothin'. But, by dad, th' first thing that feller knowed he was dead. Yes, he was dead – stone dead. So, yeh wanta watch out. Yeh might have some queer kind 'ahurt yerself. Yeh can't never tell. Where is your'n located?'

The youth had been wriggling since the introduction of this topic. He now gave a cry of exasperation and made a furious motion with his hand. 'Oh, don't bother me!' he said. He was enraged against the tattered man, and could have strangled him. His companions seemed ever to play intolerable parts. They were ever upraising the ghost of shame on the stick of their curiousity. He turned toward the tattered man as one at bay. 'Now, don't bother me,' he repeated with desperate menace.

'Well, Lord knows I don't wanta bother anybody,' said the other. There was a little accent of despair in his voice as he replied, 'Lord knows I've gota 'nough m' own t' tend to.'

The youth, who had been holding a bitter debate with himself and casting glances of hatred and contempt at the tattered man, here spoke in a hard voice. 'Good-by,' he said.

The tattered man looked at him in gaping amazement. 'Why – why, pardner, where yeh goin'?' he asked unsteadily. The youth looking at him, could see that he, too, like that other one, was beginning to act dumb and animal-like. His thoughts seemed to be floundering about in his head. 'Now – now – look – a – here, you Tom Jamison – now – I won't have this – this here won't do. Where – where yeh goin'?'

The youth pointed vaguely. 'Over there,' he replied.

'Well, now look – a – here – now,' said the tattered man, rambling on in idiot fashion. His head was hanging forward and his words were slurred. 'This thing won't do, now, Tom Jamison. It won't do. I know yeh, yeh pig-headed devil. Yeh wanta go trompin' off with a bad hurt. It ain't right – now – Tom Jamison – it ain't. Yeh wanta leave me take keer of yeh, Tom Jamison. It ain't – right – it ain't – fer yeh t' go – trompin' off – with a bad hurt – it ain't – ain't – ain't right – it ain't.'

In reply the youth climbed a fence and started away. He could hear the tattered man bleating plaintively.

Once he faced about angrily. 'What?'

'Look – a – here, now, Tom Jamison – now – it ain't –'

The youth went on. Turning at a distance he saw the tattered man wandering about helplessly in the field.

He now thought that he wished he was dead. He believed that he envied those men whose bodies lay strewn over the grass of the fields and on the fallen leaves of the forest.

The simple questions of the tattered man had been knife thrusts to him. They asserted a society that probes pitilessly at secrets until all is apparent. His late companion's chance persistency made him feel that he could not keep his crime concealed in his bosom. It was sure to be brought plain by one of those arrows which cloud the air and are constantly pricking, discovering, proclaiming those things which are willed to be forever hidden. He admitted that he could not defend himself against this agency. It was not within the power of vigilance.

Chapter Eleven

HE BECAME AWARE THAT THE furnace roar of the battle was growing louder. Great brown clouds had floated to the still heights of air before him. The noise, too, was approaching. The woods filtered men and the fields became dotted.

As he rounded a hillock, he perceived that the roadway was now a crying mass of wagons, teams, and men. From the heaving tangle issued exhortations, commands, imprecations. Fear was sweeping it all along. The cracking whips bit and horses plunged and tugged. The white-topped wagons strained and stumbled in their exertions like fat sheep.

The youth felt comforted in a measure by this sight. They were all retreating. Perhaps, then, he was not so bad after all. He seated himself and watched the terror-stricken wagons. They fled like soft, ungainly animals. All the roarers and lashers served to help him to magnify the dangers and horrors of the engagement that he might try to prove to himself that the thing with which men could charge him was in truth a symmetrical act. There was an amount of pleasure to him in watching the wild march of this vindication.

Presently the calm head of a forward-going column of infantry appeared in the road. It came swiftly on. Avoiding the obstructions gave it the sinuous movement of a serpent. The men at the head butted mules with their musket stocks. They prodded teamsters indifferent to all howls. The men forced their way through parts of the dense mass by strength. The blunt head of the column pushed. The raving teamsters swore many strange oaths.

The commands to make way had the ring of a great importance in them. The men were going forward to the heart of the din. They were to confront the eager rush of the enemy. They felt the pride of their onward movement when the remainder of the army seemed trying to dribble down this road. They tumbled teams about with a fine feeling that it was no matter so long as their column got to the front in time. This importance made their faces grave and stern. And the backs of the officers were very rigid.

As the youth looked at them the black weight of his woe returned to him. He felt that he was regarding a procession of chosen beings. The separation was as great to him as if they had marched with weapons of flame and banners of sunlight. He could never be like them. He could have wept in his longings.

He searched about in his mind for an adequate malediction for the indefinite cause, the thing upon which men turn the words of final blame. It – whatever it was – was responsible for him, he said. There lay the fault.

The haste of the column to reach the battle seemed to the forlorn young man to be something much finer than stout fighting. Heroes, he thought, could find excuses in that long seething lane. They could retire with perfect self-respect and make excuses to the stars.

He wondered what those men had eaten that they could be in such haste to force their way to grim chances of death. As he watched his envy grew until he thought that he wished to change the lives with one of them. He would have liked to have used a tremendous force, he said, throw off himself and become a better. Swift pictures of himself, apart, yet in himself, came to him – a blue desperate figure leading lurid charges with one knee forward and a broken blade high – a blue, determined figure standing before a crimson and steel assault, getting calmly killed on a high place before the eyes of all. He thought of the magnificent pathos of his dead body.

These thoughts uplifted him. He felt the quiver of war desire. In his ears, he heard the ring of victory. He knew the frenzy of a rapid successful charge. The music of the trampling feet, the sharp voices, the clanking arms of the column near him made him soar on the red wings of war. For a few moments he was sublime.

He thought that he was about to start for the front. Indeed, he saw a picture of himself, dust-stained, haggard, panting, flying to the front at the proper moment to seize and throttle the dark, leering witch of calamity.

Then the difficulties of the thing began to drag at him. He hesitated, balancing awkwardly on one foot.

He had no rifle; he could not fight with his hands, said he resentfully to his plan. Well, rifles could be had for the picking. They were extraordinarily profuse.

Also, he continued, it would be a miracle if he found his regiment. Well, he could fight with any regiment.

He started forward slowly. He stepped as if he expected to tread on some explosive thing. Doubts and he were struggling.

He would truly be a worm if any of his comrades should see him returning thus, the marks of his flight upon him. There was a reply that the intent fighters did not care for what happened rearward saving that no hostile bayonets appeared there. In the battle-blur his face would, in a way be hidden, like the face of a cowled man.

But then he said that his tireless fate would bring forth, when the strife lulled for a moment, a man to ask of him an explanation. In imagination he felt the scrutiny of his companions as he painfully labored through some lies.

Eventually, his courage expended itself upon these objections. The debates drained him of his fire.

He was not cast down by this defeat of his plan, for, upon studying the affair carefully, he could not but admit that the objections were very formidable.

Furthermore, various ailments had begun to cry out. In their presence he could not persist in flying high with the wings of war; they rendered it almost impossible for him to see himself in a heroic light. He tumbled headlong.

He discovered that he had a scorching thirst. His face was so dry and grimy that he thought he could feel his skin crackle. Each bone of his body had an ache in it, and seemingly threatened to break with each movement. His feet were like two sores. Also, his body was calling for food. It was more powerful than a direct hunger. There was a dull, weightlike feeling in his stomach, and, when he tried to walk, his head swayed and he tottered. He could not see with distinctness. Small patches of green mist floated before his vision.

While he had been tossed by many emotions, he had not been aware of his ailments. Now they beset him and made clamor. As he was at last compelled to pay attention to them, his capacity for self-hate was multiplied. In despair, he declared that he was not like those others. He now conceded it to be impossible that he should ever become a hero. He was a craven loon. Those pictures of glory were piteous things. He groaned from his heart and went staggering off.

A certain mothlike quality within him kept him in the vicinity of the battle. He had a great desire to see, and to get news. He wished to know who was winning.

He told himself that, despite his unprecedented suffering, he had never lost his greed for a victory, yet, he said, in a half-apologetic manner to his conscience, he could not but know that a defeat for the army this time might mean many favorable things for him. The blows of the enemy would splinter regiments into fragments. Thus, many men of courage, he considered, would be obliged to desert the colors and scurry like chickens. He would appear as one of them. They would be sullen brothers in distress, and he could then easily believe he had not run any farther or faster than they. And if he himself could believe in his virtuous perfection, he conceived that there would be small trouble in convincing all others.

He said, as if in excuse for this hope, that previously the army had encountered great defeats and in a few months had shaken off all blood and tradition of them, emerging as bright and valiant as a new one; thrusting out of sight the memory of disaster, and appearing with the valor and confidence of unconquered legions. The shrilling voices of the people at home would pipe dismally for a time, but various generals were usually compelled to listen to these ditties. He of course felt no compunctions for proposing a general as a sacrifice. He could not tell who the chosen for the barbs might be, so he could center no direct sympathy upon him. The people were afar and he did not conceive public opinion to be accurate at long range. It was quite probable they would hit the wrong man who, after he had recovered from his amazement would perhaps spend the rest of his days in writing replies to the songs of his alleged failure. It would be very unfortunate, no doubt, but in this case a general was of no consequence to the youth.

In a defeat there would be a roundabout vindication of himself. He thought it would prove, in a manner, that he had fled early because of his superior powers of perception. A serious prophet upon predicting a flood should be the first man to climb a tree. This would demonstrate that he was indeed a seer.

A moral vindication was regarded by the youth as a very important thing. Without salve, he could not, he thought, wear the sore badge of his dishonor through life. With his heart continually assuring him that he was despicable, he could not exist without making it, through his actions, apparent to all men.

If the army had gone gloriously on he would be lost. If the din meant that now his army's flags were tilted forward he was a condemned wretch. He would be compelled to doom himself to isolation. If the men were advancing, their indifferent feet were trampling upon his chances for a successful life.

As these thoughts went rapidly through his mind, he turned upon them and tried to thrust them away. He denounced himself as a villain. He said that he was the most unutterably selfish man in existence. His mind pictured the soldiers who would place their defiant bodies before the spear of the yelling battle fiend, and as he saw their dripping corpses on an imagined field, he said that he was their murderer.

Again he thought that he wished he was dead. He believed that he envied a corpse. Thinking of the slain, he achieved a great contempt for some of them, as if they were guilty for thus becoming lifeless. They might have been killed by lucky chances, he said, before they had had opportunities to flee or before they had been really tested. Yet they would receive laurels from tradition. He cried out bitterly that their crowns were stolen and their robes of glorious memories were shams. However, he still said that it was a great pity he was not as they.

A defeat of the army had suggested itself to him as a means of escape from the consequences of his fall. He considered, now, however, that it was useless to think of such a possibility. His education had been that success for that mighty blue machine was certain; that it would make victories as a contrivance turns out buttons. He presently discarded all his speculations in the other direction. He returned to the creed of soldiers.

When he perceived again that it was not possible for the army to be defeated, he tried to bethink him of a fine tale which he could take back to his regiment, and with it turn the expected shafts of derision.

But, as he mortally feared these shafts, it became impossible for him to invent a tale he felt he could trust. He experimented with many schemes, but threw them aside one by one as flimsy. He was quick to see vulnerable places in them all.

Furthermore, he was much afraid that some arrow of scorn might lay him mentally low before he could raise his protecting tale.

He imagined the whole regiment saying: 'Where's Henry Fleming? He run, didn't 'e? Oh, my!' He recalled various persons who would be quite sure to leave him no peace about it. They would doubtless question him with sneers, and laugh at his stammering hesitation. In the next engagement they would try to keep watch of him to discover when he would run.

Wherever he went in camp, he would encounter insolent and lingeringly cruel stares. As he imagined himself passing near crowds of comrades, he could hear someone say, 'There he goes!'

Then, as if the heads were moved by one muscle, all the faces were turned toward him with wide, derisive grins. He seemed to hear some one make a humorous remark in a low tone. At it the others all crowed and cackled. He was a slang phrase.

Chapter Twelve

THE COLUMN THAT HAD BUTTED stoutly at the obstacles in the roadway was barely out of the youth's sight before he saw dark waves of men come sweeping out of the woods and down through the fields. He knew at once that the steel fibers had been washed from their hearts. They were bursting from their coats and their equipments as from entanglements. They charged down upon him like terrified buffaloes.

Behind them blue smoke curled and clouded above the treetops, and through the thickets he could sometimes see a distant pink glare. The voices of the cannon were clamoring in interminable chorus.

The youth was horrorstricken. He stared in agony and amazement. He forgot that he was engaged in combating the universe. He threw aside his mental pamphlets on the philosophy of the retreated and rules for the guidance of the damned.

The fight was lost. The dragons were coming with invincible strides. The army, helpless in the matted thickets and blinded by the overhanging night, was going to be swallowed. War, the red animal, war, the blood-swollen god, would have bloated fill.

Within him something bade to cry out. He had the impulse to make a rallying speech, to sing a battle hymn, but he could only get his tongue to call into the air: 'Why – why – what – what's th' matter?'

Soon he was in the midst of them. They were leaping and scampering all about him. Their blanched faces shone in the dusk. They seemed, for the most part, to be very burly men. The youth turned from one to another of them as they galloped along. His incoherent questions were lost. They were heedless of his appeals. They did not seem to see him.

They sometimes gabbled insanely. One huge man was asking of the sky: 'Say, where de plank road? Where de plank road!' It was as if he had lost a child. He wept in his pain and dismay.

Presently, men were running hither and thither in all ways. The artillery booming, forward, rearward, and on the flanks made jumble of ideas of direction. Landmarks had vanished into the gathered gloom. The youth began to imagine that he had got into the center of the tremendous quarrel, and he could perceive no way out of it. From the mouths of the fleeing men came a thousand wild questions, but no one made answers.

The youth, after rushing about and throwing interrogations at the heedless bands of retreating infantry, finally clutched a man by the arm. They swung around face to face.

'Why – why –' stammered the youth struggling with his balking tongue.

The man screamed: 'Let go me! Let go me!' His face was livid and his eyes were rolling uncontrolled. He was heaving and panting. He still grasped his rifle, perhaps having forgotten to release his hold upon it. He tugged frantically, and the youth being compelled to lean forwards was dragged several paces.

'Let go me! Let go me!'

'Why – why –' stuttered the youth.

'Well, then!' bawled the man in a lurid rage. He adroitly and fiercely swung his rifle. It crushed upon the youth's head. The man ran on.

The youth's fingers had turned to paste upon the other's arms. The energy was smitten from his muscles. He saw the flaming wings of lightning flash before his vision. There was a deafening rumble of thunder within his head.

Suddenly his legs seemed to die. He sank writhing to the ground. He tried to arise. In his efforts against the numbing pain he was like a man wrestling with a creature of the air.

There was a sinister struggle.

Sometimes he would achieve a position half erect, battle with the air for a moment, and then fall again, grabbing at the grass. His face was of a clammy pallor. Deep groans were wrenched from him.

At last, with a twisting movement, he got upon his hands and knees, and from thence, like a babe trying to walk, to his feet. Pressing his hands to his temples, he went lurching over the grass.

He fought an intense battle with his body. His dulled senses wished him to swoon and he opposed them stubbornly, his mind portraying unknown dangers and mutilations if he should fall upon the field. He went tall soldier fashion. He imagined secluded spots where he could fall and be unmolested. To search for one he strove against the tide of his pain.

Once he put his hand to the top of his head and timidly touched the wound. The scratching pain of the contact made him draw a long breath through his clinched teeth. His fingers were dabbled with blood. He regarded them with a fixed stare.

Around him he could hear the grumble of jolted cannon as the scurrying horses were lashed toward the front. Once, a young officer on a besplashed charger nearly ran him down. He turned and watched the mass of guns, men, and horses sweeping in a wide curve toward a gap in a fence. The officer was making excited motions with a gauntleted hand. The guns followed the teams with an air of unwillingness, of being dragged by the heels.

Some officers of the scattered infantry were cursing and railing like fishwives. Their scolding voices could be heard above the din. Into the unspeakable jumble in the roadway road a squadron of cavalry. The faded yellow of their facings shone bravely. There was a mighty altercation.

The artillery were assembling as if for a conference.

The blue haze of evening was upon the field. The lines of forest were long purple shadows. One cloud lay along the western sky partly smothering the red.

As the youth left the scene behind him, he heard the guns suddenly roar out. He imagined them shaking in black rage. They belched and howled like brass devils guarding a gate. The soft air was filled with the tremendous remonstrance. With it came the shattering peal of opposing infantry. Turning to look behind him, he could see sheets of orange light illumine the shadowy distance. There were subtle and sudden lightnings in the far air. At times he thought he could see heaving masses of men.

He hurried on in the dusk. The day had faded until he could barely distinguish place for his feet. The purple darkness was filled with men who lectured and jabbered. Sometimes he could see them gesticulating against the blue and somber sky. There seemed to be a great ruck of men and munitions spread about in the forest and in the fields.

The little narrow roadway now lay lifeless. There were overturned wagons like sun-dried bowlders. The bed of the former torrent was choked with the bodies of horses and splintered parts of war machines.

It had come to pass that his wound pained him but little. He was afraid to move rapidly, however, for a dread of disturbing it. He held his head very still and took many precautions against stumbling. He was filled with anxiety, and his face was pinched and drawn in anticipation of the pain of any sudden mistake of his feet in the gloom.

His thoughts, as he walked, fixed intently upon his hurt. There was a cool, liquid feeling about it and he imagined blood moving slowly down under his hair. His head seemed swollen to a size that made him think his neck to be inadequate.

The new silence of his wound made much worriment. The little blistering voices of pain that had called out from his scalp were, he thought, definite in their expression of danger. By them he believed that he could measure his plight. But when they remained ominously silent he became frightened and imagined terrible fingers that clutched into his brain.

Amid it he began to reflect upon various incidents and conditions of the past. He bethought him of certain meals his mother had cooked at home, in which those dishes of which he was particularly fond had occupied prominent positions. He saw the spread table. The pine walls of the kitchen were glowing in the warm light from the stove. Too, he remembered how he and his companions used to go from the schoolhouse to the bank of a shaded pool. He saw his clothes in disorderly array upon the grass of the bank. He felt the swash of the fragrant water upon his body. The leaves of the overhanging maple rustled with melody in the wind of youthful summer.

He was overcome presently by a dragging weariness. His head hung forward and his shoulders were stooped as if he were bearing a great bundle. His feet shuffled along the ground.

He held continuous arguments as to whether he should lie down and sleep at some near spot, or force himself on until he reached a certain haven. He often tried to dismiss the questions, but his body persisted in rebellion and his senses nagged at him like pampered babies.

At last he heard a cheery voice near his shoulder: 'Yeh seem t' be in a pretty bad way, boy?'

The youth did not look up, but he assented with thick tongue. 'Uh!'

The owner of the cheery voice took him firmly by the arm. 'Well,' he said, with a round laugh, 'I'm goin' your way. Th' hull gang is goin' your way. An' I guess I kin give yeh a lift.' They began to walk like a drunken man and his friend.

As they went along, the man questioned the youth and assisted him with the replies like one manipulating the mind of a child. Sometimes he interjected anecdotes. 'What reg'ment do yeh b'long teh? Eh? What's that? Th' 304th N' York? Why, what corps is that in? Oh, it is? Why, I thought they wasn't engaged t'-day – they're 'way over in the center. Oh, they was eh? Well, pretty nearly everybody got their fair share a' fightin' t'-day. By dad, I give myself up fer dead any number 'a times. There was shootin' here an' shootin' there, an' hollerin' here an' hollerin' there, in th' damn' darkness, until I couldn't tell t' save m' soul which side I was on. Sometimes I thought I was sure 'nough from Ohier, an' other times I could 'a swore I was from th' bitter end of Florida. It was th' most mixed up dern thing I ever see. An' these here hull woods is a reg'lar mess. It'll be a miracle if we find our reg'ments t'-night. Pretty soon, though, we'll meet a-plenty of guards an' provost-guards, an' one thing an' another. Ho! there they go with an off'cer, I guess. Look at his hand a-draggin'. He's got all th' war he wants, I bet. He won't be talkin' so big about his reputation an' all when they go t' sawin' off his leg. Poor feller! My brother's got whiskers jest like that. How did yeh git 'way over here, anyhow? Your reg'ment is a long way from here, ain't it? Well, I guess we can find it. Yeh know there was a boy killed in my comp'ny t'-day that I thought th' world an' all of. Jack was a nice feller. By ginger, it hurt like thunder t' see ol' Jack jest git knocked flat. We was a-standin' purty peaceable fer a spell, 'though there was men runnin' ev'ry way all 'round us, an' while we was a-standin' like that, 'long come a big fat feller. He began t' peck at Jack's elbow, an' he ses: "Say, where's th' road t' th' river?" An' Jack, he never paid no attention, an' th' feller kept on a-peckin' at his elbow an' sayin': "Say, where's th' road t' th' river?" Jack was a-lookin' ahead all th' time tryin' t' see th' Johnnies comin' through th' woods, an' he never paid no attention t' this big fat feller fer a long time, but at last he turned 'round an' he ses: "Ah, go t' hell an' find th' road t' th' river!" An' jest then a shot slapped him bang on th' side th' head. He was a sergeant, too. Them was his last words. Thunder, I wish we was sure 'a findin' our reg'ments t'-night. It's goin' t' be long huntin'. But I guess we kin do it.'

In the search which followed, the man of the cheery voice seemed to the youth to possess a wand of a magic kind. He threaded the mazes of the tangled forest with a strange fortune. In encounters with guards and patrols he displayed the keenness of a detective and the valor of a gamin. Obstacles fell before him and became of assistance. The youth, with his chin still on his breast, stood woodenly by while his companion beat ways and means out of sullen things.

The forest seemed a vast hive of men buzzing about in frantic circles, but the cheery man conducted the youth without mistakes, until at last he began to chuckle with glee and self-satisfaction. 'Ah, there yeh are! See that fire?'

The youth nodded stupidly.

'Well, there's were your reg'ment is. An' now, good-by, ol' boy, good luck t' yeh.'

A warm and strong hand clasped the youth's languid fingers for an instant, and then he heard a cheerful and audacious whistling as the man strode away. As he who had so befriended him was thus passing out of his life, it suddenly occurred to the youth that he had not once seen his face.

Chapter Thirteen

THE YOUTH WENT SLOWLY TOWARD the fire indicated by his departed friend. As he reeled, he bethought him of the welcome his comrades would give him. He had a conviction that he would soon feel in his sore heart the barbed missiles of ridicule. He had no strength to invent a tale; he would be a soft target.

He made vague plans to go off into the deeper darkness and hide, but they were all destroyed by the voices of exhaustion and pain from his body. His ailments, clamoring, forced him to see the place of food and rest, at whatever cost.

He swung unsteadily toward the fire. He could see the forms of men throwing black shadows in the red light, and as he went nearer it became known to him in some way that the ground was strewn with sleeping men.

Of a sudden he confronted a black and monstrous figure. A rifle barrel caught some glinting beams. 'Halt! halt!' He was dismayed for a moment, but he presently thought he recognized the nervous voice. As he stood tottering before the rifle barrel, he called out: 'Why, hello, Wilson, you – you here?'

The rifle was lowered to a position of caution and the loud soldier came slowly forward. He peered into the youth's face. 'That you, Henry?'

'Yes, it's – it's me.'

'Well, well, 'ol boy,' said the other, 'by ginger, I'm glad t' see yeh! I give yeh up fer a goner. I thought yeh was dead sure enough.' There was husky emotion in his voice.

The youth found that now he could barely stand upon his feet. There was a sudden sinking of his forces. He thought that he must hasten to produce his tale to protect him from the missiles already at the lips of his redoubtable comrades. So, staggering before the loud soldier, he began: 'Yes, yes. I've – I've had an awful time. I've been all over. Way over on th' right. Ter'ble fightin' over there. I had an awful time. I got separated from th' reg'ment. Over on th' right, I got shot. In th' head. I never see sech fightin'. Awful time. I don't see how I could a' got separated from th' reg'ment. I got shot, too.'

His friend had stepped forward quickly. 'What? Got shot? Why didn't yeh say so first? Poor ol' boy, we must – hol' on a minnit; what am I doin'. I'll call Simpson.'

Another figure at that moment loomed in the gloom. They could see that it was the corporal. 'Who yeh talkin' to, Wilson?' he demanded. His voice was anger-toned. 'Who yeh talkin' to? Yeh th' derndest sentinel – why – hello, Henry, you here? Why, I thought you was dead four hours ago! Great Jerusalem, they keep turnin' up every ten minutes or so! We thought we'd lost forty-two men by straight count, but if they keep on a-comin' this way, we'll git th' comp'ny all back by mornin' yit. Where was yeh?'

'Over on th' right. I got separated –' began the youth with considerable glibness.

But his friend had interrupted hastily. 'Yes, an' he got shot in th' head an' he's in a fix, an' we must see t' him right away.' He rested his rifle in the hollow of his left arm and his right around the youth's shoulder.

'Gee, it must hurt like thunder!' he said.

The youth leaned heavily upon his friend. 'Yes, it hurts – hurts a good deal,' he replied. There was a faltering in his voice.

'Oh,' said the corporal. He linked his arm in the youth's and drew him forward. 'Come on, Henry. I'll take keer 'a yeh.'

As they went on together the loud private called out after them: 'Put 'im t' sleep in my blanket, Simpson. An' – hol' on a minnit – here's my canteen. It's full 'a coffee. Look at his head by th' fire an' see how it looks. Maybe it's a pretty bad un. When I git relieved in a couple 'a minnits, I'll be over an' see t' him.'

The youth's senses were so deadened that his friend's voice sounded from afar and he could scarcely feel the pressure of the corporal's arm. He submitted passively to the latter's directing strength. His head was in the old manner hanging forward upon his breast. His knees wobbled.

The corporal led him into the glare of the fire. 'Now, Henry,' he said, 'let's have a look at yer ol' head.'

The youth sat down obediently and the corporal, laying aside his rifle, began to fumble in the bushy hair of his comrade. He was obliged to turn the other's head so that the full flush of the fire light would beam upon it. He puckered his mouth with a critical air. He drew back his lips and whistled through his teeth when his fingers came in contact with the splashed blood and the rare wound.

'Ah, here were are!' he said. He awkwardly made further investigations. 'Jest as I thought,' he added, presently. 'Yeh've been grazed by a ball. It's raised a queer lump jest as if some feller had lammed yeh on th' head with a club. It stopped a-bleedin' long time ago. Th' most about it is that in th' mornin' yeh'll feel that a number ten hat wouldn't fit yeh. An' your head'll be all het up an' feel as dry as burnt pork. An' yeh may git a lot 'a other sicknesses, too, by mornin'. Yeh can't never tell. Still, I don't much think so. It's jest a damn' good belt on th' head, an' nothin' more. Now, you jest sit here an' don't move, while I go rout out th' relief. Then I'll send Wilson t' take keer 'a yeh.'

The corporal went away. The youth remained on the ground like a parcel. He stared with a vacant look into the fire.

After a time he aroused, for some part, and the things about him began to take form. He saw that the ground in the deep shadows was cluttered with men, sprawling in every conceivable posture. Glancing narrowly into the more distant darkness, he caught occasional glimpses of visages that loomed pallid and ghostly, lit with a phospherescent glow. These faces expressed in their lines the deep stupor of the tired soldiers. They made them appear like men drunk with wine. This bit of forest might have appeared to an ethereal wanderer as a scene of the result of some frightful debauch.

On the other side of the fire the youth observed an officer asleep, seated bolt upright, with his back against a tree. There was something perilous in his position. Badgered by dreams, perhaps, he swayed with little bounces and starts, like an old, toddy-stricken grandfather in a chimney corner. Dust and stains were upon his face. His lower jaw hung down as if lacking strength to assume its normal position. He was the picture of an exhausted soldier after a feast of war.

He had evidently gone to sleep with his sword in his arms. These two had slumbered in an embrace, but the weapon had been allowed in time to fall unheeded to the ground. The brass-mounted hilt lay in contact with some parts of the fire.

Within the gleam of rose and orange light from the burning sticks were other soldiers snoring and heaving, or lying deathlike in slumber. A few pairs of legs were stuck forth, rigid and straight. The shoes displayed the mud or dust of marches and bits of rounded trousers, protruding from the blankets, showed rents and tears from hurried pitchings through the dense brambles.

The fire crackled musically. From it swelled light smoke. Overhead the foliage moved softly. The leaves, with their faces turned toward the blaze, were colored shifting hues of silver, often edged with red. Far off to the right, through a window in the forest could be seen a handful of stars lying, like glittering pebbles, on the black level of the night.

Occasionally, in this low-arched hall, a soldier would arouse and turn his body to a new position, the experience of his sleep having taught him of uneven and objectionable places upon the ground under him. Or, perhaps, he would lift himself to a sitting posture, blink at the fire for an unintelligent moment, throw a swift glance at his prostrate companion, and then cuddle down again with a grunt of sleepy content.

The youth sat in a forlorn heap until his friend the loud young soldier came, swinging two canteens by their light strings. 'Well, now, Henry, ol' boy,' said the latter, 'we'll have yeh fixed up in jest about a minnit.'

He had the bustling ways of an amateur nurse. He fussed around the fire and stirred the sticks to brilliant exertions. He made his patient drink largely from the canteen that contained the coffee. It was to the youth a delicious draught. He tilted his head afar back and held the canteen long to his lips. The cool mixture went caressingly down his blistered throat. Having finished, he sighed with comfortable delight.

The loud young soldier watched his comrade with an air of satisfaction. He later produced an extensive handkerchief from his pocket. He folded it into a manner of bandage and soused water from the other canteen upon the middle of it. This crude arrangement he bound over the youth's head, tying the ends in a queer knot at the back of the neck.

'There,' he said, moving off and surveying his deed, 'yeh look like th' devil, but I bet yeh feel better.'

The youth contemplated his friend with grateful eyes. Upon his aching and swelling head the cold cloth was like a tender woman's hand.

'Yeh don't holler ner say nothin',' remarked his friend approvingly. 'I know I'm a blacksmith at takin' keer 'a sick folks, an' yeh never squeaked. Yer a good un, Henry. Most 'a men would a' been in th' hospital long ago. A shot in th' head ain't foolin' business.'

The youth made no reply, but began to fumble with the buttons of his jacket.

'Well, come, now,' continued his friend, 'come on. I must put yeh t' bed an' see that yeh git a good night's rest.'

The other got carefully erect, and the loud young soldier led him among the sleeping forms lying in groups and rows. Presently he stooped and picked up his blankets. He spread the rubber one upon the ground and placed the woolen one about the youth's shoulders.

'There now,' he said, 'lie down an' git some sleep.'

The youth, with his manner of doglike obedience, got carefully down like a crone stooping. He stretched out with a murmur of relief and comfort. The ground felt like the softest couch.

But of a sudden he ejaculated: 'Hol' on a minnit! Where you goin' t' sleep?'

His friend waved his hand impatiently. 'Right down there by yeh.'

'Well, but hol' on a minnit,' continued the youth. 'What yeh goin' t' sleep in? I've got your —'

The loud young soldier snarled: 'Shet up an' go on t' sleep. Don't be makin' a damn' fool 'a yerself,' he said severely.

After the reproof the youth said no more. An exquisite drowsiness had spread through him. The warm comfort of the blanket enveloped him and made a gentle languor. His head fell forward on his crooked arm and his weighted lids went softly down over his eyes. Hearing a splatter of musketry from the distance, he wondered indifferently if those men sometimes slept. He gave a long sigh, snuggled down into his blanket, and in a moment was like his comrades.

Chapter Fourteen

WHEN THE YOUTH AWOKE IT seemed to him that he had been asleep for a thousand years, and he felt sure that he opened his eyes upon an unexpected world. Gray mists were slowly shifting before the first efforts of the sun rays. An impending splendor could be seen in the eastern sky. An icy dew had chilled his face, and immediately upon arousing he curled farther down into his blanket. He stared for a while at the leaves overhead, moving in a heraldic wind of the day.

The distance was splintering and blaring with the noise of fighting. There was in the sound an expression of a deadly persistency, as if it had not began and was not to cease.

About him were the rows and groups of men that he had dimly seen the previous night. They were getting a last draught of sleep before the awakening. The gaunt, careworn features and dusty figures were made plain by this quaint light at the dawning, but it dressed the skin of the men in corpselike hues and made the tangled limbs appear pulseless and dead. The youth started up with a little cry when his eyes first swept over this motionless mass of men, thickspread upon the ground, pallid, and in strange postures. His disordered mind interpreted the hall of the forest as a charnel place. He believed for an instant that he was in the house of the dead, and he did not dare to move lest these corpses start up, squalling and squawking. In a second, however, he achieved his proper mind. He swore a complicated oath at himself. He saw that this somber picture was not a fact of the present, but a mere prophecy.

He heard then the noise of a fire crackling briskly in the cold air, and, turning his head, he saw his friend pottering busily about a small blaze. A few other figures moved in the fog, and he heard the hard cracking of axe blows.

Suddenly there was a hollow rumble of drums. A distant bugle sang faintly. Similar sounds, varying in strength, came from near and far over the forest. The bugles called to each other like brazen gamecocks. The near thunder of the regimental drums rolled.

The body of men in the woods rustled. There was a general uplifting of heads. A murmuring of voices broke upon the air. In it there was much bass of grumbling oaths. Strange gods were addressed in condemnation of the early hours necessary to correct war. An officer's peremptory tenor rang out and quickened the stiffened movement of the men. The tangled limbs unraveled. The corpse-hued faces were hidden behind fists that twisted slowly in the eye sockets.

The youth sat up and gave vent to an enormous yawn. 'Thunder!' he remarked petulantly. He rubbed his eyes, and then putting up his hand felt carefully of the bandage over his wound. His friend, perceiving him to be awake, came from the fire. 'Well, Henry, ol' man, how do yeh feel this mornin'?' he demanded.

The youth yawned again. Then he puckered his mouth to a little pucker. His head, in truth, felt precisely like a melon, and there was an unpleasant sensation in his stomach.

'Oh, Lord, I feel pretty bad,' he said.

'Thunder!' exclaimed the other. 'I hoped ye'd feel all right this mornin'.

Let's see th' bandage – I guess it's slipped.' He began to tinker at the wound in rather a clumsy way until the youth exploded.

'Gosh-dern it!' he said in sharp irritation; 'you're the hangdest man I ever saw! You wear muffs on your hands. Why in thunderation can't you be more easy? I'd rather you'd stand off an' throw guns at it. Now, go slow, an' don't act as if you was nailing down carpet.'

He glared with insolent command at his friend, but the latter answered soothingly. 'Well, well, come now, an' git some grub,' he said. 'Then, maybe, yeh'll feel better.'

At the fireside the loud young soldier watched over his comrade's wants with tenderness and care. He was very busy marshaling the little black vagabonds of tin cups and pouring into them the streaming, iron colored mixture from a small and sooty tin pail. He had some fresh meat, which he roasted hurriedly upon a stick. He sat down then and contemplated the youth's appetite with glee.

The youth took note of a remarkable change in his comrade since those days of camp life upon the river bank. He seemed no more to be continually regarding the proportions of his personal prowess. He was not furious at small words that pricked his conceits. He was no more a loud young soldier. There was about him now a fine reliance. He showed a quiet belief in his purposes and his abilities. And this inward confidence evidently enabled him to be indifferent to little words of other men aimed at him.

The youth reflected. He had been used to regarding his comrade as a blatant child with an audacity grown from his inexperience, thoughtless, headstrong, jealous, and filled with a tinsel courage. A swaggering babe accustomed to strut in his own dooryard. The youth wondered where had been born these new eyes; when his comrade had made the great discovery that there were many men who would refuse to be subjected by him. Apparently, the other had now climbed a peak of wisdom from which he could perceive himself as a very wee thing. And the youth saw that ever after it would be easier to live in his friend's neighborhood.

His comrade balanced his ebony coffee-cup on his knee. 'Well, Henry,' he said, 'what d'yeh think th' chances are? D'yeh think we'll wallop 'em?'

The youth considered for a moment. 'Day-b'fore-yesterday,' he finally replied, with boldness, 'you would 'a' bet you'd lick the hull kit-an'-boodle all by yourself.'

His friend looked a trifle amazed. 'Would I?' he asked. He pondered. 'Well, perhaps I would,' he decided at last. He stared humbly at the fire.

The youth was quite disconcerted at this surprising reception of his remarks. 'Oh, no, you wouldn't either,' he said, hastily trying to retrace.

But the other made a deprecating gesture. 'Oh, yeh needn't mind, Henry,' he said. 'I believe I was a pretty big fool in those days.' He spoke as after a lapse of years.

There was a little pause.

'All th' officers say we've got th' rebs in a pretty tight box,' said the friend, clearing his throat in a commonplace way. 'They all seem t' think we've got 'em jest were we want 'em.'

'I don't know about that,' the youth replied. 'What I seen over on th' right makes me think it was th' other way about. From where I was, it looked as if we was gettin' a good poundin' yestirday.'

'D'yeh think so?' inquired the friend. 'I thought we handled 'em pretty rough yestirday.'

'Not a bit,' said the youth. 'Why, lord, man, you didn't see nothing of the fight. Why!' Then a sudden thought came to him. 'Oh! Jim Conklin's dead.'

His friend started. 'What? Is he? Jim Conklin?'

The youth spoke slowly. 'Yes. He's dead. Shot in th' side.'

'Yeh don't say so. Jim Conklin. . . . poor cuss!'

All about them were other small fires surrounded by men with their little black utensils. From one of these near came sudden sharp voices in a row. It appeared that two light-footed soldiers had been teasing a huge, bearded man, causing him to spill coffee upon his blue knees. The man had gone into a rage and had sworn comprehensively. Stung by his language, his tormentors had immediately bristled at him with a great show of resenting unjust oaths. Possibly there was going to be a fight.

The friend arose and went over to them, making pacific motions with his arms. 'Oh, here, now, boys, what's th' use?' he said. 'We'll be at th' rebs in less'n an hour. What's th' good fightin' 'mong ourselves?'

One of the light-footed soldiers turned upon him red-faced and violent. 'Yeh needn't come around here with yer preachin'. I s'pose yeh don't approve 'a fightin' since Charley Morgan licked yeh; but I don't see what business this here is 'a yours or anybody else.'

'Well, it ain't,' said the friend mildly. 'Still I hate t' see –'

There was a tangled argument.

'Well, he –' said the two, indicating their opponent with accusative forefingers.

The huge soldier was quite purple with rage. He pointed at the two soldiers with his great hand, extended clawlike. 'Well, they –'

But during this argumentative time the desire to deal blows seemed to pass, although they said much to each other. Finally the friend returned to his old seat. In a short while the three antagonists could be seen together in an amiable bunch.

'Jimmie Rogers ses I'll have t' fight him after th' battle t'-day,' announced the friend as he again seated himself. 'He ses he don't allow no interferin' in his business. I hate t' see th' boys fightin' 'mong themselves.'

The youth laughed. 'Yer changed a good bit. Yeh ain't at all like yeh was. I remember when you an' that Irish feller –' He stopped an laughed again.

'No, I didn't used t' be that way,' said his friend thoughtfully. 'That's true 'nough.'

'Well, I didn't mean –' began the youth.

The friend made another deprecatory gesture. 'Oh, yeh needn't mind, Henry.'

There was another little pause.

'Th' reg'ment lost over half th' men yestirday,' remarked the friend eventually. 'I thought 'a course they was all dead, but, laws, they kep' a-comin' back last night until it seems, after all, we didn't lose but a few. They'd been scattered all over, wanderin' around in th' woods, fightin' with other reg'ments, an' everything. Jest like you done.'

'So?' said the youth.

Chapter Fifteen

THE REGIMENT WAS STANDING at order arms at the side of a lane, waiting for the command to march, when suddenly the youth remembered the little packet enwrapped in a faded yellow envelope which the loud young soldier with lugubrious words had intrusted to him. It made him start. He uttered an exclamation and turned toward his comrade.

'Wilson!'

'What?'

His friend, at his side in the ranks, was thoughtfully staring down the road. From some cause his expression was at that moment very meek. The youth, regarding him with sidelong glances, felt impelled to change his purpose. 'Oh, nothing,' he said.

His friend turned his head in some surprise, 'Why, what was yeh goin' t' say?'

'Oh, nothing,' repeated the youth.

He resolved not to deal the little blow. It was sufficient that the fact made him glad. It was not necessary to knock his friend on the head with the misguided packet.

He had been possessed of much fear of his friend, for he saw how easily questionings could make holes in his feelings. Lately, he had assured himself that the altered comrade would not tantalize him with a persistent curiosity, but he felt certain that during the first period of leisure his friend would ask him to relate his adventures of the previous day.

He now rejoiced in the possession of a small weapon with which he could prostrate his comrade at the first signs of a cross-examination. He was master. It would now be he who could laugh and shoot the shafts of derision.

The friend had, in a weak hour, spoken with sobs of his own death. He had delivered a melancholy oration previous to his funeral, and had doubtless in the packet of letters, presented various keepsakes to relatives. But he had not died, and thus he had delivered himself into the hands of the youth.

The latter felt immensely superior to his friend, but he inclined to condescension. He adopted toward him an air of patronizing good humor.

His self-pride was now entirely restored. In the shade of its flourishing growth he stood with braced and self-confident legs, and since nothing could now be discovered he did not shrink from an encounter with the eyes of judges, and allowed no thoughts of his own to keep him from an attitude of manfulness. He had performed his mistakes in the dark, so he was still a man.

Indeed, when he remembered his fortunes of yesterday, and looked at them from a distance he began to see something fine there. He had a license to be pompous and veteranlike.

His panting agonies of the past he put out of his sight.

In the present, he declared to himself that it was only the doomed and the damned who roared with sincerity at circumstance. Few but they ever did it. A man with a full stomach and the respect of his fellows had no business to scold about anything that he might think to be wrong in the ways of the universe, or even with the ways of society. Let the unfortunates rail; the others may play marbles.

He did not give a great deal of thought to these battles that lay directly before him. It was not essential that he should plan his ways in regard to them. He had been taught that many obligations of a life were easily avoided. The lessons of yesterday had been that retribution was a laggard and blind. With these facts before him he did not deem it necessary that he should become feverish over the possibilities of the ensuing twenty-four hours. He could leave much to chance. Besides, a faith in himself had secretly blossomed. There was a little flower of confidence growing within him. He was now a man of experience. He had been out among the dragons, he said, and he assured himself that they were not so hideous as he had imagined them. Also, they were inaccurate; they did not sting with precision. A stout heart often defied, and defying, escaped.

And, furthermore, how could they kill him who was the chosen of gods and doomed to greatness?

He remembered how some of the men had run from the battle. As he recalled their terror-stricken faces he felt a scorn for them. They had surely been more fleet and more wild than was absolutely necessary. They were weak mortals. As for himself, he had fled with discretion and dignity.

He was aroused from this reverie by his friend, who, having hitched about nervously and blinked at the trees for a time, suddenly coughed in an introductory way, and spoke.

'Fleming!'

'What?'

The friend put his hand up to his mouth and coughed again. He fidgeted in his jacket.

'Well,' he gulped, at last, 'I guess yeh might as well give me back them letters.' Dark, prickling blood had flushed into his cheeks and brow.

'All right, Wilson,' said the youth. He loosened two buttons of his coat, thrust in his hand, and brought forth the packet. As he extended it to his friend the latter's face was turned from him.

He had been slow in the act of producing the packet because during it he had been trying to invent a remarkable comment upon the affair. He could conjure nothing of sufficient point. He was compelled to allow his friend to escape unmolested with his packet. And for this he took unto himself considerable credit. It was a generous thing.

His friend at his side seemed suffering great shame. As he contemplated him, the youth felt his heart grow more strong and stout. He had never been compelled to blush in such manner for his acts; he was an individual of extraordinary virtues.

He reflected, with condescending pity: 'Too bad! Too bad! The poor devil, it makes him feel tough!'

After this incident, and as he reviewed the battle pictures he had seen, he felt quite competent to return home and make the hearts of the people glow with stories of war. He could see himself in a room of warm tints telling tales to listeners. He could exhibit laurels. They were insignificant; still, in a district where laurels were infrequent, they might shine.

He saw his gaping audience picturing him as the central figure in blazing scenes. And he imagined the consternation and the ejaculations of his mother and the young lady at the seminary as they drank his recitals. Their vague feminine formula for beloved ones doing brave deeds on the battle without risk of life would be destroyed.

Chapter Sixteen

A SPUTTERING OF MUSKETRY WAS always to be heard. Later, the cannon had entered the dispute. In the fog-filled air their voices made a thudding sound. The reverberations were continued. This part of the world led a strange, battleful existence.

The youth's regiment was marched to relieve a command that had lain long in some damp trenches. The men took positions behind a curving line of rifle pits that had been turned up, like a large furrow, along the line of woods. Before them was a level stretch, peopled with short, deformed stumps. From the woods beyond came the dull popping of the skirmishers and pickets, firing in the fog. From the right came the noise of a terrific fracas.

The men cuddled behind the small embankment and sat in easy attitudes awaiting their turn. Many had their backs to the firing. The youth's friend lay down, buried his face in his arms, and almost instantly, it seemed, he was in a deep sleep.

The youth leaned his breast against the brown dirt and peered over at the woods and up and down the line. Curtains of trees interfered with his ways of vision. He could see the low line of trenches but for a short distance. A few idle flags were perched on the dirt hills. Behind them were rows of dark bodies with a few heads sticking curiously over the top.

Always the noise of skirmishers came from the woods on the front and left, and the din on the right had grown to frightful proportions. The guns were roaring without an instant's pause for breath. It seemed that the cannon had come from all parts and were engaged in a stupendous wrangle. It became impossible to make a sentence heard.

The youth wished to launch a joke – a quotation from newspapers. He desired to say, 'All quiet on the Rappahannock,' but the guns refused to permit even a comment upon their uproar. He never successfully concluded the sentence. But at last the guns stopped, and among the men in the rifle pits rumors again flew, like birds, but they were now for the most part black creatures who flapped their wings drearily near to the ground and refused to rise on any wings of hope. The men's faces grew doleful from the interpreting of omens. Tales of hesitation and uncertainty on the part of those high in place and responsibility came to their ears. Stories of disaster were borne into their minds with many proofs. This din of musketry on the right, growing like a released genie of sound, expressed and emphasized the army's plight.

The men were disheartened and began to mutter. They made gestures expressive of the sentence: 'Ah, what more can we do?' And it could always be seen that they were bewildered by the alleged news and could not fully comprehend a defeat.

Before the gray mists had been totally obliterated by the sun rays, the regiment was marching in a spread column that was retiring carefully through the woods. The disordered, hurrying lines of the enemy could sometimes be seen down through the groves and little fields. They were yelling, shrill and exultant.

At this sight the youth forgot many personal matters and became greatly enraged. He exploded in loud sentences. 'B'jiminy, we're generaled by a lot 'a lunkheads.'

'More than one feller has said that t'-day,' observed a man.

His friend, recently aroused, was still very drowsy. He looked behind him until his mind took in the meaning of the movement. Then he sighed. 'Oh, well, I s'pose we got licked,' he remarked sadly.

The youth had a thought that it would not be handsome for him to freely condemn other men. He made an attempt to restrain himself, but the words upon his tongue were too bitter. He presently began a long and intricate denunciation of the commander of the forces.

'Mebbe, it wa'n't all his fault – not all together. He did th' best he knowed. It's our luck t' git licked often,' said his friend in a weary tone. He was trudging along with stooped shoulders and shifting eyes like a man who has been caned and kicked.

'Well, don't we fight like the devil? Don't we do all that men can?' demanded the youth loudly.

He was secretly dumbfounded at this sentiment when it came from his lips. For a moment his face lost its valor and he looked guiltily about him. But no one questioned his right to deal in such words, and presently he recovered his air of courage. He went on to repeat a statement he had heard going from group to group at the camp that morning. 'The brigadier said he never saw a new reg'ment fight the way we fought yestirday, didn't he? And we didn't do better than many another reg'ment, did we? Well, then, you can't say it's th' army's fault, can you?'

In his reply, the friend's voice was stern. ''A course not,' he said. 'No man dare say we don't fight like th' devil. No man will ever dare say it. Th' boys fight like hell-roosters. But still – still, we don't have no luck.'

'Well, then, if we fight like the devil an' don't ever whip, it must be the general's fault,' said the youth grandly and decisively. 'And I don't see any sense in fighting and fighting and fighting, yet always losing through some derned old lunkhead of a general.'

A sarcastic man who was tramping at the youth's side, then spoke lazily. 'Mebbe yeh think yeh fit th' hull battle yestirday, Fleming,' he remarked.

The speech pierced the youth. Inwardly he was reduced to an abject pulp by these chance words. His legs quaked privately. He cast a frightened glance at the sarcastic man.

'Why, no,' he hastened to say in a conciliating voice, 'I don't think I fought the whole battle yesterday.'

But the other seemed innocent of any deeper meaning. Apparently, he had no information. It was merely his habit. 'Oh!' he replied in the same tone of calm derision.

The youth, nevertheless, felt a threat. His mind shrank from going near to the danger, and thereafter he was silent. The significance of the sarcastic man's words took from him all loud moods that would make him appear prominent. He became suddenly a modest person.

There was low-toned talk among the troops. The officers were impatient and snappy, their countenances clouded with the tales of misfortune. The troops, sifting through the forest, were sullen. In the youth's company once a man's laugh rang out. A dozen soldiers turned their faces quickly toward him and frowned with vague displeasure.

The noise of firing dogged their footsteps. Sometimes, it seemed to be driven a little way, but it always returned again with increased insolence. The men muttered and cursed, throwing black looks in its direction.

In a clear space the troops were at last halted. Regiments and brigades, broken and detached through their encounters with thickets, grew together again and lines were faced toward the pursuing bark of the enemy's infantry.

This noise, following like the yellings of eager, metallic hounds, increased to a loud and joyous burst, and then, as the sun went serenely up the sky, throwing illuminating rays into the gloomy thickets, it broke forth into prolonged pealings. The woods began to crackle as if afire.

'Whoop-a-dadee,' said a man, 'here we are! Everybody fightin'. Blood an' destruction.'

'I was willin' t' bet they'd attack as soon as th' sun got fairly up,' savagely asserted the lieutenant who commanded the youth's company. He jerked without mercy at his little mustache. He strode to and fro with dark dignity in the rear of his men, who were lying down behind whatever protection they had collected.

A battery had trundled into position in the rear and was thoughtfully shelling at a distance. The regiment, unmolested as yet, awaited the moment when the gray shadows of the wood before them should be slashed by the lines of flame. There was much growling and swearing.

'Good Gawd,' the youth grumbled, 'we're always being chased around like rats! It makes me sick. Nobody seems to know where we go or why we go. We just get fired around from pillar to post and get licked here and get licked there, and nobody knows what it's done for. It makes a man feel like a damn' kitten in a bag. Now, I'd like to know what the eternal thunders we was marched into these woods for anyhow, unless it was to give the rebs a regular pot shot at us. We came in here and got our legs all tangled up in these cussed briers, and then we begin to fight and the rebs had an easy time of it. Don't tell me it's just luck! I know better. It's this derned old –'

The friend seemed jaded, but he interrupted his comrade with a voice of calm confidence. 'It'll turn out all right in th' end,' he said.

'Oh, the devil it will! You always talk like a doghanged parson. Don't tell me! I know –'

At this time there was an interposition by the savage-minded lieutenant, who was obliged to vent some of his inward dissatisfaction upon his men. 'You boys shut right up! There no need 'ayour wastin' your breath in long-winded arguments about this an' that an' th' other. You've been jawin' like a lot 'a old hens. All you've got t' do is fight, an' you'll get plenty 'a that t' do in about ten minutes. Less talkin' an' more fightin' is what's best for you boys. I neveer saw sech gabbling jackasses.'

He paused, ready to pounce upon any man who might have the temerity to reply. No words being said, he resumed his dignified pacing.

'There's too much chin music an' too little fightin' in this war, anyhow,' he said to them, turning his head for a final remark.

The day had grown more white, until the sun shed his full radiance upon the thronged forest. A sort of gust of battle came sweeping toward that part of the line where lay the youth's regiment. The front shifted a trifle to meet it squarely. There was a wait. In this part of the field there passed slowly the intense moments that precede the tempest.

A single rifle flashed in a thicket before the regiment. In an instant it was joined by many others. There was a mighty song of clashes and crashes that went sweeping through the woods. The guns in the rear, aroused and enraged by shells that had been thrown burrlike at them, suddenly involved themselves in a hideous altercation with another band of guns. The battle roar settled to a rolling thunder, which was a single, long explosion.

In the regiment there was a peculiar kind of hesitation denoted in the attitudes of the men. They were worn, exhausted, having slept but little and labored much. They rolled their eyes toward the advancing battle as they stood awaiting the shock. Some shrank and flinched. They stood as men tied to stakes.

Chapter Seventeen

THIS ADVANCE OF THE ENEMY had seemed to the youth like a ruthless hunting. He began to fume with rage and exasperation. He beat his foot upon the ground, and scowled with hate at the swirling smoke that was approaching like a phantom flood. There was a maddening quality in this seeming resolution of the foe to give him no rest, to give him no time to sit down and think. Yesterday he had fought and had fled rapidly. There had been many adventures. For to-day he felt that he had earned opportunities for contemplative repose. He could have enjoyed portraying to uninitiated listeners various scenes at which he had been a witeness or ably discussing the processes of war with other proved men. Too it was important that he should have time for physical recuperation. He was sore and stiff from his experiences. He had received his fill of all exertions, and he wished to rest.

But those other men seemed never to grow weary; they were fighting with their old speed. He had a wild hate for the relentless foe. Yesterday, when he had imagined the universe to be against him, he had hated it, little gods and big gods; to-day he hated the army of the foe with the same great hatred. He was not going to be badgered of his life, like a kitten chased by boys, he said. It was not well to drive men into final corners; at those moments they could all develop teeth and claws.

He leaned and spoke into his friend's ear. He menaced the woods with a gesture. 'If they keep on chasing us, by Gawd, they'd better watch out. Can't stand *too* much.'

The friend twisted his head and made a calm reply. 'If they keep on a-chasin' us they'll drive us all inteh th' river.'

The youth cried out savagely at this statement. He crouched behind a little tree, with his eyes burning hatefully and his teeth set in a curlike snarl. The awkward bandage was still about his head, and upon it, over his wound, there was a spot of dry blood. His hair was wondrously tousled, and some straggling, moving locks hung over the cloth of the bandage down toward his forehead. His jacket and shirt were open at the throat, and exposed his young bronzed neck. There could be seen spasmodic gulpings at his throat.

His fingers twined nervously about his rifle. He wished that it was an engine of annihilating power. He felt that he and his companions were being taunted and derided from sincere convictions that they were poor and puny. His knowledge of his inability to take vengeance for it made his rage into a dark and stormy specter, that possessed him and made him dream of abominable cruelties. The tormentors were flies sucking insolently at his blood, and he thought that he would have given his life for a revenge of seeing their faces in pitiful plight.

The winds of battle had swept all about the regiment, until the one rifle, instantly followed by others, flashed in its front. A moment later the regiment roared forth in sudden and valiant retort. A dense wall of smoke settled slowly down. It was furiously slit and slashed by the knifelike fire from the rifles.

To the youth the fighters resembled animals tossed for a death struggle into a dark pit. There was a sensation that he and his fellows, at bay, were pushing back, always pushing fierce onslaughts of creatures who were slippery. Their beams of crimson seemed to get no purchase upon the bodies of their foes; the latter seemed to evade them with ease, and come through, between, around, and about with unopposed skill.

When, in a dream, it occurred to the youth that his rifle was an impotent stick, he lost sense of everything but his hate, his desire to smash into pulp the glittering smile of victory which he could feel upon the faces of his enemies.

The blue smoke-swallowed line curled and writhed like a snake stepped upon. It swung its ends to and fro in an agony of fear and rage.

The youth was not conscious that he was erect upon his feet. He did not know the direction of the ground. Indeed, once he even lost the habit of balance and fell heavily. He was up again immediately. One thought went through the chaos of his brain at the time. He wondered if he had fallen because he had been shot. But the suspicion flew away at once. He did not think more of it.

He had taken up a first position behind the little tree, with a direct determination to hold it against the world. He had not deemed it possible that his army could that day succeed, and from this he felt the ability to fight harder. But the throng had surged in all ways, until he lost directions and locations, save that he knew where lay the enemy.

The flames bit him, and the hot smoke broiled his skin. His rifle barrel grew so hot that ordinarily he could not have borne it upon his palms; but he kept on stuffing cartridges into it, and pounding them with his clanking, bending ramrod. If he aimed at some changing form through the smoke, he pulled his trigger with a fierce grunt, as if he were dealing a blow of the fist with all his strength.

When the enemy seemed falling back before him and his fellows, he went instantly forward, like a dog who, seeing his foes lagging, turns and insists upon being pursued. And when he was compelled to retire again, he did it slowly, sullenly, taking steps of wrathful despair.

Once he, in his intent hate, was almost alone, and was firing, when all those near him had ceased. He was so engrossed in his occupation that he was not aware of a lull.

He was recalled by a hoarse laugh and a sentence that came to his ears in a voice of contempt and amazement. 'Yeh infernal fool, don't yeh know enough t' quit when there ain't anything t' shoot at? Good Gawd!'

He turned then and, pausing with his rifle thrown half into position, looked at the blue line of his comrades. During this moment of leisure they seemed all to be engaged in staring with astonishment at him. They had become spectators. Turning to the front again, he saw, under the lifted smoke, a deserted ground.

He looked bewildered for a moment. Then there appeared upon the glazed vacancy of his eyes a diamond point of intelligence. 'Oh,' he said, comprehending.

He returned to his comrades and threw himself upon the ground. He sprawled like a man who had been thrashed. His flesh seemed strangely on fire, and the sounds of battle continued in his ears. He groped blindly for his canteen.

The lieutenant was crowing. He seemed drunk with fighting. He called out to the youth: 'By heavens, if I had ten thousand wild cats like you I could tear th' stomach outa this war in less'n a week!' He puffed out his chest with large dignity as he said it.

Some of the men muttered and looked at the youth in awe-struck ways. It was plain that as he had gone on loading and firing and cursing without the proper intermission, they had found time to regard him. And they now looked upon him as a war devil.

The friend came staggering to him. There was some fright and dismay in his voice. 'Are yeh all right, Fleming? Do yeh feel all right? There ain't nothin' th' matter with yeh, Henry, is there?'

'No,' said the youth with difficulty. His throat seemed full of knobs and burrs.

These incidents made the youth ponder. It was revealed to him that he had been a barbarian, a beast. He had fought like a pagan who defends his religion. Regarding it, he saw that it was fine, wild, and, in some ways, easy. He had been a tremendous figure, no doubt. By this struggle he had overcome obstacles which he had admitted to be mountains. They had fallen like paper peaks, and he was now what he called a hero. And he had not been aware of the process. He had slept and, awakening, found himself a knight.

He lay and basked in the occasional stares of his comrades. Their faces were varied in degrees of blackness from the burned powder. Some were utterly smudged. They were reeking with perspiration, and their breaths came hard and wheezing. And from these soiled expanses they peered at him.

'Hot work! Hot work!' cried the lieutenant deliriously. He walked up and down, restless and eager. Sometimes his voice could be heard in a wild, incomprehensible laugh.

When he had a particularly profound thought upon the science of war he always unconsciously addressed himself to the youth.

There was some grim rejoicing by the men. 'By thunder, I bet this army'll never see another new reg'ment like us!'

'You bet!'

> 'A dog, a woman, an' a walnut tree,
> Th' more yeh beat 'em, th' better they be!

That's like us.'

'Lost a piler men, they did. If an' ol' woman swep' up th' woods, she'd git a dustpanful.'

'Yes, an' if she'll come around ag'in in 'bout an' hour she'll git a pile more.'

The forest still bore its burden of clamor. From off under the trees came the rolling clatter of the musketry. Each distant thicket seemed a strange porcupine with quills of flame. A cloud of dark smoke, as from smoldering ruins, went up toward the sun now bright and gay in the blue, enameled sky.

Chapter Eighteen

THE RAGGED LINE HAD RESPITE for some minutes, but during its pause the struggle in the forest became magnified until the trees seemed to quiver from the firing and the ground to shake from the rushing of the men. The voices of the cannon were mingled in a long and interminable row. It seemed difficult to live in such an atmosphere. The chests of the men strained for a bit of freshness, and their throats craved water.

There was one shot through the body, who raised a cry of bitter lamentation when came this lull. Perhaps he had been calling out during the fighting also, but at that time no one had heard him. But now the men turned at the woeful complaints of him upon the ground.

'Who is it? Who is it?'

'It's Jimmie Rogers. Jimmie Rogers.'

When their eyes first encountered him there was a sudden halt, as if they feared to go near. He was thrashing about in the grass, twisting his shuddering body into many strange postures. He was screaming loudly. This instant's hesitation seemed to fill him with a tremendous, fantastic contempt, and he damned them in shrieked sentences.

The youth's friend had a geographical illusion concerning a stream, and he obtained permission to go for some water. Immediately canteens were showered upon him. 'Fill mine, will yeh?' 'Bring me some, too.' 'And me, too.' He departed, ladened. The youth went with his friend, feeling a desire to throw his heated body into the stream and, soaking there, drink quarts.

They made a hurried search for the supposed stream, but did not find it. 'No water here,' said the youth. They turned without delay and began to retrace their steps.

From their position as they again faced toward the place of the fighting, they could of course comprehend a greater amount of the battle than when their visions had been blurred by the hurling smoke of the line. They could see dark stretches winding along the land, and on one cleared space there was a row of guns making gray clouds, which were filled with large flashes of orange-colored flame. Over some foliage they could see the roof of a house. One window, glowing a deep murder red, shone squarely through the leaves. From the edifice a tall leaning tower of smoke went far into the sky.

Looking over their own troops, they saw mixed masses slowly getting into regular form. The sunlight made twinkling points of the bright steel. To the rear there was a glimpse of a distant roadway as it curved over a slope. It was crowded with retreating infantry. From all the interwoven forest arose the smoke and bluster of the battle. The air was always occupied by a blaring.

Near where they stood shells were flip-flapping and hooting. Occasional bullets buzzed in the air and spanged into tree trunks. Wounded men and other stragglers were slinking through the woods.

Looking down an aisle of the grove, the youth and his companion saw a jangling general and his staff almost ride upon a wounded man, who was crawling on his hands and knees. The general reined strongly at his charger's opened and foamy mouth and guided it with dexterous horsemanship past the man. The latter scrambled in wild and torturing haste. His strength evidently failed him as he reached a place of safety. One of his arms suddenly weakened, and he fell, sliding over upon his back. He lay stretched out, breathing gently.

A moment later the small, creaking cavalcade was directly in front of the two soldiers. Another officer, riding with the skilful abandon of a cowboy, galloped his horse to a position directly before the general. The two unnoticed foot soldiers made a little show of going on, but they lingered near in the desire to overhear the conversation. Perhaps, they thought, some great inner historical things would be said.

The general, whom the boys knew as the commander of their division, looked at the other officer and spoke coolly, as if he were criticizing his clothes. 'Th' enemy's formin' over there for another charge,' he said. 'It'll be directed against Whiterside, an' I fear they'll break through there unless we work like thunder t' stop them.'

The other swore at his restive horse, and then cleared his throat. He made a gesture toward his cap. 'It'll be hell t' pay stoppin' them,' he said shortly.

'I presume so,' remarked the general. Then he began to talk rapidly and in a lower tone. He frequently illustrated his words with a pointing finger. The two infantrymen could hear nothing until finally he asked: 'What troops can you spare?'

The officer who rode like a cowboy reflected for an instant. 'Well,' he said, 'I had to order in th' 12th to help th' 76th, an' I haven't really got any. But there's th' 304th. They fight like a lot 'a mule drivers. I can spare them best of any.'

The youth and his friend exchanged glances of astonishment.

The general spoke sharply. 'Get 'em ready, then. I'll watch developments from here, an' send you word when t' start them. It'll happen in five minutes.'

As the other officer tossed his fingers toward his cap and wheeling his horse, started away, the general called out to him in a sober voice: 'I don't believe many of your mule drivers will get back.'

The other shouted something in reply. He smiled.

With scared faces, the youth and his companion hurried back to the line.

These happenings had occupied an incredibly short time, yet the youth felt that in them he had been made aged. New eyes were given to him. And the most startling thing was to learn suddenly that he was very insignificant. The officer spoke of the regiment as if he referred to a broom. Some part of the woods needed sweeping, perhaps, and he merely indicated a broom in a tone properly indifferent to its fate. It was war, no doubt, but it appeared strange.

As the two boys approached the line, the lieutenant perceived them and swelled with wrath. 'Fleming – Wilson – how long does it take yeh to git water, anyhow – where yeh been to.'

But his oration ceased as he saw their eyes, which were large with great tales. 'We're goin' t' charge – we're goin' t' charge!' cried the youth's friend, hastening with his news.

'Charge?' said the lieutenant. 'Charge? Well, b'Gawd! Now, this is real fightin'.' Over his soiled countenance there went a boastful smile. 'Charge? Well, b'Gawd!'

A little group of soldiers surrounded the two youths. 'Are we, sure 'nough? Well, I'll be derned! Charge? What fer? What at? Wilson, you're lyin'.'

'I hope to die,' said the youth, pitching his tones to the key of angry remonstrance. 'Sure as shooting, I tell you.'

And his friend spoke in re-enforcement. 'Not by a blame sight, he ain't lyin'. We heard 'em talkin'.'

They caught sight of two mounted figures a short distance from them. One was the colonel of the regiment and the other was the officer who had received order from the commander of the division. They were gesticulating at each other. The soldier, pointing at them, interpreted the scene.

One man had a final objection: 'How could yeh hear 'em talkin'?' But the men, for a large part, nodded, admitting that previously the two friends had spoken truth.

They settled back into reposeful attitudes with airs of having accepted the matter. And they mused upon it, with a hundred varieties of expression. It was an engrossing thing to think about. Many tightened their belts carefully and hitched at their trousers.

A moment later the officers began to bustle among the men, pushing them into a more compact mass and into a better alignment. They chased those that straggled and fumed at a few men who seemed to show by their attitudes that they had decided to remain at that spot. They were like critical shepherds struggling with sheep.

Presently, the regiment seemed to draw itself up and heave a deep breath. None of the men's faces were mirrors of large thoughts. The soldiers were bended and stooped like sprinters before a signal. Many pairs of glinting eyes peered from the grimy faces toward the curtains of the deeper woods. They seemed to be engaged in deep calculations of time and distance.

They were surrounded by the noises of the monstrous altercation between the two armies. The world was fully interested in other matters. Apparently, the regiment had its small affair to itself.

The youth, turning, shot a quick, inquiring glance at his friend. The latter returned to him the same manner of look. They were the only ones who possessed an inner knowledge. 'Mule drivers – hell t' pay – don't believe many will get back.' It was an ironical secret. Still, they saw no hesitation in each other's faces, and they nodded a mute and unprotesting assent when a shaggy man near them said in a meek voice: 'We'll git swallowed.'

Chapter Nineteen

THE YOUTH STARED AT THE LAND in front of him. Its foliages now seemed to veil powers and horrors. He was unaware of the machinery of orders that started the charge, although from the corners of his eyes he saw an officer, who looked like a boy a-horseback, come galloping, waving his hat. Suddenly he felt a straining and heaving among the men. The line fell slowly forward like a toppling wall, and, with a convulsive gasp that was intended for a cheer, the regiment began its journey. The youth was pushed and jostled for a moment before he understood the movement at all, but directly he lunged ahead and began to run.

He fixed his eye upon a distant and prominent clump of trees where he had concluded the enemy were to be met, and he ran toward it as toward a goal. He had believed throughout that it was a mere question of getting over an unpleasant matter as quickly as possible, and he ran desperately, as if pursued for a murder. His face was drawn hard and tight with the stress of his endeavour. His eyes were fixed in a lurid glare. And with his soiled and disordered dress, his red and inflamed features surmounted by the dingy rag with its spot of blood, his wildly swinging rifle and banging accouterments, he looked to be an insane soldier.

As the regiment swung from its position out into a cleared space the woods and thickets before it awakened. Yellow flames leaped towards it from many directions. The forest made a tremendous objection.

The line lurched straight for a moment. Then the right wing swung forward; it in turn was surpassed by the left. Afterward the center careered to the front until the regiment was a wedge-shaped mass, but an instant later the opposition of the bushes, trees, and uneven places on the ground split the command and scattered it into detached clusters.

The youth, light-footed, was unconsciously in advance. His eyes still kept note of the clump of trees. From all places near it the clannish yell of the enemy could be heard. The little flames of rifles leaped from it. The song of the bullets was in the air and shells snarled among the treetops. One tumbled directly into the middle of a hurrying group and exploded in crimson fury. There was an instant's spectacle of a man, almost over it, throwing up his hands to shield his eyes.

Other men, punched by bullets, fell in grotesque agonies. The regiment left a coherent trail of bodies.

They had passed into a clearer atmosphere. There was an effect like a revelation in the new appearance of the landscape. Some men working madly at a battery were plain to them, and the opposing infantry's lines were defined by the gray walls and fringes of smoke.

It seemed to the youth that he saw everything. Each blade of the green grass was bold and clear. He thought that he was aware of every change in the thin, transparent vapor that floated idly in sheets. The brown or gray trunks of the trees showed each roughness of their surfaces. And the men of the regiment, with their starting eyes and sweating faces, running madly, or falling, as if thrown headlong, to queer, heaped-up corpses – all were comprehended. His mind took a mechanical but firm impression, so that afterward everything was pictured and explained to him, save why he himself was there.

But there was a frenzy made from this furious rush. The men, pitching forward insanely, had burst into cheerings, moblike and barbaric, but tuned in strange keys that can arouse the dullard and the stoic. It made a mad enthusiasm that, it seemed, would be incapable of checking itself before granite and brass. There was the delirium that encounters despair and death, and is heedless and blind to the odds. It is a temperory but sublime absence of selfishness. And because it was of this order was the reason, perhaps, why the youth wondered, afterward, what reasons he could have had for being there.

Presently the straining pace ate up the energies of the men. As if by agreement, the leaders began to slacken their speed. The volleys directed against them had had a seeming windlike effect. The regiment snorted and blew. Among some stolid trees it began to falter and hesitate. The men, staring intently, began to wait for some of the distant walls of smoke to move and disclose to them the scene. Since much of their strength and their breath had vanished, they returned to caution. They were become men again.

The youth had a vague belief that he had run miles, and he thought, in a way, that he was now in some new and unknown land.

The moment the regiment ceased its advance the protesting splutter of musketry became a steadied roar. Long and accurate fringes of smoke spread out. From the top of a small hill came level belchings of yellow flame that caused an inhuman whistling in the air.

The men, halted, had opportunity to see some of their comrades dropping with moans and shrieks. A few lay under foot, still or wailing. And now for an instant the men stood, their rifles slack in their hands, and watched the regiment dwindle. They appeared dazed and stupid. This spectacle seemed to paralyze them, overcome them with a fatal fascination. They stared woodenly at the sights, and, lowering their eyes, looked from face to face. It was a strange pause, and a strange silence.

Then, above the sounds of the outside commotion, arose the roar of the lieutenant. He strode suddenly forth, his infantile features black with rage. 'Come on, yeh fools!' he bellowed. 'Come on' Yeh can't stay here. Yeh must come on.' He said more, but much of it could not be understood.

He started rapidly forward, with his head turned toward the men. 'Come on,' he was shouting. The men stared with blank and yokel-like eyes at him. He was obliged to halt and retrace his steps. He stood then with his back to the enemy and delivered gigantic curses into the faces of the men. His body vibrated from the weight and force of his imprecations. And he could string oaths with the facility of a maiden who strings beads.

The friend of the youth aroused. Lurching suddenly forward and dropping to his knees, he fired an angry shot at the persistent woods. This action awakened the men. They huddled no more like sheep. They seemed suddenly to bethink them of their weapons, and at once commenced firing. Belabored by their officers, they began to move forward. The regiment, involved like a cart involved in mud and muddle, started unevenly with many jolts and jerks. The men stopped now every few paces to fire and load, and in this manner moved slowly on from trees to trees.

The flaming opposition in their front grew with their advance until it seemed that all forward ways were barred by the thin leaping tongues, and off to the right an ominous demonstration could sometimes be dimly discerned.

The smoke lately generated was in confusing clouds that made it difficult for the regiment to proceed with intelligence. As he passed through each curling mass the youth wondered what would confront him on the farther side.

The command went painfully forward until an open space interposed between them and the lurid lines. Here, crouching and cowering behind some trees, the men clung with desperation, as if threatened by a wave. They looked wild-eyed, and as if amazed at this furious disturbance they had stirred. In the storm there was an ironical expression of their importance. The faces of the men, too, showed a lack of a certain feeling of responsibility for being there. It was as if they had been driven. It was the dominant animal failing to remember in the supreme moment the forceful causes of various superficial qualities. The whole affair seemed incomprehensible to many of them.

As they halted thus the lieutenant again began to bellow profanely. Regardless of the vindictive threats of the bullets, he went about coaxing, berating, and bedamning. His lips, that were habitually in a soft and childlike curve, were now writhed into unholy contortions. He swore by all possible deities.

Once he grabbed the youth by the arm. 'Come on, yeh lunkhead!' he roared. 'Come on! We'll all git killed if we stay here. We've on'y got t' go across that lot. An' then' – the remainder of his idea disappeared in a blue haze of curses.

The youth stretched forth his arm. 'Cross there?' His mouth was puckered in doubt and awe.

'Certainly. Jest 'cross th' lot! We can't stay here,' screamed the lieutenant. He poked his face close to the youth and waved his bandaged hand. 'Come on!' Presently he grappled with him as if for a wrestling bout. It was as if he planned to drag the youth by the ear on to the assault.

The private felt a sudden unspeakable indignation against his officer. He wrenched fiercely and shook him off.

'Come on yerself, then,' he yelled. There was a bitter challenge in his voice.

They galloped together down the regimental front. The friend scrambled after them. In front of the colors the three men began to bawl: 'Come on! come on!' They danced and gyrated like tortured savages.

The flag, obedient to these appeals, bended its glittering form and swept towards them. The men wavered in indecision for a moment, and then with a long, wailful cry the dilapidated regiment surged forward and began its new journey.

Over the field went the scurrying mass. It was a handful of men splattered into the faces of the enemy. Toward it instantly sprang the yellow tongues. A vast quantity of blue smoke hung before them. A mighty banging made ears valueless.

The youth ran like a madman to reach the woods before a bullet could discover him. He ducked his head low, like a football player. In his haste his eyes almost closed, and the scene was a wild blur. Pulsating saliva stood at the corners of his mouth.

Within him, as he hurled himself forward, was born a love, a despairing fondness for this flag which was near him. It was a creation of beauty and invulnerability. It was a goddess, radiant, that bended its form with an imperious gesture to him. It was a woman, red and white, hating and loving, that called him with the voice of his hopes. Because no harm could come to it he endowed it with power. He kept near, as if it could be a saver of lives, and an imploring cry went from his mind.

In the mad scramble he was aware that the color sergeant flinched suddenly, as if struck by a bludgeon. He faltered, and then became motionless, save for his quivering knees.

He made a spring and a clutch at the pole. At the same instant his friend grabbed it from the other side. They jerked at it, stout and furious, but the color sergeant was dead, and the corpse would not relinquish its trust. For a moment there was a grim encounter. The dead man, swinging with bended back, seemed to be obstinately tugging, in ludicrous and awful ways, for the possession of the flag.

It was past in an instant of time. They wrenched the flag furiously from the dead man, and, as they turned again, the corpse swayed forward with bowed head. One arm swung high, and the curved hand fell with heavy protest on the friend's unheeding shoulder.

Chapter Twenty

WHEN THE TWO YOUTHS TURNED with the flag they saw that much of the regiment had crumbled away, and the dejected remnant was coming slowly back. The men, having hurled themselves in projectile fashion, had presently expended their forces. They slowly retreated, with their faces still toward the spluttering woods, and their hot rifles still replying to the din. Several officers were giving orders, their voices keyed to screams.

'Where in hell yeh goin'?' the lieutenant was asking in a sarcastic howl. And a red-bearded officer, whose voice of triple brass could plainly be heard, was commanding: 'Shoot into 'em! Shoot into 'em, Gawd damn their souls!' There was a *mêlée* of screeches, in which the men were ordered to do conflicting and impossible things.

The youth and his friend had a small scuffle over the flag. 'Give it t' me!' 'No, let me keep it!' Each felt satisfied with the other's possession of it, but each felt bound to declare, by an offer to carry the emblem, his willingness to further risk himself. The youth roughly pushed his friend away.

The regiment fell back to the stolid trees. There it halted for a moment to blaze at some dark forms that had begun to steal upon its track. Presently it resumed its march again, curving among the tree trunks. By the time the depleted regiment had again reached the first open space they were receiving a fast and merciless fire. There seemed to be mobs all about them.

The greater part of the men, discouraged, their spirits worn by the turmoil, acted as if stunned. They accepted the pelting of the bullets with bowed and weary heads. It was of no purpose to strive against walls. It was of no use to batter themselves against granite. And from this consciousness that they had attempted to conquer an unconquerable thing there seemed to arise a feeling that they had been betrayed. They glowered with bent brows, but dangerously, upon some of the officers, more particularly upon the red-bearded one with the voice of triple brass.

However, the rear of the regiment was fringed with men, who continued to shoot irritably at the advancing foes. They seemed resolved to make every trouble. The youthful lieutenant was perhaps the last man in the disordered mass. His forgotten back was toward the enemy. He had been shot in the arm. It hung straight and rigid. Occasionally he would cease to remember it, and be about to emphasize an oath with a sweeping gesture. The multiplied pain caused him to swear with incredible power.

The youth went along with slipping, uncertain feet. He kept watchful eyes rearward. A scowl of mortification and rage was upon his face. He had thought of a fine revenge upon the officer who had referred to him and his fellows as mule drivers. But he saw that it could not come to pass. His dreams had collapsed when the mule drivers, dwindling rapidly, had wavered and hesitated on the little clearing, and then had recoiled. And now the retreat of the mule drivers was a march of shame to him.

A dagger-pointed gaze from without his blackened face was held toward the enemy, but his greater hatred was riveted upon the man, who, not knowing him, had called him a mule driver.

When he knew that he and his comrades had failed to do anything in successful ways that might bring the little pangs of a kind of remorse upon the officer, the youth allowed the rage of the baffled to possess him. This cold officer upon a monument, who dropped epithets unconcernedly down, would be finer as a dead man, he thought. So grievous did he think it that he could never possess the secret right to taunt truly in answer.

He had pictured red letters of curious revenge. 'We are mule drivers, are we?' And now he was compelled to throw them away.

He presently wrapped his heart in the cloak of his pride and kept the flag erect. He harangued his fellows, pushing against their chests with his free hand. To those he knew he made frantic appeals, beseeching them by name. Between him and the lieutenant, scolding and near to losing his mind with rage, there was felt a subtle fellowship and equality. They supported each other in all manner of hoarse, howling protests.

But the regiment was a machine run down. The two men babbled at a forceless thing. The soldiers who had heart to go slowly were continually shaken in their resolves by the knowledge that comrades were slipping with speed back to the lines. It was difficult to think of reputation when others were thinking of skins. Wounded men were left crying on this black journey.

The smoke fringes and flames blustered always. The youth, peering once through a sudden rift in a cloud, saw a brown mass of troops, interwoven and magnified until they appeared to be thousands. A fierce-hued flag flashed before his vision.

Immediately, as if the uplifting of the smoke had been prearranged, the discovered troops burst into a rasping yell, and a hundred flames jetted toward the retreating band. A rolling gray cloud again interposed as the regiment doggedly replied. The youth had to depend again upon his misused ears, which were trembling and buzzing from the mêlée of musketry and yells.

The way seemed eternal. In the clouded haze men became panicstricken with the thought that the regiment had lost its path, and was proceeding in a perilous direction. Once the men who headed the wild procession turned and came pushing back against their comrades, screaming that they were being fired upon from points which they had considered to be toward their own lines. At this cry a hysterical fear and dismay beset the troops. A soldier, who heretofore had been ambitious to make the regiment into a wise little band that would proceed calmly amid the huge-appearing difficulties, suddenly sank down and buried his face in his arms with an air of bowing to a doom. From another a shrill lamentation rang out filled with profane allusions to a general. Men ran hither and thither, seeking with their eyes roads of escape. With serene regularity, as if controlled by a schedule, bullets buffed into men.

The youth walked stolidly into the midst of the mob, and with his flag in his hands took a stand as if he expected an attempt to push him to the ground. He unconsciously assumed the attitude of the color bearer in the fight of the preceding day. He passed over his brow a hand that trembled. His breath did not come freely. He was choking during this small wait for the crisis.

His friend came to him. 'Well, Henry, I guess this is goodby – John.'

'Oh, shut up, you damned fool!' replied the youth, and he would not look at the other.

The officers labored like politicians to beat the mass into a proper circle to face the menaces. The ground was uneven and torn. The men curled into depressions and fitted themselves snugly behind whatever would frustrate a bullet.

The youth noted with vague surprise that the lieutenant was standing mutely with his legs far apart and his sword held in the manner of a cane. The youth wondered what had happened to his vocal organs that he no more cursed.

There was something curious in this little intent pause of the lieutenant. He was like a babe which, having wept its fill, raises its eyes and fixes them upon a distant toy. He was engrossed in this contemplation, and the soft under lip quivered from self-whispered words.

Some lazy and ignorant smoke curled slowly. The men, hiding from the bullets, waited anxiously for it to lift and disclose the plight of the regiment.

The silent ranks were suddenly thrilled by the eager voice of the youthful lieutenant bawling out: 'Here they come! Right onto us, b'Gawd!' His further words were lost in a roar of wicked thunder from the men's rifles.

The youth's eyes had instantly turned in the direction indicated by the awakened and agitated lieutenant, and he had seen the haze of treachery disclosing a body of soldiers of the enemy. They were so near that he could see their features. There was a recognition as he looked at the types of faces. Also he perceived with dim amazement that their uniforms were rather gay in effect, being light gray, accented with a brilliant-hued facing. Too, the clothes seemed new.

These troops had apparently been going forward with caution, their rifles held in readiness, when the youthful lieutenant had discovered them and their movement had been interrupted by the volley from the blue regiment. From the moment's glimpse, it was derived that they had been unaware of the proximity of their dark-suited foes or had mistaken the direction. Almost instantly they were shut utterly from the youth's sight by the smoke from the energetic rifles of his companions. He strained his vision to learn the accomplishment of the volley, but the smoke hung before him.

The two bodies of troops exchanged blows in the manner of a pair of boxers.

The fast angry firings went back and forth. The men in blue were intent with the despair of their circumstances and they seized upon the revenge to be had at close range. Their thunder swelled loud and valiant. Their curving front bristled with flashes and the place resounded with the clangor of their ramrods. The youth ducked and dodged for a time and achieved a few unsatisfactory views of the enemy. There appeared to be many of them and they were replying swiftly. They seemed moving toward the blue regiment, step by step. He seated himself gloomily on the ground with his flag between his knees.

As he noted the vicious, wolflike temper of his comrades he had a sweet thought that if the enemy was about to swallow the regimental broom as a large prisoner, it could at least have the consolation of going down with bristles forward.

But the blows of the antagonist began to grow more weak. Fewer bullets ripped the air, and finally, when the men slackened to learn of the fight, they could see only dark, floating smoke. The regiment lay still and gazed. Presently some chanced whim came to the pestering blur, and it began to coil heavily away. The man saw a ground vacant of fighters. It would have been an empty stage if it were not for a few corpses that lay thrown and twisted into fantastic shapes upon the sward.

At sight of this tableau, many of the men in blue sprang from behind their covers and made an ungainly dance of joy. Their eyes burned and a hoarse cheer of elation broke from their dry lips.

It had begun to seem to them that events were trying to prove that they were impotent. These little battles had evidently endeavored to demonstrate that the men could not fight well. When on the verge of submission to these opinions, the small duel had showed them that the proportions were not impossible, and by it they had revenged themselves upon their misgivings and upon the foe.

The impetus of enthusiasm was theirs again. They gazed about them with looks of uplifted pride, feeling new trust in the grim, always confident weapons in their hands. And they were men.

Chapter Twenty One

PRESENTLY THEY KNEW THAT NO FIRING threatened them. All ways seemed once more opened to them. The dusty blue lines of their friends were disclosed a short distance away. In the distance there were many colossal noises, but in all this part of the field there was a sudden stillness.

They perceived that they were free. The depleted band drew a long breath of relief and gathered itself into a bunch to complete its trip.

In this last length of journey the men began to show strange emotions. They hurried with nervous fear. Some who had been dark and unfaltering in the grimmest moments now could not conceal an anxiety that made them frantic. It was perhaps that they dreaded to be killed in insignificant ways after the times for proper military deaths had passed. Or, perhaps, they thought it would be too ironical to get killed at the portals of safety. With backward looks of perturbation, they hastened.

As they approached their own lines there was some sarcasm exhibited on the part of a gaunt and bronzed regiment that lay resting in the shade of trees. Questions were wafted to them.

'Where th' hell yeh been?'

'What yeh comin' back fer?'

'Why didn't yeh stay there?'

'Was it warm out there, sonny?'

'Goin' home now, boys?'

One shouted in taunting mimicry: 'Oh, mother, come quick an' look at th' sojers!'

There was no reply from the bruised and battered regiment, save that one man made broadcast challenges to fist fights and the red-bearded officer walked rather near and glared in great swashbuckler style at a tall captain in the other regiment. But the lieutenant suppressed the man who wished to fist fight, and the tall captain, flushing at the little fanfare of the red-bearded one, was obliged to look intently at some trees.

The youth's tender flesh was deeply stung by these remarks. From under his creased brows he glowered with hate at the mockers. He meditated upon a few revenges. Still, many in the regiment hung their heads in criminal fashion, so that it came to pass that the men trudged with sudden heaviness, as if they bore upon their bended shoulders the coffin of their honor. And the youthful lieutenant, recollecting himself, began to mutter softly in black curses.

They turned when they arrived at their old position to regard the ground over which they had charged.

The youth in this contemplation was smitten with a large astonishment. He discovered that the distances, as compared with the brilliant measurings of his mind, were trivial and ridiculous. The stolid trees, where much had taken place, seemed incredibly near. The time, too, now that he reflected, he saw to have been short. He wondered at the number of emotions and events that had been crowded into such little spaces. Elfin thoughts must have exaggerated and enlarged everything, he said.

It seemed, then, that there was bitter justice in the speeches of the gaunt and bronzed veterans. He veiled a glance of disdain at his fellows who strewed the ground, choking with dust, red from perspiration, misty-eyed, disheveled.

They were gulping at their canteens, fierce to wring every mite of water from them, and they polished at their swollen and watery features with coat sleeves and bunches of grass.

However, to the youth there was a considerable joy in musing upon his performances during the charge. He had had very little time previously in which to appreciate himself, so that there was now much satisfaction in quietly thinking of his actions. He recalled bits of color that in the flurry had stamped themselves unawares upon his engaged senses.

As the regiment lay heaving from its hot exertions the officer who had named them as mule drivers came galloping along the line. He had lost his cap. His tousled hair streamed wildly, and his face was dark with vexation and wrath. His temper was displayed with more clearness by the way in which he managed his horse. He jerked and wrenched savagely at his bridle, stopping the hard-breathing animal with a furious pull near the colonel of the regiment. He immediately exploded in reproaches which came unbidden to the ears of the men. They were suddenly alert, being always curious about black words between officers.

'Oh, thunder, MacChesnay, what an awful bull you made of this thing!' began the officer. He attempted low tones, but his indignation caused certain of the men to learn the sense of his words. 'What an awful mess you made! Good Lord, man, you stopped about a hundred feet this side of a very pretty success! If your men had gone a hundred feet farther you would have made a great charge, but as it is – what a lot of mud diggers you've got anyway!'

The men, listening with bated breath, now turned their curious eyes upon the colonel. They had a ragamuffin interest in this affair.

The colonel was seen to straighten his form and put one hand forth in oratorical fashion. He wore an injured air; it was as if a deacon had been accused of stealing. The men were wiggling in an ecstasy of excitement.

But of a sudden the colonel's manner changed from that of a deacon to that of a Frenchman. He shrugged his shoulders. 'Oh, well, general, we went as far as we could,' he said calmly.

'As far as you could? Did you, b'Gawd?' snorted the other. 'Well, that wasn't very far, was it?' he added, with a glance of cold contempt into the other's eyes. 'Not very far, I think. You were intended to make a diversion in favor of Whiterside. How well you succeeded your own ears can now tell you.' He wheeled his horse and rode stiffly away.

The colonel, bidden to hear the jarring noise of an engagement in the woods to the left, broke out in vague damnations.

The lieutenant, who had listened with an air of impotent rage to the interview, spoke suddenly in firm and undaunted tones. 'I don't care what a man is – whether he is a general or what – if he says th' boys didn't put up a good fight out there he's a damned fool.'

'Lieutenant,' began the colonel, severely, 'this is my own affair, and I'll trouble you –'

The lieutenant made an obedient gesture. 'All right, colonel, all right,' he said. He sat down with an air of being content with himself.

The news that the regiment had been reproached went along the line. For a time the men were bewildered by it. 'Good thunder!' they ejaculated, staring at the vanishing form of the general. They conceived it to be a huge mistake.

Presently, however, they began to believe that in truth their efforts had been called light. The youth could see this conviction weigh upon the entire regiment until the men were like cuffed and cursed animals, but withal rebellious.

The friend, with a grievance in his eye, went to the youth. 'I wonder what he does want,' he said. 'He must think we went out there an' played marbles! I never see sech a man!'

The youth developed a tranquil philosophy for these moments of irritation. 'Oh, well,' he rejoined, 'he probably didn't see nothing of it at all and got mad as blazes, and concluded we were a lot of sheep, just because we didn't do what he wanted done. It's a pity old Grandpa Henderson got killed yestirday – he'd have known that we did our best and fought good. It's just our awful luck, that's what.'

'I should say so,' replied the friend. He seemed to be deeply wounded at an injustice. 'I should say we did have awful luck! There's no fun in fightin' fer people when everything yeh do – no matter what – ain't done right. I have a notion t' stay behind next time an' let 'em take their ol' charge an' go t' th' devil with it.'

The youth spoke soothingly to his comrade. 'Well, we both did good. I'd like to see the fool what'd say we both didn't do as good as we could!'

'Of couse we did,' declared the friend stoutly. 'An' I'd break th' feller's neck if he was as big as a church. But we're all right, anyhow, for I heard one feller say that we two fit th' best in th' reg'ment, an' they had a great argument 'bout it. Another feller, 'a course, he had t' up an' say it was a lie – he seen all what was goin' on an' he never seen us from th' beginnin' t' th' end. An' a lot more struck in an' ses it wasn't a lie – we did fight like thunder, an' they give us quite a send-off. But this is what I can't stand – these everlastin' ol' soldiers, titterin' an laughin', an' then the general, he's crazy.'

The youth exclaimed with sudden exasperation: 'He's a lunkhead! He makes me mad. I wish he'd come along next time. We'd show 'im what –'

He ceased because several men had come hurrying up. Their faces expressed a bringing of great news.

'O Flem, yeh jest oughta heard!' cried one, eagerly.

'Heard what?' said the youth.

'Yeh jest oughta heard!' repeated the other, and he arranged himself to tell his tidings. The others made an excited circle. 'Well, sir, th' colonel met your lieutenant right by us – it was the damnedest thing I ever heard – an' he ses: "Ahem! ahem!" he ses. "Mr Hasbrouck!" he ses, "by th' way, who was that lad what carried th' flag?" he ses. There, Flemin', what d'yeh think 'a that? "Who was th' lad what carried th' flag?" he ses, an' th' lieutenant, he speaks up right away: "That's Flemin', an' he's a jimhickey," he ses right away. What? I say he did. "A jimhickey," he ses – those 'r his words. He did, too. I say he did. If you kin tell this story better than I kin, go ahead an' tell it. Well, then, keep yer mouth shet. Th' lieutenant, he ses: "He's a jimhickey," an' th' colonel, he ses: "Ahem! ahem! he is, indeed, a very good man t' have, ahem! He kep' th' flag 'way t' th' front. I saw 'im. He's a good un," ses the colonel. "You bet," ses th' lieutenant, "he an' a feller named Wilson was at th' head 'a th' charge, an' howlin' like Indians all th' time," he ses. "Head 'a th' charge all th' time," he ses. "A feller named Wilson," he ses. There, Wilson, m'boy, put that in a letter an' send it hum t' yer mother, hay? "A feller named Wilson," he ses. An' th' colonel, he ses: 'Were they, indeed? Ahem! ahem! My sakes!" he ses. "At th' head 'a th' reg'ment?" he ses. "They were," ses th' lieutenant. "My sakes!" ses th' colonel. He ses: " Well, well, well," he ses, "those two babies?" "They were," ses th' lieutenant. "Well, well," ses th' colonel, "they deserve t' be major generals," he ses. "They deserve t' be major generals."'

The youth and his friend had said: 'Huh!' 'Yer lyin', Thompson.' 'Oh, go t' blazes!' 'He never sed it.' 'Oh, what a lie!' 'Huh!' But despite these youthful scoffings and embarrassments, they knew that their faces were deeply flushing from thrills of pleasure. They exchanged a secret glance of joy and congratulation.

They speedily forgot many things. The past held no pictures of error and disappointment. They were very happy, and their hearts swelled with grateful affection for the colonel and the youthful lieutenant.

Chapter Twenty Two

WHEN THE WOODS AGAIN BEGAN to pour forth the dark-hued masses of the enemy the youth felt serene self-confidence. He smiled briefly when he saw men dodge and duck at the long screechings of shells that were thrown in giant handfuls over them. He stood, erect and tranquil, watching the attack begin against a part of the line that made a blue curve along the side of an adjacent hill. His vision being unmolested by smoke from the rifles of his companions, he had opportunities to see parts of the hard fight. It was a relief to perceive at last from whence came some of these noises which had been roared into his ears.

Off a short way he saw two regiments fighting a little separate battle with two other regiments. It was in a cleared space, wearing a set-apart look. They were blazing as if upon a wager, giving and taking tremendous blows. The firings were incredibly fierce and rapid. These intent regiments apparently were oblivious of all larger purposes of war, and were slugging each other as if at a matched game.

In another direction he saw a magnificent brigade going with the evident intention of driving the enemy from a wood. They passed in out of sight and presently there was a most awe-inspiring racket in the wood. The noise was unspeakable. Having stirred this prodigious uproar, and, apparently, finding it too prodigious, the brigade, after a little time, came marching airily out again with its fine formation in nowise disturbed. There were no traces of speed in its movements. The brigade was jaunty and seemed to point a proud thumb at the yelling wood.

On a slope to the left there was a long row of guns, gruff and maddened, denouncing the enemy, who, down through the woods, were forming for another attack in the pitiless monotony of conflicts. The round red discharges from the guns made a crimson flare and a high, thick smoke. Occasional glimpses could be caught of groups of the toiling artillerymen. In the rear of this row of guns stood a house, calm and white, amid bursting shells. A congregation of horses, tied to a long railing, were tugging frenziedly at their bridles. Men were running hither and thither.

The detached battle between the four regiments lasted for some time. There chanced to be no interference, and they settled their dispute by themselves. They struck savagely and powerfully at each other for a period of minutes, and then the lighter-hued regiments faltered and drew back, leaving the dark-blue lines shouting. The youth could see the two flags shaking with laughter amid the smoke remnants.

Presently there was a stillness, pregnant with meaning. The blue lines shifted and changed a trifle and stared expectantly at the silent woods and fields before them. The hush was solemn and churchlike, save for a distant battery that, evidently unable to remain quiet, sent a faint rolling thunder over the ground. It irritated, like the noises of unimpressed boys. The men imagined that it would prevent their perched ears from hearing the first words of the new battle.

Of a sudden the guns on the slope roared out a message of warning. A spluttering sound had begun in the woods. It swelled with amazing speed to a profound clamor that involved the earth in noises. The splitting crashes swept along the lines until an interminable roar was developed. To those in the midst of it it became a din fitted to the universe. It was the whirring and thumping of gigantic machinery, complications among the smaller stars. The youth's ears were filled up. They were incapable of hearing more.

On an incline over which a road wound he saw wild and desperate rushes of men perpetually backward and forward in riotous surges. These parts of the opposing armies were two long waves that pitched upon each other madly at dictated points. To and fro they swelled. Sometimes, one side by its yells and cheers would proclaim decisive blows, but a moment later the other side would be all yells and cheers. Once the youth saw a spray of light forms go in houndlike leaps toward the waving blue lines. There was much howling, and presently it went away with a vast mouthful of prisoners. Again, he saw a blue wave dash with such thunderous force against a gray obstruction that it seemed to clear the earth of it and leave nothing but trampled sod. And always in their swift and deadly rushes to and fro the men screamed and yelled like maniacs.

Particular pieces of fence or secure positions behind collections of trees were wrangled over, as gold thrones or pearl bedsteads. There were desperate lunges at these chosen spots seemingly every instant, and most of them were bandied like light toys between the contending forces. The youth could not tell from the battle flags flying like crimson foam in many directions which color of cloth was winning.

His emaciated regiment bustled forth with undiminished fierceness when its time came. When assaulted again by bullets, the men burst out in a barbaric cry of rage and pain. They bent their heads in aims of intent hatred behind the projected hammers of their guns. Their ramrods clanged loud with fury as their eager arms pounded the cartridges into the rifle barrels. The front of the regiment was a smoke-wall penetrated by the flashing points of yellow and red.

Wallowing in the fight, they were in an astonishingly short time resmudged. They surpassed in stain and dirt all their previous appearances. Moving to and fro with strained exertion, jabbering the while, they were, with their swaying bodies, black faces, and glowing eyes, like strange and ugly fiends jigging heavily in the smoke.

The lieutenant, returning from a tour after a bandage, produced from a hidden receptacle of his mind new and portentous oaths suited to the emergency. Strings of expletives he swung lashlike over the backs of his men, and it was evident that his previous efforts had in nowise impaired his resources.

The youth, still the bearer of the colors, did not feel his idleness. He was deeply absorbed as a spectator. The crash and swing of the great drama made him lean forward, intent-eyed, his face working in small contortions. Sometimes he prattled, words coming unconsciously from him in grotesque exclamations. He did not know that he breathed; that the flag hung silently over him, so absorbed was he.

A formidable line of the enemy came within dangerous range. They could be seen plainly – tall, gaunt men with excited faces running with long strides toward a wandering fence.

At sight of this danger the men suddenly ceased their cursing monotone. There was an instant of strained silence before they threw up their rifles and fired a plumping volley at the foes. There had been no order given; the men, upon recognizing the menace, had immediately let drive their flock of bullets without waiting for word of command.

But the enemy were quick to gain the protection of the wandering line of fence. They slid down behind it with remarkable celerity, and from this position they began briskly to slice up the blue men.

These latter braced their energies for a great struggle. Often, white clinched teeth shone from the dusky faces. Many heads surged to and fro, floating upon a pale sea of smoke. Those behind the fence frequently shouted and yelped in taunts and gibelike cries, but the regiment maintained a stressed silence. Perhaps, at this new assault the men recalled the fact that they had been named mud diggers, and it made their situation thrice bitter. They were breathlessly intent upon keeping the ground and thrusting away the rejoicing body of the enemy. They fought swiftly and with a despairing savageness denoted in their expressions.

The youth had resolved not to budge whatever should happen. Some arrows of scorn that had buried themselves in his heart had generated strange and unspeakable hatred. It was clear to him that his final and absolute revenge was to be achieved by his dead body lying, torn and gluttering, upon the field. This was to be a poignant retaliation upon the officer who had said 'mule drivers,' and later 'mud diggers,' for in all the wild graspings of his mind for a unit responsible for his sufferings and commotions he always seized upon the man who had dubbed him wrongly. And it was his idea, vaguely formulated, that his corpse would be for those eyes a great and salt reproach.

The regiment bled extravagantly. Grunting bundles of blue began to drop. The orderly sergeant of the youth's company was shot through the cheeks. Its supports being injured, his jaw hung afar down, disclosing in the wide cavern of his mouth a pulsing mass of blood and teeth. And with it all he made attempts to cry out. In his endeavor there was a dreadful earnestness, as if he conceived that one great shriek would make him well.

The youth saw him presently go rearward. His strength seemed in nowise impaired. He ran swiftly, casting wild glances for succor.

Others fell down about the feet of their companions. Some of the wounded crawled out and away, but many lay still, their bodies twisted into impossible shapes.

The youth looked once for his friend. He saw a vehement young man, powder-smeared and frowzled, whom he knew to be him. The lieutenant, also, was unscathed in his position at the rear. He had continued to curse, but it was now with the air of a man who was using his last box of oaths.

For the fire of the regiment had begun to wane and drip. The robust voice, that had come strangely from the thin ranks, was growing rapidly weak.

Chapter Twenty Three

THE COLONEL CAME RUNNING ALONG back of the line. There were other officers following him. 'We must charge'm!' they shouted. 'We must charge'm!' they cried with resentful voices, as if anticipating a rebellion against this plan by the men.

The youth, upon hearing the shouts, began to study the distance between him and the enemy. He made vague calculations. He saw that to be firm soldiers they must go forward. It would be death to stay in the present place, and with all the circumstances to go backward would exalt too many others. Their hope was to push the galling foes away from the fence.

He expected that his companions, weary and stiffened, would have to be driven to this assault, but as he turned toward them he perceived with a certain surprise that they were giving quick and unqualified expressions of assent. There was an ominous, clanging overture to the charge when the shafts of the bayonets rattled upon the rifle barrels. At the yelled words of command the soldiers sprang forward in eager leaps. There was new and unexpected force in the movement of the regiment. A knowledge of its faded and jaded condition made the charge appear like a paroxysm, a display of the strength that comes before a final feebleness. The men scampered in insane fever of haste, racing as if to achieve a sudden success before an exhilarating fluid should leave them. It was a blind and despairing rush by the collection of men in dusty and tattered blue, over a green sward and under a sapphire sky, toward a fence, dimly outlined in smoke, from behind which spluttered the fierce rifles of enemies.

The youth kept the bright colors to the front. He was waving his free arm in furious circles, the while shrieking mad calls and appeals, urging on those that did not need to be urged, for it seemed that the mob of blue men hurling themselves on the dangerous group of rifles were again grown suddenly wild with an enthusiasm of unselfishness. From the many firings starting toward them, it looked as if they would merely succeed in making a great sprinkling of corpses on the grass between the former position and the fence. But they were in a state of frenzy, perhaps because of forgotten vanities, and it made an exhibition of sublime recklessness. There was no obvious questioning, nor figurings, nor diagrams. There were, apparently, no considered loopholes. It appeared that the swift wings of their desires would have shattered against the iron gates of the impossible.

He himself felt the daring spirit of a savage religionmad. He was capable of profound sacrifices, a tremendous death. He had no time for dissections, but he knew that he thought of the bullets only as things that could prevent him from reaching the place of his endeavor. There were subtle flashings of joy within him that thus should be his mind.

He strained all his strength. His eyesight was shaken and dazzled by the tension of thought and muscle. He did not see anything excepting the mist of smoke gashed by the little knives of fire, but he knew that in it lay the aged fence of a vanished farmer protecting the snuggled bodies of the gray men.

As he ran a thought of the shock of contact gleamed in his mind. He expected a great concussion when the two bodies of troops crashed together. This became a part of his wild battle madness. He could feel the onward swing of the regiment about him and he conceived of a thunderous, crushing blow that would prostrate the resistance and spread consternation and amazement for miles. The flying regiment was going to have a catapultian effect. This dream made him run faster among his comrades, who were giving vent to hoarse and frantic cheers.

But presently he could see that many of the men in gray did not intend to abide the blow. The smoke, rolling, disclosed men who ran, their faces still turned. These grew to a crowd, who retired stubbornly. Individuals wheeled frequently to send a bullet at the blue wave.

But at one part of the line there was a grim and obdurate group that made no movement. They were settled firmly down behind posts and rails. A flag, ruffled and fierce, waved over them and their rifles dinned fiercely.

The blue whirl of men got very near, until it seemed that in truth there would be a close and frightful scuffle. There was an expressed disdain in the opposition of the little group, that changed the meaning of the cheers of the men in blue. They became yells of wrath, directed, personal. The cries of the two parties were now in sound an interchange of scathing insults.

They in blue showed their teeth; their eyes shone all white. They launched themselves as at the throats of those who stood resisting. The space between dwindled to an insignificant distance.

The youth had centered the gaze of his soul upon that other flag. Its possession would be high pride. It would express bloody minglings, near blows. He had a gigantic hatred for those who made great difficulties and complications. They caused it to be as a craved treasure of mythology, hung amid tasks and contrivances of danger.

He plunged like a mad horse at it. He was resolved it should not escape if wild blows and darings of blows could seize it. His own emblem, quivering and aflare, was winging toward the other. It seemed there would shortly be an encounter of strange beaks and claws, as of eagles.

The swirling body of blue men came to a sudden halt at close and disastrous range and roared a swift volley. The group in gray was split and broken by this fire, but its riddled body still fought. The men in blue yelled again and rushed upon it.

The youth, in his leapings, saw, as through a mist, a picture of four or five men stretched upon the ground or writhing upon their knees with bowed heads as if they had been stricken by bolts from the sky. Tottering among them was the rival color bearer, whom the youth saw had been bitten vitally by the bullets of the last formidable volley. He perceived this man fighting a last struggle, the struggle of one whose legs are grasped by demons. It was a ghastly battle. Over his face was the bleach of death, but set upon it was the dark and hard lines of desperate purpose. With this terrible grin of resolution he hugged his precious flag to him and was stumbling and staggering in his design to go the way that led to safety for it.

But his wounds always made it seem that his feet were retarded, held, and he fought a grim fight, as with invisible ghouls fastened greedily upon his limbs. Those in advance of the scampering blue men, howling cheers, leaped at the fence. The despair of the lost was in his eyes as he glanced back at them.

The youth's friend went over the obstruction in a tumbling heap and sprang at the flag as a panther at prey. He pulled at it and, wrenching it free, swung up its red brilliancy with a mad cry of exultation even as the color bearer, gasping, lurched over in a final throe and, stiffening convulsively, turned his dead face to the ground. There was much blood upon the grass blades.

At the place of success there began more wild clamorings of cheers. The men gesticulated and bellowed in an ecstasy. When they spoke it was as if they considered their listener to be a mile away. What hats and caps were left to them they often slung high in the air.

At one part of the line four men had been swooped upon, and they now sat as prisoners. Some blue men were about them in an eager and curious circle. The soldiers had trapped strange birds, and there was an examination. A flurry of fast questions was in the air.

One of the prisoners was nursing a superficial wound in the foot. He cuddled it, baby-wise, but he looked up from it often to curse with an astonishing utter abandon straight at the noses of his captors. He consigned them to red regions; he called upon the pestilential wrath of strange gods. And with it all he was singularly free from recognition of the finer points of the conduct of prisoners of war. It was as if a clumsy clod had trod upon his toe and he conceived it to be his privilege, his duty, to use deep, resentful oaths.

Another, who was a boy in years, took his plight with great calmness and apparent good nature. He conversed with the men in blue, studying their faces with his bright and keen eyes. They spoke of battles and conditions. There was an acute interest in all their faces during this exchange of view points. It seemed a great satisfaction to hear voices from where all had been darkness and speculation.

The third captive sat with a morose countenance. He preserved a stoical and cold attitude. To all advances he made one reply without variation, 'Ah, go t' hell!'

The last of the four was always silent and, for the most part, kept his face turned in unmolested directions. From the views the youth received he seemed to be in a state of absolute dejection. Shame was upon him, and with it profound regret that he was, perhaps, no more to be counted in the ranks of his fellows. The youth could detect no expression that would allow him to believe that the other was giving a thought to his narrowed future, the pictured dungeons, perhaps, and starvations and brutalities, liable to the imagination. All to be seen was shame for captivity and regret for the right to antagonize.

After the men had celebrated sufficiently they settled down behind the old rail fence, on the opposite side to the one from which their foes had been driven. A few shot perfunctorily at distant marks.

There was some long grass. The youth nestled in it and rested, making a convenient rail support the flag. His friend, jubilant and glorified, holding his treasure with vanity, came to him there. They sat side by side and congratulated each other.

Chapter Twenty Four

THE ROARINGS THAT HAD STRETCHED in a long line of sound across the face of the forest began to grow intermittent and weaker. The stentorian speeches of the artillery continued in some distant encounter, but the crashes of the musketry had almost ceased. The youth and his friend of a sudden looked up, feeling a deadened form of distress at the waning of these noises, which had become a part of life. They could see changes going on among the troops. There were marchings this way and that way. A battery wheeled leisurely. On the crest of a small hill was the thick gleam of many departing muskets.

The youth arose. 'Well, what now, I wonder?' he said. By his tone he seemed to be preparing to resent some new monstrosity in the way of dins and smashes. He shaded his eyes with his grimy hand and gazed over the field.

His friend also arose and stared. 'I bet we're goin' t' git along out of this an' back over th' river,' said he.

'Well, I swan!' said the youth.

They waited, watching. Within a little while the regiment received orders to retrace its way. The men got up grunting from the grass, regretting the soft repose. They jerked their stiffened legs, and stretched their arms over their heads. One man swore as he rubbed his eyes. They all groaned 'O Lord!' They had as many objections to this change as they would have had to a proposal for a new battle.

They trampled slowly back over the field across which they had run in a mad scamper.

The regiment marched until it had joined its fellows. The reformed brigade, in column, aimed through a wood at the road. Directly they were in a mass of dust-covered troops, and were trudging along in a way parallel to the enemy's lines as these had been defined by the previous turmoil.

They passed within view of a stolid white house, and saw in front of it groups of their comrades lying in wait behind a neat breastwork. A row of guns were booming at a distant enemy. Shells thrown in reply were raising clouds of dust and splinters. Horsemen dashed along the line of intrenchments.

At this point of its march the division curved away from the field and went winding off in the direction of the river. When the significance of this movement had impressed itself upon the youth he turned his head and looked over his shoulder toward the trampled and *débris*-strewed ground. He breathed a breath of new satisfaction. He finally nudged his friend. 'Well, it's all over,' he said to him.

His friend gazed backward. 'B'Gawd, it is,' he assented. They mused.

For a time the youth was obliged to reflect in a puzzled and uncertain way. His mind was undergoing a subtle change. It took moments for it to cast off its battleful ways and resume its accustomed course of thought. Gradually his brain emerged from the clogged clouds, and at last he was enabled to more closely comprehend himself and circumstance.

He understood then that the existence of shot and countershot was in the past. He had dwelt in a land of strange, squalling upheavals and had come forth. He had been where there was red of blood and black of passion, and he was escaped. His first thoughts were given to rejoicings at this fact.

Later he began to study his deeds, his failures, and his achievements. Thus, fresh from scenes where many of his usual machines of reflection had been idle, from where he had proceeded sheeplike, he struggled to marshal all his acts.

At last they marched before him clearly. From this present view point he was enabled to look upon them in spectator fashion and to criticize them with some correctness, for his new condition had already defeated certain sympathies.

Regarding his procession of memory he felt gleeful and unregretting, for in it his public deeds were paraded in great and shining prominence. Those performances which had been witnessed by his fellows marched now in wide purple and gold, having various deflections. They went gayly with music. It was pleasure to watch these things. He spent delightful minutes viewing the gilded images of memory.

He saw that he was good. He recalled with a thrill of joy the respectful comments of his fellows upon his conduct.

Nevertheless, the ghost of his flight from the first engagement appeared to him and danced. There were small shoutings in his brain about these matters. For a moment he blushed, and the light of his soul flickered with shame.

A specter of reproach came to him. There loomed the dogging memory of the tattered soldier – he who, gored by bullets and faint for blood, had fretted concerning an imagined wound in another; he who had loaned his last of strength and intellect for the tall soldier; he who, blind with weariness and pain, had been deserted in the field.

For an instant a wretched chill of sweat was upon him at the thought that he might be detected in the thing. As he stood persistently before his vision, he gave vent to a cry of sharp irritation and agony.

His friend turned. 'What's the matter, Henry?' he demanded. The youth's reply was an outburst of crimson oaths.

As he marched along the little branch-hung roadway among his prattling companions this vision of cruelty brooded over him. It clung near him always and darkened his view of these deeds in purple and gold. Whichever way his thoughts turned they were followed by the somber phantom of the desertion in the fields. He looked steathily at his companions, feeling sure that they must discern in his face evidences of this pursuit. But they were plodding in ragged array, discussing with quick tongues the accomplishments of the late battle.

'Oh, if a man should come up an' ask me, I'd say we got a dum good lickin'.'

'Lickin' – in yer eye! We ain't licked, sonny. We're goin' down here aways, swing aroun', an' come in behint 'em.'

'Oh, hush, with your comin' in behint 'em. I've seen all 'a that I wanta. Don't tell me about comin' in behint –'

'Bill Smithers, he ses he'd rather been in ten hundred battles than been in that heluva hospital. He ses they got shootin' in th' night-time, an' shells dropped plum among 'em in th' hospital. He ses sech hollerin' he never see.'

'Hasbrouck? He's th' best off'cer in this here reg'ment. He's a whale.'

'Didn't I tell yeh we'd come aroun' in behint 'em? Didn't I tell yeh so? We –'

'Oh, shet yeh mouth!'

For a time this pursuing recollection of the tattered man took all elation from the youth's veins. He saw his vivid error, and he was afraid that it would stand before him all his life. He took no share in the chatter of his comrades, nor did he look at them or know them, save when he felt sudden suspicion that they were seeing his thoughts and scrutinizing each detail of the scene with the tattered soldier.

Yet gradually he mustered force to put the sin at a distance. And at last his eyes seemed to open to some new ways. He found that he could look back upon the brass and bombast of his earlier gospels and see them truly. He was gleeful when he discovered that he now despised them.

With this conviction came a store of assurance. He felt a quiet manhood, nonassertive but a sturdy and strong blood. He knew that he would no more quail before his guides wherever they should point. He had been to touch the great death, and found that, after all, it was but the great death. He was a man.

So it came to pass that as he trudged from the place of blood and wrath his soul changed. He came from hot plowshares to prospects of clover tranquilly, and it was as if hot plowshares were not. Scars faded as flowers.

It rained. The procession of weary soldiers became a bedraggled train, despondent and muttering, marching with churning effort in a trough of liquid brown mud under a low, wretched sky. Yet the youth smiled, for he saw that the world was a world for him, though many discovered it to be made of oaths and walking sticks. He had rid himself of the red sickness of battle. The sultry nightmare was in the past. He had been an animal blistered and sweating in the heat and pain of war. He turned now with a lover's thirst to images of tranquil skies, fresh meadows, cool brooks – an existence of soft and eternal peace.

Over the river a golden ray of sun came through the hosts of leaden rain clouds.

TALES
OF
SOLDIERS
AND
CIVILIANS

IN THE MIDST OF LIFE

BY

AMBROSE BIERCE

SOLDIERS

A Horseman in the Sky

I

One sunny afternoon in the autumn of the year 1861 a soldier lay in a clump of
laurel by the side of a road in western Virginia. He lay at full length upon his
stomach, his feet resting upon the toes, his head upon the left forearm. His
extended right hand loosely grasped his rifle. But for the somewhat
methodical disposition of his limbs and a slight rhythmic movement of the
cartridge-box at the back of his belt he might have been thought to be dead. He
was asleep at his post of duty. But if detected he would be dead shortly
afterward, death being the just and legal penalty of his crime.

The clump of laurel in which the criminal lay was in the angle of a road
which after ascending southward a steep acclivity to that point turned sharply
to the west, running along the summit for perhaps one hundred yards. There it
turned southward again and went zigzagging downward through the forest. At
the salient of that second angle was a large flat rock, jutting out northward,
overlooking the deep valley from which the road ascended. The rock capped a
high cliff; a stone dropped from its outer edge would have fallen sheer
downward one thousand feet to the tops of the pines. The angle where the
soldier lay was on another spur of the same cliff. Had he been awake he would
have commanded a view, not only of the short arm of the road and the jutting
rock, but of the entire profile of the cliff below it. It might well have made him
giddy to look.

The country was wooded everywhere except at the bottom of the valley to
the northward, where there was a small natural meadow, through which
flowed a stream scarcely visible from the valley's rim. This open ground
looked hardly larger than an ordinary door-yard, but was really several acres
in extent. Its green was more vivid than that of the inclosing forest. Away
beyond it rose a line of giant cliffs similar to those upon which we are supposed
to stand in our survey of the savage scene, and through which the road had
somehow made its climb to the summit. The configuration of the valley,
indeed, was such that from this point of observation it seemed entirely shut in,
and one could but have wondered how the road which found a way out of it
had found a way into it, and whence came and whither went the waters of the
stream that parted the meadow more than a thousand feet below.

No country is so wild and difficult but men will make it a theatre of war;
concealed in the forest at the bottom of that military rat-trap, in which half a
hundred men in possession of the exits might have starved an army to
submission, lay five regiments of Federal infantry. They had marched all the
previous day and night and were resting. At night-fall they would take to the
road again, climb to the place where their unfaithful sentinel now slept, and

descending the other slope of the ridge fall upon a camp of the enemy at about midnight. Their hope was to surprise it, for the road led to the rear of it. In case of failure, their position would be perilous in the extreme; and fail they surely would should accident or vigilance apprise the enemy of the movement.

II

The sleeping sentinel in the clump of laurel was a young Virginian named Carter Druse. He was the son of wealthy parents, an only child, and had known such ease and cultivation and high living as wealth and taste were able to command in the mountain country of western Virginia. His home was but a few miles from where he now lay. One morning he had risen from the breakfast-table and said, quietly but gravely: 'Father, a Union regiment has arrived at Grafton. I am going to join it.'

The father lifted his leonine head, looked at the son a moment in silence, and replied: 'Well, go, sir, and whatever may occur do what you conceive to be your duty. Virginia, to which you are a traitor, must get on without you. Should we both live to the end of the war, we will speak further of the matter. Your mother, as the physician has informed you, is in a most critical condition; at the best she cannot be with us longer than a few weeks, but that time is precious. It would be better not to disturb her.'

So Carter Druse, bowing reverently to his father, who returned the salute with a stately courtesy that masked a breaking heart, left the home of his childhood to go soldiering. By conscience and courage, by deeds of devotion and daring, he soon commended himself to his fellows and his officers; and it was to these qualities and to some knowledge of the country that he owed his selection for his present perilous duty at the extreme outpost. Nevertheless, fatigue had been stronger than resolution and he had fallen asleep. What good or bad angel came in a dream to rouse him from his state of crime, who shall say? Without a movement, without a sound, in the profound silence and the languor of the late afternoon, some invisible messenger of fate touched with unsealing finger the eyes of his consciousness – whispered into the ear of his spirit the mysterious awakening word which no human lips ever have spoken, no human memory ever has recalled. He quietly raised his forehead from his arm and looked between the masking stems of the laurels, instinctively closing his right hand about the stock of his rifle.

His first feeling was a keen artistic delight. On a colossal pedestal, the cliff, – motionless at the extreme edge of the capping rock and sharply outlined against the sky, – was an equestrian statue of impressive dignity. The figure of the man sat the figure of the horse, straight and soldierly, but with the repose of a Grecian god carved in the marble which limits the suggestion of activity. The gray costume harmonized with its aerial background; the metal of accoutrement and caparison was softened and subdued by the shadow; the animal's skin had no points of high light. A carbine strikingly foreshortened lay across the pommel of the saddle, kept in place by the right hand grasping it at the 'grip'; the left hand, holding the bridle rein, was invisible. In silhouette against the sky the profile of the horse was cut with the sharpness of a cameo; it looked across the heights of air to the confronting cliffs beyond. The face of the rider, turned slightly away, showed only an outline of temple and beard; he was looking downward to the bottom of the valley. Magnified by its lift against the sky and by the soldier's testifying sense of the formidableness of a near enemy the group appeared of heroic, almost colossal, size.

For an instant Druse had a strange, half-defined feeling that he had slept to the end of the war and was looking upon a noble work of art reared upon that eminence to commemorate the deeds of an heroic past of which he had been an inglorious part. The feeling was dispelled by a slight movement of the group: the horse, without moving its feet, had drawn its body slightly backward from the verge; the man remained immobile as before. Broad awake and keenly alive to the significance of the situation, Druse now brought the butt of his rifle against his cheek by cautiously pushing the barrel forward through the bushes, cocked the piece, and glancing through the sights covered a vital spot of the horseman's breast. A touch upon the trigger and all would have been well with Carter Druse. At that instant the horseman turned his head and looked in the direction of his concealed foeman – seemed to look into his very face, into his eyes, into his brave, compassionate heart.

Is it then so terrible to kill an enemy in war – an enemy who has surprised a secret vital to the safety of one's self and comrades – an enemy more formidable for his knowledge than all his army for its numbers? Carter Druse grew pale; he shook in every limb, turned faint, and saw the statuesque group before him as black figures, rising, falling, moving unsteadily in arcs of circles in a fiery sky. His hand fell away from his weapon, his head slowly dropped until his face rested on the leaves in which he lay. This courageous gentleman and hardy soldier was near swooning from intensity of emotion.

It was not for long; in another moment his face was raised from earth, his hands resumed their places on the rifle, his forefinger sought the trigger; mind, heart, and eyes were clear, conscience and reason sound. He could not hope to capture that enemy; to alarm him would but send him dashing to his camp with his fatal news. The duty of the soldier was plain: the man must be shot dead from ambush – without warning, without a moment's spiritual preparation, with never so much as an unspoken prayer, he must be sent to his account. But no – there is a hope; he may have discovered nothing – perhaps he is but admiring the sublimity of the landscape. If permitted, he may turn and ride carelessly away in the direction whence he came. Surely it will be possible to judge at the instant of his withdrawing whether he knows. It may well be that his fixity of attention – Druse turned his head and looked through the deeps of air downward, as from the surface to the bottom of a translucent sea. He saw creeping across the green meadow a sinuous line of figures of men and horses – some foolish commander was permitting the soldiers of his escort to water their beasts in the open, in plain view from a dozen summits!

Druse withdrew his eyes from the valley and fixed them again upon the group of man and horse in the sky, and again it was through the sights of his rifle. But this time his aim was at the horse. In his memory, as if they were a divine mandate, rang the words of his father at their parting: 'Whatever may occur, do what you conceive to be your duty.' He was calm now. His teeth were firmly but not rigidly closed; his nerves were as tranquil as a sleeping babe's – not a tremor affected any muscle of his body; his breathing, until suspended in the act of taking aim, was regular and slow. Duty had conquered; the spirit had said to the body: 'Peace, be still.' He fired.

III

An officer of the Federal force, who in a spirit of adventure or in quest of knowledge had left the hidden *bivouac* in the valley, and with aimless feet had made his way to the lower edge of a small open space near the foot of the cliff, was considering what he had to gain by pushing his exploration further. At a distance of a quarter-mile before him, but apparently at a stone's throw, rose from its fringe of pines the gigantic face of rock, towering to so great a height above him that it made him giddy to look up to where its edge cut a sharp, rugged line against the sky. It presented a clean, vertical profile against a background of blue sky to a point half the way down, and of distant hills, hardly less blue, thence to the tops of the trees at its base. Lifting his eyes to the dizzy altitude of its summit the officer saw an astonishing sight – a man on horseback riding down into the valley through the air!

Straight upright sat the rider, in military fashion, with a firm seat in the saddle, a strong clutch upon the rein to hold his charger from too impetuous a plunge. From his bare head his long hair streamed upward, waving like a plume. His hands were concealed in the cloud of the horse's lifted mane. The animal's body was as level as if every hoof-stroke encountered the resistant earth. Its motions were those of a wild gallop, but even as the officer looked they ceased, with all the legs thrown sharply forward as in the act of alighting from a leap. But this was a flight!

Filled with amazement and terror by this apparition of a horseman in the sky – half believing himself the chosen scribe of some new Apocalypse, the officer was overcome by the intensity of his emotions; his legs failed him and he fell. Almost at the same instant he heard a crashing sound in the trees – a sound that died without an echo – and all was still.

The officer rose to his feet, trembling. The familiar sensation of an abraded shin recalled his dazed faculties. Pulling himself together he ran rapidly obliquely away from the cliff to a point distant from its foot; thereabout he expected to find his man; and thereabout he naturally failed. In the fleeting instant of his vision his imagination had been so wrought upon by the apparent grace and ease and intention of the marvelous performance that it did not occur to him that the line of march of aerial cavalry is directly downward, and that he could find the objects of his search at the very foot of the cliff. A half-hour later he returned to camp.

This officer was a wise man; he knew better than to tell an incredible truth. He said nothing of what he had seen. But when the commander asked him if in his scout he had learned anything of advantage to the expedition he answered:

'Yes, sir; there is no road leading down into this valley from the southward.'

The commander, knowing better, smiled.

IV

After firing his shot, Private Carter Druse reloaded his rifle and resumed his watch. Ten minutes had hardly passed when a Federal sergeant crept cautiously to him on hands and knees. Druse neither turned his head nor looked at him, but lay without motion or sign of recognition.

'Did you fire?' the sergeant whispered.

'Yes.'

'At what?'

'A horse. It was standing on yonder rock – pretty far out. You see it is no longer there. It went over the cliff.'

The man's face was white, but he showed no other sign of emotion. Having answered, he turned away his eyes and said no more. The sergeant did not understand.

'See here, Druse,' he said, after a moment's silence, 'it's no use making a mystery. I order you to report. Was there anybody on the horse?'

'Yes.'

'Well?'

'My father.'

The sergeant rose to his feet and walked away. 'Good God!' he said.

An Occurrence At Owl Creek Bridge

I

A man stood upon a railroad bridge in northern Alabama, looking down into a swift water twenty feet below. The man's hands were behind his back, the wrists bound with a cord. A rope closley encircled his neck. It was attached to a stout cross-timber above his head and the slack fell to the level of his knees. Some loose boards laid upon the sleepers supporting the metals of the railway supplied a footing for him and his executioners – two private soldiers of the Federal army, directed by a sergeant who in civil life may have been a deputy sheriff. At a short remove upon the same temporary platform was an officer in the uniform of his rank, armed. He was a captain. A sentinel at each end of the bridge stood with his rifle in the position known as 'support,' that is to say, vertical in front of the left shoulder, the hammer resting on the forearm thrown straight across the chest – a formal and unnatural position, enforcing an erect carriage of the body. It did not appear to be the duty of these two men to know what was occurring at the centre of the bridge; they merely blockaded the two ends of the foot planking that traversed it.

Beyond one of the sentinels nobody was in sight; the railroad ran straight away into a forest for a hundred yards, then, curving, was lost to view. Doubtless there was an outpost farther along. The other bank of the stream was open ground – a gentle acclivity topped with a stockade of vertical tree trunks, loop-holed for rifles, with a single embrasure through which protruded the muzzle of a brass cannon commanding the bridge. Midway of the slope between bridge and fort were the spectators – a single company of infantry in line, at 'parade rest,' the butts of the rifles on the ground, the barrels inclining slightly backward against the right shoulder, the hands crossed upon the stock. A lieutenant stood at the right of the line, the point of his sword upon the ground, his left hand resting upon his right. Excepting the group of four at the centre of the bridge, not a man moved. The company faced the bridge, staring stonily, motionless. The sentinels, facing the banks of the stream, might have been statues to adorn the bridge. The captain stood with folded arms, silent, observing the work of his subordinates, but making no sign. Death is a dignitary who when he comes announced is to be received with formal manifestations of respect, even by those most familar with him. In the code of military etiquette silence and fixity are forms of deference.

The man who was engaged in being hanged was apparently about thirty-five years of age. He was a civilian, if one might judge from his habit, which was that of a planter. His features were good – a straight nose, firm mouth, broad forehead, from which his long, dark hair was combed straight back, falling behind his ears to the collar of his well-fitting frock-coat. He wore a mustache and pointed beard, but no whiskers; his eyes were large and dark gray, and had a kindly expression which one would hardly have expected in one whose neck was in the hemp. Evidently this was no vulgar assassin. The liberal military code makes provision for hanging many kinds of persons, and gentlemen are not excluded.

The preparations being complete, the two private soldiers stepped aside and each drew away the plank upon which he had been standing. The sergeant turned to the captain, saluted and placed himself immediately behind that officer, who in turn moved apart one pace. These movements left the condemned man and the sergeant standing on the two ends of the same plank, which spanned three of the cross-ties of the bridge. The end upon which the civilian stood almost, but not quite, reached a fourth. This plank had been held in place by the weight of the captain; it was now held by that of the sergeant. At a signal from the former the latter would step aside, the plank would tilt and the condemned man go down between two ties. The arrangement commended itself to his judgment as simple and effective. His face had not been covered nor his eyes bandaged. He looked a moment at his 'unsteadfast footing,' then let his gaze wander to the swirling water of the stream racing madly beneath his feet. A piece of dancing driftwood caught his attention and his eyes followed it down the current. How slowly it appeared to move! What a sluggish stream!

He closed his eyes in order to fix his last thoughts upon his wife and children. The water, touched to gold by the early sun, the brooding mists under the banks at some distance down the stream, the fort, the soldiers, the piece of drift – all had distracted him. And now he became conscious of a new disturbance. Striking through the thought of his dear ones was a sound which he could neither ignore nor understand, a sharp, distinct, metallic percussion like the stroke of a blacksmith's hammer upon the anvil; it had the same ringing quality. He wondered what it was, and whether immeasurably distant or near by – it seemed both. Its recurrence was regular, but as slow as the tolling of a death knell. He awaited each stroke with impatience and – he knew not why – apprehension. The intervals of silence grew progressively longer; the delays became maddening. With their greater infrequency the sounds increased in strengh and sharpness. They hurt his ear like the thrust of a knife; he feared he would shriek. What he heard was the ticking of his watch.

He unclosed his eyes and saw again the water below him. 'If I could free my hands,' he thought, 'I might throw off the noose and spring into the stream. By diving I could evade the bullets and, swimming vigorously, reach the bank, take to the woods and get away home. My home, thank God, is as yet outside their lines; my wife and little ones are still beyond the invader's farthest advance.'

As these thoughts, which have here to be set down in words, were flashed into the doomed man's brain rather than evolved from it the captain nodded to the sergeant. The sergeant stepped aside.

II

Peyton Farquhar was a well-to-do planter, of an old and highly respected Alabama family. Being a slave owner and like other slave owners a politician he was naturally an original secessionist and ardently devoted to the Southern cause. Circumstances of an imperious nature, which it is unnecessary to relate here, had prevented him from taking service with the gallant army that had fought the disastrous campaigns ending with the fall of Corinth, and he chafed under the inglorious restraint, longing for the release of his energies, the larger life of the soldier, the opportunity for distinction. That opportunity, he felt, would come, as it comes to all in war time. Meanwhile he did what he could. No service was too humble for him to perform in aid of the South, no adventure too perilous for him to undertake if consistent with the character of a civilian who was at heart a soldier, and who in good faith and without too much qualification assented to at least a part of the frankly villainous dictum that all is fair in love and war.

One evening while Farquhar and his wife were sitting on a rustic bench near the entrance to his grounds, a gray-clad soldier rode up to the gate and asked for a drink of water. Mrs Farquhar was only too happy to serve him with her own white hands. While she was fetching the water her husband approached the dusty horseman and inquired eagerly for news from the front.

'The Yanks are repairing the railroads,' said the man, 'and are getting ready for another advance. They have reached the Owl Creek bridge, put it in order and built a stockade on the north bank. The commandant has issued an order, which is posted everywhere, declaring that any civilian caught interfering with the railroad, its bridges, tunnels or trains will be summarily hanged. I saw the order.'

'How far is it to the Owl Creek bridge?' Farquhar asked.

'About thirty miles.'

'Is there no force on this side the creek?'

'Only a picket post half a mile out, on the railroad, and a single sentinel at this end of the bridge.'

'Suppose a man – a civilian and student of hanging – should elude the picket post and perhaps get the better of the sentinel,' said Farquhar, smiling, 'what could he accomplish?'

The soldier reflected. 'I was there a month ago,' he replied. 'I observed that the flood of last winter had lodged a great quantity of driftwood against the wooden pier at this end of the bridge. It is now dry and would burn like tow.'

The lady had now brought the water, which the soldier drank. He thanked her ceremoniously, bowed to her husband and rode away. An hour later, after nightfall, he repassed the plantation, going northward in the direction from which he had come. He was a Federal scout.

III

As Peyton Farquhar fell straight downward through the bridge he lost consciousness and was as one already dead. From this state he was awakened – ages later, it seemed to him – by the pain of a sharp pressure upon his throat, followed by a sense of suffocation. Keen, poignant agonies seemed to shoot from his neck downward through every fibre of his body and limbs. These pains appeared to flash along well-defined lines of ramification and to beat with an inconceivably rapid periodicity. They seemed like streams of pulsating fire heating him to an intolerable temperature. As to his head, he was conscious of nothing but a feeling of fulness – of congestion. These sensations were unaccompanied by thought. The intellectual part of his nature was already effaced; he had power only to feel, and feeling was torment. He was conscious of motion. Encompassed in a luminous cloud, of which he was now merely the fiery heart, without material substance, he swung through unthinkable arcs of oscillation, like a vast pendulum. Then all at once, with terrible suddenness, the light about him shot upward with the noise of a loud plash; a frightful roaring was in his ears, and all was cold and dark. The power of thought was restored; he knew that the rope had broken and he had fallen into the stream. There was no additional strangulation; the noose about his neck was already suffocating him and kept the water from his lungs. To die of hanging at the bottom of a river! – the idea seemed to him ludicrous. He opened his eyes in the darkness and saw above him a gleam of light, but how distant, how inaccessible! He was still sinking, for the light became fainter and fainter until it was a mere glimmer. Then it began to grow and brighten, and he knew that he was rising toward the surface – knew it with reluctance, for he was now very comfortable. 'To be hanged and drowned,' he thought, 'that is not so bad; but I do not wish to be shot. No; I will not be shot; that is not fair.'

He was not conscious of an effort, but a sharp pain in his wrist apprised him that he was trying to free his hands. He gave the struggle his attention, as an idler might observe the feat of a juggler, without interest in the outcome. What splendid effort! – what magnificent, what super-human strength! Ah, that was a find endeavour! Bravo! The cord fell away; his arms parted and floated upwards, the hands dimly seen on each side in the growing light. He watched them with a new interest as first one and then the other pounced upon the noose at his neck. They tore it away and thrust it fiercely aside, its undulations resembling those of a water-snake. 'Put it back, put it back!' He thought he shouted these words to his hands, for the undoing of the noose had been succeeded by the direst pang that he had yet experienced. His neck ached horribly; his brain was on fire; his heart, which had been fluttering faintly, gave a great leap, tryng to force itself out at his mouth. His whole body was racked and wrenched with an insupportable anguish! But his disobedient hands gave no heed to the command. They beat the water vigorously with quick, downward strokes, forcing him to the surface. He felt his head emerge; his eyes were blinded by the sunlight; his chest expanded convulsively, and with a supreme and crowning agony his lungs engulfed a great draught of air, which instantly he expelled in a shriek!

He was now in full possession of his physical senses. They were, indeed, preternaturally keen and alert. Something in the awful disturbance of his organic system had so exalted and refined them that they made record of things never before perceived. He felt the ripples upon his face and heard their separate sounds as they struck. He looked at the forest on the bank of the stream, saw the individual trees, the leaves and the veining of each leaf – saw the very insects upon them: the locusts, the brilliant-bodied flies, the gray spiders stretching their webs from twig to twig. He noted the prismatic colors in all the dewdrops upon a million blades of grass. The humming of the gnats that danced above the eddies of the stream, the beating of the dragon-flies' wings, the strokes of the water-spiders' legs, like oars which had lifted their boat – all these made audible music. A fish slid along beneath his eyes and he heard the rush of its body parting the water.

He had come to the surface facing down the stream; in a moment the visible world seemed to wheel slowly round, himself the pivotal point, and he saw the bridge, the fort, the soldiers upon the bridge, the captain, the sergeant, the two privates, his executioners. They were in silhouette against the blue sky. They shouted and gesticulated, pointing at him. The captain had drawn his pistol, but did not fire; the others were unarmed. Their movements were grotesque and horrible, their forms gigantic.

Suddenly he heard a sharp report and something struck the water smartly within inches of his head, spattering his face with spray. He heard a second report, and saw one of the sentinels with his rifle at his shoulder, a light cloud of blue smoke rising from the muzzle. The man in the water saw the eye of the man on the bridge gazing into his own through the sights of the rifle. He observed that it was a gray eye and remembered having read that gray eyes were keenest, and that all famous markmen had them. Nevertheless, this one had missed.

A counter-swirl had caught Farquhar and turned him half round; he was again looking into the forest on the bank opposite the fort. The sound of a clear, high voice in a monotonous singsong now rang out behind him and came across the water with a distinctness that pierced and subdued all other sounds, even the beating of the ripples in his ears. Although no soldier, he had frequented camps enough to know the dread significance of that deliberate, drawling, aspirated chant; the lieutenant on shore was taking a part in the morning's work. How coldly and pitilessly – with what an even, calm intonation, presaging, and enforcing tranquillity in the men – with what accurately measured intervals fell those cruel words:

'Attention, company! . . . Shoulder arms! . . . Ready! . . . Aim! . . . Fire!'

Farquhar dived – dived as deeply as he could. The water roared in his ears like the voice of Niagara, yet he heard the dulled thunder of the volley and, rising again toward the surface, met shining bits of metal, singularly flattened, oscillating slowly downward. Some of them touched him on the face and hands, then fell away, continuing their descent. One lodged between his collar and neck; it was uncomfortably warm and he snatched it out.

As he rose to the surface, gasping for breath, he saw that he had been a long time under water; he was perceptibly father down stream – nearer to safety. The soldiers had almost finished reloading; the metal ramrods flashed all at once in the sunshine as they were drawn from the barrels, turned in the air, and thrust into their sockets. The two sentinels fired again, independently and ineffectually.

The hunted man saw all this over his shoulder; he was now swimming vigorously with the current. His brain was as energetic as his arms and legs; he thought with the rapidity of lightning.

'The officer,' he reasoned, 'will not make that martinet's error a second time. It is as easy to dodge a volley as a single shot. He has probably already given the command to fire at will. God help me, I cannot dodge them all!'

An appalling plash within two yards of him was followed by a loud rushing sound, *diminuendo*, which seemed to travel back through the air to the fort and died in an explosion which stirred the very river to its deeps! A rising sheet of water curved over him, fell down upon him, blinded him, strangled him! The cannon had taken a hand in the game. As he shook his head free from the commotion of the smitten water he heard the deflected shot humming through the air ahead, and in an instant it was cracking and smashing the branches in the forest beyond.

'They will not do that again,' he thought; 'the next time they will use a charge of grape. I must keep my eye upon the gun; the smoke will apprise me – the report arrives too late; it lags behind the missile. That is a good gun.'

Suddenly he felt himself whirled round and round – spinning like a top. The water, the banks, the forests, the now distant bridge, fort and men – all were commingled and blurred. Objects were represented by their colors only; circular horizontal streaks of color – that was all he saw. He had been caught in a vortex and was being whirled on with a velocity of advance and gyration that made him giddy and sick. In a few moments he was flung upon the gravel at the foot of the left bank of the stream – the southern bank – and behind a projecting point which concealed him from his enemies. The sudden arrest of his motion, the abrasion of one of his hands on the gravel, restored him, and he wept with delight. He dug his fingers into the sand, threw it over himself in handfuls and audibly blessed it. It looked like diamonds, rubies, emeralds; he could think of nothing beautiful which it did not resemble. The trees upon the bank were giant garden plants; he noted a definite order in their arrangement, inhaled the fragrance of their blooms. A strange, roseate light shone through the spaces among their trunks and the wind made in their branches the music of æolian harps. He had no wish to perfect his escape – was content to remain in that enchanting spot until retaken.

A whiz and rattle of grapeshot among the branches high above his head roused him from his dream. The baffled cannoneer had fired him a random farewell. He sprang to his feet, rushed up the sloping bank, and plunged into the forest.

All that day he traveled, laying his course by the rounding sun. The forest seemed interminable; nowhere did he discover a break in it, not even a woodman's road. He had not known that he lived in so wild a region. There was something uncanny in the revelation.

By nightfall he was fatigued, footsore, famishing. The thought of his wife and children urged him on. At last he found a road which led him in what he knew to be the right direction. It was as wide and straight as a city street, yet it seemed untraveled. No fields bordered it, no dwelling anywhere. Not so much as the barking of a dog suggested human habitation. The black bodies of the trees formed a straight wall on both sides, terminating on the horizon in a point, like a diagram in a lesson in perspective. Overhead, as he looked up through his rift in the wood, shone great golden stars looking unfamiliar and grouped in strange constellations. He was sure they were arranged in some order which had a secret and malign significance. The wood on either side was full of singular noises, among which – once, twice, and again – he distinctly heard whispers in an unknown tongue.

His neck was in pain and lifting his hand to it he found it horribly swollen. He knew that it had a circle of black where the rope had bruised it. His eyes felt congested; he could no longer close them. His tongue was swollen with thirst; he relieved its fever by thrusting it forward from between his teeth into the cold air. How softly the turf had carpeted the untraveled avenue – he could no longer feel the roadway beneath his feet!

Doubtless, despite his suffering, he had fallen asleep while walking, for now he sees another scene – perhaps he has merely recovered from a delirium. He stands at the gate of his own home. All is as he left it, and all bright and beautiful in the morning sunshine. He must have traveled the entire night. As he pushes open the gate and passes up the wide white walk, he sees a flutter of female garments; his wife, looking fresh and cool and sweet, steps down from the veranda to meet him. At the bottom of the steps she stands waiting, with a smile of ineffable joy, an attitude of matchless grace and dignity. Ah, how beautiful she is! He springs forward with extended arms. As he is about to clasp her he feels a stunning blow upon the back of the neck; a blinding white light blazes all about him with a sound like the shock of a cannon – then all is darkness and silence!

Peyton Farquhar was dead; his body, with a broken neck, swung gently from side to side beneath the timbers of the Owl Creek bridge.

Chickamauga

One sunny autumn afternoon a child strayed away from its rude home in a small field and entered a forest unobserved. It was happy in a new sense of freedom from control, happy in the opportunity of exploration and adventure; for this child's spirit, in bodies of its ancestors, had for thousands of years been trained to memorable feats of discovery and conquest – victories in battles whose critical moments were centuries, whose victors' camps were cities of hewn stone. From the cradle of its race it had conquered its way through two continents and passing a great sea had penetrated a third, there to be born to war and dominion as a heritage.

The child was a boy aged about six years, the son of a poor planter. In his younger manhood the father had been a soldier, had fought against naked savages and followed the flag of his country into the capital of a civilized race to the far South. In the peaceful life of a planter the warrior-fire survived; once kindled, it is never extinguished. The man loved military books and pictures and the boy had understood enough to make himself a wooden sword, though even the eye of his father would hardly have known it for what it was. This weapon he now bore bravely, as became the son of an heroic race, and pausing now and again in the sunny space of the forest assumed, with some exaggeration, the postures of aggression and defense that he had been taught by the engraver's art. Made reckless by the ease with which he overcame invisible foes attempting to stay his advance, he committed the common enough military error of pushing the pursuit to a dangerous extreme, until he found himself upon the margin of a wide but shallow brook, whose rapid waters barred his direct advance against the flying foe that had crossed with illogical ease. But the intrepid victor was not to be baffled; the spirit of the race which had passed the great sea burned unconquerable in that small breast and would not be denied. Finding a place where some bowlders in the bed of the stream lay but a step or a leap apart, he made his way across and fell again upon the rear-guard of his imaginary foe, putting all to the sword.

Now that the battle had been won, prudence required that he withdraw to his base of operations. Alas; like many a mightier conqueror, and like one, the mightiest, he could not

> curb the lust for war,
> Nor learn that tempted Fate will leave the loftiest star.

Advancing from the bank of the creek he suddenly found himself confronted with a new and more formidable enemy: in the path that he was following, sat, bolt upright, with ears erect and paws suspended before it, a rabbit! With a startled cry the child turned and fled, he knew not in what direction, calling with inarticulate cries for his mother, weeping, stumbling, his tender skin cruelly torn by brambles, his little heart beating hard with terror – breathless, blind with tears – lost in the forest! Then, for more than an hour, he wandered with erring feet through the tangled undergrowth, till at last, overcome by fatigue, he lay down in a narrow space between two rocks, within a few yards of the stream and still grasping his toy sword, no longer a weapon but a companion, sobbed himself to sleep. The wood birds sang merrily above his head; the squirrels, whisking their bravery of tail, ran barking from tree to tree, unconscious of the pity of it, and somewhere far away was a strange, muffled thunder, as if the partridges were drumming in celebration of nature's victory over the son of her immemorial enslavers. And back at the little plantation, where white men and black were hastily searching the fields and hedges in alarm, a mother's heart was breaking for her missing child.

Hours passed, and then the little sleeper rose to his feet. The chill of the evening was in his limbs, the fear of the gloom in his heart. But he had rested, and he no longer wept. With some blind instinct which impelled to action he struggled through the undergrowth about him and came to a more open ground – on his right the brook, to the left a gentle acclivity studded with infrequent trees; over all, the gathering gloom of twilight. A thin, ghostly mist rose along the water. It frightened and repelled him; instead of recrossing, in the direction whence he had come, he turned his back upon it, and went forward toward the dark inclosing wood. Suddenly he saw before him a strange moving object which he took to be some large animal – a dog, a pig – he could not name it; perhaps it was a bear. He had seen pictures of bears, but knew of nothing to their discredit and had vaguely wished to meet one. But something in form or movement of this object – something in the awkwardness of its approach – told him that it was not a bear, and curiosity was stayed by fear. He stood still and as it came slowly on gained courage every moment, for he saw that at least it had not the long, menacing ears of the rabbit. Possibly his impressionable mind was half conscious of something familiar in its shambling, awkward gait. Before it had approached near enough to resolve his doubts he saw that it was followed by another and another. To right and left were many more; the whole open space about him was alive with them – all moving toward the brook.

They were men. They crept upon their hands and knees. They used their hands only, dragging their legs. They used their knees only, their arms hanging idle at their sides. They strove to rise to their feet, but fell prone in the attempt. They did nothing naturally, and nothing alike, save only to advance foot by foot in the same direction. Singly, in pairs and in little groups, they came on through the gloom, some halting now and again while others crept slowly past them, then resuming their movement. They came by dozens and by hundreds; as far on either hand as one could see in the deepening gloom they extended and the black wood behind them appeared to be inexhaustible. The very ground seemed in motion toward the creek. Occasionally one who had paused did not again go on, but lay motionless. He was dead. Some, pausing, made strange gestures with their hands, erected their arms and lowered them again, clasped their heads; spread their palms upward, as men are sometimes seen to do in public prayer.

Not all of this did the child note; it is what would have been noted by an elder observer; he saw little but that these were men, yet crept like babes. Being men, they were not terrible, though unfamiliarly clad. He moved among them freely, going from one to another and peering into their faces with childish curiosity. All their faces were singularly white and many were streaked and gouted with red. Something in this – something too, perhaps, in their grotesque attitude and movements – reminded him of the painted clown whom he had seen last summer in the circus, and he laughed as he watched them. But on and ever on they crept, these maimed and bleeding men, as heedless as he of the dramatic contrast between his laughter and their own ghastly gravity.To him it was a merry spectacle. He had seen his father's Negroes creep upon their hands and knees for his amusement had ridden them so 'making believe' they were his horses. He now approached one of these crawling figures from behind and with an agile movement mounted it astride. The man sank upon his breast, recovered, flung the small boy fiercely to the ground as an unbroken colt might have done, then turned upon him a face that lacked a lower jaw – from the upper teeth to the throat was a great red gap fringed with hanging shreds of flesh and splinters of bone. The unnatural prominence of nose, the absence of chin, the fierce eyes, gave this man the appearance of a great bird of prey crimsoned in throat and breast by the blood of its quarry. The man rose to his knees, the child to his feet. The man shook his fist at the child; the child, terrified at last, ran to a tree near by, got upon the farther side of it and took a more serious view of the situation. And so the clumsy multitude dragged itself slowly and painfully along in hideous pantomime – moved forward down the slope like a swarm of great black beetles, with never a sound of going – in silence profound, absolute.

Instead of darkening, the haunted landscape began to brighten. Through the belt of trees beyond the brook shone a strange red light,the trunks and branches of the trees making a black lacework against it. It struck the creeping figures and gave them monstrous shadows, which caricatured their move-ments on the lit grass. It fell upon their faces, touching their whiteness with a ruddy tinge, accentuating the stains with which so many of them were freaked and maculated. It sparkled on buttons and bits of metal in their clothing. Instinctively the child turned toward the growing splendor and moved down the slope with his horrible companions; in a few moments had passed the foremost of the throng – not much of a feat, considering his advantages. He placed himself in the lead, his wooden sword still in hand, and solemnly directed the march, conforming his pace to theirs and occasionally turning as if to see that his forces did not straggle.Surely such a leader never before had such a following.

Scattered about upon the ground now slowly narrowing by the encroach-ment of this awful march to water, were certain articles to which, in the leader's mind, were coupled no significant associations: an occasional blanket, tightly rolled lengthwise, doubled and the ends bound together with a string; a heavy knapsack here, and there a broken rifle – such things, in short, as are found in the rear of retreating troops, the 'spoor' of men flying from their hunters. Everywhere near the creek, which here had a margin of lowland, the earth was trodden into mud by the feet of men and horses. An observer of better experience in the use of his eyes would have noticed that these footprints pointed in both directions; the ground had been twice passed over – in advance and in retreat. A few hours before, these desperate, stricken men, with their more fortunate and now distant comrades, had penetrated the forest in thousands. Their successive battalions, breaking into swarms and reforming in lines, had passed the child on every side – had almost trodden on him as he slept. The rustle and murmur of their march had not awakened him. Almost within a stone's throw of where he lay they had fought a battle; but all unheard by him were the roar of the musketry, the shock of the cannon, 'the thunder of the captains and the shouting.' He had slept through it all, grasping his little wooden sword with perhaps a tighter clutch in unconscious sympathy with his martial environment, but as heedless of the grandeur of the struggle as the dead who had died to make the glory.

The fire beyond the belt of woods on the farther side of the creek, reflected to earth from the canopy of its own smoke, was now suffusing the whole landscape. It transformed the sinuous line of mist to the vapor of gold. The water gleamed with dashes of red, and red, too, were many of the stones protruding above the surface. But that was blood; the less desperately wounded had stained them in crossing. On them, too, the child now crossed with eager steps; he was going to the fire. As he stood upon the farther bank he turned about to look at the companions of his march. The advance was arriving at the creek. The stronger had already drawn themselves to the brink and plunged their faces into the flood. Three or four who lay without motion appeared to have no heads. At this the child's eyes expanded with wonder; even his hospitable understanding could not accept a phenomenon implying such vitality as that. After slaking their thirst these men had not had the strengh to back away from the water, nor to keep their heads above it. They were drowned. In rear of these, the open spaces of the forest showed the leader as many formless figures of his grim command as at first; but not nearly so many were in motion. He waved his cap for their encouragement and smilingly pointed with his weapon in the direction of the guiding light – a pillar of fire to this strange exodus.

Confident of the fidelity of his forces, he now entered the belt of woods, passed through it easily in the red illumination, climbed a fence, ran across a field, turning now and again to coquet with his responsive shadow, and so approached the blazing ruin of a dwelling. Desolation everywhere! In all the wide glare not a living thing was visible. He cared nothing for that; the spectacle pleased, and he danced with glee in imitation of the wavering flames. He ran about, collecting fuel, but every object that he found was too heavy for him to cast in from the distance to which the head limited his approach. In despair he flung in his sword – a surrender to the superior forces of nature. His military career was at an end.

Shifting his position, his eyes fell upon some outbuildings which had an oddly familar appearance, as if he had dreamed of them. He stood considering them with wonder, when suddenly the entire plantation, with its inclosing forest, seemed to turn as if upon a pivot. His little world swung half around; the points of the compass were reversed. He recognized the blazing building as his own home!

For a moment he stood stupefied by the power of the revelation, then ran with stumbling feet, making a half-circuit of the ruin. There, conspicuous in the light of the conflagration, lay the dead body of a woman – the white face turned upward, the hands thrown out and clutched full of grass, the clothing deranged, the long dark hair in tangles and full of clotted blood. The greater part of the forehead was torn away, and from the jagged hole the brain protruded, overflowing the temple, a frothy mass of gray, crowned with clusters of crimson bubbles – the work of a shell.

The child moved his little hands, making wild, uncertain gestures. He uttered a series of inarticulate and indescribable cries – something between the chattering of an ape and the gobbling of a turkey – a startling, soulless, unholy sound, the language of a devil. The child was a deaf mute.

Then he stood motionless, with quivering lips, looking down upon the wreck.

A Son Of The Gods
A Study in the Present Tense

A breezy day and a sunny landscape. An open country to right and left and forward; behind, a wood. In the edge of this wood, facing the open but not venturing into it, long lines of troops, halted. The wood is alive with them, and full of confused noises – the occasional rattle of wheels as a battery of artillery goes into position to cover the advance; the hum and murmur of the soldiers talking; a sound of innumerable feet in the dry leaves that strew the interspaces among the trees; hoarse commands of officers. Detached groups of horsemen are well in front – not altogether exposed – many of them intently regarding the crest of a hill a mile away in the direction of the interrupted advance. For this powerful army, moving in battle order through a forest, has met with a formidable obstacle – the open country. The crest of that gentle hill a mile away has a sinister look; it says, Beware! Along it runs a stone wall extending to left and right a great distance. Behind the wall is a hedge; behind the hedge are seen the tops of trees in rather straggling order. Among the trees – what? It is neccessary to know.

Yesterday, and for many days and nights previously, we were fighting somewhere; always there was cannonading, with occasional keen rattlings of musketry, mingled with cheers, our own or the enemy's, we seldon knew, attesting some temporary advantage. This morning at daybreak the enemy was gone. We have moved forward across his earthworks, across which we have so often vainly attempted to move before, through the débris of his abandoned camps, among the graves of his fallen, into the woods beyond.

How curiously we had regarded everything! how odd it all had seemed! Nothing had appeared quite familar; the most commonplace objects – an old saddle, a splintered wheel, a forgotten canteen – everything had related something of the mysterious personality of those strange men who had been killing us. The soldier never becomes wholly familiar with the conception of his foes as men like himself; he cannot divest himself of the feeling that they are another order of beings, differently conditioned, in an environment not altogether of the earth. The smallest vestiges of them rivet his attention and engage his interest. He thinks of them as inaccessible; and, catching an unexpected glimpse of them, they appear farther away, and therefore larger, than they really are – like objects in a fog. He is somewhat in awe of them.

From the edge of the wood leading up the acclivity are the tracks of horses and wheels – the wheels of cannon. The yellow grass is beaten down by the feet of infantry. Clearly they have passed this way in thousands; they have not withdrawn by the country roads. This is significant – it is the difference between retiring and retreating.

That group of horsemen is our commander, his staff and escort. He is facing the distant crest, holding his field-glass against his eyes with both hands, his elbows needlessly elevated. It is a fashion; it seems to dignify the act; we are all addicted to it. Suddenly he lowers the glass and says a few words to those about him. Two or three aides detach themselves from the group and canter away into the woods, along the lines in each direction. We did not hear his words, but we know them: 'Tell General X. to send forward the skirmish line.'

Those of us who have been out of place resume our positions; the men resting at ease straighten themselves and the ranks are re-formed without a command. Some of us staff officers dismount and look at our saddle girths; those already on the ground remount.

Galloping rapidly along in the edge of the open ground comes a young officer on a snow-white horse. His saddle blanket is scarlet. What a fool! No one who has ever been in action but remembers how naturally every rifle turns toward the man on a white horse; no one but has observed how a bit of red enrages the bull of battle. That such colors are fashionable in military life must be accepted as the most astonishing of all the phenomena of human vanity. They would seem to have been devised to increase the death-rate.

This young officer is in full uniform, as if on parade. He is all agleam with bullion -- a blue-and-gold edition of the Poetry of War. A wave of derisive laughter runs abreast of him all along the line. But how handsome he is! – with what careless grace he sits his horse!

He reins up within a respectful distance of the corps commander and salutes. The old soldier nods familiarly; he evidently knows him. A brief colloquy between them is going on; the young man seems to be preferring some request which the elder one is indisposed to grant. Let us ride a little nearer. Ah! too late – it is ended. The young officer salutes again, wheels his horse, and rides straight toward the crest of the hill!

A thin line of skirmishers, the men deployed at six paces or so apart, now pushes from the wood into the open. The commander speaks to his bugler, who claps his instrument to his lips. *Tra-la-la! Tra-la-la!* The skirmishers halt in their tracks.

Meantime the young horseman has advanced a hundred yards. He is riding at a walk, straight up the long slope, with never a turn of the head. How glorious! Gods! what would we not give to be in his place – with his soul! He does not draw his sabre; his right hand hangs easily at his side. The breeze catches the plume in his hat and flutters it smartly. The sunshine rests upon his shoulder-straps, lovingly, like a visible benediction. Straight on he rides. Ten thousand pairs of eyes are fixed upon him with an intensity that he can hardly fail to feel; ten thousand hearts keep quick time to the inaudible hoof-beats of his snowy steed. He is not alone – he draws all souls after him. But we remember that we laughed! On and on, straight for the hedge-lined wall, he rides. Not a look backward. O, if he would but turn – if he could but see the love, the adoration, the atonement!

Not a word is spoken; the populous depths of the forest still murmur with their unseen and unseeing swarm, but all along the fringe is silence. The burly commander is an equestrian statue of himself. The mounted staff officers, their field-glasses up, are motionless all. The line of battle in the edge of the wood stands at a new kind of 'attention,' each man in the attitude in which he was caught by the consciousness of what is going on. All these hardened and impenitent man-killers, to whom death in its awfulest forms is a fact familiar to their every-day observation; who sleep on hills trembling with the thunder of great guns, dine in the midst of streaming missiles, and play at cards among the dead faces of their dearest friends – all are watching with suspended breath and beating hearts the outcome of an act involving the life of one man. Such is the magnetism of courage and devotion.

If now you should turn your head you would see a simultaneous movement among the spectators – a start, as if they had received an electric shock – and looking forward again to the now distant horseman you would see that he has in that instant altered his direction and is riding at an angle to his former course. The spectators suppose the sudden deflection to be caused by a shot, perhaps a wound; but take this field-glass and you will observe that he is riding toward a break in the wall and hedge. He means, if not killed, to ride through and overlook the country beyond.

You are not to forget the nature of this man's act; it is not permitted to you to think of it as an instance of bravado, nor, on the other hand, a needless sacrifice of self. If the enemy has not retreated he is in force on that ridge. The investigator will encounter nothing less than a line-of-battle; there is no need of pickets, videttes, skirmishers, to give warning of our approach; our attacking lines will be visible, conspicuous, exposed to an artillery fire that will shave the ground the moment they break from cover, and for half the distance to a sheet of rifle bullets in which nothing can live. In short, if the enemy is there, it would be madness to attack him in front; he must be manoeuvred out by the immemorial plan of threatening his line of communication, as necessary to his existence as to the diver at the bottom of the sea his air tube. But how ascertain if the enemy is there? There is but one way, – somebody must go and see. The natural and customary thing to do is to send forward a line of skirmishers. But in this case they will answer in the affirmative with all their lives; the enemy, crouching in double ranks behind the stone wall and in cover of the hedge, will wait until it is possible to count each assailant's teeth. At the first volley a half of the questioning line will fall, the other half before it can accomplish the predestined retreat. What a price to pay for gratified curiosity! At what a dear rate an army must sometimes purchase knowledge! 'Let me pay all,' says this gallant man – this military Christ!

There is no hope except the hope against hope that the crest is clear. True, he might prefer capture to death. So long as he advances, the line will not fire – why should it? He can safely ride into the hostile ranks and become a prisoner of war. But this would defeat his object. It would not answer our question; it is necessary either that he return unharmed or be shot to death before our eyes. Only so shall we know how to act. It captured – why, that might have been done by a half-dozen stragglers.

Now begins an extraordinary contest of intellect between a man and an army. Our horseman, now within a quarter of a mile of the crest, suddenly wheels to the left and gallops in a direction parallel to it. He has caught sight of his antagonist; he knows all. Some slight advantage of ground has enabled him to overlook a part of the line. If he were here he could tell us in words. But that is now hopeless; he must make the best use of the few minutes of life remaining to him, by compelling the enemy himself to tell us as much and as plainly as possible – which, naturally, that discreet power is reluctant to do. Not a rifleman in those crouching ranks, not a cannoneer at those masked and shotted guns, but knows the needs of the situation, the imperative duty of forbearance. Besides, there has been time enough to forbid them all to fire. True, a single rifle-shot might drop him and be no great disclosure. But firing is infectious – and see how rapidly he moves, with never a pause except as he whirls his horse about to take a new direction, never directly backward toward us, never directly forward toward his executioners. All this is visible through the glass; it seems occurring within pistol-shot; we see all but the enemy, whose presence, whose thoughts, whose motives we infer. To the unaided eye there is nothing but a black figure on a white horse, tracing slow zigzags against the slope of a distant hill – so slowly they seem almost to creep.

Now – the glass again – he has tired of his failure, or sees his error, or has gone mad; he is dashing directly forward at the wall, as if to take it at a leap, hedge and all! One moment only and he wheels right about and is speeding like the wind straight down the slope – toward his friends, toward his death! Instantly the wall is topped with a fierce roll of smoke for a distance of hundreds of yards to right and left. This is as instantly dissipated by the wind, and before the rattle of the rifle reaches us he is down. No, he recovers his seat; he has but pulled his horse upon its haunches. They are up and away! A tremendous cheer bursts from our ranks, relieving the insupportable tension of our feelings. And the horse and its rider? Yes, they are up and away. Away, indeed – they are making directly to our left, parallel to the now steadily blazing and smoking wall. The rattle of the musketry is continuous, and every bullet's target is that courageous heart.

Suddenly a great bank of white smoke pushes upward from behind the wall. Another and another – a dozen roll up before the thunder of the explosions and the humming of the missiles reach our ears and the missiles themselves come bounding through clouds of dust into our covert, knocking over here and there a man and causing a temporary distraction, a passing thought of self.

The dust drifts away. Incredible! – that enchanted horse and rider have passed a ravine and are climbing another slope to unveil another conspiracy of silence, to thwart the will of another armed host. Another moment and that crest too is in eruption. The horse rears and strikes the air with its forefeet. They are down at last. But look again – the man has detached himself from the dead animal. He stands erect, motionless, holding his sabre in his right hand straight above his head. His face is toward us. Now he lowers his hand to a level with his face and moves it outward, the blade of the sabre describing a downward curve. It is a sign to us, to the world, to posterity. It is a hero's salute to death and history.

Again the spell is broken; our men attempt to cheer; they are choking with emotion; they utter hoarse, discordant cries; they clutch their weapons and press tumultuously forward into the open. The skirmishers, without orders, against orders, are going forward at a keen run, like hounds unleashed. Our cannon speak and the enemy's now open in full chorus; to right and left as far as we can see, the distant crest, seeming now so near, erects its towers of cloud and the great shot pitch roaring down among our moving masses. Flag after flag of ours emerges from the wood, line after line sweeps forth, catching the sunlight on its burnished arms. The rear battalions alone are in obedience; they preserve their proper distance from the insurgent front.

The commander has not moved. He now removes his field-glass from his eyes and glances to the right and left. He sees the human current flowing on either side of him and his huddled escort, like tide waves parted by a rock. Not a sign of feeling in his face; he is thinking. Again he directs his eyes forward; they slowly traverse that malign and awful crest. He addresses a calm word to his bugler. *Tra-la-la! Tra-la-la!* The injuction has an imperiousness which enforces it. It is repeated by all the bugles of all the subordinate commanders; the sharp metallic notes assert themselves above the hum of the advance and penetrate the sound of the cannon. To halt is to withdraw. The colors move slowly back; the lines face about and sullenly follow, bearing their wounded; the skirmishers return, gathering up the dead.

Ah, those many, many needless dead! That great soul whose beautiful body is lying over yonder, so conspicuous against the sere hillside – could it not have been spared the bitter consciousness of a vain devotion? Would one exception have marred too much the pitiless perfection of the divine, eternal plan?

One of the Missing

Jerome Searing, a private soldier of General Sherman's army, then confronting the enemy at and about Kennesaw Mountain, Georgia, turned his back upon a small group of officers with whom he had been talking in low tones, stepped across a light line of earthworks, and disappeared in a forest. None of the men in line behind the works had said a word to him, nor had he so much as nodded to them in passing, but all who saw understood that this brave man had been intrusted with some perilous duty. Jerome Searing, though a private, did not serve in the ranks; he was detailed for service at division headquarters, being borne upon the rolls as an orderly. 'Orderly' is a word covering a multitude of duties. An orderly may be a messenger, a clerk, an officer's servant – anything. He may perform services for which no provision is made in orders and army regulations. Their nature may depend upon his aptitude, upon favor, upon accident. Private Searing, an incomparable marksman, young, hardy, intelligent and insensible to fear, was a scout. The general commanding his division was not content to obey orders blindly without knowing what was in his front, even when his command was not on detached service, but formed a fraction of the line of the army; nor was he satisfied to receive his knowledge of his *vis-à-vis* through the customary channels; he wanted to know more than he was apprised of by the corps commander and the collisions of pickets and skirmishers. Hence Jerome Searing, with his extraordinary daring, his woodcraft, his sharp eyes, and truthful tongue. On this occasion his instructions were simple: to get as near the enemy's lines as possible and learn all that he could.

In a few moments he had arrived at the picket-line, the men on duty there lying in groups of two and four behind little banks of earth scooped out of the slight depression in which they lay, their rifles protruding from the green boughs with which they had masked their small defenses. The forest extended without a break toward the front, so solemn and silent that only by an effort of the imagination could it be conceived as populous with armed men, alert and vigilant – a forest formidable with possibilities of battle. Pausing a moment in one of these rifle-pits to apprise the men of his intention Searing crept stealthily forward on his hands and knees and was soon lost to view in a dense thicket of underbrush.

'That is the last of him,' said one of the men; 'I wish I had his rifle; those fellows will hurt some of us with it.'

Searing crept on, taking advantage of every accident of ground and growth to give himself better cover. His eyes penetrated everywhere, his ears took note of every sound. He stilled his breathing, and at the cracking of a twig beneath his knee stopped his progress and hugged the earth. It was slow work, but not tedious; the danger made it exciting, but by no physical signs was the excitement manifest. His pulse was as regular, his nerves were as steady as if he were trying to trap a sparrow.

'It seems a long time,' he thought, 'but I cannot have come very far; I am still alive.'

He smiled at his own method of estimating distance, and crept forward. A moment later he suddenly flattened himself upon the earth and lay motionless, minute after minute. Through a narrow opening in the bushes he had caught sight of a small mound of yellow clay – one of the enemy's rifle-pits. After some little time he cautiously raised his head, inch by inch, then his body upon his hands, spread out on each side of him, all the while intently regarding the hillock of clay. In another moment he was upon his feet, rifle in hand, striding rapidly forward with little attempt at concealment. He had rightly interpreted the signs, whatever they were; the enemy was gone.

To assure himself beyond a doubt before going back to report upon so important a matter, Searing pushed forward across the line of abandoned pits, running from cover to cover in the more open forest, his eyes vigilant to discover possible stragglers. He came to the edge of a plantation – one of those forlorn, deserted homesteads of the last years of the war, upgrown with brambles, ugly with broken fences and desolate with vacant buildings having blank apertures in place of doors and windows. After a keen reconnoissance from the safe seclusion of a clump of young pines Searing ran lightly across a field and through an orchard to a small structure which stood apart from the other farm buildings, on a slight elevation. This he thought would enable him to overlook a large scope of country in the direction that he supposed the enemy to have taken in withdrawing. This building, which had originally consisted of a single room elevated upon four posts about ten feet high, was now little more than a roof; the floor had fallen away, the joists and planks loosely piled on the ground below or resting on end at various angles, not wholly torn from their fastenings above. The supporting posts were themselves no longer vertical. It looked as if the whole edifice would go down at the touch of a finger.

Concealing himself in the débris of joists and flooring Searing looked across the open ground between his point of view and a spur of Kennesaw Mountain, a half-mile away. A road leading up and across this spur was crowded with troops – the rear-guard of the retiring enemy, their gun-barrels gleaming in the morning sunlight.

Searing had now learned all that he could hope to know. It was his duty to return to his own command with all possibhle speed and report his discovery. But the gray column of Confederates toiling up the mountain road was singularly tempting. His rifle – an ordinary 'Springfield,' but fitted with a globe sight and hair-trigger – would easily send its ounce and a quarter of lead hissing into their midst. That would probably not affect the duration and result of the war, but it is the business of a soldier to kill. It is also his habit if he is a good soldier. Searing cocked his rifle and 'set' the trigger.

But it was decreed from the beginning of time that Private Searing was not to murder anybody that bright summer morning, nor was the Confederate retreat to be announced by him. For countless ages events had been so matching themselves together in that wondrous mosaic to some parts of which, dimly discernible, we give the name of history, that the acts which he had in will would have marred the harmony of the pattern. Some twenty-five years previously the Power charged with the execution of the work according to the design had provided against that mischance by causing the birth of a certain male child in a little village at the foot of the Carpathian Mountains, had carefully reared it, supervized its education, directed its desires into a military channel, and in due time made it an officer of artillery. By the concurrence of an infinite number of favoring influences and their preponderance over an infinite number of opposing ones, this officer of artillery had been made to commit a breach of discipline and flee from his native country to avoid punishment. He had been directed to New Orleans (instead of New York), where a recruiting officer awaited him on the wharf. He was enlisted and promoted, and things were so ordered that he now commanded a Confederate battery some two miles along the line from where Jerome Searing, the Federal scout, stood cocking his rifle. Nothing had been neglected – at every step in the progress of both these men's lives, and in the lives of their contemporaries and ancestors, the right thing had been done to bring about the desired result. Had anything in all this vast concatenation been overlooked Private Searing might have fired on the retreating Confederates that morning, and would perhaps have missed. As it fell out, a Confederate captain of artillery, having nothing better to do while awaiting his turn to pull out and be off, amused himself by sighting a field-piece obliquely to his right at what he mistook for some Federal officers on the crest of a hill, and discharged it. The shot flew high of its mark.

As Jerome Searing drew back the hammer of his rifle and with his eyes upon the distant Confederates considered where he could plant his shot with the best hope of making a widow or an orphan or a childless mother, – perhaps all three, for Private Searing, although he had repeatedly refused promotion, was not without a certain kind of ambition, – he heard a rushing sound in the air, like that made by the wings of a great bird swooping down upon its prey. More quickly than he could apprehend the gradation, it increased to a hoarse and horrible roar, as the missile that made it sprang at him out of the sky, striking with a deafening impact one of the posts supporting the confusion of timbers above him, smashing it into matchwood, and bringing down the crazy edifice with a loud clatter, in clouds of blinding dust!

When Jerome Searing recovered consciousness he did not at once understand what had occurred. It was, indeed, some time before he opened his eyes. For a while he believed that he had died and been buried, and he tried to recall some portions of the burial service. He thought that his wife was kneeling upon his grave, adding her weight to that of the earth upon his breast. The two of them, widow and earth, had crushed his coffin. Unless the children should persuade her to go home he would not much longer be able to breathe. He felt a sense of wrong. 'I cannot speak to her,' he thought; 'the dead have no voice; and if I open my eyes I shall get them full of earth.'

He opened his eyes. A great expanse of blue sky, rising from a fringe of the tops of trees. In the foreground, shutting out some of the trees, a high, dun mound, angular in outline and crossed by an intricate, patternless system of straight lines; the whole an immeasurable distance away – a distance so inconceivably great that it fatigued him, and he closed his eyes. The moment that he did so he was conscious of an insufferable light. A sound was in his ears like the low, rhythmic thunder of a distant sea breaking in successive waves upon the beach, and out of this noise, seeming a part of it, or possibly coming from beyond it, and intermingled with its ceaseless undertone, came the articulate words: 'Jerome Searing, you are caught like a rat in a trap – in a trap, trap, trap.'

Suddenly there fell a great silence, a black darkness, an infinite tranquillity, and Jerome Searing, perfectly conscious of his rathood, and well assured of the trap that he was in, remembering all and nowise alarmed, again opened his eyes to reconnoitre, to note the strengh of his enemy, to plan his defense.

He was caught in a reclining posture, his back firmly supported by a solid beam. Another lay across his breast, but he had been able to shrink a little away from it so that it no longer oppressed him, though it was immovable. A brace joining it at an angle had wedged him against a pile of boards on his left, fastening the arm on that side. His legs, slightly parted and straight along the ground, were covered upward to the knees with a mass of débris which towered above his narrow horizon. His head was as rigidly fixed as in a vise; he could move his eyes, his chin – no more. Only his right arm was partly free. 'You must help us out of this,' he said to it. But he could not get it from under the heavy timber athwart his chest, nor move it outward more than six inches at the elbow.

Searing was not seriously injured, nor did he suffer pain. A smart rap on the head from a flying fragment of the splintered post, incurred simultaneously with the frightfully sudden shock to the nervous system, had momentarily dazed him. His term of unconsciousness, including the period of recovery, during which he had had the strange fancies, had probably not exceeded a few seconds, for the dust of the wreck had not wholly cleared away as he began an intelligent survey of the situation.

With his partly free right hand he now tried to get hold of the beam that lay across, but not quite against, his breast. In no way could he do so. He was unable to depress the shoulder so as to push the elbow beyond that edge of the timber which was nearest his knees; failing in that, he could not raise the forearm and hand to grasp the beam. The brace that made an angle with it downward and backward prevented him from doing anything in that direction, and between it and his body the space was not half so wide as the length of his forearm. Obviously he could not get his hand under the beam nor over it; the hand could not, in fact, touch it at all. Having demonstrated his inability, he desisted, and began to think whether he could reach any of the débris piled upon his legs.

In surveying the mass with a view to determining that point, his attention was arrested by what seemed to be a ring of shining metal immediately in front of his eyes. It appeared to him at first to surround some perfectly black substance, and it was somewhat more than a half inch in diameter. It suddenly occurred to his mind that the blackness was simply shadow and that the ring was in fact the muzzle of his rifle protruding from the pile of débris. He was not long in satisfying himself that this was so – if it was a satisfaction. By closing either eye he could look a little way along the barrel – to the point where it was hidden by the rubbish that held it. He could see the one side, with the corresponding eye, at apparently the same angle as the other side with the other eye. Looking with the right eye, the weapon seemed to be directed at a point to the left of his head, and *vice versa*. He was unable to see the upper surface of the barrel, but could see the under surface of the stock at a slight angle. The piece was, in fact, aimed at the exact centre of his forehead.

In the perception of this circumstance, in the recollection that just previously to the mischance of which this uncomfortable situation was the result he had cocked the rifle and set the trigger so that a touch would discharge it, Private Searing was affected with a feeling of uneasiness. But that was as far as possible from fear; he was a brave man, somewhat familiar with the aspect of rifles from that point of view, and of cannon too. And now he recalled, with something like amusement, an incident of his experience at the storming of

Missionary Ridge, where, walking up to one of the enemy's embrasures from which he had seen a heavy gun throw charge after charge of grape among the assailants he had thought for a moment that the piece had been withdrawn; he could see nothing in the opening but a brazen circle. What that was he had understood just in time to step aside as it pitched another peck of iron down that swarming slope. To face firearms is one of the commonest incidents in a soldier's life – firearms, too, with malevolent eyes blazing behind them. That is what a soldier is for. Still, Private Searing did not altogether relish the situation, and turned away his eyes.

After groping, aimless, with his right hand for a time he made an ineffectual attempt to release his left. Then he tried to disengage his head, the fixity of which was the more annoying from his ignorance of what held it. Next he tried to free his feet, but while exerting the powerful muscles of his legs for that purpose it occurred to him that a disturbance of the rubbish which held them might discharge the rifle; how it could have endured what had already befallen it he could not understand, although memory assisted him with several instances in point. One in particular he recalled, in which in a moment of mental abstraction he had clubbed his rifle and beaten out another gentleman's brains, observing afterward that the weapon which he had been diligently swinging by the muzzle was loaded, capped, and at full cock – knowledge of which circumstance would doubtless have cheered his antagonist to longer endurance. He had always smiled in recalling that blunder of his 'green and salad days' as a soldier, but now he did not smile. He turned his eyes again to the muzzle of the rifle and for a moment fancied that it had moved; it seemed somewhat nearer.

Again he looked away. The tops of the distant trees beyond the bounds of the plantation interested him: he had not before observed how light and feathery they were, nor how darkly blue the sky was, even among their branches, where they somewhat paled it with their green; above him it appeared almost black. 'It will be uncomfortably hot here,' he thought, 'as the day advances. I wonder which way I am looking.'

Judging by such shadows as he could see, he decided that his face was due north; he would at least not have the sun in his eyes, and north – well, that was toward his wife and children.

'Bah!' he exclaimed aloud, 'what have they to do with it?'

He closed his eyes. 'As I can't get out I may as well go to sleep. The rebels are gone and some of our fellows are sure to stray out here foraging. They'll find me.'

But he did not sleep. Gradually he became sensible of a pain in his forehead – a dull ache, hardly perceptible at first, but growing more and more uncomfortable. He opened his eyes and it was gone – closed them and it returned. 'The devil!' he said, irrelevantly, and stared again at the sky. He heard the singing of birds, the strange metallic note of the meadow lark, suggesting the clash of vibrant blades. He fell into pleasant memories of his childhood, played again with his brother and sister, raced across the fields, shouting to alarm the sedentary larks, entered the sombre forest beyond and with timid steps followed the faint path to Ghost Rock, standing at last with audible heart-throbs before the Dead Man's Cave and seeking to penetrate its awful mystery. For the first time he observed that the opening of the haunted cavern was encircled by a ring of metal. Then all else vanished and left him gazing into the barrel of his rifle as before. But whereas before it had seemed nearer, it now seemed an inconceivable distance away, and all the more sinister for that. He cried out and, startled by something in his own voice – the note of fear – lied to himself in denial: 'If I don't sing out I may stay here till I die.'

He now made no further attempt to evade the menacing stare of the gun barrel. If he turned away his eyes an instant it was to look for assistance (although he could not see the ground on either side the ruin), and he permitted them to return, obedient to the imperative fascination. If he closed them it was from weariness, and instantly the poignant pain in his forehead – the prophecy and menace of the bullet – forced him to reopen them.

The tension of nerve and brain was too severe; nature came to his relief with intervals of unconciousness. Reviving from one of these he became sensible of a sharp, smarting pain in his right hand, and when he worked his fingers together, or rubbed his palm with them, he could feel that they were wet and slippery. He could not see the hand, but he knew the sensation; it was running blood. In his delirium he had beaten it against the jagged fragments of the wreck, had clutched it full of splinters. He resolved that he would meet his fate more manly. He was a plain, common soldier, had no religion and not much philosophy; he could not die like a hero, with great and wise last words, even if there had been some one to hear them, but he could die 'game,' and he would. But if he could only know when to expect the shot!

Some rats which had probably inhabited the shed came sneaking and scampering about. One of them mounted the pile of débris that held the rifle; another followed and another. Searing regarded them at first with indifference, then with friendly interest; then as the thought flashed into his bewildered mind that they might touch the trigger of his rifle, he cursed them and ordered them to go away. 'It is no business of yours,' he cried.

The creatures went away; they would return later, attack his face, gnaw away his nose, cut his throat – he knew that, but he hoped by that time to be dead.

Nothing could now unfix his gaze from the little ring of metal with its black interior. The pain in his forehead was fierce and incessant. He felt it gradually penetrating the brain more and more deeply, until at last its progress was arrested by the wood at the back of his head. It grew momentarily more insufferable: he began wantonly beating his lacerated hand against the splinters again to counteract that horrible ache. It seemed to throb with a slow, regular recurrence, each pulsation sharper than the preceding, and sometimes he cried out, thinking he felt the fatal bullet. No thoughts of home, of wife and children, of country, of glory. The whole record of memory was effaced. The world had passed away – not a vestage remained. Here in this confusion of timbers and boards is the sole universe. Here is immortality in time – each pain an everlasting life. The throbs tick off eternities.

Jerome Searing, the man of courage, the formidable enemy, the strong, resolute warrior, was as pale as a ghost. His jaw was fallen; his eyes protruded; he trembled in every fibre; a cold sweat bathed his entire body; he screamed with fear. He was not insane – he was terrified.

In groping about with his torn and bleeding hand he seized at last a strip of board, and, pulling, felt it give way. It lay parallel with his body, and by bending his elbow as much as the contracted space would permit, he could draw it a few inches at a time. Finally it was altogether loosened from the wreckage covering his legs; he could lift it clear of the ground its whole length.

A great hope came into his mind: perhaps he could work it upward, that is to say backward, far enough to lift the end and push aside the rifle; or, if that were too tightly wedged, so place the strip of board as to deflect the bullet. With this object he passed it backward inch by inch, hardly daring to breathe lest that act somehow defeat his intent, and more than ever unable to remove his eyes from the rifle, which might perhaps now hasten to improve its waning opportunity. Something as least had been gained: in the occupation of his mind in this attempt at self-defense he was less sensible of the pain in his head and had ceased to wince. But he was still dreadfully frightened and his teeth rattled like castanets.

The strip of board ceased to move to the suasion of his hand. He tugged at it with all his strengh, changed the direction of its length all he could, but it had met some extended obstruction behind him and the end in front was still too far away to clear the pile of débris and reach the muzzle of the gun. It extended, indeed, nearly as far as the trigger guard, which, uncovered by the rubbish, he could imperfectly see with his right eye. He tried to break the strip with his hand, but had no leverage. In his defeat, all his terror returned, augmented tenfold. The black aperture of the rifle appeared to threaten a sharper and more imminent death in punishment of his rebellion. The track of the bullet through his head ached with an intenser anguish. He began to tremble again.

Suddenly he became composed. His tremor subsided. He clenched his teeth and drew down his eyebrows. He had not exhausted his means of defense; a new design had shaped itself in his mind – another plan of battle. Raising the front end of the strip of board, he carefully pushed it forward through the wreckage at the side of the rifle until it pressed against the trigger guard. Then he moved the end slowly outward until he could feel that it had cleared it, then, closing his eyes, thrust it against the trigger with all his strength! There was no explosion; the rifle had been discharged as it dropped from his hand when the building fell. But it did its work.

Lieutenant Adrian Searing, in command of the picket-guard on that part of the line through which his brother Jerome had passed on his mission, sat with attentive ears in his breastwork behind the line. Not the faintest sound escaped him; the cry of a bird, the barking of a squirrel, the noise of the wind among the pines – all were anxiously noted by his overstrained sense. Suddenly, directly in front of his line, he heard a faint, confused rumble, like the clatter of a falling building translated by distance. The lieutenant mechanically looked at his watch. Six o'clock and eighteen minutes. At the same moment an officer approached him on foot from the rear and saluted.

'Lieutenant,' said the officer, 'the colonel directs you to move forward your line and feel the enemy if you find him. If not, continue the advance until directed to halt. There is reason to think that the enemy has retreated.'

The lieutenant nodded and said nothing; the other officer retired. In a moment the men, apprised of their duty by the non-commissioned officers in low tones, had deployed from their rifle-pits and were moving forward in skirmishing order, with set teeth and beating hearts.

This line of skirmishers sweeps across the plantation toward the mountain. They pass on both sides of the wrecked building, observing nothing. At a short distance in their rear their commander comes. He casts his eyes curiously upon the ruin and sees a dead body half buried in boards and timbers. It is so covered with dust that its clothing is Confederate gray. Its face is yellowish white; the cheeks are fallen in, the temples sunken, too, with sharp ridges about them, making the forehead forbiddingly narrow; the upper lip, slightly lifted, shows the white teeth, rigidly clenched. The hair is heavy with moisture, the face as wet as the dewy grass all about. From this point of view the officer does not observe the rifle; the man apparently killed by the fall of the building.

'Dead a week,' said the officer curtly, moving on and absently pulling out his watch as if to verify his estimate of time. Six o'clock and forty minutes.

Killed At Resaca

The best soldier of our staff was Lieutenant Herman Brayle, one of the two aides-de-camp. I don't remember where the general picked him up; from some Ohio regiment, I think; none of us had previously known him, and it would have been strange if we had, for no two of us came from the same State, nor even from adjoining States. The general seemed to think that a position on his staff was a distinction that should be so judiciously conferred as not to beget any sectional jealousies and imperil the integrity of that part of the country which was still an integer. He would not even choose officers from his own command, but by some jugglery at department headquarters obtained them from other brigades. Under such circumstances, a man's services had to be very distinguished indeed to be heard of by his family and the friends of his youth; and 'the speaking trump of fame' was a trifle hoarse from loquacity, anyhow.

Lieutenant Brayle was more than six feet in height and of splendid proportions, with the light hair and gray-blue eyes which men so gifted usually find associated with a high order of courage. As he was commonly in full uniform, especially in action, when most officers are content to be less flamboyantly attired, he was a very striking and conspicuous figure. As to the rest, he had a gentleman's manners, a scholar's head, and a lion's heart. His age was about thirty.

We all soon came to like Brayle as much as we admired him, and it was with sincere concern that in the engagement at Stone's River – our first action after he joined us – we observed that he had one most objectionable and unsoldierly quality: he was vain of his courage. During all the vicissitudes and mutations of that hideous encounter, whether our troops were fighting in the open cotton fields, in the cedar thickets, or behind the railway embankment, he did not once take cover, except when sternly commanded to do so by the general, who usually had other things to think of than the lives of his staff officers – or those of his men, for that matter.

In every later engagement while Brayle was with us it was the same way. He would sit his horse like an equestrian statue, in a storm of bullets and grape, in the most exposed places – wherever, in fact, duty, requiring him to go, permitted him to remain – when, without trouble and with distinct advantage to his reputation for common sense, he might have been in such security as is possible on a battlefield in the brief intervals of personal inaction.

On foot, from necessity or in deference to his dismounted commander or associates, his conduct was the same. He would stand like a rock in the open when officers and men alike had taken to cover; while men older in service and years, higher in rank and of unquestionable intrepidity, were loyally preserving behind the crest of a hill lives infinitely precious to their country, this fellow would stand, equally idle, on the ridge, facing in the direction of the sharpest fire.

When battles are going on in open ground it frequently occurs that the opposing lines, confronting each other within a stone's throw for hours, hug the earth as closely as if they loved it. The line officers in their proper places flatten themselves no less, and the field officers, their horse all killed or sent to the rear, crouch beneath the infernal canopy of hissing lead and screaming iron without a thought of personal dignity.

In such circumstances the life of a staff officer of a brigade is distinctly 'not a happy one,' mainly because of its precarious tenure and the unnerving alternations of emotion to which he is exposed. From a position of that comparative security from which a civilian would ascribe his escape to a 'miracle,' he may be despatched with an order to some commander of a prone regiment in the front line – a person for the moment inconspicuous and not always easy to find without a deal of search among men somewhat preoccupied, and in a din in which question and answer alike must be imparted in the sign language. It is customary in such cases to duck the head and scuttle away on a keen run, an object of lively interest to some thousands of admiring marksmen. In returning – well, it is not customary to return.

Brayle's practice was different. He would consign his horse to the care of an orderly, – he loved his horse, – and walk quietly away on his perilous errand with never a stoop of the back, his splendid figure, accentuated by his uniform, holding the eye with a strange fascination. We watched him with suspended breath, our hearts in our mouths. On one occasion of this kind, indeed, one of our number, an impetuous stammerer, was so possessed by his emotion that he shouted at me:

'I'll b-b-bet you t-two d-d-dollars they d-drop him b-b-before he g-gets to that d-d-ditch!'

I did not accept the brutal wager; I thought they would.

Let me do justice to a brave man's memory; in all these needless exposures of life there was no visible bravado nor subsequent narration. In the few instances when some of us had ventured to remonstrate, Brayle had smiled pleasantly and made some light reply, which, however, had not encouraged a further pursuit of the subject. Once he said:

'Captain, if ever I come to grief by forgetting your advice, I hope my last moments will be cheered by the sound of your beloved voice breathing into my ear the blessed words, "I told you so."'

We laughed at the captain – just why we could probably not have explained – and that afternoon when he was shot to rags from an ambuscade Brayle remained by the body for some time, adjusting the limbs with needless care – there in the middle of a road swept by gusts of grape and canister! It is easy to condemn this kind of thing, and not very difficult to refrain from imitation, but it is impossible not to respect, and Brayle was liked none the less for the weakness which had so heroic an expression. We wished he were not a fool, but he went on that way to the end, sometimes hard hit, but always returning to duty about as good as new.

Of course, it came at last; he who ignores the law of probabilities challenges an adversary that is seldom beaten. It was at Resaca, in Georgia, during the movement that resulted in the taking of Atlanta. In front of our brigade the enemy's line of earthworks ran through open fields along a slight crest. At each end of this open ground we were close up to him in the woods, but the clear ground we could not hope to occupy until night, when darkness would enable us to burrow like moles and throw up earth. At this point our line was a quarter-mile away in the edge of a wood. Roughly, we formed a semicircle, the enemy's fortified line being the chord of the arc.

'Lieutenant, go tell Colonel Ward to work up as close as he can get cover, and not to waste much ammunition in unnecessary firing. You may leave your horse.'

When the general gave this direction we were in the fringe of the forest, near the right extremity of the arc. Colonel Ward was at the left. The suggestion to leave the horse obviously enough meant that Brayle was to take the longer line, through the woods and among the men. Indeed, the suggestion was needless; to go by the short route meant absolutely certain failure to deliver the message. Before anybody could interpose, Brayle had cantered lightly into the field and the enemy's works were in crackling conflagration.

'Stop that damned fool!' shouted the general.

A private of the escort, with more ambition than brains, spurred forward to obey, and within ten yards left himself and his horse dead on the field of honor.

Brayle was beyond recall, galloping easily along, parallel to the enemy and less than two hundred yards distant. He was a picture to see! His hat had been blown or shot from his head, and his long, blond hair rose and fell with the motion of his horse. He sat erect in the saddle, holding the reins lightly in his left hand, his right hanging carelessly at his side. An occasional glimpse of his handsome profile as he turned his head one way or the other proved that the interest which he took in what was going on was natural and without affectation.

The picture was intensely dramatic, but in no degree theatrical. Successive scores of rifles spat at him viciously as he came within range, and our own line in the edge of the timber broke out in visible and audible defense. No longer regardful of themselves or their orders, our fellows sprang to their feet, and swarming into the open sent broad sheets of bullets against the blazing crest of the offending works, which poured an answering fire into their unprotected groups with deadly effect. The artillery on both sides joined the battle, punctuating the rattle and roar with deep, earth-shaking explosions and tearing the air with storms of screaming grape, which from the enemy's side splintered the trees and spattered them with blood, and from ours defiled the smoke of his arms with banks and clouds of dust from his parapet.

My attention had been for a moment drawn to the general combat, but now, glancing down the unobscured avenue between these two thunderclouds, I saw Brayle, the cause of the carnage. Invisible now from either side, and equally doomed by friend and foe, he stood in the shot-swept space, motionless, his face toward the enemy. At some little distance lay his horse. I instantly saw what had stopped him.

As topographical engineer I had, early in the day, made a hasty examination of the ground, and now remembered that at that point was a deep and sinuous gully, crossing half the field from the enemy's line, its general course at right angles to it. From where we now were it was invisible, and Brayle had evidently not known about it. Clearly, it was impassable. Its salient angles would have afforded him absolute security if he had chosen to be satisfied with the miracle already wrought in his favor and leapt into it. He could not go forward, he would not turn back; he stood awaiting death. It did not keep him long waiting.

By some mysterious coincidence, almost instantaneously as he fell, the firing ceased, a few desultory shots at long intervals serving rather to accentuate than break the silence. It was as if both sides had suddenly repented of their profitless crime. Four stretcher-bearers of ours, following a sergeant with a white flag, soon afterward moved unmolested into the field, and made straight for Brayle's body. Several Confederate officers and men came out to meet them, and with uncovered heads assisted them to take up their sacred burden. As it was borne toward us we heard beyond the hostile works fifes and a muffled drum – a dirge. A generous enemy honored the fallen brave.

Amongst the dead man's effects was a soiled Russia-leather pocket book. In the distribution of mementoes of our friend, which the general, as administrator, decreed, this fell to me.

A year after the close of the war, on my way to California, I opened and idly inspected it. Out of an overlooked compartment fell a letter without envelope or address. It was in a woman's handwriting, and began with words of endearment, but no name.

It had the following date line: 'San Francisco, Cal., July 9, 1862.' The signature was 'Darling,' in marks of quotation. Incidentally, in the body of the text, the writer's full name was given – Marian Mendenhall.

The letter showed evidence of cultivation and good breeding, but it was an ordinary love letter, if a love letter can be ordinary. There was not much in it, but there was something. It was this:

'Mr Winters, whom I shall always hate for it, has been telling that at some battle in Virginia, where he got his hurt, you were seen crouching behind a tree. I think he wants to injure you in my regard, which he knows the story would do if I believed it. I could bear to hear of my soldier lover's death, but not of his cowardice.'

These were the words which on that sunny afternoon, in a distant region, had slain a hundred men. Is woman weak?

One evening I called on Miss Mendenhall to return the letter to her. I intended, also, to tell her what she had done – but not that she did it. I found her in a handsome dwelling on Rincon Hill. She was beautiful, well bred – in a word, charming.

'You knew Lieutenant Herman Brayle,' I said, rather abruptly. 'You know, doubtless, that he fell in battle. Among his effects was found this letter from you. My errand here is to place it in your hands.'

She mechanically took the letter, glanced through it with deepening color, and then, looking at me with a smile, said:

'It is very good of you, though I am sure it was hardly worth while.' She started suddenly and changed color. 'This stain,' she said, 'is it – surely it is not – '

'Madam,' I said, 'pardon me, but that is the blood of the truest and bravest heart that ever beat.'

She hastily flung the letter on the blazing coals. 'Uh! I cannot bear the sight of blood!' she said. 'How did he die?'

I had involuntarily risen to rescue that scrap of paper, sacred even to me, and now stood partly behind her. As she asked the question she turned her face about and slightly upward. The light of the burning letter was reflected in her eyes and touched her cheek with a tinge of crimson like the stain upon its page. I had never seen anything so beautiful as this detestable creature.

'He was bitten by a snake,' I replied.

The Affair at Coulter's Notch

'Do you think, Colonel, that your brave Coulter would like to put one of his guns in here?' the general asked.

He was apparently not altogether serious; it certainly did not seem a place where any artillerist, however brave, would like to put a gun. The colonel thought that possibly his division commander meant good humoredly to intimate that in a recent conversation between them Captain Coulter's courage had been too highly extolled.

'General,' he replied warmly, 'Coulter would like to put a gun anywhere within reach of those people,' with a motion of his hand in the direction of the enemy.

'It is the only place,' said the general. He was serious, then.

The place was a depression, a 'notch,' in the sharp crest of a hill. It was a pass, and through it ran a turnpike, which reaching this highest point in its course by a sinuous ascent through a thin forest made a similar, though less steep, descent toward the enemy. For a mile to the left and a mile to the right, the ridge, though occupied by Federal infantry lying close behind the sharp crest and appearing as if held in place by atmospheric pressure, was inaccessible to artillery. There was no place but the bottom of the notch, and that was barely wide enough for the roadbed. From the Confederate side this point was commanded by two batteries posted on a slightly lower elevation beyond a creek, and a half-mile away. All the guns but one were masked by the trees of an orchard; that one – it seemed a bit of impudence – was on an open lawn directly in front of a rather grandiose building, the planter's dwelling. The gun was safe enough in its exposure – but only because the Federal infantry had been forbidden to fire. Coulter's Notch – it came to be called so – was not, that pleasant summer afternoon, a place where one would 'like to put a gun.'

Three or four dead horses lay there sprawling in the road, three or four dead men in a trim row at one side of it, and a little back, down the hill. All but one were cavalrymen belonging to the Federal advance. One was a quartermaster. The general commanding the division and the colonel commanding the brigade, with their staffs and escorts, had ridden into the notch to have a look at the enemy's guns – which had straightway obscured themselves in towering clouds of smoke. It was hardly profitable to be curious about guns which had the trick of the cuttlefish, and the season of observation had been brief. At its conclusion – a short remove backward from where it began – occurred the conversation already partly reported. 'It is the only place,' the general repeated thoughtfully, 'to get at them.'

The colonel looked at him gravely. 'There is room for only one gun, General – one against twelve.'

'That is true – for only one at a time,' said the commander with something like, yet not altogether like, a smile. 'But then, your brave Coulter – a whole battery in himself.'

The tone of irony was now unmistakable. It angered the colonel, but he did not know what to say. The spirit of military subordination is not favorable to retort, nor even to deprecation.

At this moment a young officer of artillery came riding slowly up the road attended by his bugler. It was Captain Coulter. He could not have been more than twenty-three years of age. He was of medium height, but very slender and lithe, and sat his horse with something of the air of a civilian. In fact he was of a type singularly unlike the men about him; thin, high-nosed, gray-eyed, with a slight blond mustache, and long, rather straggling hair of the same color. There was an apparent negligence in his attire. His cap was worn with the visor a trifle askew; his coat was buttoned only at the sword-belt, showing a considerable expanse of white shirt, tolerably clean for that stage of the campaign. But the negligence was all in his dress and bearing; in his face was a look of intense interest in his surroundings. His gray eyes, which seemed occasionally to strike right and left across the landscape, like search-lights, were for the most part fixed upon the sky beyond the Notch; until he should arrive at the summit of the road there was nothing else in that direction to see. As he came opposite his division and brigade commanders at the roadside he saluted mechanically and was about to pass on. The colonel signed to him to halt.

'Captain Coulter,' he said, 'the enemy has twelve pieces over there on the next ridge. If I rightly understand the general, he directs that you bring up a gun and engage them.'

There was a blank silence; the general looked stolidly at a distant regiment swarming slowly up the hill through rough undergrowth, like a torn and draggled cloud of blue smoke; the captain appeared not to have observed him. Presently the captain spoke, slowly and with apparent effort:

'On the next ridge, did you say, sir? Are the guns near the house?'

'Ah, you have been over this road before. Directly at the house.'

'And it is – necessary – to engage them? The order is imperative?'

His voice was husky and broken. He was visibly paler. The colonel was astonished and mortified. He stole a glance at the commander. In that set, immobile face was no sign; it was as hard as bronze. A moment later the general rode away, followed by his staff and escort. The colonel, humiliated and indignant, was about to order Captain Coulter in arrest, when the latter spoke a few words in a low tone to his bugler, saluted, and rode straight forward into the Notch, where, presently, at the summit of the road, his field-glass at his eyes, he showed against the sky, he and his horse, sharply defined and statuesque. The bugler had dashed down the speed and disappeared behind a wood. Presently his bugle was heard singing in the cedars, and in an incredibly short time a single gun with its caisson, each drawn by six horses and manned by its full complement of gunners, came bounding and banging up the grade in a storm of dust, unlimbered under cover, and was run forward by hand to the fatal crest among the dead horses. A gesture of the captain's arm, some strangely agile movements of the men in loading, and almost before the troops along the way had ceased to hear the rattle of the wheels, a great white cloud sprang forward down the slope, and with a deafening report the affair at Coulter's Notch had begun.

It is not intended to relate in detail the progress and incidents of that ghastly contest – a contest without vicissitudes, its alternations only different degrees of despair. Almost at the instant when Captain Coulter's gun blew its challenging cloud twelve answering clouds rolled upward from among the trees about the plantation house, a deep multiple report roared back like a broken echo, and thenceforth to the end the Federal cannoneers fought their hopeless battle in an atmosphere of living iron whose thoughts were lightnings and whose deeds were death.

Unwilling to see the efforts which he could not aid and the slaughter which he could not stay, the colonel ascended the ridge at a point a quarter of a mile to the left, whence the Notch, itself invisible, but pushing up successive masses of smoke, seemed the crater of a volcano in thundering eruption. With his glass he watched the enemy's guns, noting as he could the effects of Coulter's fire – if Coulter still lived to direct it. He saw that the Federal gunners, ignoring those of the enemy's pieces whose positions could be determined by their smoke only, gave their whole attention to the one that maintained its place in the open –the lawn in front of the house. Over and about that hardy piece the shells exploded at intervals of a few seconds. Some exploded in the house, as could be seen by thin ascensions of smoke from the breached roof. Figures of prostrate men and horses were plainly visible.

'If our fellows are doing so good work with a single gun,' said the colonel to an aide who happened to be nearest, 'they must be suffering like the devil from twelve. Go down and present the commander of that piece with my congratulations on the accuracy of his fire.'

Turning to his adjutant-general he said, 'Did you observe Coulter's damned reluctance to obey orders?'

'Yes, sir, I did.'

'Well, say nothing about it, please. I don't think the general will care to make any accusations. He will probably have enough to do in explaining his own connection with this uncommon way of amusing the rearguard of a retreating enemy.'

A young officer approached from below, climbing breathless up the acclivity. Almost before he had saluted, he gasped out:

'Colonel, I am directed by Colonel Harmon to say that the enemy's guns are within easy reach of our rifles, and most of them visible from several points along the ridge.'

The brigade commander looked at him without a trace of interest in his expression. 'I know it,' he said quietly.

The young adjutant was visibly embarrassed. 'Colonel Harmon would like to have permission to silence those guns,' he stammered.

'So should I,' the colonel said in the same tone. 'Present my compliments to Colonel Harmon and say to him that the general's orders for the infantry not to fire are still in force.'

The adjutant saluted and retired. The colonel ground his heel into the earth and turned to look again at the enemy's guns.

'Colonel,' said the adjutant-general, 'I don't know that I ought to say anything, but there is something wrong in all this. Do you happen to know that Captain Coulter is from the South?'

'No: *was* he, indeed?'

'I heard that last summer the division which the general then commanded was in the vicinity of Coulter's home – camped there for weeks, and – '

'Listen!' said the colonel, interrupting with an upward gesture. 'Do you hear *that?*'

'That' was the silence of the Federal gun. The staff, the orderlies, the lines of infantry behind the crest – all had 'heard,' and were looking curiously in the direction of the crater, whence no smoke now ascended except desultory cloudlets from the enemy's shells. Then came the blare of a bugle, a faint rattle of wheels; a minute later the sharp reports recommenced with double activity. The demolished gun had been replaced with a sound one.

'Yes,' said the adjutant-general, resuming his narrative, 'the general made the acquaintance of Coulter's family. There was trouble – I don't know the exact nature of it – something about Coulter's wife. She is a red-hot Secessionist, as they all are, except Coulter himself, but she is a good wife and high-bred lady. There was a complaint to army head-quarters. The general was transferred to this division. It is odd that Coulter's battery should afterward have been assigned to it.'

The colonel has risen from the rock upon which they had been sitting. His eyes were blazing with a generous indignation.

'See here, Morrison,' said he, looking his gossiping staff officer straight in the face, 'did you get that story from a gentleman or a liar?'

'I don't want to say how I got it, Colonel, unless it is necessary' – he was blushing a trifle – 'but I'll stake my life upon its truth in the main.'

The colonel turned toward a small knot of officers some distance away. 'Lieutenant Williams!' he shouted.

One of the officers detached himself from the group and coming forward saluted, saying: 'Pardon me, Colonel, I thought you had been informed. Williams is dead down there by the gun. What can I do, sir?'

Lieutenant Williams was the aide who had had the pleasure of conveying to the officer in charge of the gun his brigade commander's congratulations.

'Go,' said the colonel, 'and direct the withdrawal of that gun instantly. No – I'll go myself.'

He strode down the declivity toward the rear of the Notch at a breakneck pace, over rocks and through brambles, followed by his little retinue in tumultuous disorder. At the foot of the declivity they mounted their waiting animals and took to the road at a lively trot, round a bend and into the Notch. The spectacle which they encountered there was appalling!

Within that defile, barely broad enough for a single gun, were piled the wrecks of no fewer than four. They had noted the silencing of only the last one disabled – there had been a lack of men to replace it quickly with another. The débris lay on both sides of the road; the men had managed to keep an open way between, through which the fifth piece was now firing. The men? – they looked like demons of the pit! All were hatless, all stripped to the waist, their reeking skins black with blotches of powder and spattered with gouts of blood. They worked like madmen, with rammer and cartridge, lever and lanyard. They set their swollen shoulders and bleeding hands against the wheels at each recoil and heaved the heavy gun back to its place. There were no commands; in that awful environment of whooping shot, exploding shells, shrieking fragments of iron, and flying splinters of wood, none could have been heard. Officers, if officers there were, were indistinguishable; all worked together – each while he lasted – governed by the eye. When the gun was sponged, it was loaded; when loaded, aimed and fired. The colonel observed something new to his military experience – something horrible and unnatural: the gun was bleeding at the mouth! In temporary default of water, the man sponging had dipped his sponge into a pool of comrade's blood. In all this work there was no clashing; the duty of the instant was obvious. When one fell, another, looking a trifle cleaner, seemed to rise from the earth in the dead man's tracks, to fall in his turn.

With the ruined guns lay the ruined men – alongside the wreckage, under it and atop of it; and back down the road – a ghastly procession! – crept on hands and knees such of the wounded as were able to move. The colonel – he had compassionately sent his cavalcade to the right about – had to ride over those who were entirely dead in order not to crush those who were partly alive. Into that hell he tranquilly held his way, rode up alongside the gun, and, in the obscurity of the last discharge, tapped upon the cheek the man holding the rammer – who straightway fell, thinking himself killed. A fiend seven times damned sprang out of the smoke to take his place, but paused and gazed up at the mounted officer with an unearthly regard, his teeth flashing between his black lips, his eyes, fierce and expanded, burning like coals beneath his bloody brow. The colonel made an authoritative gesture and pointed to the rear. The fiend bowed in token of obedience. It was Captain Coulter.

Simultaneously with the colonel's arresting sign, silence fell upon the whole field of action. The procession of missiles no longer streamed into that defile of death, for the enemy also had ceased firing. His army had been gone for hours, and the commander of his rear-guard, who had held his position perilously long in hope to silence the Federal fire, at that strange moment had silenced his own. 'I was not aware of the breadth of my authority,' said the colonel to anybody, riding forward to the crest to see what had really happened.

An hour later his brigade was in bivouac on the enemy's ground, and its idlers were examining, with something of awe, as the faithful inspect a saint's relics, a score of straddling dead horses and three disabled guns, all spiked. The fallen men had been carried away; their torn and broken bodies would have given too great satisfaction.

Naturally, the colonel established himself and his military family in the plantation house. It was somewhat shattered, but it was better than the open air. The furniture was greatly deranged and broken. Walls and ceilings were knocked away here and there, and a lingering odor of powder smoke was everywhere. The beds, the closets of women's clothing, the cupboards were not greatly damaged. The new tenants for a night made themselves comfortable, and the virtual effacement of Coulter's battery supplied them with an interesting topic.

During supper an orderly of the escort showed himself into the dining-room and asked permission to speak to the colonel.

'What is it, Barbour?' said the officer pleasantly, having overheard the request.

'Colonel, there is something wrong in the cellar; I don't know what – somebody there. I was down there rummaging about.'

'I will go down and see,' said a staff officer, rising.

'So will I,' the colonel said; 'let the others remain. Lead on, orderly.'

They took a candle from the table and descended the cellar stairs, the orderly in visible trepidation. The candle made but a feeble light, but presently, as they advanced, its narrow circle of illumination revealed a human figure seated on the ground against the black stone wall which they were skirting, its knees elevated, its head bowed sharply forward. The face, which should have been seen in profile, was invisble, for the man was bent so far forward that his long hair concealed it; and, strange to relate, the beard, of a much darker hue, fell in a great tangled mass and lay along the ground at his side. They involuntarily paused; then the colonel, taking the candle from the orderly's shaking hand, approached the man and attentively considered him. The long dark beard was the hair of a woman – dead. The dead woman clasped in her arms a dead babe. Both were clasped in the arms of the man, pressed against his breast, against his lips. There was blood in the hair of the woman; there was blood in the hair of the man. A yard away, near an irregular depression in the beaten earth which formed the cellar's floor – a fresh excavation with a convex bit of iron, having jagged edges, visible in one of the sides – lay an infant's foot. The colonel held the light as high as he could. The floor of the room above was broken through, the splinters pointing at all angles downward. 'This casemate is not bomb-proof,' said the colonel gravely. It did not occur to him that his summing up of the matter had any levity in it.

They stood about the group awhile in silence; the staff officer was thinking of his unfinished supper, the orderly of what might possibly be in one of the casks on the other side of the cellar. Suddenly the man whom they had thought dead raised his head and gazed tranquilly into their faces. His complexion was coal black; the cheeks were apparently tattooed in irregular sinuous lines from the eyes downward. The lips, too, were white, like those of a stage Negro. There was blood upon his forehead.

The staff officer drew back a pace, the orderly two paces.

'What are you doing here, my man?' said the colonel, unmoved.

'This house belongs to me, sir,' was the reply, civilly delivered.

'To you? Ah, I see! And these?'

'My wife and child. I am Captain Coulter.'

The Coup De Grâce

The fighting had been hard and continuous; that was attested by all the senses. The very taste of battle was in the air. All was now over; it remained only to succor the wounded and bury the dead – to 'tidy up a bit,' as the humorist of a burial squad put it. A good deal of 'tidying up' was required. As far as one could see through the forests, among the splintered trees, lay wrecks of men and horses. Among them moved the stretcher-bearers, gathering and carrying away the few who showed signs of life. Most of the wounded had died of neglect while the right to minister to their wants was in dispute. It is an army regulation that the wounded must wait; the best way to care for them is to win the battle. It must be confessed that victory is a distinct advantage to a man requiring attention, but many do not live to avail themselves of it.

The dead were collected in groups of a dozen or a score and laid side by side in rows while the trenches were dug to receive them. Some, found at too great a distance from these rallying points, were buried where they lay. There was little attempt at identification, though in most cases, the burial parties being detailed to glean the same ground which they had assisted to reap, the names of the victorious dead were known and listed. The enemy's fallen had to be content with counting. But of that they got enough: many of them were counted several times, and the total, as given afterward in the official report of the victorious commander, denoted rather a hope than a result.

At some little distance from the spot where one of the burial parties had established its 'bivouac of the dead,' a man in the uniform of a Federal officer stood leaning against a tree. From his feet upward to his neck his attitude was that of weariness reposing; but he turned his head uneasily from side to side; his mind was apparently not at rest. He was perhaps uncertain in which direction to go; he was not likely to remain long where he was, for already the level rays of the setting sun straggled redly through the open spaces of the wood and the weary soldiers were quitting their task for the day. He would hardly make a night of it alone there among the dead. Nine men in ten whom you meet after a battle inquire the way to some fraction of the army – as if any one could know. Doubtless this officer was lost. After resting himself a moment he would presumably follow one of the retiring burial squads.

When all were gone he walked straight away into the forest toward the red west, its light staining his face like blood. The air of confidence with which he now strode along showed that he was on familiar ground; he had recovered his bearing. The dead on his right and on his left were unregarded as he passed. An occasional low moan from some sorely-stricken wretch whom the relief-parties had not reached, and who would have to pass a comfortless night beneath the stars with his thirst to keep him company, was equally unheeded. What, indeed, could the officer have done, being no surgeon and having no water?

At the head of a shallow ravine, a mere depression of the ground, lay a small group of bodies. He saw, and swerving suddenly from his course walked rapidly toward them. Scanning each one sharply as he passed, he stopped at last above one which lay at a slight remove from the others, near a clump of small trees. He looked at it narrowly. It seemed to stir. He stooped and laid his hand upon its face. It screamed.

The officer was Captain Downing Madwell, of a Massachusetts regiment of infantry, a daring and intelligent soldier, an honorable man.

In the regiment were two brothers named Halcrow – Caffal and Creede Halcrow. Caffal Halcrow was a sergeant in Captain Madwell's company, and these two men, the sergeant and the captain, were devoted friends. In so far as disparity of rank, difference in duties and considerations of military discipline would permit they were commonly together. They had, indeed, grown up together from childhood. A habit of the heart is not easily broken off. Caffal Halcrow had nothing military in his taste nor disposition, but the thought of separation from his friend was disagreeable; he enlisted in the company in which Madwell was second-lieutenant. Each had taken two steps upward in rank, but between the highest non-commissioned and the lowest commissioned officer the gulf is deep and wide and the old relation was maintained with difficulty and a difference.

Creede Halcrow, the brother of Caffal, was the major of the regiment – a cynical, saturnine man, between whom and Captain Madwell there was a natural antipathy which circumstances had nourished and strengthened to an active animosity. But for the restraining influence of their mutual relation to Caffal these two patriots would doubtless have endeavored to deprive their country of each other's services.

At the opening of the battle that morning the regiment was performing outpost duty a mile away from the main army. It was attacked and nearly surrounded in the forest, but stubbornly held its ground. During a lull in the fighting, Major Halcrow came to Captain Madwell. The two exchanged formal salutes, and the major said: 'Captain, the colonel directs that you push your company to the head of this ravine and hold your place there until recalled. I need hardly apprise you of the dangerous character of the movement, but if you wish, you can, I suppose, turn over the command to your first-lieutenant. I was not, however, directed to authorize the substitution; it is merely a suggestion of my own, unofficially made.'

To this deadly insult Captain Madwell coolly replied:

'Sir, I invite you to accompany the movement. A mounted officer would be a conspicuous mark, and I have long held the opinion that it would be better if you were dead.'

The art of repartee was cultivated in military circles as early as 1862.

A half-hour later Captain Madwell's company was driven from its position at the head of the ravine, with a loss of one-third its number. Among the fallen was Sergeant Halcrow. The regiment was soon afterward forced back to the main line, and at the close of the battle was miles away. The captain was now standing at the side of his subordinate and friend.

Sergeant Halcrow was mortally hurt. His clothing was deranged; it seemed to have been violently torn apart, exposing the abdomen. Some of the buttons of his jacket had been pulled off and lay on the ground beside him and fragments of his other garments were strewn about. His leather belt was parted and had apparently been dragged from beneath him as he lay. There had been no great effusion of blood. The only visible wound was a wide, ragged opening in the abdomen. It was defiled with earth and dead leaves. Protruding from it was a loop of small intestine. In all his experience Captain Madwell had not seen a wound like this. He could neither conjecture how it was made nor explain the attendant circumstances – the strangely torn clothing, the parted belt, the besmirching of the white skin. He knelt and made a closer examination. When he rose to his feet, he turned his eyes in different directions as if looking for an enemy. Fifty yards away, on the crest of a low, thinly wooded hill, he saw several dark objects moving about among the fallen men – a herd of swine. One stood with its back to him, its shoulders sharply elevated. Its forefeet were upon a human body, its head was depressed and invisible. The bristly ridge of its chine showed black against the red west. Captain Madwell drew away his eyes and fixed them again upon the thing which had been his friend.

The man who had suffered these monstrous mutilations was alive. At intervals he moved his limbs; he moaned at every breath. He stared blankly into the face of his friend and if touched screamed. In his giant agony he had torn up the ground on which he lay; his clenched hands were full of leaves and twigs and earth. Articulate speech was beyond his power; it was impossible to know if he were sensible to anything but pain. The expression of his face was an appeal; his eyes were full of prayer. For what?

There was no misreading that look; the captain had too frequently seen it in eyes of those whose lips had still the power to formulate it by an entreaty for death. Consciously or unconsciously, this writhing fragment of humanity, this type and example of acute sensation, this handiwork of man and beast, this humble, unheroic Prometheus, was imploring everything, all, the whole non-ego, for the boon of oblivion. To the earth and the sky alike, to the trees, to the man, to whatever took form in sense or consciousness, this incarnate suffering addressed that silent plea.

For what, indeed? For that which we accord to even the meanest creature without sense to demand it, denying it only to the wretched of our own race: for the blessed release, the rite of uttermost compassion, the *coup de grâce*.

Captain Madwell spoke the name of his friend. He repeated it over and over without effect until emotion choked his utterance. His tears splashed upon the livid face beneath his own and blinded himself. He saw nothing but a blurred and moving object, but the moans were more distinct than ever, interrupted at briefer intervals by sharper shrieks. He turned away, struck his hand upon his forehead, and strode from the spot. The swine, catching sight of him, threw up their crimson muzzles, regarding him suspiciously a second, and then with a gruff, concerted grunt, raced away out of sight. A horse, its foreleg splintered by a cannon-shot, lifted its head sidewise from the ground and neighed piteously. Madwell stepped foreard, drew his revolver and shot the poor beast between the eyes, narrowly observing its death-struggle, which, contrary to his expectation, was violent and long; but at last it lay still. The tense muscles of its lips, which had uncovered the teeth in a horrible grin, relaxed; the sharp, clean-cut profile took on a look of profound peace and rest.

Along the distant, thinly wooded crest to westward the fringe of sunset fire had now nearly burned itself out. The light upon the trunks of the trees had faded to a tender gray; shadows were in their tops, like great dark birds aperch. Night was coming and there were miles of haunted forest between Captain Madwell and camp. Yet he stood here at the side of the dead animal, apparently lost to all sense of his surroundings. His eyes were bent upon the earth at his feet; his left hand hung loosely at his side, his right still held the pistol. Presently he lifted his face, turned it toward his dying friend and walked rapidly back to his side. He knelt upon one knee, cocked the weapon, placed the muzzle against the man's forehead, and turning away his eyes pulled the trigger. There was no report. He had used his last cartridge for the horse.

The sufferer moaned and his lips moved convulsively. The froth that ran from them had a tinge of blood.

Captain Madwell rose to his feet and drew his sword from the scabbard. He passed the fingers of his left hand along the edge from hilt to point. He held it out straight before him, as if to test his nerves. There was no visible tremor of the blade; the ray of bleak skylight that it reflected was steady and true. He stooped and with his left hand tore away the dying man's shirt, rose and placed the point of the sword just over the heart. This time he did not withdraw his eyes. Grasping the hilt with both hands, he thrust downward with all his strengh and weight. The blade sank into the man's body – through his body into the earth; Captain Madwell came near falling forward upon his work. The dying man drew up his knees and at the same time threw his right arm across his breast and grasped the steel so tightly that the knuckles of the hand visibly whitened. By a violent but vain effort to withdraw the blade the wound was enlarged; a rill of blood escaped, running sinuously down into the deranged clothing. At that moment three men stepped silently forward from behind the clump of young trees which had concealed their approach. Two were hospital attendants and carried a stretcher.

The third was Major Creede Halcrow.

Parker Adderson, Philosopher

'Prisoner, what is your name?'

'As I am to lose it at daylight to-morrow morning it is hardly worth while concealing it. Parker Adderson.'

'Your rank?'

'A somewhat humble one; commissioned officers are too precious to be risked in the perilous business of a spy. I am a sergeant.'

'Of what regiment?'

'You must excuse me; my answer might, for anything I know, give you an idea of whose forces are in your front. Such knowledge as that is what I came into your lines to obtain, not to impart.'

'You are not without wit.'

'If you have the patience to wait you will find me dull enough tomorrow.'

'How do you know that you are to die to-morrow morning?'

'Among spies captured by night that is the custom. It is one of the nice observances of the profession.'

The general so far laid aside the dignity appropriate to a Confederate officer of high rank and wide renown as to smile. But no one in his power and out of his favor would have drawn any happy augury from that outward and visible sign of approval. It was neither genial nor infectious; it did not communicate itself to the other persons exposed to it – the caught spy who had provoked it and the armed guard who had brought him into the tent and now stood a little apart, watching his prisoner in the yellow candle-light. It was no part of that warrior's duty to smile; he had been detailed for another purpose. The conversation was resumed; it was in character a trial for a capital offense.

'You admit, then, that you are a spy – that you came into my camp, disguised as you are in the uniform of a Confederate soldier, to obtain information secretly regarding the numbers and disposition of my troops.'

'Regarding, particularly, their numbers. Their disposition I already knew. It is morose.'

The general brightened again; the guard, with a severer sense of his responsibility, accentuated the austerity of his expression and stood a trifle more erect than before. Twirling his gray slouch hat round and round upon his forefinger, the spy took a leisurely survey of his surroundings. They were simple enough. The tent was a common 'wall tent,' about eight feet by ten in dimensions, lighted by a single tallow candle stuck into the haft of a bayonet, which was itself stuck into a pine table at which the general sat, now busily writing and apparently forgetful of his unwilling guest. An old rag carpet covered the earthen floor; an older leather trunk, a second chair and a roll of blankets were about all else that the tent contained; in General Clavering's command Confederate simplicity and penury of 'pomp and circumstance' had attained their highest development. On a large nail driven into the tent pole at the entrance was suspended a sword-belt supporting a long sabre, a pistol in its holster and, absurdly enough, a bowie-knife. Of that most unmilitary weapon it was the general's habit to explain that it was a souvenir of the peaceful days when he was a civilian.

It was a stormy night. The rain cascaded upon the canvas in torrents, with the dull, drum-like sound familiar to dwellers in tents. As the whooping blasts charged upon it the frail structure shook and swayed and strained at its confining stakes and ropes.

The general finished writing, folded the half-sheet of paper and spoke to the soldier guarding Adderson: 'Here, Tassman, take that to the adjutant-general; then return.'

'And the prisoner, General?' said the soldier, saluting, with an inquiring glance in the direction of that unfortunate.

'Do as I said,' replied the officer, curtly.

The soldier took the note and ducked himself out of the tent. General Clavering turned his handsome face toward the Federal spy, looked him in the eyes, not unkindly, and said: 'It is a bad night, my man.'

'For me, yes.'

'Do you guess what I have written?'

'Something worth reading, I dare say. And – perhaps it is my vanity – I venture to suppose that I am mentioned in it.'

'Yes; it is a memorandum for an order to be read to the troops at *reveille* concerning your execution. Also some notes for the guidance of the provost-marshal in arranging the details of that event.'

'I hope, General, the spectacle will be intelligently arranged, for I shall attend it myself.'

'Have you any arrangements of your own that you wish to make? Do you wish to see a chaplain, for example?'

'I could hardly secure a longer rest for myself by depriving him of some of his.'

'Good God, man! do you mean to go to your death with nothing but jokes upon your lips? Do you know that this is a serious matter?'

'How can I know that? I have never been dead in all my life. I have heard that death is a serious matter, but never from any of those who have experienced it.'

The general was silent for a moment; the man interested, perhaps amused him – a type not previously encountered.

'Death,' he said, 'is at least a loss – a loss of such happiness as we have, and of opportunities for more.'

'A loss of which we shall never be conscious can be borne with composure and therefore expected without apprehension. You must have observed, General, that of all the dead men with whom it is your soldierly pleasure to strew your path none shows signs of regret.'

'If the being dead is not a regrettable condition, yet the becoming so – the act of dying – appears to be distinctly disagreeable to one who has not lost the power to feel.'

'Pain is disagreeable, no doubt. I never suffer it without more or less discomfort. But he who lives longest is most exposed to it. What you call dying is simply the last pain – there is really no such thing as dying. Suppose, for illustration, that I attempt to escape. You lift the revolver that you are courteously concealing in your lap, and – '

The general blushed like a girl, then laughed softly, disclosing his brilliant teeth, made a slight inclination of his handsome head and said nothing. The spy continued: 'You fire, and I have in my stomach what I did not swallow. I fall, but am not dead. After a half-hour of agony I am dead. But at any given instant of that half-hour I was either alive or dead. There is no transition period.

'When I am hanged to-morrow morning it will be quite the same; while conscious I shall be living; when dead, unconscious. Nature appears to have ordered the matter quite in my interest – the way that I should have ordered it myself. It is so simple,' he added with a smile, 'that it seems hardly worth while to be hanged at all.'

At the finish of his remarks there was a long silence. The general sat impassive, looking into the man's face, but apparently not attentive to what had been said. It was as if his eyes had mounted guard over the prisoner while his mind concerned itself with other matters. Presently he drew a long, deep breath, shuddered, as one awakened from a dreadful dream, and exclaimed almost inaudibly: 'Death is horrible!' – this man of death.

'It was horrible to our savage ancestors,' said the spy, gravely, 'because they had not enough intelligence to dissociate the idea of consciousness from the idea of the physical forms in which it is manifested – as an even lower order of intelligence, that of the monkey, for example, may be unable to imagine a house without inhabitants, and seeing a ruined hut fancies a suffering occupant. To us it is horrible because we have inherited the tendency to think it so, accounting for the notion by wild and fanciful theories of another world – as names of places give rise to legends explaining them and reasonless conduct to philosophies in justification. You can hang me, General, but there your power of evil ends; you cannot condemn me to heaven.'

The general appeared not to have heard; the spy's talk had merely turned his thoughts into an unfamiliar channel, but there they pursued their will independently to conclusions of their own. The storm had ceased, and something of the solemn spirit of the night had imparted itself to his reflections, giving them the sombre tinge of a supernatural dread. Perhaps there was an element of prescience in it. 'I should not like to die,' he said – 'not to-night.'

He was interrupted – if, indeed, he had intended to speak further – by the entrance of an officer of his staff, Captain Hasterlick, the provost-marshal. This recalled him to himself; the absent look passed away from his face.

'Captain,' he said, acknowledging the officer's salute, 'this man is a Yankee spy captured inside our lines with incriminating papers on him. He has confessed. How is the weather?'

'The storm is over, sir, and the moon shining.'

'Good; take a file of men, conduct him at once to the parade ground, and shoot him.'

A sharp cry broke from the spy's lips. He threw himself forward, thrust out his neck, expanded his eyes, clenched his hands.

'Good God!' he cried hoarsely, almost inarticulately; 'you do not mean that! You forget – I am not to die until morning.'

'I have said nothing of morning,' replied the general, coldly; 'that was an assumption of your own. You die now.'

'But, General, I beg – I implore you to remember; I am to hang! It will take some time to erect the gallows – two hours – an hour. Spies are hanged; I have rights under military law. For Heaven's sake, General, consider how short –'

'Captain, observe my directions.'

The officer drew his sword and fixing his eyes upon the prisoner pointed silently to the opening of the tent. The prisoner hesitated; the officer grasped him by the collar and pushed him gently forward. As he approached the tent pole the frantic man sprang to it and with cat-like agility seized the handle of the bowie-knife, plucked the weapon from the scabbard and thrusting the captain aside leaped upon the general with the fury of a madman, hurling him to the ground and falling headlong upon him as he lay. The table was overturned, the candle extinguished and they fought blindly in the darkness. The provost-marshal sprang to the assistance of his superior officer and was himself prostrated upon the struggling forms. Curses and inarticulate cries of rage and pain came from the welter of limbs and bodies; the tent came down upon them and beneath its hampering and enveloping folds the struggle went on. Private Tassman, returning from his errand and dimly conjecturing the situation, threw down his rifle and laying hold of the flouncing canvas at random vainly tried to drag it off the men under it; and the sentinel who paced up and down in front, not daring to leave his beat though the skies should fall, discharged his rifle. The report alarmed the camp; drums beat the long roll and bugles sounded the assembly, bringing swarms of half-clad men into the moonlight, dressing as they ran, and falling into line at the sharp commands of their officers. This was well; being in line the men were under control; they stood at arms while the general's staff and the men of his escort brought order out of confusion by lifting off the fallen tent and pulling apart the breathless and bleeding actors in that strange contention.

Breathless, indeed, was one: the captain was dead; the handle of the bowie-knife, protruding from his throat, was pressed back beneath his chin until the end had caught in the angle of the jaw and the hand that delivered the blow had been unable to remove the weapon. In the dead man's hand was his sword, clenched with a grip that defied the strength of the living. Its blade was streaked with red to the hilt.

Lifted to his feet, the general sank back to the earth with a moan and fainted. Besides his bruises he had two sword-thrusts – one through the thigh, the other through the shoulder.

The spy had suffered the least damage. Apart from a broken right arm, his wounds were such only as might have been incurred in an ordinary combat with nature's weapons. But he was dazed and seemed hardly to know what had occurred. He shrank away from those attending him, cowered upon the ground and uttered unintelligible remonstrances. His face, swollen by blows and stained with gouts of blood, nevertheless showed white beneath his disheveled hair – as white as that of a corpse.

'The man is not insane,' said the surgeon, preparing bandages and replying to a question; 'he is suffering from fright. Who and what is he?'

Private Tassman began to explain. It was the opportunity of his life; he omitted nothing that could in any way accentuate the importance of his own relation to the night's events. When he had finished his story and was ready to begin it again nobody gave him any attention.

The general had now recovered consciousness. He raised himself upon his elbow, looked about him, and, seeing the spy crouching by a camp-fire, guarded, said simply:

'Take that man to the parade ground and shoot him.'

'The general's mind wanders,' said an officer standing near.

'His mind does *not* wander,' the adjutant-general said. 'I have a memorandum from him about this business; he had given that same order to Hasterlick'

– with a motion of the hand toward the dead provost-marshal –' 'and, by God! it shall be executed.'

Ten minutes later Sergeant Parker Adderson, of the Federal army, philosopher and wit, kneeling in the moonlight and begging incoherently for his life, was shot to death by twenty men. As the volley rang out upon the keen air of the midnight, General Clavering, lying white and still in the red glow of the camp-fire, opened his big blue eyes, looked pleasantly upon those about him and said: 'How silent it all is!'

The surgeon looked at the adjutant-general, gravely and significantly. The patient's eyes slowly closed, and thus he lay for a few moments; then, his face suffused with a smile of ineffable sweetness, he said, faintly: 'I suppose this must be death,' and so passed away.

An Affair of Outposts

Concerning the wish to be dead

Two men sat in conversation. One was the Governor of the State. The year was 1861; the war was on and the Governor already famous for the intelligence and zeal with which he directed all the powers and resources of his State to the service of the Union.

'What! *you?*' the Governor was saying in evident surprise – 'you too want a military commission? Really, the fifing and drumming must have effected a profound alteration in your convictions. In my character of recruiting sergeant I suppose I ought not to be fastidious, but' – there was a touch of irony in his manner – 'well, have you forgotten that an oath of allegiance is required?'

'I have altered neither my convictions nor my sympathies,' said the other, tranquilly. 'While my sympathies are with the South, as you do me the honor to recollect, I have never doubted that the North was in the right. I am a Southerner in fact and in feeling, but it is my habit in matters of importance to act as I think, not as I feel.'

The Governor was absently tapping his desk with a pencil; he did not immediately reply. After a while he said: I have heard that there are all kinds of men in the world, so I suppose there are some like that, and doubtless you think yourself one. I've known you a long time and – pardon me – I don't think so.'

'Then I am to understand that my application is denied?'

'Unless you can remove my belief that your Southern sympathies are in some degree a disqualification, yes. I do not doubt your good faith, and I know you to be abundantly fitted by intelligence and special training for the duties of an officer. Your convictions, you say, favor the Union cause, but I prefer a man with his heart in it. The heart is what men fight with.'

'Look here, Governor,' said the younger man, with a smile that had more light than warmth: 'I have something up my sleeve – a qualification which I had hoped it would not be necessary to mention. A great miltary authority has given a simple recipe for being a good soldier: "Try always to get yourself killed." It is with that purpose that I wish to enter the service. I am not, perhaps, much of a patriot, but I wish to be dead.'

The Governor looked at him rather sharply, then a little coldly. 'There is a simpler and franker way,' he said.

'In my family, sir,' was the reply, ' we do not do that – no Armisted has ever done that.'

A long silence ensued and neither man looked at the other. Presently the Governor lifted his eyes from the pencil, which had resumed its tapping, and said:

'Who is she?'

'My wife.'

The Governor tossed the pencil into the desk, rose and walked two or three times across the room. Then he turned to Armisted, who also had risen, looked at him more coldly than before and said: 'But the man – would it not be better that he – could not the country spare him better than it can spare you?

Or are the Armisteds opposed to "the unwritten law"?'

The Armisteds, apparently, could feel an insult: the face of the younger man flushed, then paled, but he subdued himself to the service of his purpose.

'The man's identity is unknown to me,' he said, calmly enough.

'Pardon me,' said the Governor, with even less of visible contrition than commonly underlies those words. After a moment's reflection he added: 'I shall send you to-morrow a captain's commission in the Tenth Infantry, now at Nashville, Tennessee. Good night.'

'Good night, sir. I thank you.'

Left alone, the Governor remained for a time motionless, leaning against his desk. Presently he shrugged his shoulders as if throwing off a burden. 'This is a bad business,' he said.

Seating himself at a reading-table before the fire, he took up the book nearest his hand, absently opening it. His eyes fell upon this sentence:

'When God made it necessary for an unfaithful wife to lie about her husband in justification of her own sins He had the tenderness to endow men with the folly to believe her.'

He looked at the title of the book; it was, *His Excellency the Fool.*

He flung the volume into the fire.

II

How to say what is worth hearing

The enemy, defeated in two days of battle at Pittsburg Landing, had sullenly retired to Corinth, whence he had come. For manifest incompetence Grant, whose beaten army had been saved from destruction and capture by Buell's soldierly activity and skill, had been relieved of his command, which nevertheless had not been given to Buell, but to Halleck, a man of unproved powers, a theorist, sluggish, irresolute. Foot by foot his troops, always deployed in line-of-battle to resist the enemy's bickering skirmishers, always entrenching against the columns that never came, advanced across the thirty miles of forest and swamp toward an antagonist prepared to vanish at contact, like a ghost at cock-crow. It was a campaign of 'excursions and alarums,' of reconnoissances and counter-marches, of cross-purposes and countermanded orders. For weeks the solemn farce held attention, luring distinguished civilians from fields of political ambition to see what they safely could of the horrors of war. Among these was our friend the Governor. At the head-quarters of the army and in the camps of the troops from his State he was a familiar figure, attended by the several members of his personal staff, showily horsed, faultlessly betailored and bravely silk-hatted. Things of charm they were, rich in suggestions of peaceful lands beyond a sea of strife. The bedraggled soldier looked up from his trench as they passed, leaned upon his spade and audibly damned them to signify his sense of their ornamental irrelevance to the austerities of his trade.

'I think, Governor,' said General Masterson one day, going into informal session atop of his horse and throwing one leg across the pommel of his saddle, his favorite posture – 'I think I would not ride any farther in that direction if I were you. We've nothing out there but a line of skirmishers. That, I presume, is why I was directed to put these siege guns here: if the skirmishers are driven in the enemy will die of dejection at being unable to haul them away – they're a trifle heavy.'

There is reason to fear that the unstrained quality of this military humor dropped not as the gentle rain from heaven upon the place beneath the civilian's silk hat. Anyhow he abated none of his dignity in recognition.

'I understand,' he said, gravely, 'that some of my men out there – a company of the Tenth, commanded by Captain Armisted. I should like to meet him if you do not mind.'

'He is worth meeting. But there's a bad bit of jungle out there, and I should advise that you leave your horse and' – with a look at the Governor's retinue – 'your other impedimenta.'

The Governor went forward alone and on foot. In a half-hour he had pushed through a tangled undergrowth covering a boggy soil and entered upon firm and more open ground. Here he found a half-company of infantry lounging behind a line of stacked rifles. The men wore their accoutrements – their belts, cartridge-boxes, haversacks and canteens. Some lying at full length on the dry leaves were fast asleep: others in small groups gossiped idly of this and that; a few played at cards; none was far from the line of stacked arms. To the civilian's eye the scene was one of carelessness, confusion, indifference; a soldier would have observed expectancy and readiness.

At a little distance apart an officer in fatigue uniform, armed, sat on a fallen tree noting the approach of the visitor, to whom a sergeant, rising from one of the groups, now came forward.

'I wish to see Captain Armisted,' said the Governor.

The sergeant eyed him narrowly, saying nothing, pointed to the officer, and taking a rifle from one of the stacks, accompanied him.

'This man wants to see you, sir,' said the sergeant, saluting. The officer rose.

It would have been a sharp eye that would have recognized him. His hair, which but a few months before had been brown, was streaked with gray. His face, tanned by exposure, was seamed as with age. A long livid scar across the forehead marked the stroke of a sabre; one cheek was drawn and puckered by the work of a bullet. Only a woman of the loyal North would have thought the man handsome.

'Armisted – Captain,' said the Governor, extending his hand, 'do you not know me?'

'I know you, sir, and I salute you – as the Governor of my State.'

Lifting his right hand to the level of his eyes he threw it outward and downward. In the code of military etiquette there is no provision for shaking hands. That of the civilian was withdrawn. If he felt either surprise or chagrin his face did not betray it.

'It is the hand that signed your commission,' he said.

'And it is the hand – '

The sentence remains unfinished. The sharp report of a rifle came from the front, followed by another and another. A bullet hissed through the forest and struck a tree near by. The men sprang from the ground and even before the captain's high, clear voice was done intoning the command 'At-ten-tion!' had fallen into line in rear of the stacked arms. Again – and now through the din of a crackling fusillade – sounded the strong, deliberate sing-song of authority:

'Take . . . arms!' followed by the rattle of unlocking bayonets.

Bullets from the unseen enemy were now flying thick and fast, though mostly well spent and emitting the humming sound which signified interference by twigs and rotation in the plane of flight. Two or three of the men in the line were already struck and down. A few wounded men came limping awkwardly out of the undergrowth from the skirmish line in front; most of them did not pause, but held their way with white faces and set teeth to the rear.

Suddenly there was a deep, jarring report in front, followed by the startling rush of a shell, which passing overhead exploded in the edge of a thicket, setting afire the fallen leaves. Penetrating the din – seeming to float above it like the melody of a soaring bird – rang the slow, aspirated monotones of the captain's several commands, without emphasis, without accent, musical and restful as an evensong under the harvest moon. Familiar with this tranquilizing chant in moments of imminent peril, these raw soldiers of less than a year's training yielded themselves to the spell, executing its mandates with the composure and precision of veterans. Even the distinguished civilian behind his tree, hesitating between pride and terror, was accessible to its charm and suasion. He was conscious of a fortified resolution and ran away only when the skirmishers, under orders to rally on the reserve, came out of the woods like hunted hares and formed on the left of the stiff little line, breathing hard and thankful for the boon of breath.

III

The fighting of one whose heart
was not in the quarrel

Guided in his retreat by that of the fugitive wounded, the Governor struggled bravely to the rear through the 'bad bit of jungle.' He was well winded and a trifle confused. Excepting a single rifle-shot now and again, there was no sound of strife behind him; the enemy was pulling himself together for a new onset against an antagonist of whose numbers and tactical disposition he was in doubt. The fugitive felt that he would probably be spared to his country, and only commended the arrangements of Providence to that end, but in leaping a small brook in more open ground one of the arrangements incurred the mischance of a disabling sprain at the ankle. He was unable to continue his flight, for he was too fat to hop, and after several vain attempts, causing intolerable pain, seated himself on the earth to nurse his ignoble disability and deprecate the military situation.

A brisk renewal of the firing broke out and stray bullets came flitting and droning by. Then came the crash of two clean, definite volleys, followed by a continuous rattle, through which he heard the yells and cheers of the combatants, punctuated by thunderclaps of cannon. All this told him that Armisted's little command was bitterly beset and fighting at close quarters. The wounded men whom he had distanced began to straggle by on either hand, their numbers visibly augmented by new levies from the line. Singly and by twos and threes, some supporting comrades more deperately hurt than themselves, but all deaf to his appeals for assistance, they sifted through the underbrush and disappeared. The firing was increasingly louder and more distinct, and presently the ailing fugitives were succeeded by men who strode with a firmer tread, occasionally facing about and discharging their pieces, then doggedly resuming their retreat, reloading as they walked. Two or three fell as he looked, and lay motionless. One had enough of life left in him to make a pitiful attempt to drag himself to cover. A passing comrade paused beside him long enough to fire, appraised the poor devil's disability with a look and moved sullenly on, inserting a cartridge in his weapon.

In all this was none of the pomp of war – no hint of glory. Even in his distress and peril the helpless civilian could not forbear to contrast it with the gorgeous parades and reviews held in honor of himself – with the brilliant uniforms, the music, the banners, and the marching. It was an ugly and sickening business: to all that was artistic in his nature, revolting, brutal, in bad taste.

'Ugh!' he grunted, shuddering – 'this is beastly! Where is the charm of it all? Where are the elevated sentiments, the devotion, the heroism, the – '

From a point somewhere near, in the direction of the pursuing enemy, rose the clear, deliberate sing-song of Captain Armisted.

'Stead-y, men – stead-y. Halt! Commence fir-ing.'

The rattle of fewer than a score of rifles could be distinguished through the general uproar, and again that penetrating falsetto:

'Cease fir-ing. In re-treat . . . maaarch!'

In a few moments this remnant had drifted slowly past the Governor, all to the right of him as they faced in retiring, the men deployed at intervals of a half-dozen paces. At the extreme left and a few yards behind came the captain. The civilian called out his name, but he did not hear. A swarm of men in gray now broke out of cover in pursuit, making directly for the spot where the Governor lay – some accident of the ground had caused them to converge upon that point: their line had become a crowd. In a last struggle for life and liberty the Governor attempted to rise, and looking back the captain saw him. Promptly, but with the same slow precision as before, he sang his commands:

'Skirm-ish-ers, halt!' The men stopped and according to rule turned to face the enemy.

'Ral-ly on the right!' – and they came in at a run, fixing bayonets and forming loosely on the man at that end of the line.

'Forward . . . to save the Gov-ern-or of your State . . . doub-le quick . . . maaarch!'

Only one man disobeyed this astonishing command! He was dead. With a cheer they sprang forward over the twenty or thirty paces between them and their task. The captain having a shorter distance to go arrived first – simultaneously with the enemy. A half-dozen hasty shots were fired at him, and the foremost man – a fellow of heroic stature, hatless and bare-breasted – made a vicious sweep at his head with a clubbed rifle. The officer parried the blow at the cost of a broken arm and drove his sword to the hilt into the giant's breast. As the body fell the weapon was wrenched from his hand and before he could pluck his revolver from the scabbard at his belt another man leaped upon him like a tiger, fastening both hands upon his throat and bearing him backward upon the prostrate Governor, still struggling to rise. This man was promptly spitted upon the bayonet of a Federal sergeant and his death-gripe on the captain's throat loosened by a kick upon each wrist. When the captain had risen he was at the rear of his men, who had all passed over and around him and were thrusting fiercely at their more numerous but less coherent antagonists. Nearly all the rifles on both sides were empty and in the crush there was neither time nor room to reload. The Confererates were at a disadvantage in that most of them lacked bayonets; they fought by bludgeon-ing – and a clubbed rifle is a formidable arm. The sound of the conflict was a clatter like that of the interlocking horns of battling bulls – now and then the pash of a crushed skull, an oath, or a grunt caused by the impact of a rifle's muzzle against the abdomen transfixed by its bayonet. Through an opening made by the fall of one of his men Captain Armisted sprang, with his dangling left arm; in his right hand a full-charged revolver, which he fired with rapidity and terrible effect into the thick of the gray crowd: but across the bodies of the slain the survivors in the front were pushed forward by their comrades in the rear till again they breasted the tireless bayonets. There were fewer bayonets now to breast – a beggarly half-dozen, all told. A few minutes more of this rough work – a little fighting back to back – and all would be over.

Suddenly a lively firing was heard on the right and the left: a fresh line of Federal skirmishers came forward at a run, driving before them those parts of the Confederate line that had been separated by staying the advance of the centre. And behind these new and noisy combatants, at a distance of two or three hundred yards, could be seen, indistinct among the trees a line-of-battle!

Instinctively before retiring, the crowd in gray made a tremendous rush upon its handful of antagonists, overwhelming them by mere momentum and, unable to use weapons in the crush, trampled them, stamped savagely on their limbs, their bodies, their necks, their faces; then retiring with bloody feet across its own dead it joined the general rout and the incident was at an end.

IV

The great honor the great

The Governor, who had been unconscious, opened his eyes and stared about him, slowly recalling the day's events. A man in the uniform of a major was kneeling beside him; he was a surgeon. Grouped about were the civilian members of the Governor's staff, their faces expressing a natural solicitude regarding their offices. A little apart stood General Masterson addressing another officer and gesticulating with a cigar. He was saying: 'It was the beautifulest fight ever made – by God, sir, it was great!'

The beauty and greatness were attested by a row of dead, trimly disposed, and another of wounded, less formally placed, restless, half-naked, but bravely bebandaged.

'How do you feel, sir?' said the surgeon. 'I find no wound.'

'I think I am all right,' the patient replied, sitting up. 'It is that ankle.'

The surgeon transferred his attention to the ankle, cutting away the boot. All eyes followed the knife.

In moving the leg a folded paper was uncovered. The patient picked it up and carelessly opened it. It was a letter three months old, signed 'Julia.' Catching sight of his name in it he read it. It was nothing very remarkable –

merely a weak woman's confession of unprofitable sin – the penitence of a faithless wife deserted by her betrayer. The letter had fallen from the pocket of Captain Armisted; the reader quietly transferred it to his own.

An aide-de-camp rode up and dismounted. Advancing to the Governor he saluted.

'Sir,' he said, 'I am sorry to find you wounded – the Commanding General has not been informed. He presents his compliments and I am directed to say that he has ordered for to-morrow a grand review of the reserve corps in your honor. I venture to add that the General's carriage is at your service if you are able to attend.'

'Be pleased to say to the Commanding General that I am deeply touched by his kindness. If you have the patience to wait a few moments you shall convey a more definite reply.'

He smiled brightly and glancing at the surgeon and his assistants added: 'At present – if you will permit an allusion to the horrors of peace – I am "in the hands of my friends."'

The humor of the great is infectious; all laughed who heard.

'Where is Captain Armisted?' the Governor asked, not altogether carelessly.

The surgeon looked up from his work, pointing silently to the nearest body in the row of dead, the features discreetly covered with a handkerchief. It was so near that the great man could have laid his hand upon it, but he did not. He may have feared that it would bleed.

The Story Of A Conscience

I

Captain Parrol Hartroy stood at the advanced post of his picket-guard, talking in low tones with the sentinel. This post was on a turnpike which bisected the captain's camp, a half-mile in rear, though the camp was not in sight from that point. The officer was apparently giving the soldier certain instructions – was perhaps merely inquiring if all were quiet in front. As the two stood talking a man approached them from the direction of the camp, carelessly whistling, and was promptly halted by the soldier. He was evidently a civilian – a tall person, coarsely clad in the home-made stuff of yellow gray, called 'butternut,' which was men's only wear in the latter days of the Confederacy. On his head was a slouch felt hat, once white, from beneath which hung masses of uneven hair, seemingly unacquainted with either scissors or comb. The man's face was rather striking; a broad forehead, high nose, and thin cheeks, the mouth invisible in the full dark beard, which seemed as neglected as the hair. The eyes were large and had that steadiness and fixity of attention which so frequently mark a considering intelligence and a will not easily turned from its purpose – so say those physiognomists who have that kind of eyes. On the whole, this was a man whom one would be likely to observe and be observed by. He carried a walking-stick freshly cut from the forest and his ailing cowskin boots were white with dust.

'Show your pass,' said the Federal soldier, a trifle more imperiously perhaps than he would have thought necessary if he had not been under the eye of his commander, who with folded arms looked on from the roadside.

''Lowed you'd rec'lect me, Gineral,' said the wayfarer tranquilly, while producing the paper from the pocket of his coat. There was something in his tone – perhaps a faint suggestion of irony – which made his elevation of his obstructor to exalted rank less agreeable to that worthy warrior than promotion is commonly found to be. 'You-all have to be purty pertickler, I reckon,' he added, in a more conciliatory tone, as if in half-apology for being halted.

Having read the pass, with his rifle resting on the ground, the soldier handed the document back without a word, shouldered his weapon, and returned to his commander. The civilian passed on in the middle of the road, and when he had penetrated the circumjacent Confederacy a few yards resumed his whistling and was soon out of sight beyond an angle in the road, which at that point entered a thin forest. Suddenly the officer undid his arms from his breast, drew a revolver from his belt and sprang forward at a run in the same direction, leaving his sentinel in gaping astonishment at his post. After making to the various visible forms of nature a solemn promise to be damned, that gentleman resumed the air of stolidity which is supposed to be appropriate to a state of alert military attention.

II

Captain Hartroy held an independent command. His force consisted of a company of infantry, a squadron of cavalry, and a section of artillery, detached from the army to which they belonged, to defend an important defile in the Cumberland Mountains in Tennessee. It was a field officer's command held by a line officer promoted from the ranks, where he had quietly served until 'discovered.' His post was one of exceptional peril; its defense entailed a heavy responsibility and he had wisely been given corresponding discretionary powers, all the more necessary because of his distance from the main army, the precarious nature of his communications and the lawless character of the enemy's irregular troops infesting that region. He had strongly fortified his little camp, which embraced a village of a half-dozen dwellings and a country store, and had collected a considerable quantity of supplies. To a few resident civilians of known loyalty, with whom it was desirable to trade, and of whose services in various ways he sometimes availed himself, he had given written passes admitting them within his lines. It is easy to understand that an abuse of this privilege in the interest of the enemy might entail serious consequences. Captain Hartroy had made an order to the effect that any one so abusing it would be summarily shot.

While the sentinel had been examining the civilian's pass the captain had eyed the latter narrowly. He thought his appearance familiar and had at first no doubt of having given him the pass which had satisfied the sentinel. It was not until the man had got out of sight and hearing that his identity was disclosed by a revealing light from memory. With soldierly promptness of decision the officer had acted on the revelation.

III

To any but a singularly self-possessed man the apparition of an officer of the military forces, formidably clad, bearing in one hand a sheathed sword and in the other a cocked revolver, and rushing in furious pursuit, is no doubt disquieting to a high degree; upon the man to whom the pursuit was in this instance directed it appeared to have no other effect than somewhat to intensify his tranquillity. He might easily enough have escaped into the forest to the right or the left, but chose another course of action – turned and quietly faced the captain, saying as he came up; 'I reckon ye must have something to say to me, which ye disremembered. What mout it be, neighbor?'

But the 'neighbor' did not answer, being engaged in the unneighborly act of covering him with a cocked pistol.

'Surrender,' said the captain as calmly as a slight breathlessness from exertion would permit, 'or you die.'

There was no menace in the manner of this demand; that was all in the matter and in the means of enforcing it. There was, too, something not altogether reassuring in the cold gray eyes that glanced along the barrel of the weapon. For a moment the two men stood looking at each other in silence; then the civilian, with no appearance of fear – with as great apparent unconcern as when complying with the less austere demand of the sentinel –

slowly pulled from his pocket the paper which had satisfied that humble functionary and held it out, saying:

'I reckon this 'ere parss from Mister Hartroy is – '

'The pass is a forgery,' the officer said, interrupting. 'I am Captain Hartroy – and you are Dramer Brune.'

It would have required a sharp eye to observe the slight pallor of the civilian's face at these words, and the only other manifestation attesting their significance was a voluntary relaxation of the thumb and fingers holding the dishonored paper, which, falling to the road, unheeded, was rolled by a gentle wind and then lay still, with a coating of dust, as in humiliation for the lie that it bore. A moment later the civilian, still looking unmoved into the barrel of the pistol, said:

'Yes, I am Dramer Brune, a Confederate spy, and your prisoner. I have on my person, as you will soon discover, a plan of your fort and its armament, a statement of the distribution of your men and their number, a map of the approaches, showing the positions of all your outposts. My life is fairly yours, but if you wish it taken in a more formal way than by your own hand, and if you are willing to spare me the indignity of marching into camp at the muzzle of your pistol, I promise you that I will neither resist, escape, nor remonstrate, but will submit to whatever penalty may be imposed.'

The officer lowered his pistol, uncocked it, and thrust it into its place in his belt. Brune advanced a step, extending his right hand.

'It is the hand of a traitor and a spy,' said the officer coldly, and did not take it. The other bowed.

'Come,' said the captain, 'let us go to camp; you shall not die until to-morrow morning.'

He turned his back upon his prisoner, and these two enigmatical men retraced their steps and soon passed the sentinel, who expressed his general sense of things by a needless and exaggerated salute to his commander.

IV

Early on the morning after these events the two men, captor and captive, sat in the tent of the former. A table was between them on which lay, among a number of letters, official and private, which the captain had written during the night, the incriminating papers found upon the spy. That gentleman had slept through the night in an adjoining tent, unguarded. Both, having breakfasted, were now smoking.

'Mr. Brune,' said Captain Hartroy, 'you probably do not understand why I recognized you in your disguise, nor how I was aware of your name.'

'I have not sought to learn, Captain,' the prisoner said with quiet dignity.

'Nevertheless I should like you to know – if the story will not offend. You will perceive that my knowledge of you goes back to the autumn of 1861. At that time you were a private in an Ohio regiment – a brave and trusted soldier. To the surprise and grief of your officers and comrades you deserted and went over to the enemy. Soon afterward you were captured in a skirmish, recognized, tried by court-martial and sentenced to be shot. Awaiting the execution of the sentence you were confined, unfettered, in a freight car standing on a side track of a railway.'

'At Grafton, Virginia,' said Brune, pushing the ashes from his cigar with the little finger of the hand holding it, and without looking up.

'At Grafton, Virginia,' the captain repeated. 'One dark and stormy night a soldier who had just returned from a long, fatiguing march was put on guard over you. He sat on a cracker box inside the car, near the door, his rifle loaded and the bayonet fixed. You sat in a corner and his orders were to kill you if you attempted to rise.'

'But if I *asked* to rise he might call the corporal of the guard.'

'Yes. As the long silent hours wore away the soldier yielded to the demands of nature: he himself incurred the death penalty by sleeping at his post of duty.'

'You did.'

'What! you recognize me? you have known me all along?'

The captain had risen and was walking the floor of his tent, visibly excited. His face was flushed, the gray eyes had lost the cold, pitiless look which they had shown when Brune had seen them over the pistol barrel; they had softened wonderfully.

'I knew you,' said the spy, with his customary tranquillity, 'the moment you faced me, demanding my surrender. In the circumstances it would have been hardly becoming in me to recall these matters. I am perhaps a traitor, certainly a spy; but I should not wish to seem a suppliant.'

The captain had paused in his walk and was facing his prisoner. There was a singular huskiness in his voice as he spoke again.

'Mr Brune, whatever your conscience may permit you to be, you saved my life at what you must have believed the cost of your own. Until I saw you yesterday when halted by my sentinel I believed you dead – thought that you had suffered the fate which through my own crime you might easily have escaped. You had only to step from the car and leave me to take your place before the firing-squad. You had a divine compassion. You pitied my fatigue. You let me sleep, watched over me, and as the time drew near for the relief-guard to come and detect me in my crime, you gently waked me. Ah, Brune, Brune, that was well done – that was great – that – '

The captain's voice failed him; the tears were running down his face and sparkled upon his beard and his breast. Resuming his seat at the table, he buried his face in his arms and sobbed. All else was silence.

Suddenly the clear warble of a bugle was heard sounding the 'assembly.' The captain started and raised his wet face from his arms; it had turned ghastly pale. Outside, in the sunlight, were heard the stir of the men falling into line; the voices of the sergeants calling the roll; the tapping of the drummers as they braced their drums. The captain spoke again:

'I ought to have confessed my fault in order to relate the story of your magnanimity; it might have procured you a pardon. A hundred times I resolved to do so, but shame prevented. Besides, your sentence was just and righteous. Well, Heaven forgive me! I said nothing, and my regiment was soon afterward ordered to Tennessee and I never heard about you.'

'It was all right, sir,' said Brune, without visible emotion; 'I escaped and returned to my colors – the Confederate colors. I should like to add that before deserting from the Federal service I had earnestly asked a discharge, on the ground of altered convictions. I was answered by punishment.'

'Ah, but if I had suffered the penalty of my crime – if you had not generously given me the life that I accepted without gratitude you would not be again in the shadow and imminence of death.'

The prisoner started slightly and a look of anxiety came into his face. One would have said, too, that he was surprised. At that moment a lieutenant, the adjutant, appeared at the opening of the tent and saluted. 'Captain,' he said, 'the battalion is formed.'

Captain Hartroy had recovered his composure. He turned to the officer and said: 'Lieutenant, go to Captain Graham and say that I direct him to assume command of the battalion and parade it outside the parapet. This gentleman is a deserter and a spy; he is to be shot to death in the presence of the troops. He will accompany you, unbound and unguarded.'

While the adjutant waited at the door the two men inside the tent rose and exchanged ceremonious bows, Brune immediately retiring.

Half an hour later an old Negro cook, the only person left in camp except the commander, was so startled by the sound of a volley of musketry that he dropped the kettle that he was lifting from a fire. But for his consternation and the hissing which the contents of the kettle made among the embers, he might also have heard, nearer at hand, the single pistol shot with which Captain Hartroy renounced the life which in conscience he could no longer keep.

In compliance with the terms of a note that he left for the officer who succeeded him in command, he was buried, like the deserter and spy, without military honors; and in the solemn shadow of the mountain which knows no more of war the two sleep well in long-forgotten graves.

One Kind Of Officer

I

Of the uses of civility

'Captain Ransome, it is not permitted to you to know *anything*. It is sufficient that you obey my order – which permit me to repeat. If you perceive any movement of troops in your front you are to open fire, and if attacked hold this position as long as you can. Do I make myself understood, sir?'

'Nothing could be plainer. Lieutenant Price,' – this to an officer of his own battery, who had ridden up in time to hear the order – 'the general's meaning is clear, is it not?'

'Perfectly.'

The lieutenant passed on to his post. For a moment General Cameron and the commander of the battery sat in their saddles, looking at each other in silence. There was no more to say; apparently too much had already been said. Then the superior officer nodded coldly and turned his horse to ride away. The artillerist saluted slowly, gravely, and with extreme formality. One acquainted with the niceties of military etiquette would have said that by his manner he attested a sense of the rebuke that he had incurred. It is one of the important uses of civility to signify resentment.

When the general had joined his staff and escort, awaiting him at a little distance, the whole cavalcade moved off toward the right of the guns and vanished in the fog. Captain Ransome was alone, silent, motionless as an equestrian statue. The gray fog, thickening every moment, closed in about him like a visible doom.

II

Under what circumstances men do not
wish to be shot

The fighting of the day before had been desultory and indecisive. At the points of collision the smoke of battle had hung in blue sheets among the branches of the trees till beaten into nothing by the falling rain. In the softened earth the wheels of cannon and ammunition wagons cut deep, ragged furrows, and movements of infantry seemed impeded by the mud that clung to the soldiers' feet as, with soaken garments and rifles imperfectly protected by capes of overcoats they went dragging in sinuous lines hither and thither through dripping forest and flooded field. Mounted officers, their heads protruding from rubber ponchos that glittered like black armor, picked their way, singly and in loose groups, among the men, coming and going with apparent aimlessness and commanding attention from nobody but one another. Here and there a dead man, his clothing defiled with earth, his face covered with a blanket or showing yellow and claylike in the rain, added his dispiriting influence to that of the other dismal features of the scene and augmented the general discomfort with a particular dejection. Very repulsive these wrecks looked – not at all heroic, and nobody was accessible to the infection of their patriotic example. Dead upon the field of honor, yes; but the field of honor was so very wet! It makes a difference.

The general engagement that all expected did not occur, none of the small advantages accruing, now to this side and now to that, in isolated and accidental collisions being followed up. Half-hearted attacks provoked a sullen resistance which was satisfied with mere repulse. Orders were obeyed with mechanical fidelity; no one did any more than his duty.

'The army is cowardly to-day,' said General Cameron, the commander of a Federal brigade, to his adjutant-general.

'The army is cold,' replied the officer addressed, 'and – yes, it doesn't wish to be like that.'

He pointed to one of the dead bodies, lying in a thin pool of yellow water, its face and clothing bespattered with mud from hoof and wheel.

The army's weapons seemed to share its military delinquency. The rattle of rifles sounded flat and contemptible. It had no meaning and scarcely roused to attention and expectancy the unengaged parts of the line-of-battle and the waiting reserves. Heard at a little distance, the reports of cannon were feeble in volume and *timbre*: they lacked sting and resonance. The guns seemed to be fired with light charges, unshotted. And so the futile day wore on to its dreary close, and then to a night of discomfort succeeded a day of apprehension.

An army has a personality. Beneath the individual thoughts and emotions of its component parts it thinks and feels as a unit. And in this large, inclusive sense of things lies a wiser wisdom than the mere sum of all that it knows. On that dismal morning this great brute force, groping at the bottom of a white ocean of fog among trees that seemed as sea weeds, had a dumb consciousness that all was not well; that a day's manœuvring had resulted in a faulty disposition of its parts, a blind diffusion of its strength. The men felt insecure and talked among themselves of such tactical errors as with their meager military vocabulary they were able to name. Field and line officers gathered in groups and spoke more learnedly of what they apprehended with no greater clearness. Commanders of brigades and divisions looked anxiously to their connections on the right and on the left, sent staff officers on errands of inquiry and pushed skirmish lines silently and cautiously forward into the dubious region between the known and the unknown. At some points on the line the troops, apparently of their own volition, constructed such defenses as they could without the silent spade and the noisy ax.

One of these points was held by Captain Ransome's battery of six guns. Provided always with intrenching tools, his men had labored with diligence during the night, and now his guns thrust their black muzzles through the embrasures of a really formidable earthwork. It crowned a slight acclivity devoid of undergrowth and providing an unobstructed fire that would sweep the ground for an unknown distance in front. The position could hardly have been better chosen. It had this peculiarity, which Captain Ransome, who was greatly addicted to the use of the compass, had not failed to observe; it faced northward, whereas he knew that the general line of the army must face eastward. In fact, that part of the line was 'refused' – that is to say, bent backward, away from the enemy. This implied that Captain Ransome's battery was somewhere near the left flank of the army; for an army in line of battle retires its flanks if the nature of the ground will permit, they being its vulnerable points. Actually, Captain Ransome appeared to hold the extreme left of the line, no troops being visible in that direction beyond his own. Immediately in rear of his guns occurred that conversation between him and his brigade commander, the concluding and more picturesque part of which is reported above.

III

How to play the cannon without notes

Captain Ransome sat motionless and silent on horseback. A few yards away his men were standing at their guns. Somewhere – everywhere within a few miles – were a hundred thousand men, friends and enemies. Yet he was alone. The mist had isolated him as completely as if he had been in the heart of a desert. His world was a few square yards of wet and trampled earth about the feet of his horse. His comrades in that ghostly domain were invisible and inaudible. These were conditions favorable to thought, and he was thinking. Of the nature of his thoughts his clear-cut handsome features yielded no attesting sign. His face was as inscrutable as that of the sphinx. Why should it have made a record which there was none to observe? At the sound of a footstep he merely turned his eyes in the direction whence it came; one of his sergeants, looking a giant in stature in the false perspective of the fog, approached, and when clearly defined and reduced to his true dimensions by propinquity, saluted and stood at attention.

'Well, Morris,' said the officer, returning his subordinate's salute.

'Lieutenant Price directed me to tell you, sir, that most of the infantry has been withdrawn. We have not sufficient support.'

'Yes, I know.'

'I am to say that some of our men have been out over the works a hundred yards and report that our front is not picketed.'

'Yes.'

'They were so far forward that they heard the enemy.'

'Yes.'

'They heard the rattle of the wheels of artillery and the commands of officers.'

'Yes.'

'The enemy is moving toward our works.'

Captain Ransome, who had been facing to the rear of his line – toward the point where the brigade commander and his cavalcade had been swallowed up by the fog – reined his horse about and faced the other way. Then he sat motionless as before.

'Who are the men who made that statement?' he inquired, without looking at the sergeant; his eyes were directed straight into the fog over the head of his horse.

'Corporal Hassman and Gunner Manning.'

Captain Ransome was a moment silent. A slight pallor came into his face, a slight compression affected the lines of his lips, but it would have required a closer observer than Sergeant Morris to note the change. There was none in the voice.

'Sergeant, present my compliments to Lieutenant Price and direct him to open fire with all the guns. Grape.'

The sergeant saluted and vanished in the fog.

IV

To introduce general masterson

Searching for his division commander, General Cameron and his escort had followed the line of battle for nearly a mile to the right of Ransome's battery, and there learned that the division commander had gone in search of the corps commander. It seemed that everybody was looking for his immediate superior – an ominous circumstance. It meant that nobody was quite at ease. So General Cameron rode on for another half-mile, where by good luck he met General Masterson, the division commander, returning.

'Ah, Cameron,' said the higher officer, reining up, and throwing his right leg across the pommel of his saddle in a most unmilitary way – 'anything up? Found a good position for your battery, I hope – if one place is better than another in a fog.'

'Yes, general,' said the other, with the greater dignity appropriate to his less exalted rank, 'my battery is very well placed. I wish I could say that it is as well commanded.'

'Eh, what's that? Ransome? I think him a fine fellow. In the army we should be proud of him.'

It was customary for officers of the regular army to speak of it as 'the army.' As the greatest cities are most provincial, so the self-complacency of aristocracies is most frankly plebeian.

'He is too fond of his opinion. By the way, in order to occupy the hill that he holds I had to extend my line dangerously. The hill is on my left – that is to say the left flank of the army.'

'Oh, no, Hart's brigade is beyond. It was ordered up from Drytown during the night and directed to hook on to you. Better go and – '

The sentence was unfinished: a lively cannonade had broken out on the left, and both officers, followed by their retinues of aides and orderlies making a great jingle and clank, rode rapidly toward the spot. But they were soon impeded, for they were compelled by the fog to keep within sight of the line-of-battle, behind which were swarms of men, all in motion across their way. Everywhere the line was assuming a sharper and harder definition, as the men sprang to arms and the officers, with drawn swords, 'dressed' the ranks. Color-bearers unfurled the flags, buglers blew the 'assembly,' hospital attendants appeared with stretchers. Field officers mounted and sent their impedimenta to the rear in care of Negro servants. Back in the ghostly spaces of the forest could be heard the rustle and murmur of the reserves, pulling themselves together.

Nor was all this preparation vain, for scarcely five minutes had passed since Captain Ransome's guns had broken the truce of doubt before the whole region was aroar: the enemy had attacked nearly everywhere.

V

How sounds can fight shadows

Captain Ransome walked up and down behind his guns, which were firing rapidly but with steadiness. The gunners worked alertly, but without haste or apparent excitement. There was really no reason for excitement; it is not much to point a cannon into a fog and fire it. Anybody can do as much as that.

The men smiled at their noisy work, performing it with a lessening alacrity. They cast curious regards upon their captain, who had now mounted the banquette of the fortification and was looking across the parapet as if observing the effect of his fire. But the only visible effect was the substitution of wide, low-lying sheets of smoke for their bulk of fog. Suddenly out of the obscurity burst a great sound of cheering, which filled the intervals between the reports of the guns with startling distinctness! To the few with leisure and opportunity to observe, the sound was inexpressibly strange – so loud, so near, so menacing, yet nothing seen! The men who had smiled at their work smiled no more, but performed it with a serious and feverish activity.

From his station at the parapet Captain Ransome now saw a great multitude of dim gray figures taking shape in the mist below him and swarming up the slope. But the work of the guns was now fast and furious. They swept the populous declivity with gusts of grape and canister, the whirring of which could be heard through the thunder of the explosions. In this awful tempest of iron the assailants struggled forward foot by foot across their dead, firing into the embrasures, reloading, firing again, and at last falling in their turn, a little in advance of those who had fallen before. Soon the smoke was dense enough to cover all. It settled down upon the attack and, drifting back, involved the defense. The gunners could hardly see to serve their pieces, and when occasional figures of the enemy appeared upon the parapet – having had the good luck to get near enough to it, between two embrasures, to be protected from the guns – they looked so unsubstantial that it seemed hardly worth while for the few infantrymen to go to work upon them with the bayonet and tumble them back into the ditch.

As the commander of a battery in action can find something better to do than cracking individual skulls, Captain Ransome had retired from the parapet to his proper post in rear of his guns, where he stood with folded arms, his bugler beside him. Here, during the hottest of the fight, he was approached by Lieutenant Price, who had just sabred a daring assailant inside the work. A spirited colloquy ensued between the two officers – spirited, at least, on the part of the lieutenant, who gesticulated with energy and shouted again and again into his commander's ear in the attempt to make himself heard above the infernal din of the guns. His gestures, if coolly noted by an actor, would have been pronounced to be those of protestation: one would have said that he was opposed to the proceedings. Did he wish to surrender?

Captain Ransome listened without a change of countenance or attitude, and when the other man had finished his harangue, looked him coldly in the eyes and during a seasonable abatement of the uproar said:

'Lieutenant Price, it is not permitted to you to know *anything*. It is sufficient that you obey my orders.'

The lieutenant went to his post, and the parapet being now apparently clear

Captain Ransome returned to it to have a look over. As he mounted the banquette a man sprang upon the crest, waving a great brilliant flag. The captain drew a pistol from his belt and shot him dead. The body, pitching forward, hung over the inner edge of the embankment, the arms straight downward, both hands still grasping the flag. The man's few followers turned and fled down the slope. Looking over the parapet, the captain saw no living thing. He observed also that no bullets were coming into the work.

He made a sign to the bugler, who sounded the command to cease firing. At all other points the action had already ended with a repulse of the Confederate attack; with the cessation of this cannonade the silence was absolute.

VI

Why, being affronted by A, it is not best to affront B

General Masterson rode into the redoubt. The men, gathered in groups, were talking loudly and gesticulating. They pointed at the dead, running from one body to another. They neglected their foul and heated guns and forgot to resume their outer clothing. They ran to the parapet and looked over, some of them leaping down into the ditch. A score were gathered about a flag rigidly held by a dead man.

'Well, my men,' said the general cheerily, 'you have had a pretty fight of it.'

They stared; nobody replied; the presence of the great man seemed to embarrass and alarm.

Getting no response to his pleasant condescension, the easy-mannered officer whistled a bar or two of a popular air, and riding forward to the parapet, looked over at the dead. In an instant he had whirled his horse about and was spurring along in rear of the guns, his eyes everywhere at once. An officer sat on the trail of one of the guns, smoking a cigar. As the general dashed up he rose and tranquilly saluted.

'Captain Ransome!' – the words fell sharp and harsh, like the clash of steel blades – 'you have been fighting our own men – our own men, sir: do you hear? Hart's brigade!'

'General, I know that.'

'You know it – you know that, and you sit here smoking? Oh, damn it, Hamilton, I'm losing my temper,' – this to his provost-marshal. 'Sir – Captain Ransome, be good enough to say – to say why you fought our own men.'

'That I am unable to say. In my orders that information was withheld.'

Apparently the general did not comprehend.

'Who was the aggressor in this affair, you or General Hart?' he asked.

'I was.'

'And could you not have known – could you not see, sir, that you were attacking our own men?'

The reply was astounding!

'I knew that, general. It appeared to be none of my business.'

Then, breaking the dead silence that followed his answer, he said:

'I must refer you to General Cameron.'

'General Cameron is dead, sir – as dead as he can be – as dead as any man in this army. He lies back yonder under a tree. Do you mean to say that he had anything to do with this horrible business?'

Captain Ransome did not reply. Observing the altercation his men had gathered about to watch the outcome. They were greatly excited. The fog, which had been partly dissipated by the firing, had again closed in so darkly about them that they drew more closely together till the judge on horseback and the accused standing calmly before him had but a narrow space free from intrusion. It was the most informal of courts-martial, but all felt that the formal one to follow would but affirm its judgement. It had no jurisdiction, but it had the significance of prophecy.

'Captain Ransome,' the general cried impetuously, but with something in his voice that was almost entreaty, 'if you can say anything to put a better light upon your incomprehensible conduct I beg you will do so.'

Having recovered his temper this generous soldier sought for something to justify his naturally sympathetic attitude toward a brave man in the imminence of a dishonorable death.

'Where is Lieutenant Price?' the captain said.

That officer stood forward, his dark saturnine face looking somewhat forbidding under a bloody hankerchief bound about his brow. He understood the summons and needed no invitation to speak. He did not look at the captain, but addressed the general:

'During the engagement I discovered the state of affairs, and apprised the commander of the battery. I ventured to urge that the firing cease. I was insulted and ordered to my post.'

'Do you know anything of the orders under which I was acting?' asked the captain.

'Of any orders under which the commander of the battery was acting,' the lieutenant continued, still addressing the general, 'I know nothing.'

Captain Ransome felt his world sink away from his feet. In those cruel words he heard the murmur of the centuries breaking upon the shore of eternity. He heard the voice of doom; it said, in cold, mechanical, and measured tones: 'Ready, aim, fire!' and he felt the bullets tear his heart to shreds. He heard the sound of the earth upon his coffin and (if the good God was so merciful) the song of a bird above his forgotten grave. Quietly detaching his sabre from its supports, he handed it up to the provost-marshal.

One officer, One man

Captain Graffenreid stood at the head of his company. The regiment was not engaged. It formed a part of the front line-of-battle, which stretched away to the right with a visible length of nearly two miles through the open ground. The left flank was veiled by woods; to the right also the line was lost to sight, but it extended many miles. A hundred yards in rear was a second line; behind this, the reserve brigades and divisions in column. Batteries of artillery occupied the spaces between and crowned the low hills. Groups of horsemen – generals with their staffs and escorts, and field officers of regiments behind the colors – broke the regularity of the lines and columns. Numbers of these figures of interest had field-glasses at their eyes and sat motionless, stolidly scanning the country in front; others came and went at a slow canter, bearing orders. There were squads of strecher-bearers, ambulances, wagon-trains with ammunition, and officers' servants in rear of all – of all that was visible – for still in rear of these, along the roads, extended for many miles all that vast multitude of non-combatants who with their various impedimenta are assigned to the inglorious but important duty of supplying the fighters' many needs.

An army in line-of-battle awaiting attack, or prepared to deliver it, presents strange contrasts. At the front are precision, formality, fixity, and silence. Toward the rear these characteristics are less and less conspicuous, and finally, in point of space, are lost altogether in confusion, motion and noise. The homogeneous becomes heterogeneous. Definition is lacking; repose is replaced by an apparently purposeless activity; harmony vanishes in hubbub, form in disorder. Commotion everywhere and ceaseless unrest. The men who do not fight are never ready.

From his position at the right of his company in the front rank, Captain Graffenreid had an unobstructed outlook toward the enemy. A half-mile of open and nearly level ground lay before him, and beyond it an irregular wood, covering a slight acclivity; not a human being anywhere visible. He could imagine nothing more peaceful than the appearance of that pleasant landscape with its long stretches of brown fields over which the atmosphere was beginning to quiver in the heat of the morning sun. Not a sound came from forest or field – not even the barking of a dog or the crowing of a cock at the half-seen plantation house on the crest among the trees. Yet every man in those miles of men knew that he and death were face to face.

Captain Graffenreid had never in his life seen an armed enemy, and the war in which his regiment was one of the first to take the field was two years old. He had had the rare advantage of a military education, and when his comrades had marched to the front he had been detached for administrative service at the capital of his State, where it was thought that he could be most useful. Like a bad soldier he protested, and like a good one obeyed. In close official and personal relations with the governor of his State, and enjoying his confidence and favor, he had firmly refused promotion and seen his juniors elevated above him. Death had been busy in his distant regiment; vacancies among the field officers had occurred again and again; but from a chivalrous feeling that war's rewards belonged of right to those who bore the storm and stress of battle he had held his humble rank and generously advanced the fortunes of others. His silent devotion to principle had conquered at last: he had been relieved of his hateful duties and ordered to the front, and now, untried by fire, stood in the van of battle in command of a company of hardy veterans, to whom he had been only a name, and that name a byword. By none – not even by those of his brother officers in whose favor he had waived his rights – was his devotion to duty understood. They were too busy to be just; he was looked upon as one who had shirked his duty, until forced unwillingly into the field. Too proud to explain, yet not too insensible to feel, he could only endure and hope.

Of all the Federal Army on that summer morning none had accepted battle more joyously than Anderton Graffenreid. His spirit was buoyant, his faculties were riotous. He was in a state of mental exaltation and scarcely could endure the enemy's tardiness in advancing to the attack. To him this was opportunity – for the result he cared nothing. Victory or defeat, as God might will; in one or in the other he should prove himself a soldier and a hero; he should vindicate his right to the respect of his men and the companionship of his brother officers – to the consideration of his superiors. How his heart leaped in his breast as the bugle sounded the stirring notes of the 'assembly'! With what a light tread, scarcely conscious of the earth beneath his feet, he strode forward at the head of his company, and how exultingly he noted the tactical dispositions which placed his regiment in the front line! And if perchance some memory came to him of a pair of dark eyes that might take on a tenderer light in reading the account of that day's doings, who shall blame him for the unmartial thought or count it a debasement of soldierly ardor?

Suddenly, from the forest a half-mile in front – apparently from among the upper branches of the trees, but really from the ridge beyond – rose a tall column of white smoke. A moment later came a deep, jarring explosion, followed – almost attended – by a hideous rushing sound that seemed to leap forward across the intervening space with inconceivable rapidity, rising from whisper to roar with too quick a gradation for attention to note the successive stages of its horrible progression! A visible tremor ran along the lines of men; all were startled into motion. Captain Graffenreid dodged and threw up his hands to one side of his head, palms outward. As he did so he heard a keen, ringing report, and saw on a hillside behind the line a fierce roll of smoke and dust – the shell's explosion. It had passed a hundred feet to his left! He heard, or fancied he heard, a low, mocking laugh and turning in the direction whence it came saw the eyes of his first lieutenant fixed upon him with an unmistakable look of amusement. He looked along the line of faces in the front ranks. The men were laughing. At him? The thought restored the color to his bloodless face – restored too much of it. His cheeks burned with a fever of shame.

The enemy's shot was not answered: the officer in command at that exposed part of the line had evidently no desire to provoke a cannonade. For the forbearance Captain Graffenreid was conscious of a sense of gratitude. He had not known that the flight of a projectile was a phenomenon of so appalling character. His conception of war had already undergone a profound change, and he was conscious that his new feeling was manifesting itself in visible perturbation. His blood was boiling in his veins; he had a choking sensation and felt that if he had a command to give it would be inaudible, or at least unintelligible. The hand in which he held his sword trembled; the other moved automatically, clutching at various parts of his clothing. He found a difficulty in standing still and fancied that his men observed it. Was it fear? He feared it was.

From somewhere away to the right came, as the wind served, a low, intermittent murmur like that of ocean in a storm – like that of a distant railway train – like that of wind among the pines – three sounds so nearly alike that the ear, unaided by the judgement, cannot distinguish them one from another. The eyes of the troops were drawn in that direction; the mounted officers turned their field-glasses that way. Mingled with the sound was an irregular throbbing. He thought it, at first, the beating of his fevered blood in his ears; next, the distant tapping of a bass drum.

'The ball is opened on the right flank,' said an officer.

Captain Graffenreid understood: the sounds were musketry and artillery. He nodded and tried to smile. There was apparently nothing infectious in the smile.

Presently a light line of blue smoke-puffs broke out along the edge of the wood in front, succeeded by a crackle of rifles. There were keen, sharp hissings in the air, terminating abruptly with a thump near by. The man at Captain Graffenreid's side dropped his rifle; his knees gave way and he pitched awkwardly forward, falling upon his face. Somebody shouted 'Lie down!' and the dead man was hardly distinguishable from the living. It looked as if those few rifle-shots had slain ten thousand men. Only the field officers remained erect; their concession to the emergency consisted in dismounting and sending their horses to the shelter of the low hills immediately in rear.

Captain Graffenreid lay alongside the dead man, from beneath whose breast flowed a little rill of blood. It had a faint, sweetish odor that sickened him. The face was crushed into earth and flattened. It looked yellow already, and was repulsive. Nothing suggested the glory of a soldier's death nor mitigated the loathsomeness of the incident. He could not turn his back upon the body without facing away from his company.

He fixed his eyes upon the forest, where all again was silent. He tried to imagine what was going on there – the lines of troops forming to attack, the guns being pushed forward by hand to the edge of the open. He fancied he could see their black muzzles protruding from the undergrowth, ready to deliver their storm of missiles – such missiles as the one whose shriek had so unsettled his nerves. The distension of his eyes became painful; a mist seemed to gather before them; he could no longer see across the field, yet would not withdraw his gaze lest he see the dead man at his side.

The fire of battle was not now burning very brightly in this warrior's soul. From inaction had come introspection. He sought rather to analyze his feelings than distinguish himself by courage and devotion. The result was profoundly disappointing. He covered his face with his hands and groaned aloud.

The hoarse murmur of battle grew more and more distinct upon the right; the murmur had, indeed, become a roar, the throbbing, a thunder. The sounds had worked round obliquely to the front; evidently the enemy's left was being driven back, and the propitious moment to move against the salient angle of his line would soon arrive. The silence and mystery in front were ominous; all felt that they boded evil to the assailants.

Behind the prostrate lines sounded the hoof-beats of galloping horses; the men turned to look. A dozen staff officers were riding to the various brigade and regimental commanders, who had remounted. A moment more and there was a chorus of voices, all uttering out of time the same words – 'Attention, battalion!' The men sprang to their feet and were aligned by the company commanders. They awaited the word 'forward' – awaited, too, with beating hearts and set teeth the gusts of lead and iron that were to smite them at their first movement in obedience to that word. The word was not given; the tempest did not break out. The delay was hideous, maddening! It unnerved like a respite at the guillotine.

Captain Graffenreid stood at the head of his company, the dead man at his feet. He heard the battle on the right – rattle and crash of musketry, ceaseless thunder of cannon, desultory cheers of invisible combatants. He marked ascending clouds of smoke from distant forests. He noted the sinister silence of the forest in front. These contrasting extremes affected the whole range of his sensibilities. The strain upon his nervous organization was insupportable. He grew hot and cold by turns. He panted like a dog, and then forgot to breathe until reminded by vertigo.

Suddenly he grew calm. Glancing downward, his eyes had fallen upon his naked sword, as he held it, point to earth. Foreshortened to his view, it resembled somewhat, he thought, the short heavy blade of the ancient Roman. The fancy was full of suggestion, malign, fateful, heroic!

The sergeant in the rear rank, immediately behind Captain Graffenreid, now observed a strange sight. His attention drawn by an uncommon movement made by the captain – a sudden reaching forward of the hands and their energetic withdrawal, throwing the elbows out, as in pulling an oar – he saw spring from between the officer's shoulders a bright point of metal which prolonged itself outward, nearly a half-arm's length – a blade! It was faintly streaked with crimson, and its point approached so near to the sergeant's breast, and with so quick a movement, that he shrank backward in alarm. That moment Captain Graffenreid pitched heavily forward upon the dead man and died.

A week later the major-general commanding the left corps of the Federal Army submitted the following official report.

'SIR: I have the honor to report, with regard to the action of the 19th inst., that owing to the enemy's withdrawal from my front to reinforce his beaten left, my command was not seriously engaged. My loss was as follows: Killed, one officer, one man.'

George Thurston

Three incidents in the life of a man

George Thurston was a first lieutenant and aide-de-camp on the staff of Colonel Brough, commanding a Federal brigade. Colonel Brough was only temporarily in command, as senior colonel, the brigadier-general having been severely wounded and granted a leave of absence to recover. Lieutenant Thurston was, I believe, of Colonel Brough's regiment, to which, with his chief, he would naturally have been relegated had he lived till our brigade commander's recovery. The aide whose place Thurston took had been killed in battle; Thurston's advent among us was the only change in the *personnel* of our staff consequent upon the change in commanders. We did not like him; he was unsocial. This, however, was more observed by others than by me. Whether in camp or on the march, in barracks, in tents, or *en bivouac*, my duties as topographical engineer kept me working like a beaver – all day in the saddle and half the night at my drawing-table, platting my surveys. It was hazardous work; the nearer to the enemy's lines I could penetrate, the more valuable were my field notes and the resulting maps. It was a business in which the lives of men counted as nothing against the chance of defining a road or sketching a bridge. Whole squadrons of cavalry escort had sometimes to be sent thundering against a powerful infantry outpost in order that the brief time between the charge and the inevitable retreat might be utilized in sounding a ford or determining the point of intersection of two roads.

In some of the dark corners of England and Wales they have an immemorial custom of 'beating the bounds' of the parish. On a certain day of the year the whole population turns out and travels in procession from one landmark to another on the boundary line. At the most important points lads are soundly beaten with rods to make them remember the place in after life. They become authorities. Our frequent engagements with the Confederate outposts, patrols, and scouting parties had, incidentally, the same educating value; they fixed in my memory a vivid and apparently imperishable picture of the locality – a picture serving instead of accurate field notes, which, indeed, it was not always convenient to take, with carbines cracking, sabres clashing, and horses plunging all about. These spirited encounters were observations entered in red.

One morning as I set out at the head of my escort on an expedition of more than the usual hazard, Lieutenant Thurston rode up alongside and asked if I had any objection to his accompanying me, the colonel commanding having given him permission.

'None whatever,' I replied rather gruffly; 'but in what capacity will you go? You are not a topographical engineer, and Captain Burling commands my escort.'

'I will go as a spectator,' he said. Removing his sword-belt and taking the pistols from his holsters he handed them to his servant, who took them back to headquarters. I realized the brutality of my remark, but not clearly seeing my way to an apology, said nothing.

That afternoon we encountered a whole regiment of the enemy's cavalry in line and a field-piece that dominated a straight mile of the turnpike by which we had approached. My escort fought deployed in the woods on both sides, but Thurston remained in the center of the road, which at intervals of a few seconds was swept by gusts of grape and canister that tore the air wide open as they passed. He had dropped the rein on the neck of his horse and sat bolt upright in the saddle, with folded arms. Soon he was down, his horse torn to pieces. From the side of the road, my pencil and field book idle, my duty forgotten, I watched him slowly disengaging himself from the wreck and rising. At that instant, the cannon having ceased firing, a burly Confederate trooper on a spirited horse dashed like a thunderbolt down the road with drawn saber. Thurston saw him coming, drew himself up to his full height, and again folded his arms. He was too brave to retreat before the sword, and my uncivil words had disarmed him. He was a spectator. Another moment and he would have been split like a mackerel, but a blessed bullet tumbled his assailant into the dusty road so near that the impetus sent the body rolling to Thurston's feet. That evening, while platting my hasty survey, I found time to frame an apology, which I think took the rude, primitive form of a confession that I had spoken like a malicious idiot.

A few weeks later a part of our army made an assault upon the enemy's left. The attack, which was made upon an unknown position and across unfamiliar ground, was led by our brigade. The ground was so broken and the underbrush so thick that all mounted officers and men were compelled to fight on foot – the brigade commander and his staff included. In the *mêlée* Thurston was parted from the rest of us, and we found him, horribly wounded, only when we had taken the enemy's last defense. He was some months in hospital at Nashville, Tennessee, but finally rejoined us. He said little about his misadventure, except that he had been bewildered and had strayed into the enemy's lines and been shot down; but from one of his captors, whom we in turn had captured, we learned the particulars. 'He came walking right upon us as we lay in line,' said this man. 'A whole company of us instantly sprang up and leveled our rifles at his breast, some of them almost touching him. "Throw down that sword and surrender, you damned Yank!" shouted some one in authority. The fellow ran his eyes along the line of rifle barrels, folded his arms across his breast, his right hand still clutching his sword, and deliberately replied, "I will not," If we had all fired he would have been torn to shreds. Some of us didn't. I didn't, for one; nothing could have induced me.'

When one is tranquilly looking death in the eye and refusing him any concession one naturally has a good opinion of one's self. I don't know if it was this feeling that in Thurston found expression in a stiffish attitude and folded arms; at the mess table one day, in his absence, another explanation was suggested by our quartermaster, an irreclaimable stammerer when the wine was in: 'It's h – is w – ay of m-m-mastering a c-c-consti-t-tu-tional t-tendency to r – un aw – ay.'

'What!' I flamed out, indignantly rising; 'you intimate that Thurston is a coward – and in his absence?'

'If he w – ere a cow – wow-ard h – e w – wouldn't t-try to m-m-master it; and if he w – ere p-present I w – wouldn't d-d-dare to d-d-discuss it,' was the mollifying reply.

This intrepid man, George Thurston, died an ignoble death. The brigade was in camp, with headquarters in a grove of immense trees. To an upper branch of one of these a venturesome climber had attached the two ends of a long rope and made a swing with a length of not less than one hundred feet. Plunging downward from a height of fifty feet, along the arc of a circle with such a radius, soaring to an equal altitude, pausing for one breathless instant, then sweeping dizzily backward – no one who has not tried it can conceive the terrors of such sport to the novice. Thurston came out of his tent one day and asked for instruction in the mystery of propelling the swing – the art of rising and sitting, which every boy has mastered. In a few moments he had acquired the trick and was swinging higher than the most experienced of us had dared. We shuddered to look at his fearful flights.

'St-t-top him,' said the quartermaster, snailing lazily along from the mess-tent, where he had been lunching; 'h – e d-doesn't know that if h – e g-g-goes c-clear over h – e'll w – ind up the sw – ing.'

With such energy was that strong man cannonading himself through the air that at each extremity of his increasing arc his body, standing in the swing, was almost horizontal. Should he once pass above the level of the rope's attachment he would be lost; the rope would slacken and he would fall vertically to a point as far below as he had gone above, and then the sudden tension of the rope would wrest it from his hands. All saw the peril – all cried out to him to desist, and gesticulated at him as, indistinct and with a noise like the rush of a cannon shot in flight, he swept past us through the lower reaches of his hideous oscillation. A woman standing at a little distance away fainted and fell unobserved. Men from the camp of a regiment near by ran in crowds to see, all shouting. Suddenly, as Thurston was on his upward curve, the shouts all ceased.

Thurston and the swing had parted – that is all that can be known; both hands at once had released the rope. The impetus of the light swing exhausted, it was falling back; the man's momentum was carrying him, almost erect, upward and forward, no longer in his arc, but with an outward curve. It could have been but an instant, yet it seemed an age. I cried out, or thought I cried out: 'My God! will he never stop going up?' He passed close to the branch of a tree. I remember a feeling of delight as I thought he would clutch it and save himself. I speculated on the possibility of it sustaining his weight. He passed above it, and from my point of view was sharply outlined against the blue. At this distance of many years I can distinctly recall that image of a man in the sky, its head erect, its feet close together, its hands – I do not see its hands. All at once, with astonishing suddenness and rapidity, it turns clear over and pitches downward. There is another cry from the crowd, which has rushed instinctively forward. The man has become merely a whirling object, mostly legs. Then there is an indescribable sound – the sound of an impact that shakes the earth, and these men, familiar with death in its most awful aspects, turn sick. Many walk unsteadily away from the spot; others support themselves against the trunks of trees or sit at the roots. Death has taken an unfair advantage; he has struck with an unfamiliar weapon; he has executed a new and disquieting stratagem. We did not know that he had so ghastly resources, possibilities of terror so dismal.

Thurston's body lay on its back. One leg, bent beneath, was broken above the knee and the bone driven into the earth. The abdomen had burst; the bowels protruded. The neck was broken.

The arms were folded tightly across the breast.

The Mocking-Bird

The time, a pleasant Sunday afternoon in the early autumn of 1861. The place, a forest's heart in the mountain region of southwestern Virginia. Private Grayrock of the Federal Army is discovered seated comfortably at the root of a great pine tree, against which he leans, his legs extended straight along the ground, his rifle lying across his thighs, his hands (clasped in order that they may not fall away to his sides) resting upon the barrel of the weapon. The contact of the back of his head with the tree has pushed his cap downward over his eyes, almost concealing them; one seeing him would say that he slept.

Private Grayrock did not sleep; to have done so would have imperiled the interest of the United States, for he was a long way outside the lines and subject to capture or death at the hands of the enemy. Moreover, he was in a frame of mind unfavourable to repose. The cause of his perturbation of spirit was this: during the previous night he had served on the picket-guard, and had been posted as a sentinel in this very forest. The night was clear, though moonless, but in the gloom of the wood the darkness was deep. Grayrock's post was at a considerable distance from those to right and left, for the pickets had been thrown out a needless distance from the camp, making the line too long for the force detailed to occupy it. The war was young, and military camps entertained the error that while sleeping they were better protected by thin lines a long way out toward the enemy than by thicker ones close in. And surely they needed as long notice as possible of an enemy's approach, for they were at that time addicted to the practice of undressing – than which nothing could be more unsoldierly. On the morning of the memorable 6th of April, at Shiloh, many of Grant's men when spitted on Confederate bayonets were as naked as civilians; but it should be allowed that this was not because of any defect in their picket line. Their error was of another sort: they had no pickets. This is perhaps a vain digression. I should not care to undertake to interest the reader in the fate of an army; what we have here to consider is that of Private Grayrock.

For two hours after he had been left at his lonely post that Saturday night he stood stockstill, leaning against the trunk of a large tree, staring into the darkness in his front and trying to recognize known objects; for he had been posted at the same spot during the day. But all was now different; he saw nothing in detail, but only groups of things, whose shapes, not observed when there was something more of them to observe, were now unfamiliar. They seemed not to have been there before. A landscape that is all trees and undergrowth, moreover, lacks definition, is confused and without accentuated points upon which attention can gain a foothold. Add the gloom of a moonless night, and something more than great natural intelligence and a city education is required to preserve one's knowledge of direction. And that is how it occurred that Private Grayrock, after vigilantly watching the spaces in his front and then imprudently executing a circumspection of his whole dimly visible environment (silently walking around his tree to accomplish it) lost his bearings and seriously impaired his usefulness as a sentinel. Lost at his post – unable to say in which direction to look for an enemy's approach, and in which lay the sleeping camp for whose security he was accountable with his life – conscious, too, of many another awkward feature of the situation and of considerations affecting his own safety, Private Grayrock was profoundly disquieted. Nor was he given time to recover his tranquillity, for almost at the moment that he realized his awkward predicament he heard a stir of leaves and a snap of fallen twigs, and turning with a stilled heart in the direction whence it came, saw in the gloom the indistinct outlines of a human figure.

'Halt!' shouted Private Grayrock, peremptorily as in duty bound, backing up the command with the sharp metallic snap of his cocking rifle – 'who goes there?'

There was no answer; at least there was an instant's hesitation, and the answer, if it came, was lost in the report of the sentinel's rifle. In the silence of the night and the forest the sound was deafening, and hardly had it died away when it was repeated by the pieces of the pickets to right and left, a sympathetic fusillade. For two hours every unconverted civilian of them had been evolving enemies from his imagination, and peopling the woods in his front with them, and Grayrock's shot had started the whole encroaching host into visible existence. Having fired, all retreated, breathless, to the reserves – all but Grayrock, who did not know in what direction to retreat. When, no enemy appearing, the roused camp two miles away had undressed and got itself into bed again, and the picket line was cautiously re-established, he was discovered bravely holding his ground, and was complimented by the officer of the guard as the one soldier of that devoted band who could rightly be considered the moral equivalent of that uncommon unit of value, 'a whoop in hell.'

In the mean time, however, Grayrock had made a close but unavailing search for the mortal part of the intruder at whom he had fired, and whom he had a marksman's intuitive sense of having hit; for he was one of those born experts who shoot without aim by an instinctive sense of direction, and are nearly as dangerous by night as by day. During a full half of his twenty-four years he had been a terror to the targets of all the shooting-galleries in three cities. Unable now to produce his dead game he had the discretion to hold his tongue, and was glad to observe in his officer and comrades the natural assumption that not having run away he had seen nothing hostile. His 'honorable mention' had been earned by not running away anyhow.

Nevertheless, Private Grayrock was far from satisfied with the night's adventure, and when the next day he made some fair enough pretext to apply for a pass to go outside the lines, and the general commanding promptly granted it in recognition of his bravery the night before, he passed out at the point where that had been displayed. Telling the sentinel then on duty there that he had lost something, – which was true enough – he renewed the search for the person whom he supposed himself to have shot, and whom if only wounded he hoped to trail by the blood. He was no more successful by daylight than he had been in the darkness, and after covering a wide area and boldly penetrating a long distance into 'the Confederacy' he gave up the search, somewhat fatigued, seated himself at the root of the great pine tree, where we have seen him, and indulged his disappointment.

It is not to be inferred that Grayrock's was the chagrin of a cruel nature balked of its bloody deed. In the clear large eyes, finely wrought lips, and broad forehead of that young man one could read quite another story, and in point of fact his character was a singularly felicitous compound of boldness and sensibility, courage and conscience.

'I find myself disappointed,' he said to himself, sitting there at the bottom of the golden haze submerging the forest like a subtler sea – 'disappointed in failing to discover a fellow-man dead by my hand! Do I then really wish that I had taken life in the performance of a duty as well performed without? What more could I wish? If any danger threatened, my shot averted it; that is what I was there to do. No, I am glad indeed if no human life was needlessly extinguished by me. But I am in a false position. I have suffered myself to be complimented by my officers and envied by my comrades. The camp is ringing with praise of my courage. That is not just; I know myself courageous, but this praise is for specific acts which I did not perform, or performed – otherwise. It is believed that I remained at my post bravely, without firing, whereas it was I who began the fusillade, and I did not retreat in the general alarm because bewildered. What, then, shall I do? Explain that I saw an enemy and fired? They have all said that of themselves, yet none believes it. Shall I tell a truth which, discrediting my courage, will have the effect of a lie? Ugh! it is an ugly business altogether. I wish to God I could find my man!'

And so wishing, Private Grayrock, overcome at last by the languor of the afternoon and lulled by the stilly sounds of insects droning and prosing in certain fragrant shrubs, so far forgot the interests of the United States as to fall asleep and expose himself to capture. And sleeping he dreamed.

He thought himself a boy, living in a far, fair land by the border of a great river upon which the tall steamboats moved grandly up and down beneath their towering evolutions of black smoke, which announced them long before they had rounded the bends and marked their movements when miles out of sight. With him always, at his side as he watched them, was one to whom he gave his heart and soul in love – a twin brother. Together they strolled along the banks of the stream; together explored the fields lying farther away from it, and gathered pungent mints and sticks of fragrant sassafras in the hills overlooking all – beyond which lay the Realm of Conjecture, and from which, looking southward across the great river, they caught glimpses of the Enchanted Land. Hand in hand and heart in heart they two, the only children of a widowed mother, walked in paths of light through valleys of peace, seeing new things under a new sun. And through all the golden days floated one unceasing sound – the rich, thrilling melody of a mocking-bird in a cage by the cottage door. It pervaded and possessed all the spiritual intervals of the dream, like a musical benediction. The joyous bird was always in song; its infinitely various notes seemed to flow from its throat, effortless, in bubbles and rills at each heart-beat, like the waters of a pulsing spring. That fresh, clear melody seemed, indeed, the spirit of the scene, the meaning and interpretation to sense of the mysteries of life and love.

But there came a time when the days of the dream grew dark with sorrow in a rain of tears. The good mother was dead, the meadowside home by the great river was broken up, and the brothers were parted between two of their kinsmen. William (the dreamer) went to live in a populous city in the Realm of Conjecture, and John, crossing the river into the Enchanted Land, was taken to a distant region whose people in their lives and ways were said to be strange and wicked. To him, in the distribution of the dead mother's estate, had fallen all that they deemed of value – the mocking-bird. They could be divided, but it could not, so it was carried away into the strange country, and the world of William knew it no more forever. Yet still through the aftertime of his loneliness its song filled all the dream, and seemed always sounding in his ear and in his heart.

The kinsmen who had adopted the boys were enemies, holding no communication. For a time letters full of boyish bravado and boastful narratives of the new and larger experience – grotesque descriptions of their widening lives and the new words they had conquered – passed between them; but these gradually became less frequent, and with William's removal to another and greater city ceased altogether. But ever through it all ran the song of the mocking-bird, and when the dreamer opened his eyes and stared through the vistas of the pine forest the cessation of its music first apprised him that he was awake.

The sun was low and red in the west; the level rays projected from the trunk of each giant pine a wall of shadow traversing the golden haze to eastward until light and shade were blended in undistinguishable blue.

Private Grayrock rose to his feet, looked cautiously about him, shouldered his rifle and set off toward camp. He had gone perhaps a half-mile, and was passing a thicket of laurel, when a bird rose from the midst of it and perching on the branch of a tree above, poured from its joyous breast so inexhaustible floods of song as but one of all God's creatures can utter in His praise. There was little in that – it was only to open the bill and breathe; yet the man stopped as if struck – stopped and let fall his rifle, looked upward at the bird, covered his eyes with his hands and wept like a child! For the moment he was, indeed, a child, in spirit and in memory, dwelling again by the great river, over-against the Enchanted Land! Then with an effort of the will he pulled himself together, picked up his weapon and audibly damning himself for an idiot strode on. Passing an opening that reached into the heart of the little thicket he looked in, and there, supine upon the earth, its arms all abroad, its gray uniform stained with a single spot of blood upon the breast, its white face turned sharply upward and backward, lay the image of himself! – the body of John Grayrock, dead of a gunshot wound, and still warm! He had found his man.

As the unfortunate soldier knelt beside that masterwork of civil war the shrilling bird upon the bough overhead stilled her song and, flushed with sunset's crimson glory, glided silently away through the solemn spaces of the wood. At roll-call that evening in the Federal camp the name William Grayrock brought no response, nor ever again thereafter.

CIVILIANS

The Man Out of the Nose

At the intersection of two certain streets in that part of San Francisco known by the rather loosely applied name of North Beach, is a vacant lot, which is rather more nearly level than is usually the case with lots, vacant or otherwise, in that region. Immediately at the back of it, to the south, however, the ground slopes steeply upward, the acclivity broken by three terraces cut into the soft rock. It is a place for goats and poor persons, several families of each class having occupied it jointly and amicably 'from the foundation of the city.' One of the humble habitations of the lowest terrace is noticeable for its rude resemblance to the human face, or rather to such a simulacrum of it as a boy might cut out of a hollowed pumpkin, meaning no offense to his race. The eyes are two circular windows, the nose is a door, the mouth an aperture caused by removal of a board below. There are no doorsteps. As a face, this house is too large; as a dwelling, too small. The blank, unmeaning stare of its lidless and browless eyes is uncanny.

Sometimes a man steps out of the nose, turns, passes the place where the right ear should be and making his way through the throng of children and goats obstructing the narrow walk between his neighbors' doors and the edge of the terrace gains the street by descending a flight of rickety stairs. Here he pauses to consult his watch and the stranger who happens to pass wonders why such a man as that can care what is the hour. Longer observations would show that the time of day is an important element in the man's movements, for it is at precisely two o'clock in the afternoon that he comes forth 365 times in every year.

Having satisfied himself that he has made no mistake in the hour he replaces the watch and walks rapidly southward up the street two squares, turns to the right and as he approaches the next corner fixes his eyes on an upper window in a three-story building across the way. This is a somewhat dingy structure, originally of red brick and now gray. It shows the touch of age and dust. Built for a dwelling, it is now a factory. I do not know what is made there; the things that are commonly made in a factory, I suppose. I only know that at two o'clock in the afternoon of every day but Sunday it is full of activity and clatter; pulsations of some great engine shake it and there are recurrent screams of wood tormented by the saw. At the window on which the man fixes an intensely expectant gaze nothing ever appears; the glass, in truth, has such a coating of dust that it has long ceased to be transparent. The man looks at it without stopping; he merely keeps turning his head more and more backward as he leaves the building behind. Passing along to the next corner, he turns to the left, goes round the block, and comes back till he reaches the point diagonally across the street from the factory – a point on his former course, which he then retraces, looking frequently backward over his right shoulder at the window while it is in sight. For many years he has not been known to vary his route nor to introduce a single innovation into his action. In a quarter of an hour he is again at the mouth of his dwelling, and a woman, who has for some time been standing in the nose, assists him to enter. He is seen no more until two o'clock the next day.

The woman is his wife. She supports herself and him by washing for the poor people among whom they live, at rates which destroy Chinese and domestic competition.

This man is about fifty-seven years of age, though he looks greatly older. His hair is dead white. He wears no beard, and is always newly shaven. His hands are clean, his nails well kept. In the matter of dress he is distinctly superior to his position, as indicated by his surroundings and the business of his wife. He is , indeed, very neatly, if not quite fashionably, clad. His silk hat has a date no earlier than the year before the last, and his boots, scrupulously polished, are innocent of patches. I am told that the suit which he wears during his daily excursions of fifteen minutes is not the one that he wears at home. Like everything else that he has, this is provided and kept in repair by the wife, and is renewed as frequently as her scanty means permit.

Thirty years ago John Hardshaw and his wife lived on Rincon Hill in one of the finest residences of that once aristocratic quarter. He had once been a physician, but having inherited a considerable estate from his father concerned himself no more about the ailments of his fellow-creatures and found as much work as he cared for in managing his own affairs. Both he and his wife were highly cultivated persons, and their house was frequented by a small set of such men and women as persons of their tastes would think worth knowing. So far as these knew, Mr and Mrs Hardshaw lived happily together; certainly the wife was devoted to her handsome and accomplished husband and exceedingly proud of him.

Among their acquaintances were the Barwells – man, wife and two young children – of Sacramento. Mr Barwell was a civil and mining engineer, whose duties took him much from home and frequently to San Francisco. On these occasions his wife commonly accompanied him and passed much of her time at the house of her friend, Mrs Hardshaw, always with her two children, of whom Mrs Hardshaw, childless herself, grew fond. Unluckily, her husband grew equally fond of their mother – a good deal fonder. Still more unluckily, that attractive lady was less wise than weak.

At about three o'clock one autumn morning Officer No. 13 of the Sacremento police saw a man stealthily leaving the rear entrance of a gentleman's residence and promptly arrested him. The man – who wore a slouched hat and shaggy overcoat – offered the policeman one hundred, then five hundred, then one thousand dollars to be released. As he had less than the first mentioned sum on his person the officer treated his proposal with virtuous contempt. Before reaching the station the prisoner agreed to give him a check for ten thousand dollars and remain ironed in the willows along the river bank until it should be paid. As this only provoked new derision he would say no more, merely giving an obviously fictitious name. When he was searched at the station nothing of value was found on him but a miniature portrait of Mrs Barwell – the lady of the house at which he was caught. The case was set with costly diamonds; and something in the quality of the man's linen sent a pang of unavailing regret through the severely incorruptible bosom of Officer No. 13. There was nothing about the prisoner's clothing nor person to identify him and he was booked for burglary under the name that he had given, the honorable name of John K. Smith. The K. was an inspiration upon which, doubtless, he greatly prided himself.

In the mean time the mysterious disappearance of John Hardshaw was agitating the gossips of Rincon Hill in San Francisco, and was even mentioned in one of the newspapers. It did not occur to the lady whom that journal considerately described as his 'widow,' to look for him in the city prison at Sacramento – a town which he was not known ever to have visited. As John K. Smith he was arraigned and, waiving examination, committed for trail.

About two weeks before the trial, Mrs Hardshaw, accidentally learning that her husband was held in Sacramento under an assumed name on a charge of burglary, hastened to that city without daring to mention the matter to any one and presented herself at the prison, asking for an interview with her husband, John K. Smith. Haggard and ill with anxiety, wearing a plain traveling wrap which covered her from neck to foot, and in which she had passed the night on the steamboat, too anxious to sleep, she hardly showed for what she was, but her manner pleaded for her more strongly than anything that she chose to say in evidence of her right to admittance. She was permitted to see him alone.

What occurred during that distressing interview has never transpired; but later events prove that Hardshaw had found means to subdue her will to his own. She left the prison, a broken-hearted woman, refusing to answer a single question, and returning to her desolate home renewed, in a half-hearted way, her inquiries for her missing husband. A week later she was herself missing: she had 'gone back to the States' – nobody knew any more than that.

On his trial the prisoner pleaded guilty – 'by advice of his counsel,' so his counsel said. Nevertheless, the judge, in whose mind several unusual circumstances had created a doubt, insisted on the district attorney placing Officer No. 13 on the stand, and the deposition of Mrs Barwell, who was too ill to attend, was read to the jury. It was very brief: she knew nothing of the matter except that the likeness of herself was her property, and had, she thought, been left on the parlor table when she had retired on the night of the arrest. She had intended it as a present to her husband, then and still absent in Europe on business for a mining company.

This witness's manner when making the deposition at her residence was afterward described by the district attorney as most extraordinary. Twice she had refused to testify, and once, when the deposition lacked nothing but her signature, she had caught it from the clerk's hands and torn it in pieces. She had called her children to the bedside and embraced them with streaming eyes, then suddenly sending them from the room, she verified her statement by oath and signature, and fainted – 'slick away,' said the district attorney. It was at that time that her physician, arriving upon the scene, took in the situation at a glance and grasping the representative of the law by the collar chucked him into the street and kicked his assistant after him. The insulted majesty of the law was not vindicated; the victim of the indignity did not even mention anything of all this in court. He was ambitious to win his case, and the circumstances of the taking of that deposition were not such as would give it weight if related; and after all, the man on trial had committed an offense against the law's majesty only less heinous than that of the irascible physician.

By suggestion of the judge the jury rendered a verdict of guilty; there was nothing else to do, and the prisoner was sentenced to the penitentiary for three years. His counsel, who had objected to nothing and had made no plea for lenity – had, in fact, hardly said a word – wrung his client's hand and left the room. It was obvious to the whole bar that he had been engaged only to prevent the court from appointing counsel who might possibly insist on making a defense.

John Hardshaw served out his term at San Quentin, and when discharged was met at the prison gates by his wife, who had returned from 'the States' to receive him. It is thought they went straight to Europe; anyhow, a general power-of-attorney to a lawyer still living among us –from whom I have many of the facts of this simple history – was executed in Paris. This lawyer in a short time sold everything that Hardshaw owned in California, and for years nothing was heard of the unfortunate couple; though many to whose ears had come vague and inaccurate intimations of their strange story, and who had known them, recalled their personality with tenderness and their misfortunes with compassion.

Some years later they returned, both broken in fortune and spirits and he in health. The purpose of their return I have not been able to ascertain. For some time they lived, under the name of Johnson, in a respectable enough quarter south of Market Street, pretty well out, and were never seen away from the vicinity of their dwelling. They must have had a little money left, for it is not known that the man had any occupation, the state of his health probably not permitting. The woman's devotion to her invalid husband was matter of remark among their nieghbors; she seemed never absent from his side and always supporting and cheering him. They would sit for hours on one of the benches in a little public park, she reading to him, his hand in hers, her light touch occasionally visiting his pale brow, her still beautiful eyes frequently lifted from the book to look into his as she made some comment on the text, or closed the volume to beguile his mood with talk of – what? Nobody ever overheard a conversation between these two. The reader who has had the patience to follow their history to this point may possibly find a pleasure in conjecture: there was probably something to be avoided. The bearing of the man was one of profound dejection; indeed, the unsympathetic youth of the neighborhood, with that keen sense for visible characteristics which ever distinguishes the young male of our species, sometimes mentioned him among themselves by the name of Spoony Glum.

It occurred one day that John Hardshaw was possessed by the spirit of unrest. God knows what led him whither he went, but he crossed Market Street and held his way northward over the hills, and downward into the region known as North Beach. Turning aimlessly to the left he followed his toes along an unfamiliar street until he was opposite what for that period was a rather grand dwelling, and for this is a rather shabby factory. Casting his eyes casually upward he saw at an open window what it had been better that he had not seen – the face and figure of Elvira Barwell. Their eyes met. With a sharp exclamation, like the cry of a startled bird, the lady sprang to her feet and thrust her body half out of the window, clutching the casing on each side. Arrested by the cry, the people in the street below looked up. Hardshaw stood motionless, speechless, his eyes two flames. 'Take care!' shouted some one in the crowd, as the woman strained further and further forward, defying the silent, implacable law of gravitation, as once she had defied that other law which God thundered from Sinai. The suddenness of her movements had tumbled a torrent of dark hair down her shoulders, and now it was blown about her cheeks, almost concealing her face. A moment so, and then – ! A fearful cry rang through the street, as, losing her balance, she pitched headlong from the window, a confused and whirling mass of skirts, limbs, hair, and white face, and struck the pavement with a horrible sound and a force of impact that was felt a hundred feet away. For a moment all eyes refused their office and turned from the sickening spectacle on the sidewalk. Drawn again to that horror, they saw it strangely augmented. A man, hatless, seated flat upon the paving stones, held the broken, bleeding body against his breast, kissing the mangled cheeks and streaming mouth through tangles of wet hair, his own features indistinguishably crimson with the blood that half-strangled him and ran in rills from his soaken beard.

The reporter's task is nearly finished. The Barwells had that very morning returned from a two years' absence in Peru. A week later the widower, now doubly desolate, since there could be no missing the significance of Hardshaw's horrible demonstration, had sailed for I know not what distant port; he has never come back to stay. Hardshaw – as Johnson no longer – passed a year in the Stockton asylum for the insane, where also, through the influence of pitying friends, his wife was admitted to care for him. When he was discharged, not cured but harmless, they returned to the city; it would seem ever to have had some dreadful fascination for them. For a time they lived near the Mission Dolores, in poverty only less abject than that which is their present lot; but it was too far away from the objective point of the man's daily pilgrimage. They could not afford car fare. So that poor devil of an angel from Heaven – wife to this convict and lunatic – obtained, at a fair enough rental, the blank-faced shanty on the lower terrace of Goat Hill. Thence to the structure that was a dwelling and is a factory the distance is not so great; it is, in fact, an agreeable walk, judging from the man's eager and cheerful look as he takes it. The return journey appears to be a trifle wearisome.

An Adventure at Brownville

I taught a little country school near Brownville, which, as every one knows who has had the good luck to live there, is the capital of a considerable expanse of the finest scenery in California. The town is somewhat frequented in summer by a class of persons whom it is the habit of the local journal to call 'pleasure seekers,' but who by a juster classification would be known as 'the sick and those in adversity.' Brownville itself might rightly enough be described, indeed, as a summer place of last resort. It is fairly well endowed with boarding-houses, at the least pernicious of which I performed twice a day (lunching at the schoolhouse) the humble rite of cementing the alliance between soul and body. From this 'hostelry' (as the local journal preferred to call it when it did not call it a 'caravanserai') to the schoolhouse the distance by the wagon road was about a mile and a half; but there was a trail, very little used, which led over an intervening range of low, heavily wooded hills, considerably shortening the distance. By this trail I was returning one evening later than usual. It was the last day of the term and I had been detained at the schoolhouse until almost dark, preparing an account of my stewardship for the trustees – two of whom, I proudly reflected, would be able to read it, and the third (an instance of the dominion of mind over matter) would be overruled in his customary antagonism to the schoolmaster of his own creation.

I had gone not more than a quarter of the way when, finding an interest in the antics of a family of lizards which dwelt thereabout and seemed full of reptilian joy for their immunity from the ills incident to life at the Brownville House, I sat upon a fallen tree to observe them. As I leaned wearily against a branch of the gnarled old trunk the twilight deepened in the somber woods and the faint new moon began casting visible shadows and gilding the leaves of the trees with a tender but ghostly light.

I heard the sound of voices – a woman's, angry, impetuous, rising against deep masculine tones, rich and musical. I strained my eyes, peering through the dusky shadows of the wood, hoping to get a view of the intruders on my solitude, but could see no one. For some yards in each direction I had an uninterrupted view of the trail, and knowing of no other within a half mile thought the persons heard must be approaching from the wood at one side. There was no sound but that of the voices, which were now so distinct that I could catch the words. That of the man gave me an impression of anger, abundantly confirmed by the matter spoken.

'I will have no threats; you are powerless, as you very well know. Let things remain as they are or, by God! you shall both suffer for it.'

'What do you mean?' this was the voice of the woman, a cultivated voice, the voice of a lady. 'You would not – murder us.'

There was no reply, at least none that was audible to me. During the silence I peered into the wood in hope to get a glimpse of the speakers, for I felt sure that this was an affair of gravity in which ordinary scruples ought not to count. It seemed to me that the woman was in peril; at any rate the man had not disavowed a willingness to murder. When a man is enacting the rôle of potential assassin he has not the right to choose his audience.

After some little time I saw them, indistinct in the moonlight among the trees. The man, tall and slender, seemed clothed in black; the woman wore, as nearly as I could make out, a gown of gray stuff. Evidently they were still unaware of my presence in the shadow, though for some reason when they renewed their conversation they spoke in lower tones and I could no longer understand. As I looked the woman seemed to sink to the ground and raise her hands in supplication, as is frequently done on the stage and never, so far as I knew, anywhere else, and I am now not altogether sure that it was done in this instance. The man fixed his eyes upon her; they seemed to glitter bleakly in the moonlight with an expression that made me apprehensive that he would turn them upon me. I do not know by what impluse I was moved, but I sprang to my feet out of the shadow. At that instant the figures vanished. I peered in vain through the spaces among the trees and clumps of undergrowth. The night wind rustled the leaves; the lizards had retired early, reptiles of exemplary habits. The little moon was already slipping behind a black hill in the west.

I went home, somewhat disturbed in mind, half doubting that I had heard or seen any living thing excepting the lizards. It all seemed a trifle odd and uncanny. It was as if among the several phenomena, objective and subjective, that made the sum total of the incident there had been an uncertain element which had diffused its dubious character over all – had leavened the whole mass with unreality. I did not like it.

At the breakfast table the next morning there was a new face; opposite me sat a young woman at whom I merely glanced as I took my seat. In speaking to the high and mighty female personage who condescended to seem to wait upon us, this girl soon invited my attention by the sound of her voice, which was like, yet not altogether like, the one still murmuring in my memory of the previous evening's adventure. A moment later another girl, a few years older, entered the room and sat at the left of the other, speaking to her a gentle 'good morning.' By *her* voice I was startled: it was without doubt the one of which the first girl's had reminded me. Here was the lady of the sylvan incident sitting bodily before me, 'in her habit as she lived.'

Evidently enough the two were sisters. With a nebulous kind of apprehension that I might be recognized as the mute inglorious hero of an adventure which had in my consciousness and conscience something of the character of eavesdropping, I allowed myself only a hasty cup of the lukewarm coffee thoughtfully provided by the prescient waitress for the emergency, and left the table. As I passed out of the house into the grounds I heard a rich, strong male voice singing an aria from 'Rigoletto.' I am bound to say that it was exquisitely sung, too, but there was something in the performance that displeased me, I could say neither what nor why, and I walked rapidly away.

Returning latter in the day I saw the elder of the two young women standing on the porch and near her a tall man in black clothing – the man whom I had expected to see. All day the desire to know something of these persons had been uppermost in my mind and I now resolved to learn what I could of them in any way that was neither dishonorable nor low.

The man was talking easily and affably to his companion, but at the sound of my footsteps on the gravel walk he ceased, and turning about looked me full in the face. He was apparently of middle age, dark and uncommonly handsome. His attire was faultless, his bearing easy and graceful, the look which he turned upon me open, free, and devoid of any suggestion of rudeness. Nevertheless it affected me with a distinct emotion which on subsequent analysis in memory appeared to be compounded of hatred and dread – I am unwilling to call it fear. A second later the man and woman had disappeared. They seemed to have a trick of disappearing. On entering the house, however, I saw them through the open doorway of the parlor as I passed; they had merely stepped through a window which opened down to the floor.

Cautiously 'approached' on the subject of her new guests my landlady proved not ungracious. Restated with, I hope, some small reverence for English grammar the facts were these: the two girls were Pauline and Eva Maynard of San Francisco; the elder was Pauline. The man was Richard Benning, their guardian, who had been the most intimate friend of their father, now deceased. Mr Benning had brought them to Brownville in the hope that the mountain climate might benefit Eva, who was thought to be in danger of consumption.

Upon these short and simple annals the landlady wrought an embroidery of eulogium which abundantly attested her faith in Mr Benning's will and ability to pay for the best that her house afforded. That he had a good heart was evident to her from his devotion to his two beautiful wards and his really touching solicitude for their comfort. The evidence impressed me as insufficient and I silently found the Scotch verdict, 'Not proven.'

Certainly Mr Benning was most attentive to his wards. In my strolls about the country I frequently encountered them – sometimes in company with other guests of the hotel – exploring the gulches, fishing, rifle shooting, and otherwise wiling away the monotony of country life; and although I watched them as closely as good manners would permit I saw nothing that would in any way explain the strange words that I had overheard in the wood. I had grown tolerably well acquainted with the young ladies and could exchange looks and even greetings with their guardian without actual repugnance.

A month went by and I had almost ceased to interest myself in their affairs when one night our entire little community was thrown into excitement by an event which vividly recalled my experience in the forest.

This was the death of the elder girl, Pauline.

The sisters had occupied the same bedroom on the third floor of the house. Waking in the gray of the morning Eva had found Pauline dead beside her. Later, when the poor girl was weeping beside the body amid a throng of sympathetic if not very considerate persons, Mr Benning entered the room and appeared to be about to take her hand. She drew away from the side of the dead and moved slowly toward the door.

'It is you,' she said – 'you who have done this. You – you – you!'

'She is raving,' he said in a low voice. He followed her, step by step, as she retreated, his eyes fixed upon hers with a steady gaze in which there was nothing of tenderness nor of compassion. She stopped; the hand that she had raised in accusation fell to her side, her dilated eyes contracted visibly, the lids slowly dropped over them, veiling their strange wild beauty, and she stood motionless and almost as white as the dead girl lying near. The man took her hand and put his arm gently about her shoulders, as if to support her. Suddenly she burst into a passion of tears and clung to him as a child to its mother. He smiled with a smile that affected me most disagreeably – perhaps any kind of smile would have done so – and led her silently out of the room.

There was an inquest – and the customary verdict: the deceased, it appeared, came to her death through 'heart disease.' It was before the invention of heart *failure*, though the heart of poor Pauline had indubitably failed. The body was embalmed and taken to San Francisco by some one summoned thence for the purpose, neither Eva nor Benning accompanying it. Some of the hotel gossips ventured to think that very strange, and a few hardy spirits went so far as to think it very strange indeed; but the good landlady generously threw herself into the breach, saying it was owing to the precarious nature of the girl's health. It is not of record that either of the two persons most affected and apparently least concerned made any explanation.

One evening about a week after the death I went out upon the veranda of the hotel to get a book that I had left there. Under some vines shutting out the moonlight from a part of the space I saw Richard Benning, for whose apparition I was prepared by having previously heard the low, sweet voice of Eva Maynard, whom also I now discerned, standing before him with one hand raised to his shoulder and her eyes, as nearly as I could judge, gazing upward into his. He held her disengaged hand and his head was bent with a singular dignity and grace. Their attitude was that of lovers, and as I stood in deep shadow to observe I felt even guiltier than on that memorable night in the wood. I was about to retire, when the girl spoke, and the contrast between her words and her attitude was so surprising that I remained, because I had merely forgotten to go away.

'You will take my life,' she said, 'as you did Pauline's. I know your intention as well as I know your power, and I ask nothing, only that you finish your work without needless delay and let me be at peace.'

He made no reply – merely let go the hand that he was holding, removed the other from his shoulder, and turning away descended the steps leading to the garden and disappeared in the shrubbery. But a moment later I heard, seemingly from a great distance, his fine clear voice in a barbaric chant, which as I listened brought before some inner spiritual sense a consciousness of some far, strange land peopled with beings having forbidden powers. The song held me in a kind of spell, but when it had died away I recovered and instantly perceived what I thought an opportunity. I walked out of my shadow to where the girl stood. She turned and stared at me with something of the look, it seemed to me, of a hunted hare. Possibly my intrusion had frightened her.

'Miss Maynard,' I said, 'I beg you to tell me who that man is and the nature of his power over you. Perhaps this is rude in me, but it is not a matter for idle civilities. When a woman is in danger any man has a right to act.'

She listened without visible emotion – almost I thought without interest, and when I had finished she closed her big blue eyes as if unspeakably weary.

'You can do nothing,' she said.

I took hold of her arm, gently shaking her as one shakes a person falling into a dangerous sleep.

'You must rouse yourself,' I said; 'something must be done and you must give me leave to act. You have said that that man killed your sister, and I believe it – that he will kill you, and I believe that.'

She merely raised her eyes to mine.

'Will you not tell me all?' I added.

'There is nothing to be done, I tell you – nothing. And if I could do anything I would not. It does not matter in the least. We shall be here only two days more; we go away then, oh, so far! If you have observed anything; I beg you to be silent.'

'But this is madness, girl.' I was trying by rough speech to break the deadly repose of her manner. 'You have accused him of murder. Unless you explain these things to me I shall lay the matter before the authorities.'

This roused her, but in a way that I did not like. She lifted her head proudly and said; 'Do not meddle, sir, in what does not concern you. This is my affair, Mr Moran, not yours.'

'It concerns every person in the country – in the world,' I answered, with equal coldness. 'If you had no love for your sister I, at least, am concerned for you.'

'Listen,' she interrupted, leaning toward me, 'I loved her, yes, God knows! But more than that – beyond all, beyond expression, I love *him*. You have overheard a secret, but you shall not make use of it to harm him. I shall deny all. Your word against mine – it will be that. Do you think your "authorities" will believe you?'

She was now smiling like an angel and, God help me! I was heels over head in love with her! Did she, by some of the many methods of divination known to her sex, read my feelings? Her whole manner had altered.

'Come,' she said, almost coaxingly, 'promise that you will not be impolite again.' She took my arm in the most friendly way. 'Come, I will walk with you. He will not know – he will remain away all night.'

Up and down the veranda we paced in the moonlight, she seemingly forgetting her recent bereavement, cooing and murmuring girl-wise of every kind of nothing in all Brownville; I silent, consciously awkward and with something of the feeling of being concerned in an intrigue. It was a revelation – this most charming and apparently blameless creature coolly and confessedly deceiving the man for whom a moment before she had acknowledged and shown the supreme love which finds even death an acceptable endearment.

'Truly,' I thought in my inexperience, 'here is something new under the moon.'

And the moon must have smiled.

Before we parted I had exacted a promise that she would walk with me the next afternoon – before going away forever – to the Old Mill, one of Brownville's revered antiquities, erected in 1860.

'If he is not about,' she added gravely, as I let go the hand she had given me at parting, and of which, may the good saints forgive me, I strove vainly to repossess myself when she had said it – so charming, as the wise Frenchman has pointed out, do we find women's infidelity when we are its objects, not its victims. In apportioning his benefactions that night the Angel of Sleep overlooked me.

The Brownville House dined early, and after dinner the next day Miss Maynard, who had not been at table, came to me on the veranda, attired in the demurest of walking costumes, saying not a word. 'He' was evidently 'not about.' We went slowly up the road that led to the Old Mill. She was apparently not strong and at times took my arm, relinquishing it and taking it again rather capriciously, I thought. Her mood, or rather her succession of moods, was as mutable as skylight in a rippling sea. She jested as if she had never heard of such a thing as death, and laughed on the lightest incitement, and directly afterward would sing a few bars of some grave melody with such tenderness of expression that I had to turn away my eyes lest she should see the evidence of her success in art, if art it was, not artlessness, as then I was compelled to think it. And she said the oddest things in the most unconventional way, skirting sometimes unfathomable abysms of thought, where I had hardly the courage to set foot. In short, she was fascinating in a thousand and fifty different ways, and at every step I executed a new and profounder emotional folly, a hardier spiritual indiscretion, incurring fresh liability to arrest by the constabulary of conscience for infractions of my own peace.

Arriving at the mill, she made no pretense of stopping, but turned into a trail leading through a field of stubble toward a creek. Crossing by a rustic bridge we continued on the trail, which now led uphill to one of the most picturesque spots in the country. The Eagle's Nest, it was called – the summit of a cliff that rose sheer into the air to a height of hundreds of feet above the forest at its base. From this elevated point we had a noble view of another valley and of the opposite hills flushed with the last rays of the setting sun. As we watched the light escaping to higher and higher planes from the encroaching flood of shadow filling the valley we heard footsteps, and in another moment were joined by Richard Benning.

'I saw you from the road,' he said carelessly; 'so I came up.'

Being a fool, I neglected to take him by the throat and pitch him into the treetops below, but muttered some polite lie instead. On the girl the effect of his coming was immediate and unmistakable. Her face was suffused with the glory of love's transfiguration: the red light of the sunset had not been more obvious in her eyes than was now the lovelight that replaced it.

'I am so glad you came!' she said, giving him both her hands; and, God help me! it was manifestly true.

Seating himself upon the ground he began a lively dissertation upon the wild flowers of the region, a number of which he had with him. In the middle of a facetious sentence he suddenly ceased speaking and fixed his eyes upon Eva, who leaned against the stump of a tree, absently plaiting grasses. She lifted her eyes in a startled way to his, as if she had *felt* his look. She then rose, cast away her grasses, and moved slowly away from him. He also rose, continuing to look at her. He had still in his hand the bunch of flowers. The girl turned, as if to speak, but said nothing. I recall clearly now something of which I was but half-conscious then – the dreadful contrast between the smile upon her lips and the terrified expression in her eyes as she met his steady and imperative gaze. I know nothing of how it happened, nor how it was that I did not sooner understand; I only know that with the smile of an angel upon her lips and that look of terror in her beautiful eyes Eva Maynard sprang from the cliff and shot crashing into the tops of the pines below!

How and how long afterward I reached the place I cannot say, but Richard Benning was already there, kneeling beside the dreadful thing that had been a woman.

'She is dead – quite dead,' he said coldly. 'I will go to town for assistance. Please do me the favor to remain.'

He rose to his feet and moved away, but in a moment had stopped and turned about.

'You have doubtless observed, my friend,' he said, 'that this was entirely her own act. I did not rise in time to prevent it, and you, not knowing her mental condition – you could not, of course, have suspected.'

His manner maddened me.

'You are as much her assassin,' I said, 'as if your damnable hands had cut her throat.'

He shrugged his shoulders without reply and, turning, walked away. A moment later I heard, through the deepening shadows of the wood into which he had disappeared, a rich, strong, baritone voice singing 'La donna e mobile,' from 'Rigoletto.'

The Famous Gilson Bequest

It was rough on Gilson. Such was the terse, cold, but not altogether unsympathetic judgment of the better public opinion at Mammon Hill – the dictum of respectability. The verdict of the opposite, or rather the opposing, element – the element that lurked red-eyed and restless about Moll Gurney's 'deadfall,' while respectability took it with sugar at Mr Jo. Bentley's gorgeous 'saloon' – was to pretty much the same general effect, though somewhat more ornately expressed by the use of picturesque expletives, which it is needless to quote. Virtually, Mammon Hill was a unit on the Gilson question. And it must be confessed that in a merely temporal sense all was not well with Mr Gilson. He had that morning been led into town by Mr Brentshaw and publicly charged with horse stealing; the sheriff meantime busying himself about The Tree with a new manila rope and Carpenter Pete being actively employed between drinks upon a pine box about the length and breadth of Mr Gilson. Society having rendered its verdict, there remained between Gilson and eternity only the decent formality of a trial.

These are the short and simple annals of the prisoner: He had recently been a resident of New Jerusalem, on the north fork of the Little Stony, but had come to the newly discovered placers of Mammon Hill immediately before the 'rush' by which the former place was depopulated. The discovery of the new diggings had occurred opportunely for Mr Gilson, for it had only just before been intimated to him by a New Jerusalem vigilance committee that it would better his prospects in, and for, life to go somewhere; and the list of places to which he could safely go did not include any of the older camps; so he naturally established himself at Mammon Hill. Being eventually followed thither by all his judges, he ordered his conduct with considerable circumspection, but as he had never been known to do an honest day's work at any industry sanctioned by the stern local code of morality except draw poker he was still an object of suspicion. Indeed, it was conjectured that he was the author of the many daring depredations that had recently been committed with pan and brush on the sluice boxes.

Prominent among those in whom this suspicion had ripened into a steadfast conviction was Mr Brentshaw. At all seasonable and unseasonable times Mr Brentshaw avowed his belief in Mr Gilson's connection with these unholy midnight enterprises, and his own willingness to prepare a way for the solar beams through the body of any one who might think it expedient to utter a different opinion – which, in his presence, no one was more careful not to do than the peace-loving person most concerned. Whatever may have been the truth of the matter, it is certain that Gilson frequently lost more 'clean dust' at Jo. Bentley's faro table than it was recorded in local history that he had ever honestly earned at draw poker in all the days of the camp's existence. But at last Mr Bentley – fearing, it may be to lose the more profitable patronage of Mr Brentshaw – peremptorily refused to let Gilson copper the queen, intimating at the same time, in his frank, forthright way, that the privilege of losing money at 'this bank' was a blessing appertaining to, proceeding logically from, and coterminous with, a condition of notorious commercial righteousness and social good repute.

The Hill thought it high time to look after a person whom its most honored citizen had felt it his duty to rebuke at a considerable personal sacrifice. The New Jerusalem contingent, particularly, began to abate something of the toleration begotten of amusement at their own, blunder in exiling an objectionable neighbor from the place which they had left to the place whither they had come. Mammon Hill was at last of one mind. Not much was said, but that Gilson must hang was 'in the air.' But at this critical juncture in his affairs he showed signs of an altered life if not a changed heart. Perhaps it was only that 'the bank' being closed against him he had no further use for gold dust. Anyhow the sluice boxes were molested no more forever. But it was impossible to repress the abounding energies of such a nature as his, and he continued, possibly from habit, the tortuous courses which he had pursued for profit of Mr Bentley. After a few tentative and resultless undertakings in the way of highway robbery – if one may venture to designate road-agency by so harsh a name – he made one or two modest essays in horse- herding, and it was in the midst of a promising enterprise of this character, and just as he had taken the tide in his affairs at its flood, that he made shipwreck. For on a misty, moonlight night Mr Brentshaw rode up alongside a person who was evidently leaving that part of the country, laid a hand upon the halter connecting Mr Gilson's wrist with Mr Harper's bay mare, tapped him familiarly on the cheek with the barrel of a navy revolver and requested the pleasure of his company in a direction opposite to that in which he was traveling.

It was indeed rough on Gilson.

On the morning after his arrest he was tried, convicted, and sentenced. It only remains, so far as concerns his earthly career, to hang him, reserving for more particular mention his last will and testament, which with great labor, he contrived in prison, and in which, probably from some confused and imperfect notion of the rights of captors, he bequeathed everything he owned to his 'lawfle execketer,' Mr Brentshaw. The bequest, however, was made conditional on the legatee taking the testator's body from the Tree and 'planting it white.'

So Mr Gilson was – I was about to say 'swung off,' but I fear there has been already something too much of slang in this straightforward statement of facts; besides, the manner in which the law took its course is more accurately described in the terms employed by the judge in passing sentence: Mr Gilson was 'strung up.'

In due season Mr Brentshaw, somewhat touched, it may well be, by the empty compliment of the bequest, repaired to The Tree to pluck the fruit thereof. When taken down the body was found to have in its waist-coat pocket a duly attested codicil to the will already noted. The nature of its provisions accounted for the manner in which it had been withheld, for had Mr Brentshaw previously been made aware of the conditions under which he was to succeed to the Gilson estate he would indubitably have declined the responsibility. Briefly stated, the purport of the codicil was as follows:

Whereas, at divers times and in sundry places, certain persons had asserted that during his life the testator had robbed their sluice boxes; therefore, if during the five years next succeeding the date of this instrument any one should make proof of such assertion before a court of law, such person was to receive as reparation the entire personal and real estate of which the testator died seized and possessed, minus the expenses of court and a stated compensation to the executor, Henry Clay Brentshaw; provided, that if more than one person made such proof the estate was to be equally divided between or among them. But in case none should succeed in so establishing the testator's guilt, then the whole property, minus court expenses, as aforesaid, should go to the said Henry Clay Brentshaw for his own use, as stated in the will.

The syntax of this remarkable document was perhaps open to critical objection, but that was clearly enough the meaning of it. The orthography conformed to no recognized system, but being mainly phonetic it was not ambiguous. As the probate judge remarked, it would take five aces to beat it. Mr Brentshaw smiled good-humoredly, and after performing the last sad rites with amusing ostentation, had himself duly sworn as executor and conditional legatee under the provisions of a law hastily passed (at the instance of the member from the Mammon Hill district) by a facetious legislature; which law was afterward discovered to have created also three or four lucrative offices and authorized the expenditure of a considerable sum of public money for the construction of a certain railway bridge that with greater advantage might perhaps have been erected on the line of some actual railway.

Of course Mr Brentshaw expected neither profit from the will nor litigation in consequence of its unusual provisions; Gilson, although frequently 'flush,' had been a man whom assessors and tax collectors were well satisfied to lose no money by. But a careless and merely formal search among his papers revealed title deeds to valuable estates in the East and certificates of deposit for incredible sums in banks less severely scrupulous than that of Mr Jo. Bentley.

The astounding news got abroad directly, throwing the Hill into a fever of excitement. The Mammon Hill *Patriot*, whose editor had been a leading spirit in the proceedings that resulted in Gilson's departure from New Jerusalem, published a most complimentary obituary notice of the deceased, and was good enough to call attention to the fact that his degraded contemporary, the Squaw Gulch *Clarion*, was bringing virtue into contempt by beslavering with flattery the memory of one who in life had spurned the vile sheet as a nuisance from his floor. Undeterred by the press, however, claimants under the will were not slow in presenting themselves with their evidence; and great as was the Gilson estate it appeared conspicuously paltry considering the vast number of sluice boxes from which it was averred to have been obtained. The country rose as one man!

Mr Brentshaw was equal to the emergency. With a shrewd application of humble auxiliary devices, he at once erected above the bones of his benefactor a costly monument, overtopping every rough headboard in the cemetery, and on this he judiciously caused to be inscribed an epitaph of his own composing, eulogizing the honesty, public spirit and cognate virtues of him who slept beneath, 'a victim to the unjust aspersions of Slander's viper brood.'

Moreover, he employed the best legal talent in the Territory to defend the memory of his departed friend, and for five long years the Territorial courts were occupied with litigation growing out of the Gilson bequest. To fine forensic abilities Mr Brentshaw opposed abilities more finely forensic; in bidding for purchasable favors he offered prices which utterly deranged the market; the judges found at his hospitable board entertainment for man and beast, the like of which had never been spread in the Territory; with mendacious witnesses he confronted witnesses of superior mendacity.

Nor was the battle confined to the temple of the blind goddess – it invaded the press, the pulpit, the drawing-room. It raged in the mart, the exchange, the school; in the gulches, and on the street corners. And upon the last day of the memorable period to which legal action under the Gilson will was limited, the sun went down upon a region in which the moral sense was dead, the social conscience callous, the intellectual capacity dwarfed, enfeebled, and con-fused! But Mr Brentshaw was victorious all along the line.

On that night it so happened that the cemetery in one corner of which lay the now honored ashes of the late Milton Gilson, Esq., was partly under water. Swollen by incessant rains, Cat Creek had spilled over its banks an angry flood which, after scooping out unsightly hollows wherever the soil had been disturbed, had partly subsided, as if ashamed of the sacrilege, leaving exposed much that had been piously concealed. Even the famous Gilson monument, the pride and glory of Mammon Hill, was no longer a standing rebuke to the 'viper brood'; succumbing to the sapping current it had toppled prone to earth. The ghoulish flood had exhumed the poor, decayed pine coffin, which now lay half-exposed, in pitiful contrast to the pompous monolith which, like a giant note of admiration, emphasized the disclosure.

To this depressing spot, drawn by some subtle influence he had sought neither to resist nor analyze, came Mr Brentshaw. An altered man was Mr Brentshaw. Five years of toil, anxiety, and wakefulness had dashed his black locks with streaks and patches of gray, bowed his fine figure, drawn sharp and angular his face, and debased his walk to a doddering shuffle. Nor had this lustrum of fierce contention wrought less upon his heart and intellect. The careless good humor that had prompted him to accept the trust of the dead man had given place to a fixed habit of melancholy. The firm, vigorous intellect had overripened into the mental mellowness of second childhood. His broad understanding had narrowed to the accommodation of a single idea; and in place of the quiet, cynical incredulity of former days, there was in him a haunting faith in the supernatural, that flitted and fluttered about his soul, shadowy, batlike, ominous of insanity. Unsettled in all else, his understanding clung to one conviction with the tenacity of a wrecked intellect. That was an unshaken belief in the entire blamelessness of the dead Gilson. He had so often sworn to this in court and asserted it in private conversation – had so frequently and so triumphantly established it by testimony that had come expensive to him (for that very day he had paid the last dollar of the Gilson estate to Mr Jo Bentley, the last witness to the Gilson good character) – that it had become to him a sort of religious faith. It seemed to him the one great central and basic truth of life – the sole serene verity in a world of lies.

On that night, as he seated himself pensively upon the prostrate monument, trying by the uncertain moonlight to spell out the epitaph which five years before he had composed with a chuckle that memory had not recorded, tears of remorse came into his eyes as he remembered that he had been mainly instrumental in compassing by a false accusation this good man's death; for during some of the legal proceedings, Mr Harper, for a consideration (forgotten) had come forward and sworn that in the little transaction with his bay mare the deceased had acted in strict accordance with the Harperian wishes, confidentially communicated to the deceased and by him faithfully concealed at the cost of his life. All that Mr Brentshaw had since done for the dead man's memory seemed pitifully inadequate – most mean, paltry, and debased with selfishness!

As he sat there, torturing himself with futile regrets, a faint shadow fell across his eyes. Looking toward the moon, hanging low in the west, he saw what seemed a vague, watery cloud obscuring her; but as it moved so that her beams lit up one side of it he perceived the clear, sharp outline of a human figure. The apparition became momentarily more distinct, and grew, visibly; it was drawing near. Dazed as were his senses, half locked up with terror and confounded with dreadful imaginings, Mr Brentshaw yet could but perceive, or think he perceived, in this unearthly shape a strange similitude to the mortal part of the late Milton Gilson, as that person had looked when taken from The Tree five years before. The likeness was indeed complete, even to the full, stony eyes, and a certain shadowy circle about the neck. It was without coat or hat, precisely as Gilson had been when laid in his poor, cheap casket by the not ungentle hands of Carpenter Pete – for whom some one had long since performed the same neighborly office. The specter, if such it was, seemed to bear something in its hands which Mr Brentshaw could not clearly make out. It drew nearer, and paused at last beside the coffin containing the ashes of the late Mr Gilson, the lid of which was awry, half disclosing the uncertain interior. Bending over this, the phantom seemed to shake into it from a basin some dark substance of dubious consistency, then glided stealthily back to the lowest part of the cemetery. Here the retiring flood had stranded a number of open coffins, about and among which it gurgled with low sobbings and stilly whispers. Stooping over one of these, the apparition carefully brushed its contents into the basin, then returning to its own casket, emptied the vessel into that, as before. This mysterious operation was repeated at every exposed coffin, the ghost sometimes dipping its laden basin into the running water, and gently agitating it to free it of the baser clay, always hoarding the residuium in its own private box. In short, the immortal part of the late Milton Gilson was cleaning up the dust of its neighbors and providently adding the same to its own.

Perhaps it was a phantasm of a disordered mind in a fevered body. Perhaps it was a solemn farce enacted by pranking existences that throng the shadows lying along the border of another world. God knows; to us is permitted only the knowledge that when the sun of another day touched with a grace of gold the ruined cemetery of Mammon Hill his kindliest beam fell upon the white, still face of Henry Brentshaw, dead among the dead.

The Applicant

Pushing his adventurous shins through the deep snow that had fallen overnight, and encouraged by the glee of his little sister, following in the open way that he made, a sturdy small boy, the son of Grayville's most distinguished citizen, struck his foot against something of which there was no visible sign on the surface of the snow. It is the purpose of this narrative to explain how it came to be there.

No one who has had the advantage of passing through Grayville by day can have failed to observe the large stone building crowning the low hill to the north of the railway station – that is to say, to the right in going toward Great Mowbray. It is a somewhat dull-looking edifice, of the Early Comatose order, and appears to have been designed by an architect who shrank from publicity, and although unable to conceal his work – even compelled, in this instance, to set it on an eminence in the sight of men – did what he honestly could to insure it against a second look. So far as concerns its outer and visible aspect, the Abersush Home for Old Men is unquestionably inhospitable to human attention. But it is a building of great magnitude, and cost its benevolent founder the profit of many a cargo of the teas and silks and spices that his ships brought up from the under-world when he was in trade in Boston; though the main expense was its endowment. Altogether, this reckless person had robbed his heirs-at-law of no less a sum than half a million dollars and flung it away in riotous giving. Possibly it was with a view to get out of sight of the silent big witness to his extravagance that he shortly afterward disposed of all his Grayville property that remained to him, turned his back upon the scene of his prodigality and went off across the sea in one of his own ships. But the gossips who got their inspiration most directly from Heaven declared that he went in search of a wife – a theory not easily reconciled with that of the village humorist, who solemnly averred that the bachelor philanthropist had departed this life (left Grayville, to wit) because the marriageable maidens had made it too hot to hold him. However this may have been, he had not returned, and although at long intervals there had come to Grayville, in a desultory way, vague rumors of his wanderings in strange lands, no one seemed certainly to know about him, and to the new generation he was no more than a name. But from above the portal of the Home for Old Men the name shouted in stone.

Despite its unpromising exterior, the Home is a fairly commodious place of retreat from the ills that its inmates have incurred by being poor and old and men. At the time embraced in this brief chronicle they were in number about a score, but in acerbity, querulousness, and general ingratitude they could hardly be reckoned at fewer than a hundred; at least that was the estimate of the superintendent, Mr Silas Tilbody. It was Mr Tilbody's steadfast conviction that always, in admitting new old men to replace those who had gone to another and a better Home, the trustees had distinctly in will the infraction of his peace, and the trial of his patience. In truth, the longer the institution was connected with him, the stronger was his feeling that the founder's scheme of benevolence was sadly impaired by providing any inmates at all. He had not much imagination, but with what he had he was addicted to the reconstruction of the Home for Old Men into a kind of 'castle in Spain,' with himself as castellan, hospitably entertaining about a score of sleek and prosperous middle-aged gentlemen, consummately good-humored and civilly willing to pay for their board and lodging. In this revised project of philanthrophy the trustees, to whom he was indebted for his office and responsible for his conduct, had not the happiness to appear. As to them, it was held by the village humorist aforementioned that in their management of the great charity Providence had thoughtfully supplied an incentive to thrift. With the inference which he expected to be drawn from that view we have nothing to do; it had neither support nor denial from the inmates, who certainly were most concerned. They lived out their little remnant of life, crept into graves neatly numbered, and were succeeded by other old men as like them as could be desired by the Adversary of Peace. If the Home was a place of punishment for the sin of unthrift the veteran offenders sought justice with a persistence that attested the sincerity of their penitence. It is to one of these that the reader's attention is now invited.

In the matter of attire this person was not altogether engaging. But for this season, which was midwinter, a careless observer might have looked upon him as a clever device of the husbandman indisposed to share the fruits of his toil with the crows that toil not, neither spin – an error that might not have been dispelled without longer and closer observation than he seemed to court; for his progress up Abersush Street, toward the Home in the gloom of the winter evening, was not visibly faster than what might have been expected of a scarecrow blessed with youth, health, and discontent. The man was indisputably ill-clad, yet not without a certain fitness and good taste, withal; for he was obviously an applicant for admittance to the Home, where poverty was a qualification. In the army of indigence the uniform is rags; they serve to distinguish the rank and file from the recruiting officers.

As the old man, entering the gate of the grounds, shuffled up the broad walk, already white with the fast-falling snow, which from time to time he feebly shook from its various coigns of vantage on his person, he came under inspection of the large globe lamp that burned always by night over the great door of the building. As if unwilling to incur its revealing beams, he turned to the left and, passing a considerable distance along the face of the building, rang at a smaller door emitting a dimmer ray that came from within, through the fanlight, and expended itself incuriously overhead. The door was opened by no less a personage than the great Mr Tilbody himself. Observing his vistor, who at once uncovered, and somewhat shortened the radius of the permanent curvature of his back, the great man gave visible token of neither surprise nor displeasure. Mr Tilbody was, indeed, in an uncommonly good humor, a phenomenon ascribable doubtless to the cheerful influence of the season; for this was Christmas Eve, and the morrow would be that blessed 365th part of the year that all Christian souls set apart for mighty feats of goodness and joy. Mr Tilbody was so full of the spirit of the season that his fat face and pale blue eyes, whose ineffectual fire served to distinguish it from an untimely summer squash, effused so genial a glow that it seemed a pity that he could not have lain down in it, basking in the consciousness of his own indentity. He was hatted, booted, overcoated, and umbrellaed, as became a person who was about to expose himself to the night and the storm on an errand of charity; for Mr Tilbody had just parted from his wife and children to go 'down town' and purchase the wherewithal to confirm the annual falsehood about the hunch-

bellied saint who frequents the chimneys to reward little boys and girls who
are good, and especially truthful. So he did not invite the old man in, but
saluted him cheerily:

'Hello! just in time; a moment later and you would have missed me. Come, I
have no time to waste; we'll walk a little way together.'

'Thank you,' said the old man, upon whose thin and white but not ignoble
face the light from the open door showed an expression that was perhaps
disappointment; 'but if the trustees – if my application – '

'The trustees,' Mr Tilbody said, closing more doors than one, and cutting
off two kinds of light, 'have agreed that your application disagrees with them.'

Certain sentiments are inappropriate to Christmastide, but Humor, like
Death, has all seasons for his own.

'Oh, my God!' cried the old man, in so thin and husky a tone that the
invocation was anything but impressive, and to at least one of his two auditors
sounded, indeed, somewhat ludicrous. To the Other – but that is a matter
which laymen are devoid of the light to expound.

'Yes,' continued Mr Tilbody, accommodating his gait to that of his
companion, who was mechanically, and not very successfully, retracing the
track that he had made through the snow; 'they have decided that, under the
circumstances – under the very peculiar circumstances, you understand – it
would be inexpedient to admit you. As superintendent and *ex officio* secretary
of the honorable board' – as Mr Tilbody 'read his title clear' the magnitude of
the big building, seen through its veil of falling snow, appeared to suffer
somewhat in comparison – 'it is my duty to inform you that, in the words of
Deacon Byram, the chairman, your presence in the Home would – under the
circumstances – be peculiarly embarrassing. I felt it my duty to submit to the
honorable board the statement that you made to me yesterday of your needs,
your physical condition, and the trials which it has pleased Providence to send
upon you in your very proper effort to present your claims in person; but,
after careful, and I may say prayerful, consideration of your case – with
something too, I trust, of the large charitableness appropriate to the season – it
was decided that we would not be justified in doing anything likely to impair
the usefulness of the institution intrusted (under Providence) to our care.'

They had now passed out of the grounds; the street lamp opposite the gate
was dimly visible through the snow. Already the old man's former track was
obliterated, and he seemed uncertain as to which way he should go. Mr
Tilbody had drawn a little away from him, but paused and turned half toward
him, apparently reluctant to forego the continuing opportunity.

'Under the circumstances,' he resumed, 'the decision – '

But the old man was inaccessible to the suasion of his verbosity; he had
crossed the street into a vacant lot and was going forward, rather deviously
toward nowhere in particular – which, he having nowhere in particular to go
to, was not so reasonless a proceeding as it looked.

And that is how it happened that the next morning, when the church bells of
all Grayville were ringing with an added unction appropriate to the day, the
sturdy little son of Deacon Byram, breaking a way through the snow to the
place of worship, struck his foot against the body of Amasa Abersush,
philanthropist.

A Watcher by the Dead

In an upper room of an unoccupied dwelling in the part of San Francisco known as North Beach lay the body of a man, under a sheet. The hour was near nine in the evening; the room was dimly lighted by a single candle. Although the weather was warm, the two windows, contrary to the custom which gives the dead plenty of air, were closed and the blinds drawn down. The furniture of the room consisted of but three pieces – an arm-chair, a small reading-stand supporting the candle, and a long kitchen table, supporting the body of the man. All these, as also the corpse, seemed to have been recently brought in, for an observer, had there been one, would have seen that all were free from dust, whereas everything else in the room was pretty thickly coated with it, and there were cobwebs in the angles of the walls.

Under the sheet the outlines of the body could be traced, even the features, these having that unnaturally sharp definition which seems to belong to faces of the dead, but is really characteristic of those only that have been wasted by disease. From the silence of the room one would rightly have inferred that it was not in the front of the house, facing a street. It really faced nothing but a high breast of rock, the rear of the building being set into a hill.

As a neighboring church clock was striking nine with an indolence which seemed to imply such an indifference to the flight of time that one could hardly help wondering why it took the trouble to strike at all, the single door of the room was opened and a man entered, advancing toward the body. As he did so the door closed, apparently of its own volition; there was a grating, as of a key turned with difficulty, and the snap of the lock bolt as it shot into its socket. A sound of retiring footsteps in the passage outside ensued, and the man was to all appearance a prisoner. Advancing to the table, he stood a moment looking down at the body; then with a slight shrug of the shoulders walked over to one of the windows and hoisted the blind. The darkness outside was absolute, the panes were covered with dust, but by wiping this away he could see that the window was fortified with strong iron bars crossing it within a few inches of the glass and imbedded in the masonry on each side. He examined the other window. It was the same. He manifested no great curiosity in the matter, did not even so much as raise the sash. If he was a prisoner he was apparently a tractable one. Having completed his examination of the room, he seated himself in the arm-chair, took a book from his pocket, drew the stand with its candle alongside and began to read.

The man was young – not more than thirty – dark in complexion, smooth-shaven, with brown hair. His face was thin and high-nosed, with a broad forehead and a 'firmness' of the chin and jaw which is said by those having it to denote resolution. The eyes were gray and steadfast, not moving except with definitive purpose. They were now for the greater part of the time fixed upon the book, but he occasionally withdrew them and turned them to the body on the table, not, apparently, from any dismal fascination which under such circumstances it might be supposed to exercise upon even a courageous person, nor with a conscious rebellion against the contrary influence which might dominate a timid one. He looked at it as if in his reading he had come upon something recalling him to a sense of his surroundings. Clearly this watcher by the dead was discharging his trust with intelligence and compo- sure, as became him.

After reading for perhaps a half-hour he seemed to come to the end of a chapter and quietly laid away the book. He then rose and taking the reading- stand from the floor carried it into a corner of the room near one of the windows, lifted the candle from it and returned to the empty fireplace before which he had been sitting.

A moment later he walked over to the body on the table, lifted the sheet and turned it back from the head, exposing a mass of dark hair and a thin face- cloth, beneath which the features showed with even sharper definition than before. Shading his eyes by interposing his free hand between them and the candle, he stood looking at his motionless companion with a serious and tranquil regard. Satisfied with his inspection, he pulled the sheet over the face again and returning to the chair, took some matches off the candlestick, put them in the side pocket of his sack-coat and sat down. He then lifted the candle from its socket and looked at it critically, as if calculating how long it would last. It was barely two inches long; in another hour he would be in darkness. He replaced it in the candlestick and blew it out.

II

In a physician's office in Kearny Street three men sat about a table, drinking punch and smoking. It was late in the evening, almost midnight, indeed, and there had been no lack of punch. The gravest of the three, Dr Helberson, was the host – it was in his rooms they sat. He was about thirty years of age; the others were even younger; all were physicians.

'The superstitious awe with which the living regard the dead,' said Dr Helberson, 'is hereditary and incurable. One needs no more be ashamed of it than of the fact that he inherits, for example, an incapacity for mathematics, or a tendency to lie.'

The others laughed. 'Oughtn't a man to be ashamed to lie?' asked the youngest of the three, who was in fact a medical student not yet graduated.

'My dear Harper, I said nothing about that. The tendency to lie is one thing; lying is another.'

'But do you think,' said the third man, 'that this superstitious feeling, this fear of the dead, reasonless as we know it to be, is universal? I am myself not conscious of it.'

'Oh, but it is "in your system" for all that,' replied Helberson; 'it needs only the right conditions – what Shakespeare calls the "confederate season" – to manifest itself in some very disagreeable way that will open your eyes. Physicians and soldiers are of course more nearly free from it than others.'

'Physicians and soldiers! – why don't you add hangmen and headsmen? Let us have in all the assassin classes.'

'No, my dear Mancher; the juries will not let the public executioners acquire sufficient familiarity with death to be altogether unmoved by it.'

Young Harper, who had been helping himself to a fresh cigar at the sideboard, resumed his seat. 'What would you consider conditions under which any man of woman born would become insupportably conscious of his share of our common weakness in this regard?' he asked, rather verbosely.

'Well, I should say that if a man were locked up all night with a corpse – alone – in a dark room – of a vacant house – with no bed covers to pull over his head – and lived through it without going altogether mad, he might justly boast himself not of woman born, nor yet, like Macduff, a product of Cæsarean section.'

'I thought you never would finish piling up conditions,' said Harper, 'but I know a man who is neither a physician nor a soldier who will accept them all, for any stake you like to name.'

'Who is he?'

'His name is Jarette – a stranger here; comes from my town in New York. I have no money to back him, but he will back himself with loads of it.'

'How do you know that?'

'He would rather bet than eat. As for fear – I dare say he thinks it some cutaneous disorder, or possibly a particular kind of religious heresy.'

'What does he look like?' Helberson was evidently becoming interested.

'Like Mancher, here – might be his twin brother.'

'I accept the challenge,' said Helberson, promptly.

'Awfully obliged to you for the compliment, I'm sure,' drawled Mancher, who was growing sleepy. 'Can't I get into this?'

'Not against me,' Helberson said. 'I don't want *your* money.'

'All right,' said Mancher; 'I'll be the corpse.'

The others laughed.

The outcome of this crazy conversation we have seen.

III

In extinguishing his meagre allowance of candle Mr Jarette's object was to preserve it against some unforeseen need. He may have thought, too, or half thought, that the darkness would be no worse at one time than another, and if the situation became insupportable it would be better to have a means of relief, or even release. At any rate it was wise to have a little reserve of light, even if only to enable him to look at his watch.

No sooner had he blown out the candle and set it on the floor at his side than he settled himself comfortably in the arm-chair, leaned back and closed his eyes, hoping and expecting to sleep. In this he was disappointed; he had never in his life felt less sleepy, and in a few minutes he gave up the attempt. But what could he do? He could not go groping about in absolute darkness at the risk of bruising himself – at the risk, too, of blundering against the table and rudely disturbing the dead. We all recognize their right to lie at rest, with immunity from all that is harsh and violent. Jarette almost succeeded in making himself believe that considerations of this kind restrained him from risking the collision and fixed him to the chair.

While thinking of this matter he fancied that he heard a faint sound in the direction of the table – what kind of sound he could hardly have explained. He did not turn his head. Why should he – in the darkness? But he listened – why should he not? And listening he grew giddy and grasped the arms of the chair for support. There was a strange ringing in his ears; his head seemed bursting; his chest was oppressed by the constriction of his clothing. He wondered why it was so, and whether these were symptoms of fear. Then, with a long and strong expiration, his chest appeared to collapse, and with the great gasp with which he refilled his exhausted lungs the vertigo left him and he knew that so intently had he listened that he had held his breath almost to suffocation. The revelation was vexatious; he rose, pushed away the chair with his foot and strode to the center of the room. But one does not stride far in darkness; he began to grope, and finding the wall followed it to an angle, turned, followed it past the two windows and there in another corner came into violent contact with the reading-stand, overturning it. It made a clatter that startled him. He was annoyed. 'How the devil could I have forgotten where it was?' he muttered, and groped his way along the third wall to the fireplace. 'I must put things to rights,' said he, feeling the floor for the candle.

Having recovered that, he lighted it and instantly turned his eyes to the table, where, naturally, nothing had undergone any change. The reading-stand lay unobserved upon the floor; he had forgotten to 'put it to rights.' He looked all about the room, dispersing the deeper shadows by movements of the candle in his hand, and crossing over to the door tested it by turning and pulling the knob with all his strength. It did not yield and this seemed to afford him a certain satisfaction; indeed, he secured it more firmly by a bolt which he had not before observed. Returning to his chair, he looked at his watch; it was half-past nine. With a start of surpirse he held the watch at his ear. It had not stopped. The candle was now visibly shorter. He again extinguished it, placing it on the floor at his side as before.

Mr Jarette was not at his ease; he was distinctly dissatisfied with his surroundings, and with himself for being so. 'What have I to fear?' he thought. 'This is ridiculous and disgraceful; I will not be so great a fool.' But courage does not come of saying, 'I will be courageous,' nor of recognizing its appropriateness to the occasion. The more Jarette condemned himself, the more reason he gave himself for condemnation; the greater the number of variations which he played upon the simple theme of the harmlessness of the dead, the more insupportable grew the discord of his emotions. 'What!' he cried aloud in the anguish of his spirit, 'what! shall I, who have not a shade of superstition in my nature – I, who have no belief in immortality – I, who know (and never more clearly than now) that the after-life is the dream of a desire – shall I lose at once my bet, my honor and my self-respect, perhaps my reason, because certain savage ancestors dwelling in caves and burrows conceived the monstrous notion that the dead walk by night? – that –' Distinctly, unmistakably, Mr Jarette heard behind him a light, soft sound of footfalls, deliberate, regular, successively nearer!

IV

Just before daybreak the next morning Dr Helberson and his young friend Harper were driving slowly through the streets of North Beach in the doctor's coupé.

'Have you still the confidence of youth in the courage or stolidity of your friend?' said the elder man. 'Do you believe that I have lost this wager?'

'I *know* you have,' replied the other, with enfeebling emphasis.

'Well, upon my soul, I hope so.'

It was spoken earnestly, almost solemnly. There was a silence for a few moments.

'Harper,' the doctor resumed, looking very serious in the shifting half-lights that entered the carriage as they passed the street lamps, 'I don't feel altogether comfortable about this business. If your friend had not irritated me by the contemptuous manner in which he treated my doubt of his endurance – a purely physical quality – and by the cool incivility of his suggestion that the corpse be that of a physician, I should not have gone on with it. If anything should happen we are ruined, as I fear we deserve to be.'

'What can happen? Even if the matter should be taking a serious turn, of which I am not at all afraid, Mancher has only to "resurrect" himself and explain matters. With a genuine "subject" from the dissecting room, or one of your late patients, it might be different.'

Dr Mancher, then, had been as good as his promise; he was the 'corpse.'

Dr Helberson was silent for a long time, as the carriage, at a snail's pace, crept along the same street it had traveled two or three times already. Presently he spoke: 'Well, let us hope that Mancher, if he has had to rise from the dead, has been discreet about it. A mistake in that might make matters worse instead of better.'

'Yes,' said Harper, 'Jarette would kill him. But, Doctor' – looking at his watch as the carriage passed a gas lamp – 'It is nearly four o'clock at last.'

A moment later the two had quitted the vehicle and were walking briskly toward the long unoccupied house belonging to the doctor in which they had immured Mr Jarette in accordance with the terms of the mad wager. As they neared it they met a man running. 'Can you tell me,' he cried, suddenly checking his speed, 'where I can find a doctor?'

'What's the matter?' Helberson asked, non-committal.

'Go and see for yourself,' said the man, resuming his running.

They hastened on. Arrived at the house, they saw several persons entering in haste and excitement. In some of the dwellings near by and across the way the chamber windows were thrown up, showing a protrusion of heads. All heads were asking questions, none heeding the questions of the others. A few of the windows with closed blinds were illuminated; the inmates of those rooms were dressing to come down. Exactly opposite the door of the house that they sought a street lamp threw a yellow, insufficient light upon the scene, seeming to say that it could disclose a good deal more if it wished. Harper paused at the door and laid a hand upon his companion's arm. 'It is all up with us, Doctor,' he said in extreme agitation, which contrasted strangely with his free-and-easy words; 'the game has gone against us all. Let's not go in there; I'm for lying low.'

'I'm a physician,' said Dr Helberson, calmly; 'there may be need of one.'

They mounted the doorsteps and were about to enter. The door was open; the street lamp opposite lighted the passage into which it opened. It was full of men. Some had ascended the stairs at the farther end, and denied admittance above, waited for better fortune. All were talking, none listening. Suddenly, on the upper landing there was a great commotion; a man had sprung out of a door and was breaking away from those endeavoring to detain him. Down through the mass of affrighted idlers he came, pushing them aside, flattening them against the wall on one side, or compelling them to cling to the rail on the other, clutching them by the throat, striking them savagely, thrusting them back down the stairs and walking over the fallen. His clothing was in disorder, he was without a hat. His eyes, wild and restless, had in them something more terrifying than his apparently superhuman strength. His face, smooth-shaven, was bloodless, his hair frost-white.

As the crowd at the foot of the stairs, having more freedom, fell away to let him pass Harper sprang forward. 'Jarette! Jarette!' he cried.

Dr Helberson seized Harper by the collar and dragged him back. The man looked into their faces without seeming to see them and sprang through the door, down the steps, into the street, and away. A stout policeman, who had had inferior success in conquering his way down the stairway, followed a moment later and started in pursuit, all the heads in the windows – those of women and children now – screaming in guidance.

The stairway being now partly cleared, most of the crowd having rushed down to the street to observe the flight and pursuit, Dr Helberson mounted to the landing, followed by Harper. At a door in the upper passage an officer denied them admittance. 'We are physicians,' said the doctor, and they passed in. The room was full of men, dimly seen, crowded about a table. The newcomers edged their way forward and looked over the shoulders of those in the front rank. Upon the table, the lower limbs covered with a sheet, lay the body of a man, brilliantly illuminated by the beam of a bull's-eye lantern held by a policeman standing at the feet. The others, excepting those near the head – the officer himself – all were in darkness. The face of the body showed yellow, repulsive, horrible! The eyes were partly open and upturned and the jaw fallen; traces of froth defiled the lips, the chin, the cheeks. A tall man, evidently a doctor, bent over the body with his hand thrust under the shirt front. He withdrew it and placed two fingers in the open mouth. 'This man has been about six hours dead,' said he. 'It is a case for the coroner.'

He drew a card from his pocket, handed it to the officer and made his way toward the door.

'Clear the room – out, all!' said the officer, sharply, and the body disappeared as if it had been snatched away, as shifting the lantern he flashed its beam of light here and there against the faces of the crowd. The effect was amazing! The men, blinded, confused, almost terrified, made a tumultuous rush for the door, pushing, crowding, and tumbling over one another as they fled, like the hosts of Night before the shafts of Apollo. Upon the struggling, trampling mass the officer poured his light without pity and without cessation. Caught in the current, Helberson and Harper were swept out of the room and cascaded down the stairs into the street.

'Good God, Doctor! did I not tell you that Jarette would kill him?' said Harper, as soon as they were clear of the crowd.

'I believe you did,' replied the other, without apparent emotion.

They walked on in silence, block after block. Against the graying east the dwellings of the hill tribes showed in silhouette. The familiar milk wagon was already astir in the steets; the baker's man would soon come upon the scene, the newspaper carrier was abroad in the land.

'It strikes me, youngster,' said Helberson, 'that you and I have been having too much of the morning air lately. It is unwholesome; we need a change.

What do you say to a tour in Europe?'

'When?'

'I'm not particular. I should suppose that four o'clock this afternoon would be early enough.'

'I'll meet you at the boat,' said Harper.

V

Seven years afterward these two men sat upon a bench in Madison Square, New York, in familiar conversation. Another man, who had been observing them for some time, himself unobserved, approached and, courteously lifting his hat from locks as white as frost, said: 'I beg your pardon, gentlemen, but when you have killed a man by coming to life, it is best to change clothes with him, and at the first opportunity make a break for liberty.'

Helberson and Harper exchanged significant glances. They were obviously amused. The former then looked the stranger kindly in the eye and replied:

'That has always been my plan. I entirely agree with you as to its advant – '

He stopped suddenly, rose and went white. He stared at the man, open-mouthed; he trembled visibly.

'Ah!', said the stranger, 'I see that you are indisposed, Doctor. If you cannot treat yourself Dr Harper can do something for you, I am sure.'

'Who the devil are you?' said Harper, bluntly.

The stranger came nearer and, bending toward them, said in a whisper: 'I call myself Jarette sometimes, but I don't mind telling you, for old friendship, that I am Dr William Mancher'

The revelation brought Harper to his feet. 'Mancher!' he cried; and Helberson added: 'It is true, by God!'

'Yes,' said the stranger, smiling vaguely, 'it is true enough, no doubt.'

He hesitated and seemed to be trying to recall something, then began humming a popular air. He had apparently forgotten their presence.

'Look here, Mancher,' said the elder of the two, 'tell us just what occurred that night – to Jarette, you know.'

'Oh, yes, about Jarette,' said the other. 'It's odd I should have neglected to tell you – I tell it so often. You see I knew, by overhearing him talking to himself, that he was pretty badly frightened. So I couldn't resist the temptation to come to life and have a bit of fun out of him – I couldn't really. That was all right, though certainly I did not think he would take it so seriously; I did not, truly. And afterward – well, it was a tough job changing places with him, and then – damn you! you didn't let me out!'

Nothing could exceed the ferocity with which these last words were delivered. Both men stepped back in alarm.

'We? – why – why,' Helberson stammered, losing his self-possession utterly, 'we had nothing to do with it.'

'Didn't I say you were Drs Hell-born and Sharper?' inquired the man, laughing.

'My name is Helberson, yes; and this gentleman is Mr Harper,' replied the former, reassured by the laugh. 'But we are not physicians now; we are – well, hang it, old man, we are gamblers.'

And that was the truth.

'A very good profession – very good, indeed; and, by the way, I hope Sharper here paid over Jarette's money like an honest stakeholder. A very good and honorable profession,' he repeated, thoughtfully, moving carelessly away; 'but I stick to the old one. I am High Supreme Medical Officer of the Bloomingdale Asylum; it is my duty to cure the superintendent.'

The Man and the Snake

It is of veritabyll report, and attested of so many that there be nowe of wyse and learned none to gaynsaye it, that ye serpente hys eye hath a magnetick propertie that whosoe falleth into its svasion is drawn forwards in despyte of his wille, and perisheth miserabyll by ye creature hys byte.

Stretched at ease upon a sofa, in gown and slippers, Harker Brayton smiled as he read the foregoing sentence in old Morryster's *Marvells of Science*. 'The only marvel in the matter,' he said to himself, 'is that the wise and learned in Morryster's day should have believed such nonsense as is rejected by most of even the ignorant in ours.'

A train of reflection followed – for Brayton was a man of thought – and he unconsciously lowered his book without altering the direction of his eyes. As soon as the volume had gone below the line of sight, something in an obscure corner of the room recalled his attention to his surroundings. What he saw, in the shadow under his bed, was two small points of light, apparently about an inch apart. They might have been reflections of the gas jet above him, in metal nail heads; he gave them but little thought and resumed his reading. A moment later something – some impulse which it did not occur to him to analyze – impelled him to lower the book again and seek for what he saw before. The points of light were still there. They seemed to have become brighter than before, shining with a greenish lustre that he had not at first observed. He thought, too, that they might have moved a trifle – were somewhat nearer. They were still too much in shadow, however, to reveal their nature and origin to an indolent attention, and again he resumed his reading. Suddenly something in the text suggested a thought that made him start and drop the book for the third time to the side of the sofa, whence, escaping from his hand, it fell sprawling to the floor, back upward. Brayton, half-risen, was staring intently into the obscurity beneath the bed, where the points of light shone with, it seemed to him, an added fire. His attention was now fully aroused, his gaze eager and imperative. It disclosed, almost directly under the foot-rail of the bed, the coils of a large serpent – the points of light were its eyes! Its horrible head, thrust flatly forth from the innermost coil and resting upon the outermost, was directed straight toward him, the definition of the wide, brutal jaw and the idiot-like forehead serving to show the direction of its malevolent gaze. The eyes were no longer merely luminous points; they looked into his own with a meaning, a malign significance.

II

A snake in a bedroom of a modern city dwelling of the better sort is, happily, not so common a phenomenon as to make explanation altogether needless. Harker Brayton, a bachelor of thirty-five, a scholar, idler and something of an athlete, rich, popular and of sound health, had returned to San Francisco from all manner of remote and unfamiliar countries. His tastes, always a trifle luxurious, had taken on an added exuberance from long privation; and the resources of even the Castle Hotel being inadequate to their perfect gratification, he had gladly accepted the hospitality of his friend, Dr Druring, the distinguished scientist. Dr Druring's house, a large, old-fashioned one in what is now an obscure quarter of the city, had an outer and visible aspect of proud reserve. It plainly would not associate with the contiguous elements of its altered enviroment, and appeared to have developed some of the eccentricities which come of isolation. One of these was a 'wing,' conspicuously irrelevant in point of architecture, and no less rebellious in matter of purpose; for it was a combination of laboratory, menagerie and museum. It was here that the doctor indulged the scientific side of his nature in the study of such forms of animal life as engaged his interest and comforted his taste – which, it must be confessed, ran rather to the lower types. For one of the higher nimbly and sweetly to recommend itself unto his gentle senses it had at least to retain certain rudimentary characteristics allying it to such 'dragons of the prime' as toads and snakes. His scientific sympathies were distinctly reptilian; he loved nature's vulgarians and described himself as the Zola of zoölogy. His wife and daughters not having the advantage to share his enlightened curiosity regarding the works and ways of our ill-starred fellow-creatures, were with needless austerity excluded from what he called the Snakery and doomed to companionship with their own kind, though to soften the rigors of their lot he had permitted them out of his great wealth to outdo the reptiles in the gorgeousness of their surroundings and to shine with a superior splendor.

Architecturally and in point of 'furnishing' the Snakery had a severe simplicity befitting the humble circumstances of its occupants, many of whom, indeed, could not safely have been intrusted with the liberty that is necessary to the full enjoyment of luxury, for they had the troublesome peculiarity of being alive. In their own apartments, however, they were under as little personal restraint as was compatible with their protection from the baneful habit of swallowing one another; and, as Brayton had thoughtfully been apprised, it was more than a tradition that some of them had at divers times been found in parts of the premises where it would have embarrassed them to explain their presence. Despite the Snakery and its uncanny associations – to which, indeed, he gave little attention – Brayton found life at the Druring mansion very much to his mind.

III

Beyond a smart shock of surprise and a shudder of mere loathing Mr Brayton was not greatly affected. His first thought was to ring the call bell and bring a servant; but although the bell cord dangled within easy reach he made no movement toward it; it had occurred to his mind that the act might subject him to the suspicion of fear, which he certainly did not feel. He was more keenly conscious of the incongruous nature of the situation than affected by its perils; it was revolting, but absurd.

The reptile was of a species with which Brayton was unfamiliar. Its length he could only conjecture; the body at the largest visible part seemed about as thick as his forearm. In what way was it dangerous, if in any way? Was it venomous? Was it a constrictor? His knowledge of nature's danger signals did not enable him to say; he had never deciphered the code.

If not dangerous the creature was at least offensive. It was *de trop* – 'matter out of place' – an impertinence. The gem was unworthy of the setting. Even the barbarous taste of our time and country, which had loaded the walls of the room with pictures, the floor with furniture and the furniture with bric-a-brac, had not quite fitted the place for this bit of the savage life of the jungle. Besides – insupportable thought! – the exhalations of its breath mingled with the atmosphere which he himself was breathing.

These thoughts shaped themselves with greater or less definition in Brayton's mind and begot action. The process is what we call consideration and decision. It is thus that we are wise and unwise. It is thus that the withered leaf in an autumn breeze shows greater or less intelligence than its fellows, falling upon the land or upon the lake. The secret of human action is an open one; something contracts our muscles. Does it matter if we give to the preparatory molecular changes the name of will?

Brayton rose to his feet and prepared to back softly away from the snake, without disturbing it if possible, and through the door. Men retire so from the presence of the great, for greatness is power and power is a menace. He knew that he could walk backward without error. Should the monster follow, the taste which had plastered the walls with paintings had consistently supplied a rack of murderous Oriental weapons from which he could snatch one to suit the occasion. In the mean time the snake's eyes burned with a more pitiless malevolence than before.

Brayton lifted his right foot free of the floor to step backward. That moment he felt a strong aversion to doing so.

'I am accounted brave,' he thought; 'is bravery, then, no more than pride? Because there are none to witness the shame shall I retreat?'

He was steadying himself with his right hand upon the back of a chair, his foot suspended.

'Nonsense!' he said aloud; 'I am not so great a coward as to fear to seem to myself afraid.'

He lifted the foot a little higher by slightly bending the knee and thrust it sharply to the floor – an inch in front of the other! He could not think how that occurred. A trial with the left foot had the same result; it was again in advance of the right. The hand upon the chair back was grasping it; the arm was straight, reaching somewhat backward. One might have said that he was reluctant to lose his hold. The snake's malignant head was still thrust forth from the inner coil as before, the neck level. It had not moved, but its eyes were now electric sparks, radiating an infinity of luminous needles.

The man had an ashy pallor. Again he took a step forward, and another, partly dragging the chair, which when finally released fell upon the floor with a crash. The man groaned; the snake made neither sound nor motion, but its eyes were two dazzling suns. The reptile itself was wholly concealed by them. They gave off enlarging rings of rich and vivid colors, which at their greatest expansion successively vanished like soap-bubbles; they seemed to approach his very face, and anon were an immeasurable distance away. He heard, somewhere, the continuous throbbing of a great drum, with desultory bursts of far music, inconceivably sweet, like the tones of an æolian harp. He knew it for the sunrise melody of Memnon's statue, and thought he stood in the

Nileside reeds hearing with exalted sense that immortal anthem through the silence of the centuries.

The music ceased; rather, it became by insensible degrees the distant roll of a retreating thunder-storm. A landscape, glittering with sun and rain, stretched before him, arched with a vivid rainbow framing in its giant curve a hundred visible cities. In the middle distance a vast serpent, wearing a crown, reared its head out of its voluminous convolutions and looked at him with his dead mother's eyes. Suddenly this enchanting landscape seemed to rise swiftly upward like the drop scene at a theatre, and vanished in a blank. Something struck him a hard blow upon the face and breast. He had fallen to the floor; the blood ran from his broken nose and his bruised lips. For a time he was dazed and stunned, and lay with closed eyes, his face against the floor. In a few moments he had recovered, and then knew that this fall, by withdrawing his eyes, had broken the spell that held him. He felt that now, by keeping his gaze averted, he would be able to retreat. But the thought of the serpent within a few feet of his head, yet unseen – perhaps in the very act of springing upon him and throwing its coils about his throat – was too horrible! He lifted his head, stared again into those baleful eyes and was again in bondage.

The snake had not moved and appeared somewhat to have lost its power upon the imagination; the gorgeous illusions of a few moments before were not repeated. Beneath that flat and brainless brow its black, beady eyes simply glittered as at first with an expression unspeakably malignant. It was as if the creature, assured of its triumph, had determined to practise no more alluring wiles.

Now ensued a fearful scene. The man, prone upon the floor, within a yard of his enemy, raised the upper part of his body upon his elbows, his head thrown back, his legs extended to their full length. His face was white between its stains of blood; his eyes were strained open to their uttermost expansion. There was froth upon his lips; it dropped off in flakes. Strong convulsions ran through his body, making almost serpentile undulations. He bent himself at the waist, shifting his legs from side to side. And every movement left him a little nearer to the snake. He thrust his hands forward to brace himself back, yet constantly advanced upon his elbows.

IV

Dr Druring and his wife sat in the library. The scientist was in rare good humor.

'I have just obtained by exchange with another collector,' he said, 'a splendid specimen of the *ophiophagus*.'

'And what may that be?' the lady inquired with a somewhat languid interest.

'Why, bless my soul, what profound ignorance! My dear, a man who ascertains after marriage that his wife does not know Greek is entitled to a divorce. The *ophiophagus* is a snake that eats other snakes.'

'I hope it will eat all yours,' she said, absently shifting the lamp. 'But how does it get the other snakes? By charming them, I suppose.'

'That is just like you, dear,' said the doctor, with an affectation of petulance. 'You know how irritating to me is any allusion to that vulgar superstition about a snake's power of fascination.'

The conversation was interrupted by a mighty cry, which rang through the silent house like the voice of a demon shouting in a tomb! Again and yet again it sounded, with terrible distinctness. They sprang to their feet, the man confused, the lady pale and speechless with fright. Almost before the echoes of the last cry had died away the doctor was out of the room, springing up the stairs two steps at a time. In the corridor in front of Brayton's chamber he met some servants who had come from the upper floor. Together they rushed at the door without knocking. It was unfastened and gave way. Brayton lay upon his stomach on the floor, dead. His head and arms were partly concealed under the foot rail of the bed. They pulled the body away, turning it upon the back. The face was daubed with blood and froth, the eyes were wide open, staring – a dreadful sight!

'Died in a fit,' said the scientist, bending his knee and placing his hand upon the heart. While in that position, he chanced to look under the bed. 'Good God!' he added, 'how did this thing get in here?'

He reached under the bed, pulled out the snake and flung it, still coiled, to the center of the room, whence with a harsh, shuffling sound it slid across the polished floor till stopped by the wall, where it lay without motion. It was a stuffed snake; its eyes were two shoe buttons.

A Holy Terror

I

There was an entire lack of interest in the latest arrival at Hurdy-Gurdy. He was not even christened with the picturesquely descriptive nick-name which is so frequently a mining camp's word of welcome to the newcomer. In almost any other camp thereabout this circumstance would of itself have secured him some such appellation as 'The White-headed Conundrum,' or 'No Sarvey' – an expression naïvely supposed to suggest to quick intelligences the Spanish *quien sabe*. He came without provoking a ripple of concern upon the social surface of Hurdy-Gurdy – a place which to the general Californian contempt of men's personal history superadded a local indifference of its own. The time was long past when it was of any importance who came there, or if anybody came. No one was living at Hurdy-Gurdy.

Two years before, the camp had boasted a stirring population of two or three thousand males and not fewer than a dozen females. A majority of the former had done a few week's earnest work in demonstrating, to the disgust of the latter, the singularly mendacious character of the person whose ingenious tales of rich gold deposits had lured them thither – work, by the way, in which there was as little mental satisfaction as pecuniary profit; for a bullet from the pistol of a public-spirited citizen had put that imaginative gentleman beyond the reach of aspersion on the third day of the camp's existence. Still, his fiction had a certain foundation in fact, and many had lingered a considerable time in and about Hurdy-Gurdy, though now all had been long gone.

But they had left ample evidence of their sojourn. From the point where Injun Creek falls into the Rio San Juan Smith, up along both banks of the former into the cañon whence it emerges, extended a double row of forlorn shanties that seemed about to fall upon one another's neck to bewail their desolation; while about an equal number appeared to have straggled up the slope on either hand and perched themselves upon commanding eminences, whence they craned forward to get a good view of the affecting scene. Most of these habitations were emaciated as by famine to the condition of mere skeletons, about which clung unlovely tatters of what might have been skin, but was really canvas. The little valley itself, torn and gashed by pick and shovel, was unhandsome with long, bending lines of decaying flume resting here and there upon the summits of sharp ridges, and stilting awkwardly across the intervals upon unhewn poles. The whole place presented that raw and forbidding aspect of arrested development which is a new country's substitute for the solemn grace of ruin wrought by time. Wherever there remained a patch of the original soil a rank overgrowth of weeds and brambles had spread upon the scene, and from its dank, unwholesome shades a visitor curious in such matters might have obtained numberless souvenirs of the camp's former glory – fellowless boots mantled with green mould and plethoric of rotting leaves; an occasional old felt hat; desultory remnants of a flannel shirt; sardine boxes inhumanly mutilated and a surprising profusion of black bottles distributed with a truly catholic impartiality, everywhere.

II

The man who had now rediscovered Hurdy-Gurdy was evidently not curious as to its archæology. Nor, as he looked about him upon the dismal evidences of wasted work and broken hopes, their dispiriting significance accentuated by the ironical pomp of a cheap gilding by the rising sun, did he supplement his sigh of weariness by one of sensibility. He simply removed from the back of his tired burro a miner's outfit a trifle larger than the animal itself, picketed that creature and selecting a hatchet from his kit moved off at once across the dry bed of Injun Creek to the top of a low, gravelly hill beyond.

Stepping across a prostrate fence of brush and boards he picked up one of the latter, split it into five parts and sharpened them at one end. He then began a kind of search, occasionally stooping to examine something with close attention. At last his patient scrutiny appeared to be rewarded with success, for he suddenly erected his figure to its full height, made a gesture of satisfaction, pronounced the word 'Scarry' and at once strode away with long, equal steps, which he counted. Then he stopped and drove one of his stakes into the earth. He then looked carefully about him, measured off a number of paces over a singularly uneven ground and hammered in another. Pacing off twice the distance at a right angle to his former course he drove down a third, and repeating the process sank home the fourth, and then a fifth. This he split at the top and in the cleft inserted an old letter envelope covered with an intricate system of pencil tracks. In short, he staked off a hill claim in strict accordance with the local mining laws of Hurdy-Gurdy and put up the customary notice.

It is necessary to explain that one of the adjuncts to Hurdy-Gurdy – one to which that metropolis became afterward itself an adjunct – was a cemetery. In the first week of the camp's existence this had been thoughtfully laid out by a committee of citizens. The day after had been signalized by a debate between two members of the committee, with reference to a more eligible site, and on the third day the necropolis was inaugurated by a double funeral. As the camp had waned the cemetery had waxed; and long before the ultimate inhabitant, victorious alike over the insidious malaria and the forthright revolver, had turned the tail of his pack-ass upon Injun Creek the outlying settlement had become a populous if not popular suburb. And now, when the town was fallen into the sere and yellow leaf of an unlovely senility, the graveyard – though somewhat marred by time and circumstance, and not altogether exempt from innovations in grammar and experiments in orthography, to say nothing of the devastating coyote – answered the humble needs of its denizens with reasonable completeness. It comprised a generous two acres of ground, which with commendable thrift but needless care had been selected for its mineral unworth, contained two or three skeleton trees (one of which had a stout lateral branch from which a weather-wasted rope still significantly dangled), half a hundred gravelly mounds, a score of rude headboards displaying the literary peculiarities above mentioned and a struggling colony of prickly pears. Altogether, God's Location, as with characteristic reverence it had been called, could justly boast of an indubitably superior quality of desolation. It was in the most thickly settled part of this interesting demesne that Mr Jefferson Doman staked off his claim. If in the prosecution of his design he should deem it expedient to remove any of the dead they would have the right to be suitably reinterred.

III

This Mr Jefferson Doman was from Elizabethtown, New Jersey, where six years before he had left his heart in the keeping of a golden-haired, demure-mannered young woman named Mary Matthews, as collateral security for his return to claim her hand.

'I just *know* you'll never get back alive – you never do succeed in anything,' was the remark which illustrated Miss Matthews's notion of what constituted success and, inferentially, her view of the nature of encouragement. She added: 'If you don't I'll go to California too. I can put the coins in little bags as you dig them out.'

This characteristically feminine theory of auriferous deposits did not commend itself to the masculine intelligence: it was Mr Doman's belief that gold was found in a liquid state. He deprecated her intent with considerable enthusiasm, suppressed her sobs with a light hand upon her mouth, laughed in her eyes as he kissed away her tears, and with a cheerful 'Ta-ta' went to California to labor for her through the long, loveless years, with a strong heart, an alert hope and a steadfast fidelity that never for a moment forgot what it was about. In the mean time, Miss Matthews had granted a monopoly of her humble talent for sacking up coins to Mr Jo. Seeman, of New York, gambler, by whom it was better appreciated than her commanding genius for unsacking and bestowing them upon his local rivals. Of this latter aptitude, indeed, he manifested his disapproval by an act which secured him the position of clerk of the laundry in the State prison, and for her the *sobriquet* of 'Split-faced Moll.' At about this time she wrote to Mr Doman a touching letter of renunciation, inclosing her photograph to prove that she had no longer a right to indulge the dream of becoming Mrs Doman, and recounting so graphically her fall from a horse that the staid 'plug' upon which Mr Doman had ridden into Red Dog to get the letter made vicarious atonement under the spur all the way back to camp. The letter failed in a signal way to accomplish its object; the fidelity which had before been to Mr Doman a matter of love and duty was thenceforth a matter of honor also; and the photograph, showing the once pretty face sadly disfigured as by the slash of a knife, was duly instated in his affections and its more comely predeccessor treated with contumelious neglect. On being informed of this, Miss Matthews, it is only fair to say, appeared less suprised than from the apparently low estimate of Mr Doman's generosity which the tone of her former letter attested one would naturally have expected her to be. Soon after, however, her letters grew infrequent, and then ceased altogether.

But Mr Doman had another correspondent, Mr Barney Bree, of Hurdy-Gurdy, formerly of Red Dog. This gentleman, although a notable figure among miners, was not a miner. His knowledge of mining consisted mainly in a marvelous command of its slang, to which he made copious contributions, enriching its vocabulary with a wealth of uncommon phrases more remarkable for their aptness than their refinement, and which impressed the unlearned 'tenderfoot' with a lively sense of the profundity of their inventor's acquirements. When not entertaining a circle of admiring auditors from San Francisco or the East he could commonly be found pursuing the comparatively obscure industry of sweeping out the various dance houses and purifying the cuspidors.

Barney had apparently but two passions in life – love of Jefferson Doman, who had once been of some service to him, and love of whisky, which certainly had not. He had been among the first in the rush to Hurdy-Gurdy, but had not prospered, and had sunk by degrees to the position of grave digger. This was not a vocation, but Barney in a desultory way turned his trembling hand to it whenever some local misunderstanding at the card table and his own partial recovery from a prolonged debauch occurred coincidently in point of time. One day Mr Doman received, at Red Dog, a letter with the simple postmark, 'Hurdy, Cal.,' and being occupied with another matter, carelessly thrust it into a chink of his cabin for future perusal. Some two years later it was accidentally dislodged and he read it. It ran as follows: –

HURDY, June 6.

FRIEND JEFF: I've hit her hard in the boneyard. She's blind and lousy. I'm on the divvy – that's me, and mum's my lay till you toot. Yours,

BARNEY.

P.S. – I've clayed her with Scarry.

With some knowledge of the general mining camp *argot* and of Mr Bree's private system for the communication of ideas Mr Doman had no difficulty in understanding by this uncommon epistle that Barney while performing his duty as grave digger had uncovered a quartz ledge with no outcroppings; that it was visibly rich in free gold; that, moved by considerations of friendship, he was willing to accept Mr Doman as a partner and awaiting that gentleman's declaration of his will in the matter would discreetly keep the discovery a secret. From the post-script it was plainly inferable that in order to conceal the treasure he had buried above it the mortal part of a person named Scarry.

From subsequent events, as related to Mr Doman at Red Dog, it would appear that before taking this precaution Mr Bree must have had the thrift to remove a modest competency of the gold; at any rate, it was at about that time that he entered upon that memorable series of potations and treatings which is still one of the cherished traditions of the San Juan Smith country, and is spoken of with respect as far away as Ghost Rock and Lone Hand. At its conclusion some former citizens of Hurdy-Gurdy, for whom he had performed the last kindly office at the cemetery, made room for him among them, and he rested well.

IV

Having finished staking off his claim Mr Doman walked back to the center of it and stood again at the spot where his search among the graves had expired in the exclamation, 'Scarry.' He bent again over the headboard that bore that name and as if to reinforce the senses of sight and hearing ran his forefinger along the rudely carved letters. Re-erecting himself he appended orally to the simple inscription the shockingly forthright epitaph, 'She was a holy terror!'

Had Mr Doman been required to make these words good with proof – as, considering their somewhat censorious character, he doubtless should have been – he would have found himself embarrassed by the absence of reputable witnesses, and hearsay evidence would have been the best he could command.

At the time when Scarry had been prevalent in the mining camps thereabout –
when, as the editor of the *Hurdy Herald* would have phrased it, she was 'in the
plenitude of her power' – Mr Doman's fortunes had been at a low ebb, and he
had led the vagrantly laborious life of a prospector. His time had been mostly
spent in the mountains, now with one companion, now with another. It was
from the admiring recitals of these casual partners, fresh from the various
camps, that his judgement of Scarry had been made up; he himself had never
had the doubtful advantage of her acquaintance and the precarious distinction
of her favor. And when, finally, on the termination of her perverse career at
Hurdy-Gurdy he had read in a chance copy of the *Herald* her column-long
obituary (written by the local humorist of that lively sheet in the highest style
of his art) Doman had paid to her memory and to her historiographer's genius
the tribute of a smile and chivalrously forgotten her. Standing now at the
grave-side of this mountain Messalina he recalled the leading events of her
turbulent career, as he had heard them celebrated at his several camp-fires, and
perhaps with an unconscious attempt at self-justification repeated that she was
a holy terror, and sank his pick into her grave up to the handle. At that
moment a raven, which had silently settled upon a branch of the blasted tree
above his head, solemnly snapped its beak and uttered its mind about the
matter with an approving croak.

Pursuing his discovery of free gold with great zeal, which he probably
credited to his conscience as a grave digger, Mr Barney Bree had made an
unusually deep sepulcher, and it was near sunset before Mr Doman, laboring
with the leisurely deliberation of one who has 'a dead sure thing' and no fear of
an adverse claimant's enforcement of a prior right, reached the coffin and
uncovered it. When he had done so he was confronted by a difficulty for
which he had made no provision; the coffin – a mere flat shell of not very well-
preserved redwood boards, apparently – had no handles, and it filled the
entire bottom of the excavation. The best he could do without violating the
decent sanctities of the situation was to make the excavation sufficiently
longer to enable him to stand at the head of the casket and getting his powerful
hands underneath erect it upon its narrower end; and this he proceeded to do.
The approach of night quickened his efforts. He had no thought of
abandoning his task at this stage to resume it on the morrow under more
advantageous conditions. The feverish stimulation of cupidity and the
fascination of terror held him to his dismal work with an iron authority. He no
longer idled, but wrought with a terrible zeal. His head uncovered, his outer
garments discarded, his shirt opened at the neck and thrown back from his
breast, down which ran sinuous rills of perspiration, this hardy and
impenitent gold-getter and grave-robber toiled with a giant energy that almost
dignified the character of his horrible purpose; and when the sun fringes had
burned themselves out along the crest line of the western hills, and the full
moon had climbed out of the shadows that lay along the purple plain, he had
erected the coffin upon its foot, where it stood propped against the end of the
open grave. Then, standing up to his neck in the earth at the opposite extreme
of the excavation, as he looked at the coffin upon which the moonlight now
fell with a full illumination he was thrilled with a sudden terror to observe
upon it the startling apparition of a dark human head – the shadow of his own.
For a moment this simple and natural circumstance unnerved him. The noise
of his labored breathing frightened him, and he tried to still it, but his bursting

lungs would not be denied. Then, laughing half-audibly and wholly without spirit, he began making movements of his head from side to side, in order to compel the apparition to repeat them. He found a comforting reassurance in asserting his command over his own shadow. He was temporizing, making, with unconscious prudence, a dilatory opposition to an impending catas-trophe. He felt that invisible forces of evil were closing in upon him, and he parleyed for time with the Inevitable.

He now observed in succession several unusual circumstances. The surface of the coffin upon which his eyes were fastened was not flat; it presented two distinct ridges, one longitudinal and the other transverse. Where these intersected at the widest part there was a corroded metallic plate that reflcted the moonlight with a dismal lustre. Along the outer edges of the coffin, at long intervals, were rust-eaten heads of nails. This frail product of the carpenter's art had been put into the grave the wrong side up!

Perhaps it was one of the humors of the camp – a practical manifestation of the facetious spirit that had found literary expression in the topsy-turvy obituary notice from the pen of Hurdy-Gurdy's great humorist. Perhaps it had some occult personal signification impenetrable to understandings unin-structed in local traditions. A more charitable hypothesis is that it was owing to a misadventure on the part of Mr Barney Bree, who, making the interment unassisted (either by choice for the conservation of his golden secret, or through public aparthy), had committed a blunder which he was afterward unable or unconcerned to rectify. However it had come about, poor Scarry had indubitably been put into the earth face downward.

When terror and absurdity make alliance, the effect is frightful. This strong-hearted and daring man, this hardy night worker among the dead, this defiant antagonist of darkness and desolation, succumbed to a ridiculous surprise. He was smitten with a thrilling chill – shivered, and shook his massive shoulders as if to throw off an icy hand. He no longer breathed, and the blood in his veins, unable to abate its impetus, surged hotly beneath his cold skin. Unleavened with oxygen, it mounted to his head and congested his brain. His physical functions had gone over to the enemy; his very heart was arrayed against him. He did not move; he could not have cried out. He needed but a coffin to be dead – as dead as the death that confronted him with only the length of an open grave and the thickness of a rotting plank between.

Then, one by one, his senses returned; the tide of terror that had over-whelmed his faculties began to recede. But with the return of his senses he became singularly unconscious of the object of his fear. He saw the moonlight gilding the coffin, but no longer the coffin that it gilded. Raising his eyes and turning his head, he noted, curiously and with surprise, the black branches of the dead tree, and tried to estimate the length of the weather-worn rope that dangled from its ghostly hand. The monotonous barking of distant coyotes affected him as something he had heard years ago in a dream. An owl flapped awkwardly above him on noiseless wings, and he tried to forecast the direction of its flight when it should encounter the cliff that reared its illuminated front a mile away. His hearing took account of a gopher's stealthy tread in the shadow of the cactus. He was intensely observant; his senses were all alert; but he saw not the coffin. As one can gaze at the sun until it looks black and then vanishes, so his mind, having exhausted its capacities of dread, was no longer conscious of the separate existence of anything dreadful. The Assassin was cloaking the sword.

It was during this lull in the battle that he became sensible of a faint, sickening odor. At first he thought it was that of a rattle-snake, and involuntarily tried to look about his feet. They were nearly invisible in the gloom of the grave. A hoarse, gurgling sound, like the death-rattle in a human throat, seemed to come out of the sky, and a moment later a great, black, angular shadow, like the same sound made visible, dropped curving from the topmost branch of the spectral tree, fluttered for an instant before his face and sailed fiercely away into the mist along the creek. It was the raven. The incident recalled him to a sense of the situation, and again his eyes sought the upright coffin, now illuminated by the moon for half its length. He saw the gleam of the metallic plate and tried without moving to decipher the inscription. Then he fell to speculating upon what was behind it. His creative imagination presented him a vivid picture. The planks no longer seemed an obstacle to his vision and he saw the livid corpse of the dead woman, standing in grave-clothes, and staring vacantly at him, with lidless, shrunken eyes. The lower jaw was fallen, the upper lip drawn away from the uncovered teeth. He could make out a mottled pattern on the hollow cheeks – the maculations of decay. By some mysterious process his mind reverted for the first time that day to the photograph of Mary Matthews. He contrasted its blond beauty with the forbidding aspect of this dead face – the most beloved object that he knew with the most hideous that he could conceive.

The Assassin now advanced and displaying the blade laid it against the victim's throat. That is to say, the man became at first dimly, then definitely, aware of an impressive coincidence – a relation – a parallel between the face on the card and the name on the headboard. The one was disfigured, the other described a disfiguration. The thought took hold of him and shook him. It transformed that face that his imagination had created behind the coffin lid; the contrast became a resemblance; the resemblance grew to identity. Remembering the many descriptions of Scarry's personal appearance that he had heard from the gossips of his camp-fire he tried with imperfect success to recall the exact nature of the disfiguration that had given the woman her ugly name; and what was lacking in his memory fancy supplied, stamping it with the validity of conviction. In the maddening attempt to recall such scraps of the woman's history as he had heard, the muscles of his arms and hands were strained to a painful tension, as by an effort to lift a great weight. His body writhed and twisted with the exertion. The tendons of his neck stood out as tense as whip-cords, and his breath came in short, sharp gasps. The catastrophe could not be much longer delayed, or the agony of anticipation would leave nothing to be done by the *coup de grâce* of verification. The scarred face behind the lid would slay him through the wood.

A movement of the coffin diverted his thought. It came forward to within a foot of his face, growing visibly larger as it approached. The rusted metallic plate, with an inscription illegible in the moonlight, looked him steadily in the eye. Determined not to shrink, he tried to brace his shoulders more firmly against the end of the excavation, and nearly fell backward in the attempt. There was nothing to support him; he had unconsciously moved upon his enemy, clutching the heavy knife that he had drawn from his belt. The coffin had not advanced and he smiled to think it could not retreat. Lifting his knife he struck the heavy hilt against the metal place with all his power. There was a sharp, ringing percussion, and with a dull clatter the whole decayed coffin lid broke in pieces and came away, falling about his feet. The quick and the dead were face to face – the frenzied, shrieking man – the woman standing tranquil in her silences. She was a holy terror!

V

Some months later a party of men and women belonging to the highest social circles of San Francisco passed through Hurdy-Gurdy on their way to the Yosemite Valley by a new trail. They halted for dinner and during its preparation explored the desolate camp. One of the party had been at Hurdy-Gurdy in the days of its glory. He had, indeed, been one of its prominent citizens; and it used to be said that more money passed over his faro table in any one night than over those of all his competitors in a week; but being now a millionaire engaged in greater enterprises, he did not deem these early successes of sufficient importance to merit the distinction of remark. His invalid wife, a lady famous in San Francisco for the costly nature of her entertainments and her exacting rigor with regard to the social position and 'antecedents' of those who attended them, accompanied the expedition. During a stroll among the shanties of the abandoned camp Mr Porfer directed the attention of his wife and friends to a dead tree on a low hill beyond Injun Creek.

'As I told you,' he said, 'I passed through this camp in 1852, and was told that no fewer than five men had been hanged here by vigilantes at different times, and all on that tree. If I am not mistaken, the rope is dangling from it yet. Let us go over and see the place.'

Mr Porfer did not add that the rope in question was perhaps the very one from whose fatal embrace his own neck had once had an escape so narrow that an hour's delay in taking himself out of that region would have spanned it.

Proceeding leisurely down the creek to a convenient crossing, the party came upon the cleanly picked skeleton of an animal which Mr Porfer after due examination pronounced to be that of an ass. The distinguishing ears were gone, but much of the inedible head had been spared by the beasts and birds, and the stout bridle of horsehair was intact, as was the riata, of similar material, connecting it with a picket pin still firmly sunken in the earth. The wooden and metallic elements of a miner's kit lay near by. The customary remarks were made, cynical on the part of the men, sentimental and refined by the lady. A little later they stood by the tree in the cemetery and Mr Porfer sufficiently unbent from his dignity to place himself beneath the rotten rope and confidently lay a coil of it about his neck, somewhat, it appeared, to his own satisfaction, but greatly to the horror of his wife, to whose sensibilities the performance gave a smart shock.

An exclamation from one of the party gathered them all about an open grave, at the bottom of which they saw a confused mass of human bones and the broken remnants of a coffin. Coyotes and buzzards had performed the last sad rites for pretty much all else. Two skulls were visible and in order to investigate this somewhat unusual redundancy one of the younger men had the hardihood to spring into the grave and hand them up to another before

Mrs Porfer could indicate her marked disapproval of so shocking an act, which, nevertheless, she did with considerable feeling and in very choice words. Pursuing his search among the dismal débris at the bottom of the grave the young man next handed up a rusted coffin plate, with a rudely cut inscription, which with difficulty Mr Porfer deciphered and read aloud with an earnest and not altogether unsuccessful attempt at the dramatic effect which he deemed befitting to the occasion and his rhetorical abilities:

> MANUELITA MURPHY.
> *Born at the Mission San Pedro – Died in*
> *Hurdy-Gurdy,*
> *Aged 47.*
> *Hell's full of such.*

In deference to the piety of the reader and the nerves of Mrs Porfer's fastidious sisterhood of both sexes let us not touch upon the painful impression produced by this uncommon inscription, further than to say that the elocutionary powers of Mr Porfer had never before met with so spontaneous and overwhelming recognition.

The next morsel that rewarded the ghoul in the grave was a long tangle of black hair defiled with clay: but this was such an anticlimax that it received little attention. Suddenly, with a short exclamation and a gesture of excitement, the young man unearthed a fragment of grayish rock, and after a hurried inspection handed it up to Mr Porfer. As the sunlight fell upon it it glittered with a yellow luster – it was thickly studded with gleaming points. Mr Portfer snatched it, bent his head over it a moment and threw it lightly away with the simple remark:

'Iron pyrites – fool's gold.'

The young man in the discovery shaft was a trifle disconcerted, apparently.

Meanwhile, Mrs Porfer, unable longer to endure the disagreeable business, had walked back to the tree and seated herself at its root. While rearranging a tress of golden hair which had slipped from its confinement she was attracted by what appeared to be and really was the fragment of an old coat. Looking about to assure herself that so unladylike an act was not observed, she thrust her jeweled hand into the exposed breast pocket and drew out a mouldy pocket-book. Its contents were as follows:

One bundle of letters, postmarked 'Elizabethtown, New Jersey.'

One circle of blonde hair tied with a ribbon.

One photograph of a beautiful girl.

One ditto of same, singularly disfigured.

One name on back of photograph – 'Jefferson Doman.'

A few moments later a group of anxious gentlemen surrounded Mrs Porfer as she sat motionless at the foot of the tree, her head dropped forward, her fingers clutching a crushed photograph. Her husband raised her head, exposing a face ghastly white, except the long, deforming cicatrice, familiar to all her friends, which no art could ever hide, and which now traversed the pallor of her countenance like a visible curse.

Mary Matthews Porfer had the bad luck to be dead.

The Suitable Surroundings.

The Night

One midsummer night a farmer's boy living about ten miles from the city of Cincinnati was following a bridle path through a dense and dark forest. He had lost himself while searching for some missing cows, and near midnight was a long way from home, in a part of the country with which he was unfamiliar. But he was a stout-hearted lad, and knowing his general direction from his home, he plunged into the forest without hesitation, guided by the stars. Coming into the bridle path, and observing that it ran in the right direction, he followed it.

The night was clear, but in the woods it was exceedingly dark. It was more by the sense of touch than by that of sight that the lad kept the path. He could not, indeed, very easily go astray; the undergrowth on both sides was so thick as to be almost impenetrable. He had gone into the forest a mile or more when he was surprised to see a feeble gleam of light shining through the foliage skirting the path on his left. The sight of it startled him and set his heart beating audibly.

'The old Breede house is somewhere about here,' he said to himself. 'This must be the other end of the path which we reach it by from our side. Ugh! what should a light be doing here?'

Nevertheless, he pushed on. A moment later he had emerged from the forest into a small, open space, mostly upgrown to brambles. There were remnants of a rotting fence. A few yards from the trail, in the middle of the 'clearing,' was the house from which the light came, through an unglazed window. The window had once contained glass, but that and its supporting frame had long ago yielded to missiles flung by hands of venturesome boys to attest alike their courage and their hostility to the supernatural; for the Breede house bore the evil reputation of being haunted. Possibly it was not, but even the hardiest sceptic could not deny that it was deserted – which in rural regions is much the same thing.

Looking at the mysterious dim light shining from the ruined window the boy remembered with apprehension that his own hand had assisted at the destruction. His penitence was of course poignant in proportion to its tardiness and inefficacy. He half expected to be set upon by all the unworldly and bodiless malevolences whom he had outraged by assisting to break alike their windows and their peace. Yet this stubborn lad, shaking in every limb, would not retreat. The blood in his veins was strong and rich with the iron of the frontiersman. He was but two removes from the generation that had subdued the Indian. He started to pass the house.

As he was going by he looked in at the blank window space and saw a strange and terrifying sight, – the figure of a man seated in the centre of the room, at a table upon which lay some loose sheets of paper. The elbows rested on the table, the hands supporting the head, which was uncovered. On each side the fingers were punched into the hair. The face showed dead-yellow in the light of a single candle a little to one side. The flame illuminated that side of the face, the other was in deep shadow. The man's eyes were fixed upon the blank window space with a stare in which an older and cooler observer might have discerned something of apprehension, but which seemed to the lad altogether soulless. He believed the man to be dead.

The situation was horrible, but not without its fascination. The boy stopped to note it all. He was weak, faint and trembling; he could feel the blood forsaking his face. Nevertheless, he set his teeth and resolutely advanced to the house. He had no conscious intention – it was the mere courage of terror. He thrust his white face forward into the illuminated opening. At that instant a strange, harsh cry, a shriek, broke upon the silence of the night – the note of a screech-owl. The man sprang to his feet, overturning the table and extinguishing the candle. The boy took to his heels.

The day before

'Good morning, Colston. I am in luck, it seems. You have often said that my commendation of your literary work was mere civility, and here you find me absorbed – actually merged – in your latest story in the *Messenger*. Nothing less shocking than your touch upon my shoulder would have roused me to consciousness.'

'The proof is stronger than you seem to know,' replied the man addressed: 'so keen is your eagerness to read my story that you are willing to renounce selfish considerations and forego all the pleasure that you could get from it.'

'I don't understand you,' said the other, folding the newspaper that he held and putting it into his pocket. 'You writers are a queer lot, anyhow. Come, tell me what I have done or omitted in this matter. In what way does the pleasure that I get, or might get, from your work depend on me?'

'In many ways. Let me ask you how you would enjoy your breakfast if you took it in this street car. Suppose the phonograph so perfected as to be able to give you an entire opera, – singing, orchestration, and all; do you think you would get much pleasure out of it if you turned it on at your office during business hours? Do you really care for a serenade by Schubert when you hear it fiddled by an untimely Italian on a morning ferryboat? Are you always cocked and primed for enjoyment? Do you keep every mood on tap, ready to any demand? Let me remind you, sir, that the story which you have done me the honor to begin as a means of becoming oblivious to the discomfort of this car is a ghost story!'

'Well?'

'Well! Has the reader no duties corresponding to his privileges? You have paid five cents for that newspaper. It is yours. You have the right to read it when and where you will. Much of what is in it is neither helped nor harmed by time and place and mood; some of it actually requires to be read at once – while it is fizzing. But my story is not of that character. It is not 'the very latest advices' from Ghostland. You are not expected to keep yourself *au courant* with what is going on in the realm of spooks. The stuff will keep until you have leisure to put yourself into the frame of mind appropriate to the sentiment of the piece – which I respectfully submit that you cannot do in a street car, even if you are the only passenger. The solitude is not of the right sort. An author has rights which the reader is bound to respect.'

'For specific example?'

'The right to the reader's undivided attention. To deny him this is immoral. To make him share your attention with the rattle of a street car, the moving panorama of the crowds on the sidewalks, and the buildings beyond – with any of the thousands of distractions which make our customary environment – is to treat him with gross injustice. By God, it is infamous!'

The speaker had risen to his feet and was steadying himself by one of the straps hanging from the roof of the car. The other man looked up at him in sudden astonishment, wondering how so trivial a grievance could seem to justify so strong language. He saw that his friend's face was uncommonly pale and that his eyes glowed like living coals.

'You know what I mean,' continued the writer, impetuously crowding his words – 'you know what I mean, Marsh. My stuff in this morning's *Messenger* is plainly subheaded "A Ghost Story." That is ample notice to all. Every honorable reader will understand it as prescribing by implication the conditions under which the work is to be read.'

The man addressed as Marsh winced a trifle, then asked with a smile: 'What conditions? You know that I am only a plain business man who cannot be supposed to understand such things. How, when, where should I read your ghost story?'

'In solitude – at night – by the light of a candle. There are certain emotions which a writer can easily enough excite – such as compassion or merriment. I can move you to tears or laughter under almost any circumstances. But for my ghost story to be effective you must be made to feel fear – at least a strong sense of the supernatural – and that is a difficult matter. I have a right to expect that if you read me at all you will give me a chance; that you will make yourself accessible to the emotion that I try to inspire.'

The car had now arrived at its terminus and stopped. The trip just completed was its first for the day and the conversation of the two early passengers had not been interrupted. The streets were yet silent and desolate; the house tops were just touched by the rising sun. As they stepped from the car and walked away together Marsh narrowly eyed his companion, who was reported, like most men of uncommon literary ability, to be addicted to various destructive vices. That is the revenge which dull minds take upon bright ones in resentment of their superiority. Mr Colston was known as a man of genius. There are honest souls who believe that genius is a mode of excess. It was known that Colston did not drink liquor, but many said that he ate opium. Something in his appearance that morning – a certain wildness of the eyes, an unusual pallor, a thickness and rapidity of speech – were taken by Mr Marsh to confirm the report. Nevertheless, he had not the self-denial to abandon a subject which he found interesting, however it might excite his friend.

'Do you mean to say,' he began, 'that if I take the trouble to observe your directions – place myself in the conditions that you demand: solitude, night and a tallow candle – you can with your ghostly work give me an uncomfortable sense of the supernatural, as you call it? Can you accelerate my pulse, make me start at sudden noises, send a nervous chill along my spine and cause my hair to rise?'

Colston turned suddenly and looked him squarely in the eyes as they walked. 'You would not dare – you have not the courage,' he said. He emphasized the words with a contemptuous gesture. 'You are brave enough to read me in a street car, but – in a deserted house – alone – in the forest – at night! Bah! I have a manuscript in my pocket that would kill you.'

Marsh was angry. He knew himself courageous, and the words stung him. 'If you know such a place,' he said, 'take me there tonight and leave me your story and a candle. Call for me when I've had time enough to read it and I'll tell you the entire plot and – kick you out of the place.'

That is how it occurred that the farmer's boy, looking in at an unglazed window of the Breede house, saw a man sitting in the light of a candle.

The day after

Late in the afternoon of the next day three men and a boy approached the Breede house from that point of the compass toward which the boy had fled the preceding night. The men were in high spirits; they talked very loudly and laughed. They made facetious and good-humored ironical remarks to the boy about his adventure, which evidently they did not believe in. The boy accepted their raillery with seriousness, making no reply. He had a sense of the fitness of things and knew that one who professes to have seen a dead man rise from his seat and blow out a candle is not a credible witness.

Arriving at the house and finding the door unlocked, the party of investigators entered without ceremony. Leading out of the passage into which this door opened was another on the right and one on the left. They entered the room on the left – the one which had the blank front window. Here was the dead body of a man.

It lay partly on one side, with the forearm beneath it, the cheek on the floor. The eyes were wide open; the stare was not an agreeable thing to encounter. The lower jaw had fallen; a little pool of saliva had collected beneath the mouth. An overthrown table, a partly burned candle, a chair and some paper with writing on it were all else that the room contained. The men looked at the body, touching the face in turn. The boy gravely stood at the head, assuming a look of ownership. It was the proudest moment of his life. One of the men said to him, 'You're a good 'un' – a remark which was received by the two others with nods of acquiescence. It was Scepticism apologizing to Truth. Then one of the men took from the floor the sheet of manuscript and stepped to the window, for already the evening shadows were glooming the forest. The song of the whip-poor-will was heard in the distance and a monstrous beetle sped by the window on roaring wings and thundered away out of hearing. The man read:

The manuscript

'Before committing the act which, rightly or wrongly, I have resolved on and appearing before my Maker for judgement, I, James R. Colston, deem it my duty as a journalist to make a statement to the public. My name is, I believe, tolerably well known to the people as a writer of tragic tales, but the somberest imagination never conceived anything so tragic as my own life and history.

Not in incident: my life has been destitute of adventure and action. But my mental career has been lurid with experiences such as kill and damn. I shall not recount them here – some of them are written and ready for publication elsewhere. The object of these lines is to explain to whomsoever may be interested that my death is voluntary – my own act. I shall die at twelve o'clock on the night of the 15th of July – a significant anniversary to me, for it was on that day, and at that hour, that my friend in time and eternity, Charles Breede, performed his vow to me by the same act which his fidelity to our pledge now entails upon me. He took his life in his little house in the Copeton woods. There was the customary verdict of "temporary insanity." Had I testified at that inquest – had I told all I knew, they would have called *me* mad!'

Here followed an evidently long passage which the man reading read to himself only. The rest he read aloud.

'I have still a week of life in which to arrange my worldly affairs and prepare for the great change. It is enough, for I have but few affairs and it is now four years since death became an imperative obligation.

'I shall bear this writing on my body; the finder will please hand it to the coroner.

'JAMES R. COLSTON.

'P.S. – Willard Marsh, on this the fatal fifteenth day of July I hand you this manuscipt, to be opened and read under the conditions agreed upon, and at the place which I designated. I forego my intention to keep it on my body to explain the manner of my death, which is not important. It will serve to explain the manner of yours. I am to call for you during the night to receive assurance that you have read the manuscript. You know me well enough to expect me. But, my friend, it *will be after twelve o'clock.* May God have mercy on our souls!

'J. R. C.'

Before the man who was reading this manuscript had finished, the candle had been picked up and lighted. When the reader had done, he quietly thrust the paper against the flame and despite the protestations of the others held it until it was burnt to ashes. The man who did this, and who afterward placidly endured a severe reprimand from the coroner, was a son-in-law of the late Charles Breede. At the inquest nothing could elicit an intelligent account of what the paper had contained.

From 'The Times'

'Yesterday the Commissioners of Lunacy committed to the asylum Mr James R. Colston, a writer of some local reputation, connected with the *Messenger*. It will be remembered that on the evening of the 15th inst. Mr Colston was given into custody by one of his fellow-lodgers in the Baine House, who had observed him acting very suspiciously, baring his throat and whetting a razor – occasionally trying its edge by actually cutting through the skin of his arm, etc.

On being handed over to the police, the unfortunate man made a desperate resistance, and has ever since been so violent that it has been necessary to keep him in a strait-jacket. Most of our esteemed contemporary's other writers are still at large.'

The Boarded Window

In 1830, only a few miles away from what is now the great city of Cincinnati, lay an immense and almost unbroken forest. The whole region was sparsely settled by people of the frontier – restless souls who no sooner had hewn fairly habitable homes out of the wilderness and attained to that degree of prosperity which today we should call indigence than impelled by some mysterious impulse of their nature they abandoned all and pushed farther westward, to encounter new perils and privations in the effort to regain the meagre comforts which they had voluntarily renounced. Many of them had already forsaken that region for the remoter settlements, but among those remaining was one who had been of those first arriving. He lived alone in a house of logs surrounded on all sides by the great forest, of whose gloom and silence he seemed a part, for no one had ever known him to smile nor speak a needless word. His simple wants were supplied by the sale or barter of skins of wild animals in the river town, for not a thing did he grow upon the land which, if needful, he might have claimed by right of undisturbed possession. There were evidences of 'improvement' – a few acres of ground immediately about the house had once been cleared of its trees, the decayed stumps of which were half concealed by the new growth that had been suffered to repair the ravage wrought by the ax. Apparently the man's zeal for agriculture had burned with a failing flame, expiring in penitential ashes.

The little log house, with its chimney of sticks, its roof of warping clapboards weighted with traversing poles and its 'chinking' of clay, had a single door and, directly opposite, a window. The latter, however, was boarded up – nobody could remember a time when it was not. And none knew why it was so closed; certainly not because of the occupant's dislike of light and air, for on those rare occasions when a hunter had passed that lonely spot the recluse had commonly been seen sunning himself on his doorstep if heaven had provided sunshine for his need. I fancy there are few persons living today who ever knew the secret of that window, but I am one, as you shall see.

The man's name was said to be Murlock. He was apparently seventy years old, actually about fifty. Something besides years had had a hand in his aging. His hair and long, full beard were white, his gray, lustreless eyes sunken, his face singularly seamed with wrinkles which appeared to belong to two intersecting systems. In figure he was tall and spare, with a stoop of the shoulders – a burden bearer. I never saw him; these particulars I learned from my grandfather, from whom also I got the man's story when I was a lad. He had known him when living near by in that early day.

One day Murlock was found in his cabin, dead. It was not a time and place for coroners and newspapers, and I suppose it was agreed that he had died from natural causes or I should have been told, and should remember. I know only that with what was probably a sense of the fitness of things the body was buried near the cabin, alongside the grave of his wife, who had preceded him by so many years that local tradition had retained hardly a hint of her existence. That closes the final chapter of this true story – excepting, indeed, the circumstances that many years afterward, in company with an equally intrepid spirit, I penetrated to the place and ventured near enough to the ruined cabin to throw a stone against it, and ran away to avoid the ghost which every well-informed boy thereabout knew haunted the spot. But there is an earlier chapter – that supplied by my grandfather.

When Murlock built his cabin and began laying sturdily about with his ax to hew out a farm – the rifle, meanwhile, his means of support – he was young, strong and full of hope. In that eastern country whence he came he had married, as was the fashion, a young woman in all ways worthy of his honest devotion, who shared the dangers and privations of his lot with a willing spirit and light heart. There is no known record of her name; of her charms of mind and person tradition is silent and the doubter is at liberty to entertain his doubt; but God forbid that I should share it! Of their affection and happiness there is abundant assurance in every added day of the man's widowed life; for what but the magnetism of a blessed memory could have chained that venturesome spirit to a lot like that?

One day Murlock returned from gunning in a distant part of the forest to find his wife prostrate with fever, and delirious. There was no physician within miles, no neighbor; nor was she in a condition to be left, to summon help. So he set about the task of nursing her back to health, but at the end of the third day she fell into unconsciousness and so passed away, apparently, with never a gleam of returning reason.

From what we know of a nature like his we may venture to sketch in some of the details of the outline picture drawn by my grandfather. When convinced that she was dead, Murlock had sense enough to remember that the dead must be prepared for burial. In performance of this sacred duty he blundered now and again, did certain things incorrectly, and others which he did correctly were done over and over. His occasional failures to accomplish some simple and ordinary act filled him with astonishment, like that of a drunken man who wonders at the suspension of familiar natural laws. He was surprised, too, that he did not weep – surprised and a little ashamed; surely it is unkind not to weep for the dead. 'Tomorrow,' he said aloud, 'I shall have to make the coffin and dig the grave; and then I shall miss her, when she is no longer in sight; but now – she is dead, of course, but it is all right – it *must* be all right, somehow. Things cannot be so bad as they seem.'

He stood over the body in the fading light, adjusting the hair and putting the finishing touches to the simple toilet, doing all mechanically, with soulless care. And still through his consciousness ran an undersense of conviction that all was right – that he should have her again as before, and everything explained. He had had no experience in grief; his capacity had not been enlarged by use. His heart could not contain it all, nor his imagination rightly conceive it. He did not know he was so hard struck; *that* knowledge would come later, and never go. Grief is an artist of powers as various as the instruments upon which he plays his dirges for the dead, evoking from some the sharpest, shrillest notes, from others the low, grave chords that throb recurrent like the slow beating of a distant drum. Some natures it startles; some it stupefies. To one it comes like the stroke of an arrow, stinging all the sensibilities to a keener life; to another as the blow of a bludgeon, which in crushing benumbs. We may conceive Murlock to have been that way affected, for (and here we are upon surer ground than that of conjecture) no sooner had he finished his pious work than, sinking into a chair by the side of the table upon which the body lay, and noting how white the profile showed in the deepening gloom, he laid his arms upon the table's edge, and dropped his face into them, tearless yet and unutterably weary. At that moment came in through the open window a long, wailing sound like the cry of a lost child in the far deeps of the darkening wood! But the man did not move. Again, and nearer than before, sounded that unearthly cry upon his failing sense. Perhaps it was a wild beast; perhaps it was a dream. For Murlock was asleep.

Some hours later, as it afterward appeared, this unfaithful watcher awoke and lifting his head from his arms intently listened – he knew not why. There in the black darkness by the side of the dead, recalling all without a shock, he strained his eyes to see – he knew not what. His senses were all alert, his breath was suspended, his blood had stilled its tides as if to assist the silence. Who – what had waked him, and where was it?

Suddenly the table shook beneath his arms, and at the same moment he heard, or fancied that he heard, a light, soft step – another – sounds as of bare feet upon the floor!

He was terrified beyond the power to cry out or move. Perforce he waited – waited there in the darkness through seeming centuries of such dread as one may know, yet live to tell. He tried vainly to speak the dead woman's name, vainly to stretch forth his hand across the table to learn if she were there. His throat was powerless, his arms and hands were like lead. Then occurred something most frightful. Some heavy body seemed hurled against the table with an impetus that pushed it against his breast so sharply as nearly to overthrow him, and at the same instant he heard and felt the fall of something upon the floor with so violent a thump that the whole house was shaken by the impact. A scuffling ensued, and a confusion of sounds impossible to describe. Murlock had risen to his feet. Fear had by excess forfeited control of his faculties. He flung his hands upon the table. Nothing was there!

There is a point at which terror may turn to madness; and madness incites to action. With no definite intent, from no motive but the wayward impulse of a madman, Murlock sprang to the wall, with a little groping seized his loaded rifle, and without aim discharged it. By the flash which lit up the room with a vivid illumination, he saw an enormous panther dragging the dead woman toward the window, its teeth fixed in her throat! Then there was darkness blacker than before, and silence; and when he returned to consciousness the sun was high and the wood vocal with songs of birds.

The body lay near the window, where the beast had left it when frightened away by the flash and report of the rifle. The clothing was deranged, the long hair in disorder, the limbs lay anyhow. From the throat, dreadfully lacerated, had issued a pool of blood not yet entirely coagulated. The ribbon with which he had bound the wrists was broken; the hands were tightly clenched. Between the teeth was a fragment of the animal's ear.

A Lady From Redhorse

I find myself more and more interested in him. It is not, I am sure, his – do you know any good noun corresponding to the adjective 'handsome'? One does not like to say 'beauty' when speaking of a man. He is beautiful enough, Heaven knows; I should not even care to trust you with him – faithfulest of all possible wives that you are – when he looks his best, as he always does. Nor do I think the fascination of his manner has much to do with it. You recollect that the charm of art inheres in that which is undefinable, and to you and me, my dear Irene, I fancy there is rather less of that in the branch of art under consideration than to girls in their first season. I fancy I know how my fine gentleman produces many of his effects and could perhaps give him a pointer on heightening them. Nevertheless, his manner is something truly delightful. I suppose what interests me chiefly is the man's brains. His conversation is the best I have ever heard and altogether unlike any one else's. He seems to know everything, as indeed he ought, for he has been everywhere, read everything, seen all there is to see – sometimes I think rather more than is good for him – and had acquaintance with the *queerest* people. And then his voice – Irene, when I hear it I actually feel as if I ought to have paid at the door, though of course it is my own door.

JULY 3.

I fear my remarks about Dr Barritz must have been, being thoughtless, very silly, or you would not have written of him with such levity, not to say disrespect. Believe me, dearest, he has more dignity and seriousness (of the kind, I mean, which is not inconsistent with a manner sometimes playful and always charming) than any of the men that you and I ever met. And young Raynor – you knew Raynor at Monterey – tells me that the men all like him and that he is treated with something like deference everywhere. There is a mystery, too – something about his connection with the Blavatsky people in Northern India. Raynor either would not or could not tell me the particulars. I infer that Dr Barritz is thought – don't you dare to laugh! – a magician. Could anything be finer than that? An ordinary mystery is not, of course, so good as a scandal, but when it relates to dark and dreadful practices – to the exercise of unearthly powers – could anything be more piquant? It explains, too, the singular influence the man has upon me. It is the undefinable in his art – black art. Seriously, dear, I quite tremble when he looks me full in the eyes with those unfathomable orbs of his, which I have already vainly attempted to describe to you. How dreadful if he has the power to make one fall in love! Do you know if the Blavatsky crowd have that power – outside of Sepoy?

JULY 16.

The strangest thing! Last evening while Auntie was attending one of the hotel hops (I hate them) Dr Barritz called. It was scandalously late – I actually believe that he had talked with Auntie in the ballroom and learned from her that I was alone. I had been all the evening contriving how to worm out of him the truth about his connection with the Thugs in Sepoy, and all of that black business, but the moment he fixed his eyes on me (for I admitted him, I'm ashamed to say) I was helpless. I trembled, I blushed, I – O Irene, Irene, I love the man beyond expression and you know how it is yourself.

Fancy! I, an ugly duckling from Redhorse – daughter (they say) of old Calamity Jim – certainly his heiress, with no living relation but an absurd old aunt who spoils me a thousand and fifty ways – absolutely destitute of everything but a million dollars and a hope in Paris, – I daring to love a god like him! My dear, if I had you here I could tear your hair out with mortification.

I am convinced that he is aware of my feeling, for he stayed but a few moments, said nothing but what another man might have said half as well, and pretending that he had an engagement went away. I learned today (a little bird told me – the bell-bird) that he went straight to bed. How does that strike you as evidence of exemplary habits?

JULY 17.

That little wretch, Raynor, called yesterday and his babble set me almost wild. He never runs down – that is to say, when he exterminates a score of reputations, more or less, he does not pause between one reputation and the next. (By the way, he inquired about you, and his manifestations of interest in you had, I confess, a good deal of *vraisemblance*.) Mr Raynor observes no game laws; like Death (which he would inflict if slander were fatal) he has all seasons for his own. But I like him, for we knew each other at Redhorse when we were young. He was known in those days as 'Giggles,' and I – O Irene, can you ever forgive me? – I was called 'Gunny.' God knows why; perhaps in allusion to the material of my pinafores; perhaps because the name is in alliteration with 'Giggles,' for Gig and I were inseparable playmates, and the miners may have thought it a delicate civility to recognize some kind of relationship between us.

Later, we took in a third – another of Adversity's brood, who, like Garrick between Tragedy and Comedy, had a chronic inability to adjudicate the rival claims of Frost and Famine. Between him and misery there was seldom anything more than a single suspender and the hope of a meal which would at the same time support life and make it insupportable. He literally picked up a precarious living for himself and an aged mother by 'chloriding the dumps,' that is to say, the miners permitted him to search the heaps of waste rock for such pieces of 'pay ore' as had been overlooked; and these he sacked up and sold at the Syndicate Mill. He became a member of our firm – 'Gunny, Giggles, and Dumps' thenceforth – through my favor; for I could not then, nor can I now, be indifferent to his courage and prowess in defending against Giggles the immemorial right of his sex to insult a strange and unprotected female – myself. After old Jim struck it in the Calamity and I began to wear shoes and go to school, and in emulation Giggles took to washing his face and became Jack Raynor, of Wells, Fargo & Co., and old Mrs Barts was herself chlorided to her fathers, Dumps drifted over to San Juan Smith and turned stage driver, and was killed by road agents, and so forth.

Why do I tell you all this, dear? Because it is heavy on my heart. Because I walk the Valley of Humility. Because I am subduing myself to permanent consciousness of my unworthiness to unloose the latchet of Dr Barritz's shoe. Because, oh dear, oh dear, there's a cousin of Dumps at this hotel! I haven't spoken to him. I never had much acquaintance with him, – but do you suppose he has recognized me? Do, please give me in your next your candid, sure-enough opinion about it, and say you don't think so. Do you suppose He knows about me already, and that is why He left me last evening when He saw that I blushed and trembled like a fool under His eyes? You know I can't bribe *all* the newspapers, and I can't go back on anybody who was civil to Gunny at Redhorse – not if I'm pitched out of society into the sea. So the skeleton sometimes rattles behind the door. I never cared much before, as you know, but now – *now* it is not the same. Jack Raynor I am sure of – he will not tell Him. He seems, indeed, to hold Him in such respect as hardly to dare speak to Him at all, and I'm a good deal that way myself. Dear, dear! I wish I had something besides a million dollars! If Jack were three inches taller I'd marry him alive and go back to Redhorse and wear sackcloth again to the end of my miserable days.

JULY 25.

We had a perfectly splendid sunset last evening and I must tell you all about it. I ran away from Auntie and everybody and was walking alone on the beach. I expect you to believe, you infidel! that I had not looked out of my window on the seaward side of the hotel and seen Him walking alone on the beach. If you are not lost to every feeling of womanly delicacy you will accept my statement without question. I soon established myself under my sunshade and had for some time been gazing out dreamily over the sea, when he approached, walking close to the edge of the water – it was ebb tide. I assure you the wet sand actually brightened about his feet! As he approached me he lifted his hat, saying, 'Miss Dement, may I sit with you? – or will you walk with me?'

The possibility that neither might be agreeable seems not to have occurred to him. Did you ever know such assurance? Assurance? My dear, it was gall, downright *gall*! Well, I didn't find it wormwood, and replied, with my untutored Redhorse heart in my throat, 'I – I shall be pleased to do *anything*.' Could words have been more stupid? There are depths of fatuity in me, friend o' my soul, that are simply bottomless!

He extended his hand, smiling, and I delivered mine into it without a moment's hesitation, and when his fingers closed about it to assist me to my feet the consciousness that it trembled made me blush worse than the red west. I got up, however, and after a while, observing that he had not let go my hand I pulled on it a little, but unsuccessfully. He simply held on, saying nothing, but looking down into my face with some kind of smile – I didn't know – how could I? – whether it was affectionate, derisive, or what, for I did not look at him. How beautiful he was! – with the red fires of the sunset burning in the depths of his eyes. Do you know, dear, if the Thugs and Experts of the Blavatsky region have any special kind of eyes? Ah, you should have seen his superb attitude, the godlike inclination of his head as he stood over me after I had got upon my feet! It was a noble picture, but I soon destroyed it, for I began at once to sink again to the earth. There was only one thing for him to do, and he did it; he supported me with an arm about my waist.

'Miss Dement, are you ill?' he said.

It was not an exclamation; there was neither alarm nor solicitude in it. If he had added: 'I suppose that is about what I am expected to say,' he would hardly have expressed his sense of the situation more clearly. His manner filled me with shame and indignation, for I was suffering acutely. I wrenched my hand out of his, grasped his arm supporting me and pushing myself free, fell plump into the sand and sat helpless. My hat had fallen off in the struggle and my hair tumbled about my face and shoulders in the most mortifying way.

'Go away from me,' I cried, half choking. 'O *please* go away, you – you Thug! How dare you think *that* when my leg is asleep?'

I actually said those identical words! And then I broke down and sobbed. Irene, I *blubbered!*

His manner altered in an instant – I could see that much through my fingers and hair. He dropped on one knee beside me, parted the tangle of hair and said in the tenderest way: 'My poor girl, God knows I have not intended to pain you. How should I? – I who love you – I who have loved you for – for years and years!'

He had pulled my wet hands away from my face and was covering them with kisses. My cheeks were like two coals, my whole face was flaming and, I think, steaming. What could I do? I hid it on his shoulder – there was no other place. And, O my dear friend, how my leg tingled and thrilled, and how I wanted to kick!

We sat so for a long time. He had released one of my hands to pass his arm about me again and I possessed myself of my handkerchief and was drying my eyes and my nose. I would not look up until that was done; he tried in vain to push me a little away and gaze into my face. Presently, when all was right, and it had grown a bit dark, I lifted my head, looked him straight in the eyes and smiled my best – my level best, dear.

'What do you mean,' I said, 'by "years and years"?'

'Dearest,' he replied, very gravely, very earnestly, 'in the absence of the sunken cheeks, the hollow eyes, the lank hair, the slouching gait, the rags, dirt, and youth, can you not – will you not understand? Gunny, I'm Dumps!'

In a moment I was upon my feet and he upon his. I seized him by the lapels of his coat and peered into his handsome face in the deepening darkness. I was breathless with excitement.

'And you are not dead?' I asked, hardly knowing what I said.

'Only dead in love, dear. I recovered from the road agent's bullet, but this, I fear, is fatal.'

'But about Jack – Mr Raynor? Don't you know –'

'I am ashamed to say, darling, that it was through that unworthy person's suggestion that I came here from Vienna.'

Irene, they have roped in your affectionate friend

MARY JANE DEMENT.

P.S. – The worse of it is that there is no mystery; that was the invention of Jack Raynor, to arouse my curiosity. James is not a Thug. He solemnly assures me that in all his wanderings he has never set foot in Sepoy.

The Eyes of the Panther

I

One does not always marry when insane

A man and a woman – nature had done the grouping – sat on a rustic seat, in the late afternoon. The man was middle-aged, slender, swarthy, with the expression of a poet and the complexion of a pirate – a man at whom one would look again. The woman was young, blonde, graceful, with something in her figure and movements suggesting the word 'lithe.' She was habited in a gray gown with odd brown markings in the texture. She may have been beautiful; one could not readily say, for her eyes denied attention to all else. They were gray-green, long and narrow, with an expression defying analysis. One could only know that they were disquieting. Cleopatra may have had such eyes.

The man and the woman talked.

'Yes,' said the woman, 'I love you, God knows! But marry you, no. I cannot, will not.'

'Irene, you have said that many times, yet always have denied me a reason. I've a right to know, to understand, to feel and prove my fortitude if I have it. Give me a reason.'

'For loving you?'

The woman was smiling through her tears and her pallor. That did not stir any sense of humor in the man.

'No: there is no reason for that. A reason for not marrying me. I've a right to know. I must know. I will know!'

He had risen and was standing before her with clenched hands, on his face a frown – it might have been called a scowl. He looked as if he might attempt to learn by strangling her. She smiled no more – merely sat looking up into his face with a fixed, set regard that was utterly without emotion or sentiment. Yet it had something in it that tamed his resentment and made him shiver.

'You are determined to have my reason?' she asked in a tone that was entirely mechanical – a tone that might have been her look made audible.

'If you please – if I'm not asking too much.'

Apparently this lord of creation was yielding some part of his dominion over his co-creature.

'Very well, you shall know; I am insane.'

The man started, then looked incredulous and was conscious that he ought to be amused. But, again, the sense of humor failed him in his need and despite his disbelief he was profoundly disturbed by that which he did not believe. Between our convictions and our feelings there is no good understanding.

'That is what the physicians would say,' the woman continued – 'if they knew. I might myself prefer to call it a case of "possession." Sit down and hear what I have to say.'

The man silently resumed his seat beside her on the rustic bench by the wayside. Over-against them on the eastern side of the valley the hills were already sunset-flushed and the stillness all about was of that peculiar quality that foretells the twilight. Something of its mysterious and significant solemnity had imparted itself to the man's mood. In the spiritual, as in the material world, are signs and presages of night. Rarely meeting her look, and whenever he did so conscious of the indefinable dread with which, despite their feline beauty, her eyes always affected him, Jenner Brading listened in silence to the story told by Irene Marlowe. In deference to the reader's possible prejudice against the artless method of an unpractised historian the author ventures to substitute his own version for hers.

II

A room may be too narrow for three,
though one is outside

In a little log house containing a single room sparely and rudely furnished, crouching on the floor against one of the walls, was a woman, clasping to her breast a child. Outside, a dense unbroken forest extended for many miles in every direction. This was at night and the room was black dark: no human eye could have discerned the woman and the child. Yet they were observed, narrowly, vigilantly, with never even a momentary slackening of attention; and that is the pivotal fact upon which this narrative turns.

Charles Marlowe was of the class, now extinct in this country, of woodmen pioneers – men who found their most acceptable surroundings in sylvan solitudes that stretched along the eastern slope of the Mississippi Valley, from the Great Lakes to the Gulf of Mexico. For more than a hundred years these men pushed ever westward, generation after generation, with rifle and ax, reclaiming from Nature and her savage children here and there an isolated acreage for the plow, no sooner reclaimed than surrendered to their less venturesome but more thrifty successors. At last they burst through the edge of the forest into the open country and vanished as if they had fallen over a cliff. The woodman pioneer is no more; the pioneer of the plains – he whose easy task it was to subdue for occupancy two-thirds of the country in a single generation – is another and inferior creation. With Charles Marlowe in the wilderness, sharing the dangers, hardships and privations of that strange, unprofitable life, were his wife and child, to whom, in the manner of his class, in which the domestic virtues were a religion, he was passionately attached. The woman was still young enough to be comely, new enough to the awful isolation of her lot to be cheerful. By withholding the large capacity for happiness which the simple satisfactions of the forest life could not have filled, Heaven had dealt honorably with her. In her light household tasks, her child, her husband and her few foolish books, she found abundant provisions for her needs.

One morning in midsummer Marlowe took down his rifle from the wooden hooks on the wall and signified his intention of getting game.

'We've meat enough,' said the wife; 'please don't go out today. I dreamed last night, O, such a dreadful thing! I cannot recollect it, but I'm almost sure that it will come to pass if you go out.'

It is painful to confess that Marlowe received this solemn statement with less of gravity than was due to the mysterious nature of the calamity foreshadowed. In truth, he laughed.

'Try to remember,' he said. 'Maybe you dreamed that Baby had lost the power of speech.'

The conjecture was obviously suggested by the fact that Baby, clinging to the fringe of his hunting-coat with all her ten pudgy thumbs was at that moment uttering her sense of the situation in a series of exultant goo-goos inspired by sight of her father's raccoon-skin cap.

The woman yielded: lacking the gift of humor she could not hold out against his kindly badinage. So, with a kiss for the mother and a kiss for the child, he left the house and closed the door upon his happiness forever.

At nightfall he had not returned. The woman prepared supper and waited. Then she put Baby to bed and sang softly to her until she slept. By this time the fire on the hearth, at which she had cooked supper, had burned out and the room was lighted by a single candle. This she afterward placed in the open window as a sign and welcome to the hunter if he should approach from that side. She had thoughtfully closed and barred the door against such wild animals as might prefer it to an open window – of the habits of beasts of prey in entering a house uninvited she was not advised, though with true female prevision she may have considered the possibility of their entrance by way of the chimney. As the night wore on she became not less anxious, but more drowsy, and at last rested her arms upon the bed by the child and her head upon the arms. The candle in the window burned down to the socket, sputtered and flared a moment and went out unobserved; for the woman slept and dreamed.

In her dreams she sat beside the cradle of a second child. The first one was dead. The father was dead. The home in the forest was lost and the dwelling in which she lived was unfamiliar. There were heavy oaken doors, always closed, and outside the windows, fastened into the thick stone walls, were iron bars, obviously (so she thought) a provision against Indians. All this she noted with an infinite self-pity, but without surprise – an emotion unknown in dreams. The child in the cradle was invisible under its coverlet which something impelled her to remove. She did so, disclosing the face of a wild animal! In the shock of this dreadful revelation the dreamer awoke, trembling in the darkness of her cabin in the wood.

As a sense of her actual surroundings came slowly back to her she felt for the child that was not a dream, and assured herself by its breathing that all was well with it; nor could she forbear to pass a hand lightly across its face. Then, moved by some impulse for which she probably could not have accounted, she rose and took the sleeping babe in her arms, holding it close against her breast. The head of the child's cot was against the wall to which the woman now turned her back as she stood. Lifting her eyes she saw two bright objects starring the darkness with a reddish-green glow. She took them to be two coals on the hearth, but with her returning sense of direction came the disquieting consciousness that they were not in that quarter of the room, moreover were too high, being nearly at the level of the eyes – of her own eyes. For these were the eyes of a panther.

The beast was at the open window directly opposite and not five paces away. Nothing but those terrible eyes was visible, but in the dreadful tumult of her feelings as the situation disclosed itself to her understanding she somehow knew that the animal was standing on its hinder feet, supporting itself with its paws on the window-ledge. That signified a malign interest – not the mere gratification of an indolent curiosity. The consciousness of the attitude was an added horror, accentuating the menace of those awful eyes, in whose steadfast fire her strength and courage were alike consumed. Under their silent questioning she shuddered and turned sick. Her knees failed her, and by degrees, instinctively striving to avoid a sudden movement that might bring the beast upon her, she sank to the floor, crouched against the wall and tried to shield the babe with her trembling body without withdrawing her gaze from the luminous orbs that were killing her. No thought of her husband came to her in her agony – no hope nor suggestion of rescue or escape. Her capacity for thought and feeling had narrowed to the dimensions of a single emotion – fear of the animal's spring, of the impact of its body, the buffeting of its great arms, the feel of its teeth in her throat, the mangling of her babe. Motionless now and in absolute silence, she awaited her doom, the moments growing to hours, to years, to ages; and still those devilish eyes maintained their watch.

Returning to his cabin late at night with a deer on his shoulders Charles Marlowe tried the door. It did not yield. He knocked; there was no answer. He laid down his deer and went round to the window. As he turned the angle of the building he fancied he heard a sound as of stealthy footfalls and a rustling in the undergrowth of the forest, but they were slight for certainty, even to his practised ear. Approaching the window, and to his surprise finding it open, he threw his leg over the sill and entered. All was darkness and silence. He groped his way to the fire-place, struck a match and lit a candle. Then he looked about. Cowering on the floor against a wall was his wife, clasping his child. As he sprang toward her she rose and broke into laughter, long, loud, and mechanical, devoid of gladness and devoid of sense – the laughter that is not out of keeping with the clanking of a chain. Hardly knowing what he did he extended his arms. She laid the babe in them. It was dead – pressed to death in its mother's embrace.

III

The theory of the defense

That is what occurred during a night in a forest, but not all of it did Irene Marlowe relate to Jenner Brading; not all of it was known to her. When she had concluded the sun was below the horizon and the long summer twilight had begun to deepen in the hollows of the land. For some moments Brading was silent, expecting the narrative to be carried forward to some definite connection with the conversation introducing it; but the narrator was as silent as he, her face averted, her hands clasping and unclasping themselves as they lay in her lap, with a singular suggestion of an activity independent of her will.

'It is a sad, a terrible story,' said Brading at last, 'but I do not understand. You call Charles Marlowe father; that I know. That he is old before his time, broken by some great sorrow, I have seen, or thought I saw. But, pardon me, you said that you – that you – '

'That I am insane,' said the girl, without a movement of head or body.

'But, Irene, you say – please, dear, do not look away from me – you say that the child was dead, not demented.'

'Yes, that one – I am the second. I was born three months after that night, my mother being mercifully permitted to lay down her life in giving me mine.'

Brading was again silent; he was a trifle dazed and could not at once think of the right thing to say. Her face was still turned away. In his embarrassment he reached impulsively toward the hands that lay closing and unclosing in her lap, but something – he could not have said what – restrained him. He then remembered, vaguely, that he had never altogether cared to take her hand.

'Is it likely,' she resumed, 'that a person born under such circumstances is like others – is what you call sane?'

Brading did not reply; he was preoccupied with a new thought that was taking shape in his mind – what a scientist would have called an hypothesis; a detective, a theory. It might throw an added light, albeit a lurid one, upon such doubt of her sanity as her own assertion had not dispelled.

The country was still new and, outside the villages, sparsely populated. The professional hunter was still a familiar figure, and among his trophies were heads and pelts of the larger kinds of game. Tales variously credible of nocturnal meetings with savage animals in lonely roads were sometimes current, passed through the customary stages of growth and decay, and were forgotten. A recent addition to these popular apocrypha, originating, apparently, by spontaneous generation in several households, was of a panther which had frightened some of their members by looking in at windows by night. The yarn had caused its little ripple of excitement – had even attained to the distinction of a place in the local newspaper; but Brading had given it no attention. Its likeness to the story to which he had just listened now impressed him as perhaps more than accidental. Was it not possible that the one story had suggested the other – that finding congenial conditions in a morbid mind and a fertile fancy, it had grown to the tragic tale that he had heard?

Brading recalled certain circumstances of the girl's history and disposition, of which, with love's incuriosity, he had hitherto been heedless – such as her solitary life with her father, at whose house no one, apparently, was an acceptable visitor and her strange fear of the night, by which those who knew her best accounted for her never being seen after dark. Surely in such a mind imagination once kindled might burn with a lawless flame, penetrating and enveloping the entire structure. That she was mad, though the conviction gave him the acutest pain, he could no longer doubt; she had only mistaken an effect of her mental disorder for its cause, bringing into imaginary relation with her own personality the vagaries of the local myth-makers. With some vague intention of testing his new 'theory,' and no very definite notion of how to set about it he said, gravely, but with hesitation:

'Irene, dear, tell me – I beg you will not take offence, but tell me –'

'I have told you,' she interrupted, speaking with a passionate earnestness that he had not known her to show – 'I have already told you that we cannot marry; is anything else worth saying?'

Before he could stop her she had sprung from her seat and without another word or look was gliding away among the trees toward her father's house. Brading had risen to detain her; he stood watching her in silence until she had vanished in the gloom. Suddenly he started as if he had been shot; his face took on an expression of amazement and alarm: in one of the black shadows into which she had disappeared he had caught a quick, brief glimpse of shining eyes! For an instant he was dazed and irresolute, then he dashed in to the wood after her, shouting: 'Irene, Irene, look out! The panther! The panther!'

In a moment he had passed through the fringe of forest into open ground and saw the girl's gray skirt vanishing into her father's door. No panther was visible.

IV

An appeal to the conscience of god

Jenner Brading, attorney-at-law, lived in a cottage at the edge of the town. Directly behind the dwelling was the forest. Being a batchelor, and therefore, by the Draconian moral code of the time and place denied the services of the only species of domestic servant known thereabout, the 'hired girl,' he boarded at the village hotel, where also was his office. The woodside cottage was merely a lodging maintained – at no great cost, to be sure – as an evidence of prosperity and respectabilty. It would hardly do for one to whom the local newspaper had pointed with pride as 'the foremost jurist of his time' to be 'homeless,' albeit he may sometimes have suspected that the words 'home' and 'house' were not strictly synonymous. Indeed, his consciousness of the disparity and his will to harmonize it were matters of logical inference, for it was generally reported that soon after the cottage was built its owner had made a futile venture in the direction of marriage – had, in truth, gone so far as to be rejected by the beautiful but eccentric daughter of Old Man Marlowe, the recluse. This was publicly believed because he had told it himself and she had not – a reversal of the usual order of things which could hardly fail to carry conviction.

Brading's bedroom was at the rear of the house, with a single window facing the forest. One night he was awakened by a noise at that window; he could hardly have said what it was like. With a little thrill of the nerves he sat up in bed and laid hold of the revolver which, with a forethought most commendable in one addicted to the habit of sleeping on the ground floor with an open window, he had put under his pillow. The room was in absolute darkness, but being unterrified he knew where to direct his eyes, and there he held them, awaiting in silence what further might occur. He could now dimly discern the aperture – a square of light black. Presently there appeared at its lower edge two gleaming eyes that burned with a malignant lustre inexpressibly terrible! Brading's heart gave a great jump, then seemed to stand still. A chill passed along his spine and through his hair; he felt the blood forsake his cheeks. He could not have cried out – not to save his life; but being a man of courage he would not, to save his life, have done so if he had been able. Some trepidation his coward body might feel, but his spirit was of sterner stuff. Slowly the shining eyes rose with a steady motion that seemed an approach, and slowly rose Brading's right hand, holding the pistol. He fired!

Blinded by the flash and stunned by the report, Brading nevertheless heard, or fancied that he heard, the wild, high scream of the panther, so human in sound, so devilish in suggestion. Leaping from the bed he hastily clothed himself and, pistol in hand, sprang from the door, meeting two or three men who came running up from the road. A brief explanation was followed by a cautious search of the house. The grass was wet with dew; beneath the window it had been trodden and partly leveled for a wide space, from which a devious trail, visible in the light of a lantern, led away into the bushes. One of the men stumbled and fell upon his hands, which as he rose and rubbed them together were slippery. On examination they were seen to be red with blood.

An encounter, unarmed, with a wounded panther was not agreeable to their taste; all but Brading turned back. He, with lantern and pistol, pushed courageously forward into the wood. Passing through a difficult undergrowth he came into a small opening, and there his courage had its reward, for there he found the body of his victim. But is was no panther. What it was is told, even to this day, upon a weather-worn headstone in the village churchyard, and for many years was attested daily at the graveside by the bent figure and sorrow-seamed face of Old Man Marlowe, to whose soul, and to the soul of his strange, unhappy child, peace. Peace and reparation.

UNCLE TOM'S CABIN

OR

LIFE AMONG THE LOWLY
(AN EXTRACT)

BY

HARRIET
BEECHER STOWE

In Which It Appears That a Senator Is But a Man

The light of the cheerful fire shone on the rug and carpet of a cosey parlor, and glittered on the sides of the tea-cups and well-brightened tea-pot, as Senator Bird was drawing off his boots, preparatory to inserting his feet in a pair of new handsome slippers, which his wife had been working for him while away on his senatorial tour. Mrs Bird, looking the very picture of delight, was superintending the arrangements of the table, ever and anon mingling admonitory remarks to a number of frolicsome juveniles, who were effervescing in all those modes of untold gambol and mischief that have astonished mothers ever since the flood.

'Tom, let the door-knob alone, – there's a man! Mary! Mary! don't pull the cat's tail, – poor pussy! Jim, you mustn't climb on that table, – no, no! – You don't know, my dear, what a surprise it is to us all, to see you here tonight!' said she, at last, when she found a space to say something to her husband.

'Yes, yes, I thought I'd just make a run down, spend the night, and have a little comfort at home. I'm tired to death, and my head aches!'

Mrs Bird cast a glance at a camphor-bottle, which stood in the half-open closet, and appeared to meditate an approach to it, but her husband interposed.

'No, no, Mary, no doctoring! a cup of your good hot tea, and some of our good home living, is what I want. It's a tiresome business, this legislating!'

And the senator smiled, as if he rather liked the idea of considering himself a sacrifice to his country.

'Well,' said his wife, after the business of the tea-table was getting rather slack, 'and what have they been doing in the Senate?'

Now, it was a very unusual thing for gentle little Mrs Bird ever to trouble her head with what was going on in the house of the state, very wisely considering that she had enough to do to mind her own. Mr Bird therefore, opened his eyes in surprise, and said,

'Not very much of importance.'

'Well; but is it true that they have been passing a law forbidding people to give meat and drink to those poor colored folks that come along? I heard they were talking of some such law, but I didn't think any Christian legislature would pass it!'

'Why, Mary, you are getting to be a politician, all at once.'

'No, nonsense! I wouldn't give a fip for all your politics, generally, but I think this is something downright cruel and unchristian. I hope, my dear, no such law has been passed.'

'There has been a law passed forbidding people to help off the slaves that come over from Kentucky, my dear; so much of that thing has been done by these reckless Abolitionists, that our brethren in Kentucky are very strongly excited, and it seems necessary, and no more than Christian and kind, that something should be done by our state to quiet the excitement.'

'And what is the law? It don't forbid us to shelter those poor creatures a night, does it, and to give 'em something comfortable to eat, and a few old clothes, and send them quietly about their business?'

'Why, yes, my dear; that would be aiding and abetting, you know.'

Mrs Bird was a timid, blushing little woman, of about four feet in height, and with mild blue eyes, and a peach-blow complexion, and the gentlest, sweetest voice in the world; – as for courage, a moderate-sized cock-turkey had been known to put her to rout at the very first gobble, and a stout house-dog, of moderate capacity, would bring her into subjection merely by a show of his teeth. Her husband and children were her entire world, and in these she ruled more by entreaty and persuasion than by command or argument. There was only one thing that was capable of arousing her, and that provocation came in on the side of her unusually gentle and sympathetic nature; – anything in the shape of cruelty would throw her into a passion, which was the more alarming and inexplicable in proportion to the general softness of her nature. Generally the most indulgent and easy to be entreated of all mothers, still her boys had a very reverent remembrance of a most vehement chastisement she once bestowed on them, because she found them leagued with several graceless boys of the neighborhood, stoning a defenceless kitten.

'I'll tell you what,' Master Bill used to say, 'I was scared that time. Mother came at me so that I thought she was crazy, and I was whipped and tumbled off to bed, without any supper, before I could get over wondering what had come about; and, after that, I heard mother crying outside the door, which made me feel worse than all the rest. I'll tell you what,' he'd say, 'we boys never stoned another kitten!'

On the present occasion, Mrs Bird rose quickly, with very red cheeks, which quite improved her general appearance, and walked up to her husband, with quite a resolute air, and said, in a determined tone:

'Now, John, I want to know if you think such a law as that is right and Christian?'

'You won't shoot me, now, Mary, if I say I do!'

'I never could have thought it of you, John; you didn't vote for it?'

'Even so, my fair politician.'

'You ought to be ashamed, John! Poor, homeless, houseless creatures! It's a shameful, wicked, abominable law, and I'll break it, for one, the first time I get a chance; and I hope I *shall* have a chance, I do! Things have got to a pretty pass, if a woman can't give a warm supper and a bed to poor, starving creatures, just because they are slaves, and have been abused and oppressed all their lives, poor things!'

'But, Mary, just listen to me. Your feelings are all quite right, dear, and interesting, and I love you for them; but, then, dear, we mustn't suffer our feelings to run away with our judgment; you must consider it's a matter of private feeling, – there are great public interests involved, – there is such a state of public agitation rising, that we must put aside our private feelings.'

'Now, John, I don't know anything about politics, but I can read my Bible; and there I see that I must feed the hungry, clothe the naked, and comfort the desolate; and that Bible I mean to follow.'

'But in cases where your doing so would involve a great public evil –'

'Obeying God never brings on public evils. I know it can't. It's always safest, all round, to *do as* He bids us.'

'Now, listen to me, Mary, and I can state to you a very clear argument, to show –'

'O, nonsense, John! – you can talk all night, but you wouldn't do it. I put it to you, John, – would *you* now turn away a poor, shivering, hungry creature from your door, because he was a runaway? *Would* you, now?'

Now, if the truth must be told, our senator had the misfortune to be a man who had a particularly humane and accessible nature, and turning away anybody that was in trouble never had been his forte; and what was worse for him in this particular pinch of the argument was, that his wife knew it, and, of course was making an assault on rather an indefensible point. So he had recourse to the usual means of gaining time for such cases made and provided; he said 'ahem,' and coughed several times, took out his pocket-handkerchief, and began to wipe his glasses. Mrs Bird, seeing the defenceless condition of the enemy's territory, had no more conscience than to push her advantage.

'I should like to see you doing that, John – I really should! Turning a woman out of doors in a snow-storm, for instance; or may be you'd take her up and put her in jail, wouldn't you? You would make a great hand at that!'

'Of course, it would be a very painful duty,' began Mr Bird, in a moderate tone.

'Duty, John! don't use that word! You know it isn't a duty – it can't be a duty! If folks want to keep their slaves from running away, let 'em treat 'em well, – that's my doctrine. If I had slaves (as I hope I never shall have), I'd risk their wanting to run away from me, or you either, John. I tell you folks don't run away when they are happy; and when they do run, poor creatures! they suffer enough with cold and hunger and fear, without everybody's turning against them; and, law or no law, I never will, so help me God!'

'Mary! Mary! My dear, let me reason with you.'

'I hate reasoning, John, – especially reasoning on such subjects. There's a way you political folks have of coming round and round a plain right thing; and you don't believe in it yourselves, when it comes to practice. I know *you* well enough, John. You don't believe it's right any more than I do; and you wouldn't do it any sooner than I.'

At this critical juncture, old Cudjoe, the black man-of-all-work, put his head in at the door, and wished 'Missis would come into the kitchen;' and our senator, tolerably relieved, looked after his little wife with a whimsical mixture of amusement and vexation, and, seating himself in the arm-chair, began to read the papers.

After a moment, his wife's voice was heard at the door, in a quick, earnest tone, – 'John! John! I do wish you'd come here, a moment.'

He laid down his paper, and went into the kitchen, and started, quite amazed at the sight that presented itself: – A young and slender woman, with garments torn and frozen, with one shoe gone, and the stocking torn away from the cut and bleeding foot, was laid back in a deadly swoon upon two chairs. There was the impress of the despised race on her face, yet none could help feeling its mournful and pathetic beauty, while its stony sharpness, its cold, fixed, deathly aspect, struck a solemn chill over him. He drew his breath short, and stood in silence. His wife, and their only colored domestic, old Aunt Dinah, were busily engaged in restorative measures; while old Cudjoe had got the boy on his knee, and was busy pulling off his shoes and stockings, and chafing his little cold feet.

'Sure, now, if she an't a sight to behold!' said old Dinah, compassionately; ''pears like 't was the heat that made her faint. She was tol'able peart when she cum in, and asked if she couldn't warm herself here a spell; and I was just a-askin' her where she cum from, and she fainted right down. Never done much hard work, guess, by the looks of her hands.'

'Poor creature!' said Mrs Bird, compassionately, as the woman slowly unclosed her large, dark eyes, and looked vacantly at her. Suddenly an expression of agony crossed her face, and she sprang up, saying, 'O, my Harry! Have they got him?'

The boy, at this, jumped from Cudjoe's knee, and running to her side put up his arms. 'O, he's here! he's here!' she exclaimed.

'O, ma'am!' said she, wildly, to Mrs Bird, 'do protect us! don't let them get him!'

'Nobody shall hurt you here, poor woman,' said Mrs Bird, encouragingly. 'You are safe; don't be afraid.'

'God bless you!' said the woman, covering her face and sobbing; while the little boy, seeing her crying, tried to get into her lap.

With many gentle and womanly offices, which none knew better how to render than Mrs Bird, the poor woman was, in time, rendered more calm. A temporary bed was provided for her on the settle, near the fire; and, after a short time, she fell into a heavy slumber, with the child, who seemed no less weary, soundly sleeping on her arm; for the mother resisted, with nervous anxiety, the kindest attempts to take him from her; and, even in sleep, her arm encircled him with an unrelaxing clasp, as if she could not even then be beguiled of her vigilant hold.

Mr and Mrs Bird had gone back to the parlor, where, strange as it may appear, no reference was made, on either side, to the preceding conversation; but Mrs Bird busied herself with her knitting-work, and Mr Bird pretended to be reading the paper.

'I wonder who and what she is!' said Mr Bird, at last, as he laid it down.

'When she wakes up and feels a little rested, we will see,' said Mrs Bird.

'I say, wife!' said Mr Bird after musing in silence over his newspaper.

'Well, dear!'

'She couldn't wear one of your gowns, could she, by any letting down, or such matter? She seems to be rather larger than you are.'

A quite perceptible smile glimmered on Mrs Bird's face, as she answered, 'We'll see.'

Another pause, and Mr Bird again broke out,

'I say, wife!'

'Well! What now?'

'Why, there's that old bombazin cloak, that you keep on purpose to put over me when I take my afternoon's nap; you might as well give her that, – she needs clothes.'

At this instant, Dinah looked in to say that the woman was awake, and wanted to see Missis.

Mr and Mrs Bird went into the kitchen, followed by the two eldest boys, the smaller fry having, by this time, been safely disposed of in bed.

The woman was now sitting up on the settle, by the fire. She was looking steadily into the blaze, with a calm, heart-broken expression, very different from her former agitated wildness.

'Did you want me?' said Mrs Bird, in gentle tones. 'I hope you feel better now, poor woman!'

A long-drawn, shivering sigh was the only answer; but she lifted her dark eyes, and fixed them on her with such a forlorn and imploring expression, that the tears came into the little woman's eyes.

'You needn't be afraid of anything; we are friends here, poor woman! Tell me where you came from, and what you want,' said she.

'I came from Kentucky,' said the woman.

'When?' said Mr Bird, taking up the interogatory.

'Tonight.'

'How did you come?'

'I crossed on the ice.'

'Crossed on the ice!' said every one present.

'Yes,' said the woman, slowly, 'I did. God helping me, I crossed on the ice; for they were behind me – right behind – and there was no other way!'

'Law, Missis,' said Cudjoe, 'the ice is all in broken-up blocks, a swinging and a tetering up and down in the water!'

'I know it was – I know it!' said she, wildly; 'but I did it! I wouldn't have thought I could, – I didn't think I should get over, but I didn't care! I could but die, if I didn't. The Lord helped me; nobody knows how much the Lord can help 'em, till they try,' said the woman, with a flashing eye.

'Were you a slave?' said Mr Bird.

'Yes, sir; I belonged to a man in Kentucky.'

'Was he unkind to you?'

'No, sir; he was a good master.'

'And was your mistress unkind to you?'

'No sir – no! my mistress was always good to me.'

'What could induce you to leave a good home, then, and run away, and go through such dangers?'

The woman looked up at Mrs Bird, with a keen, scrutinizing glance, and it did not escape her that she was dressed in deep mourning.

'Ma'am,' she said, suddenly, 'have you ever lost a child?'

The question was unexpected, and it was thrust on a new wound; for it was only a month since a darling child of the family had been laid in the grave.

Mr Bird turned around and walked to the window, and Mrs Bird burst into tears; but, recovering her voice, she said,

'Why do you ask that? I have lost a little one.'

'Then you will feel for me. I have lost two, one after another, – left 'em buried there when I came away; and I had only this one left. I never slept a night without him; he was all I had. He was my comfort and pride, day and night; and, ma'am, they were going to take him away from me, – to *sell* him, – sell him down south, ma'am, to go all alone, – a baby that had never been away from his mother in his life! I couldn't stand it, ma'am. I knew I never should be good for anything, if they did; and when I knew the papers were signed, and he was sold, I took him and came off in the night; and they chased me, – the man that bought him, and some of Mas'r's folks, – and they were coming down right behind me, and I heard 'em. I jumped right on to the ice; and how I got across, I don't know, – but, first I knew, a man was helping me up the bank.'

The woman did not sob nor weep. She had gone to a place where tears are dry; but every one around her was, in some way characteristic of themselves, showing signs of hearty sympathy.

The two little boys, after a desperate rummaging in their pockets, in search of those pocket-handkerchiefs which mothers know are never to be found there, had thrown themselves disconsolately into the skirts of their mother's gown, where they were sobbing, and wiping their eyes and noses, to their hearts' content; – Mrs Bird had her face fairly hidden in her pocket-handkerchief; and old Dinah, with tears streaming down her black, honest face, was ejaculating, 'Lord have mercy on us!' with all the fervor of a camp-meeting; – while old Cudjoe, rubbing his eyes very hard with his cuffs, and making a most uncommon variety of wry faces, occasionally responded in the same key, with great fervor. Our senator was a statesman, and of course could not be expected to cry, like other mortals; and so he turned his back to the company, and looked out of the window, and seemed particularly busy in clearing his throat and wiping his spectacle-glasses, occasionally blowing his nose in a manner that was calculated to excite suspicion, had any one been in a state to observe critically.

'How came you to tell me you had a kind master?' he suddenly exclaimed, gulping down very resolutely some kind of rising in his throat, and turning suddenly round upon the woman.

'Because he *was* a kind master; I'll say that of him, any way; – and my mistress was kind; but they couldn't help themselves. They were owing money; and there was some way, I can't tell how, that a man had a hold on them, and they were obliged to give him his will. I listened, and heard him telling mistress that, and she begging and pleading for me, – and he told her he couldn't help himself, and that the papers were all drawn; – and then it was I took him and left my home, and came away. I knew 't was no use of my trying to live, if they did it; for 't 'pears like this child is all I have.'

'Have you no husband?'

'Yes, but he belongs to another man. His master is real hard to him, and won't let him come to see me, hardly ever; and he's grown harder and harder upon us, and he threatens to sell him down south; – it's like I'll never see *him* again!'

The quiet tone in which the woman pronounced these words might have led a superficial observer to think that she was entirely apathetic; but there was a calm, settled depth of anguish in her large, dark eye, that spoke of something far otherwise.

'And where do you mean to go, my poor woman?' said Mrs Bird.

'To Canada, if I only knew where that was. Is it very far off, is Canada?' said she, looking up, with a simple, confiding air, to Mrs Bird's face.

'Poor thing!' said Mrs Bird, involuntarily.

'Is 't a very great way off, think?' said the woman, earnestly.

'Much further than you think, poor child!' said Mrs Bird; 'but we will try to think what can be done for you. Here, Dinah, make her up a bed in your own room, close by the kitchen, and I'll think what to do for her in the morning. Meanwhile, never fear, poor woman; put your trust in God; he will protect you.'

Mrs Bird and her husband reentered the parlor. She sat down in her little rocking-chair before the fire, swaying thoughtfully to and fro. Mr Bird strode up and down the room, grumbling to himself, 'Pish! pshaw! confounded awkward business!' At length, striding up to his wife, he said,

'I say, wife, she'll have to get away from here, this very night. That fellow will be down on the scent bright and early tomorrow morning: if 't was only the woman, she could lie quiet till it was over; but that little chap can't be kept still by a troop of horse and foot, I'll warrant me; he'll bring it all out, popping his head out of some window or door. A pretty kettle of fish it would be for me, too, to be caught with them both here, just now! No; they'll have to be got off tonight.'

'Tonight! How is it possible? – where to?'

'Well, I know pretty well where to,' said the senator, beginning to put on his boots, with a reflective air; and, stopping when his leg was half in, he embraced his knee with both hands, and seemed to go off in deep meditation.

'It's a confounded awkward, ugly business,' said he, at last, beginning to tug at his boot-straps again, 'and that's a fact!' After one boot was fairly on, the senator sat with the other in his hand, profoundly studying the figure of the carpet. 'It will have to be done, though, for aught I see, – hang it all!' and he drew the other boot anxiously on, and looked out of the window.

Now, little Mrs Bird was a discreet woman, – a woman who never in her life said, 'I told you so!' and, on the present occasion, though pretty well aware of the shape her husband's meditations were taking, she very prudently forbore to meddle with them, only sat very quietly in her chair, and looked quite ready to hear her liege lord's intentions, when he should think proper to utter them.

'You see,' he said, 'there's my old client, Van Trompe, has come over from Kentucky, and set all his slaves free; and he has bought a place seven miles up the creek, here, back in the woods, where nobody goes, unless they go on purpose; and it's a place that isn't found in a hurry. There she'd be safe enough; but the plague of the thing is, nobody could drive a carriage there tonight, but *me*.'

'Why not? Cudjoe is an excellent driver.'

'Ay, ay, but here it is. The creek has to be crossed twice; and the second crossing is quite dangerous, unless one knows it as I do. I have crossed it a hundred times on horseback, and know exactly the turns to take. And so, you see, there's no help for it. Cudjoe must put in the horses, as quietly as may be, about twelve o'clock, and I'll take her over; and then, to give color to the matter, he must carry me on to the next tavern to take the stage for Columbus, that comes by about three or four, and so it will look as if I had had the carriage only for that. I shall get into business bright and early in the morning. But I'm thinking I shall feel rather cheap there, after all that's been said and done; but, hang it, I can't help it!'

'Your heart is better than your head, in this case, John,' said the wife, laying her little white hand on his. 'Could I ever have loved you, had I not known you better than you know yourself?' And the little woman looked so handsome, with the tears sparkling in her eyes, that the senator thought he must be a decidedly clever fellow, to get such a pretty creature into such a passionate admiration of him; and so, what could he do but walk off soberly, to see about the carriage. At the door, however, he stopped a moment, and then coming back, he said, with some hesitation.

'Mary, I don't know how you'd feel about it, but there's that drawer full of things – of – of – poor little Henry's.' So saying, he turned quickly on his heel, and shut the door after him.

His wife opened the little bed-room door adjoining her room and, taking the candle, set it down on the top of a bureau there; then from a small recess she took a key, and put it thoughtfully in the lock of a drawer, and made a sudden pause, while two boys, who, boy like, had followed close on her heels, stood looking, with silent, significant glances, at their mother. And oh! mother that reads this, has there never been in your house a drawer, or a closet, the opening of which has been to you like the opening again of a little grave? Ah! happy mother that you are, if it has not been so.

Mrs Bird slowly opened the drawer. There were little coats of many a form and pattern, piles of aprons, and rows of small stockings; and even a pair of little shoes, worn and rubbed at the toes, were peeping from the folds of a paper. There was a toy horse and wagon, a top, a ball, – memorials gathered with many a tear and many a heart-break! She sat down by the drawer, and, leaning her head on her hands over it, wept till the tears fell through her fingers into the drawer; then suddenly raising her head, she began, with nervous haste, selecting the plainest and most substantial articles, and gathering them into a bundle.

'Mamma,' said one of the boys, gently touching her arm, 'you going to give away *those* things?'

'My dear boys,' she said, softly and earnestly, 'if our dear, loving little Henry looks down from heaven, he would be glad to have us do this. I could not find it in my heart to give them away to any common person – to anybody that was happy; but I give them to a mother more heart-broken and sorrowful than I am; and I hope God will send his blessings with them!'

There are in this world blessed souls, whose sorrows all spring up into joys for others; whose earthly hopes, laid in the grave with many tears, are the seed from which spring healing flowers and balm for the desolate and the distressed. Among such was the delicate woman who sits there by the lamp, dropping slow tears, while she prepares the memorials of her own lost one for the outcast wanderer.

After a while, Mrs Bird opened a wardrobe, and, taking from thence a plain, serviceable dress or two, she sat down busily to her work-table, and, with needle, scissors, and thimble, at hand, quietly commenced the 'letting down' process which her husband had recommended, and continued busily at it till the old clock in the corner struck twelve, and she heard the low rattling of wheels at the door.

'Mary,' said her husband, coming in, with his overcoat in his hand, 'you must wake her up now; we must be off.'

Mrs Bird hastily deposited the various articles she had collected in a small plain trunk, and locking it, desired her husband to see it in the carriage, and then proceeded to call the woman. Soon, arrayed in a cloak, bonnet, and shawl, that had belonged to her benefactress, she appeared at the door with her child in her arms. Mr Bird hurried her into the carriage, and Mrs Bird pressed on after her to the carriage steps. Eliza leaned out of the carriage, and put out her hand, – a hand as soft and beautiful as was given in return. She fixed her large, dark eyes full of earnest meaning, on Mrs Bird's face, and seemed going to speak. Her lips moved, – she tried once or twice, but there was no sound, –

and pointing upward, with a look never to be forgotten, she fell back in the seat, and covered her face. The door was shut, and the carriage drove on.

What a situation, now, for a patriotic senator, that had been all the week before spurring up the legislature of his native state to pass more stringent resolutions against escaping fugitives, their harborers and abettors!

Our good senator in his native state had not been exceeded by any of his brethren at Washington, in the sort of eloquence which has won for them immortal renown! How sublimely he had sat with his hands in his pockets, and scouted all sentimental weakness of those who would put the welfare of a few miserable fugitives before great state interests!

He was as bold as a lion about it, and 'mightily convinced' not only himself, but everybody that heard him; – but then his idea of a fugitive was only an idea of the letters that spell the word, – or at the most, the image of a little newspaper picture of a man with a stick and bundle with 'Ran away from the subscriber' under it. The magic of the real presence of distress, – the imploring human eye, the frail, trembling human hand, the despairing appeal of helpless agony, – these he had never tried. He had never thought that a fugitive might be a hapless mother, a defenceless child, – like that one which was now wearing his lost boy's little well-known cap; and so, as our poor senator was not stone or steel, – as he was a man, and a downright noble-hearted one, too, – he was, as everybody must see, in a sad case for his patriotism. And you need not exult over him, good brother of the Southern States; for we have some inklings that many of you, under similar circumstances, would not do much better. We have reason to know, in Kentucky, as in Mississippi, are noble and generous hearts, to whom never was tale of suffering told in vain. Ah, good brother! is it fair for you to expect of us services which your own brave, honorable heart would not allow you to render, were you in our place?

Be that as it may, if our good senator was a political sinner, he was in a fair way to expiate it by his night's penance. There had been a long continuous period of rainy weather, and the soft, rich earth of Ohio, as every one knows, is admirably suited to the manufacture of mud – and the road was an Ohio railroad of the good old times.

'And pray, what sort of a road may that be?' says some eastern traveller, who has been accustomed to connect no ideas with a railroad, but those of smoothness or speed.

Know, then, innocent eastern friend, that in benighted regions of the west, where the mud is of unfathomable and sublime depth, roads are made of round rough logs, arranged transversely side by side, and coated over in their pristine freshness with earth, turf, and whatsoever may come to hand, and then the rejoicing native calleth it a road, and straightway essayeth to ride thereupon. In process of time, the rains wash off all the turf and grass aforesaid, move the logs hither and thither, in picturesque positions, up, down and crosswise, with divers chasms and ruts of black mud intervening.

Over such a road as this our senator went stumbling along, making moral reflections as continuously as under the circumstances could be expected, – the carriage proceeding along much as follows, – bump! bump! bump! slush! down in the mud! – the senator, woman and child, reversing their positions so suddenly as to come, without any very accurate adjustment, against the windows of the down-hill side. Carriage sticks fast, while Cudjoe on the outside is heard making a great muster among the horses. After various ineffectual pullings and twitchings, just as the senator is losing all patience, the carriage suddenly rights itself with a bounce, – two front wheels go down into another abyss, and senator, woman, and child, all tumble promiscuously on to the front seat, – senator's hat is jammed over his eyes and nose quite unceremoniously, and he considers himself fairly extinguished; – child cries, and Cudjoe on the outside delivers animated addresses to the horses, who are kicking, and floundering, and straining under repeated cracks of the whip. Carriage springs up, with another bounce, – down go the hind wheels, – senator, woman, and child, fly over on to the back seat, his elbows encountering her bonnet, and both her feet being jammed into his hat, which flies off in the concussion. After a few moments the 'slough' is passed, and the horses stop, panting; – the senator finds his hat, the woman straightens her bonnet and hushes her child, and they brace themselves for what is yet to come.

For a while only the continuous bump! bump! intermingled, just by way of variety, with divers side plunges and compound shakes; and they begin to flatter themselves that they are not so badly off, after all. At last, with a square plunge, which puts all on to their feet and then down into their seats with incredible quickness, the carriage stops, – and, after much outside commotion, Cudjoe appears at the door.

'Please, sir, it's powerful bad spot, this yer. I don't know how we's to get clar out. I'm a thinkin' we'll have to be a gettin' rails.'

The senator despairingly steps out, picking gingerly for some firm foothold; down goes one foot an immeasurable depth, – he tries to pull it up, loses his balance, and tumbles over into the mud, and is fished out, in a very despairing condition, by Cudjoe.

But we forbear, out of sympathy to our readers' bones. Western travellers, who have beguiled the midnight hour in the interesting process of pulling down rail fences, to pry their carriages out of mud holes, will have a respectful and mournful sympathy with our unfortunate hero. We beg them to drop a silent tear, and pass on.

It was full late in the night when the carriage emerged, dripping and bespattered, out of the creek, and stood at the door of a large farm-house.

It took no inconsiderable perseverance to arouse the inmates; but at last the respectable proprietor appeared, and undid the door. He was a great, tall, bristling Orson of a fellow, full six feet and some inches in his stockings, and arrayed in a red flannel hunting-shirt. A very heavy *mat* of sandy hair, in a decidedly tousled condition, and a beard of some days' growth, gave the worthy man an appearance to say the least, not particularly prepossessing. He stood for a few minutes holding the candle aloft, and blinking on our travellers with a dismal and mystified expression that was truly ludicrous. It cost some effort of our senator to induce him to comprehend the case fully; and while he is doing his best at that, we shall give him a little introduction to our readers.

Honest old John Van Trompe was once quite a considerable land-owner and slave-owner in the State of Kentucky. Having 'nothing of the bear about him but the skin,' and being gifted by nature with a great, honest, just heart, quite equal to his gigantic frame, he had been for some years witnessing with repressed uneasiness the workings of a system equally bad for oppressor and oppressed. At last, one day, John's great heart had swelled altogether too big to wear his bonds any longer; so he just took his pocket-book out of his desk, and went over into Ohio, and bought a quarter of a township of good, rich land, made out free papers for all his people, – men, women, and children, – packed them up in wagons, and sent them off to settle down; and then honest John turned his face up the creek, and sat quietly down on a snug, retired farm, to enjoy his conscience and his reflections.

'Are you the man that will shelter a poor woman and child from slave-catchers?' said the senator, explicitly.

'I rather think I am,' said honest John, with some considerable emphasis.

'I thought so,' said the senator.

'If there's anybody comes,' said the good man, stretching his tall, muscular form upward, 'why here I'm ready for him: and I've got seven sons, each six foot high, and they'll be ready for 'em. Give our respects to 'em', said John; 'tell 'em it's no matter how soon they call, – make no kinder difference to us,' said John, running his fingers through the shock of hair that thatched his head, and bursting out into a great laugh.

Weary, jaded, and spiritless, Eliza dragged herself up to the door, with her child lying in a heavy sleep on her arm. The rough man held the candle to her face, and uttering a kind of compassionate grunt, opened the door of a small bed-room adjoining to the large kitchen where they were standing, and motioned her to go in. He took down a candle, and lighting it, set it upon the table, and then addressed himself to Eliza.

'Now, I say, gal, you needn't be a bit afeard, let who will come here. I'm up to all that sort o' thing,' said he, pointing to two or three goodly rifles over the mantelpiece; 'and most people that know me know that 't wouldn't be healthy to try to get anybody out o' my house when I'm agin it. So *now* you jist go to sleep now, as quiet as if yer mother was a rockin' ye,' said he, as he shut the door.

'Why, this is an uncommon handsome un,' he said to the senator. 'Ah, well; handsome uns has the greatest cause to run, sometimes, if they has any kind o' feelin, such as decent women should. I know all about that.'

The senator, in a few words, briefly explained Eliza's history.

'O! ou! aw! now, I want to know?' said the good man, pitifully; 'sho! now sho! That's natur now, poor crittur! hunted down now like a deer, – hunted down, jest for havin' natural feelin's, and doin' what no kind o' mother could help a doin'! I tell ye what, these yer things make me come the nighest to swearin', now, o' most anything,' said honest John, as he wiped his eyes with the back of a great, freckled, yellow hand. 'I tell yer what, stranger, it was years and years before I'd jine the church, 'cause the ministers round in our parts used to preach that the Bible went in for these ere cuttings up, – and I couldn't be up to 'em with their Greek and Hebrew, and so I took up agin 'em, Bible and all. I never jined the church till I found a minister that was up to 'em all in Greek and all that, and he said right the contrary; and then I took right hold, and jined the church, – I did now, fact,' said John who had been all this time uncorking some very frisky bottled cider, which at this juncture he presented.

'Ye'd better jest put up here, now, till daylight,' said he, heartily, 'and I'll call up the old woman, and have a bed got ready for you in no time.'

'Thank you, my good friend,' said the senator, 'I must be along, to take the night stage for Columbus.'

'Ah! well, then, if you must, I'll go a piece with you, and show you a cross road that will take you there better than the road you came on. That road's mighty bad.'

John equipped himself, and, with a lantern in hand, was soon seen guiding the senator's carriage towards a road that ran down in a hollow, back of his dwelling. When they parted, the senator put into his hand a ten-dollar bill.

'It's for her,' he said, briefly.

'Ay, ay,' said John, with equal conciseness.

They shook hands, and parted.

CHAPTER TEN

The Property Is Carried Off

The February morning looked gray and drizzling through the window of Uncle Tom's cabin. It looked on downcast faces, the images of mournful hearts. The little table stood out before the fire, covered with an ironing-cloth; a coarse but clean shirt or two, fresh from the iron, hung on the back of a chair by the fire, and Aunt Chloe had another spread out before her on the table. Carefully she rubbed and ironed every fold and every hem, with the most scrupulous exactness, every now and then raising her hand to her face to wipe off the tears that were coursing down her cheeks.

Tom sat by, with his Testament open on his knee, and his head leaning upon his hand; – but neither spoke. It was yet early, and the children lay all asleep together in their little rude trundle-bed.

Tom, who had, to the full, the gentle, domestic heart, which woe for them! has been a peculiar characteristic of his unhappy race, got up and walked silently to look at his children.

'It's the last time,' he said.

Aunt Chloe did not answer, only rubbed away over and over on the coarse shirt, already as smooth as hands could make it; and finally setting her iron suddenly down with a despairing plunge, she sat down to the table, and 'lifted up her voice and wept.'

'S'pose we must be resigned; but oh Lord! how ken I? If I know'd anything whar you 's goin', or how they'd sarve you! Missis says she'll try and 'deem ye, in a year or two; but Lor! nobody never comes up that goes down thar! They kills 'em! I've hearn 'em tell how dey works 'em up on dem ar plantations.'

'There'll be the same God there, Chloe, that there is here.'

'Well,' said Aunt Chloe, 's'pose dere will; but de Lord lets drefful things happen, sometimes. I don't seem to get no comfort dat v'ay.'

'I'm in the Lord's hands,' said Tom; 'nothin' can go no turder than he lets it; – and thar's one thing I can thank him for. It's me that's sold and going down, and not you nur the chil'en. Here you're safe; – what comes will come only on me; and the Lord, he'll help me, – I know he will.'

Ah, brave, manly heart, – smothering thine own sorrow, to comfort thy beloved ones! Tom spoke with a thick utterance, and with a bitter choking in his throat, – but he spoke brave and strong.

'Let's think on our marcies!' he added, tremulously, as if he was quite sure he needed to think on them very hard indeed.

'Marcies!' said Aunt Chloe; 'don't see no marcy in 't! 'tan't right! tan't right it should be so! Mas'r never ought ter left it so that ye *could* be took for his debts. Ye've arnt him all he gets for ye, twice over. He owed ye yer freedom, and ought ter gin 't to yer years ago. Mebbe he can't help himself now, but I feel it's wrong. Nothing can't beat that ar out o' me. Sich a faithful crittur as ye've been, – and allers sot his business 'fore yer own every way, – and reckoned on him more than yer own wife and chil'en! Them as sells heart's love and heart's blood, to get out thar scrapes, de Lord'll be up to 'em!'

'Chloe! now, if ye love me, ye won't talk so, when perhaps jest the last time we'll ever have together! And I'll tell ye, Chloe, it goes agin me to hear one word agin Mas'r. Wan't he put in my arms a baby? – it's natur I should think a heap of him. And he couldn't be spected to think so much of poor Tom. Mas'rs is used to havin' all these yer things done for 'em, and nat'lly they don't think so much on 't. They can't be spected to, no way. Set him 'longside of other Mas'rs – who's had the treatment and livin' I've had? And he never would have let this yer come on me, if he could have seed it aforehand. I know he wouldn't.'

'Wal, any way, thar's wrong about it *somewhar*,' said Aunt Chloe, in whom a stubborn sense of justice was a predominant trait; 'I can't jest make out whar 't is, but thar's wrong somewhar, I'm *clar* o' that.'

'Yer ought ter look up to the Lord above – he's above all – thar don't a sparrow fall without him.'

'It don't seem to comfort me, but I spect it orter,' said Aunt Chloe. 'But dar's no use talkin'; I'll jes wet up de corn-cake, and get ye one good breakfast, 'cause nobody knows when you'll get another.'

In order to appreciate the sufferings of the negroes sold south, it must be remembered that all the instinctive affections of that race are peculiarly strong. Their local attachments are very abiding. They are not naturally daring and enterprising, but home-loving and affectionate. Add to this all the terrors with which ignorance invests the unknown, and add to this, again, that selling to the south is set before the negro from childhood as the last severity of punishment. The threat that terrifies more than whipping or torture of any kind is the threat of being sent down the river. We have ourselves heard this feeling expressed by them, and seen the unaffected horror with which they will sit in their gossipping hours, and tell frightful stories of that 'down river,' which to them is

'That undiscovered country, from whose bourn
No traveller returns.'

A missionary figure among the fugitives in Canada told us that many of the fugitives confessed themselves to have escaped from comparatively kind masters, and that they were induced to brave the perils of escape, in almost every case, by the desperate horror with which they regarded being sold south, – a doom which was hanging either over themselves or their husbands, their wives or children. This nerves the African, naturally patient, timid and unenterprising, with heroic courage, and leads him to suffer hunger, cold, pain, the perils of the wilderness, and the more dread penalties of recapture.

The simple morning meal now smoked on the table, for Mrs Shelby had excused Aunt Chloe's attendance at the great house that morning. The poor soul had expended all her little energies on this farewell feast, – had killed and dressed her choicest chicken, and prepared her corn-cake with scrupulous exactness, just to her husband's taste, and brought out certain mysterious jars on the mantelpiece, some preserves that were never produced except on extreme occasions.

'Lor, Pete,' said Mose, triumphantly, 'han't we got a buster of a breakfast!' at the same time catching at a fragment of the chicken.

Aunt Chloe gave him a sudden box on the ear. 'Thar now! crowing over the last breakfast yer poor daddy's gwine to have to home!'

'O, Chloe!' said Tom, gently.

'Wal, I can't help it,' said Aunt Chloe, hiding her face in her apron; 'I's so tossed about it, it makes me act ugly.'

The boys stood quite still, looking first at their father and then at their mother, while the baby, climbing up her clothes, began an imperious, commanding cry.

'Thar!' said Aunt Chloe, wiping her eyes and taking up the baby; 'now I's done, I hope, – now do eat something. This yer's my nicest chicken. Thar, boys, ye shall have some, poor critturs! Yer mammy's been cross to yer.'

The boys needed no second invitation, and went in with great zeal for the eatables; and it was well they did so, as otherwise there would have been very little performed to any purpose by the party.

'Now,' said Aunt Chloe, bustling about after breakfast, 'I must put up yer clothes. Jest like as not, he'll take 'em all away. I know thar ways – mean as dirt, they is! Wal, now, yer flannels for rhumatis is in this corner; so be careful, 'cause there won't nobody make ye no more. Then here's yer old shirts, and these yer is new ones. I toed off these yer stockings last night, and put de ball in 'em to mend with. But Lor! who'll ever mend for ye?' and Aunt Chloe, again overcome, laid her head on the box side, and sobbed. 'To think on 't! no crittur to do for ye, sick or well! I don't railly think I ought ter be good now!'

The boys, having eaten everything there was on the breakfast-table, began now to take some thought of the case; and, seeing their mother crying, and their father looking very sad, began to whimper and put their hands to their eyes. Uncle Tom had the baby on his knee, and was letting her enjoy herself to the utmost extent, scratching his face and pulling his hair, and occasionally breaking out into clamorous explosions of delight, evidently arising out of her own internal reflections.

'Ay, crow away, poor crittur!' said Aunt Chloe; 'ye'll have to come to it, too! ye'll live to see yer husband sold, or mebbe be sold yerself; and these yer boys, they's to be sold, I s'pose, too, jest like as not, when dey gets good for somethin'; an't no use in niggers havin' nothin'!'

Here one of the boys called out, 'Thar's Missis a-comin' in!'

'She can't do no good; what's she coming for?' said Aunt Chloe.

Mrs Shelby entered. Aunt Chloe set a chair for her in a manner decidedly gruff and crusty. She did not seem to notice either the action or the manner. She looked pale and anxious.

'Tom,' she said, 'I come to –' and stopping suddenly, and regarding the silent group, she sat down in the chair, and, covering her face with her handkerchief, began to sob.

'Lor, now, Missis, don't – don't!' said Aunt Chloe, bursting out in her turn; and for a few moments they all wept in company. And in those tears they all shed together, the high and the lowly, melted away all the heart-burnings and anger of the oppressed. O, ye who visit the distressed, do ye know that everything your money can buy, given with a cold, averted face, is not worth one honest tear shed in real sympathy?

'My good fellow,' said Mrs Shelby, 'I can't give you anything to do you any good. If I give you money, it will only be taken from you. But I tell you solemnly, and before God, that I will keep trace of you, and bring you back as soon as I can command the money; – and, till then, trust in God!'

Here the boys called out that Mas'r Haley was coming, and then an unceremonious kick pushed open the door. Haley stood there in very ill humor, having ridden hard the night before, and being not at all pacified by his ill success in recapturing his prey.

'Come,' said he, 'ye nigger, ye'r ready? Servant, ma'am!' said he, taking off his hat, as he saw Mrs Shelby.

Aunt Chloe shut and corded the box, and, getting up, looked gruffly on the trader, her tears seeming suddenly turned to sparks of fire.

Tom rose up meekly, to follow his new master, and raised up his heavy box on his shoulder. His wife took the baby in her arms to go with him to the wagon, and the children, still crying, trailed on behind.

Mrs Shelby, walking up to the trader, detained him for a few moments, talking with him in an earnest manner; and while she was thus talking, the whole family party proceeded to a wagon, that stood ready harnessed at the door. A crowd of all the old and young hands on the place stood gathered around it, to bid farewell to their old associate. Tom had been looked up to, both as a head servant and a Christian teacher, by all the place, and there was much honest sympathy and grief about him, particularly among the women.

'Why, Chloe, you bar it better 'n we do!' said one of the women, who had been weeping freely, noticing the gloomy calmness with which Aunt Chloe stood by the wagon.

'I's done my tears!' she said, looking grimly at the trader, who was coming up. 'I does not feel to cry 'fore dat ar old limb, no how!'

'Get in!' said Haley to Tom, as he strode through the crowd of servants, who looked at him with lowering brows.

Tom got in, and Haley, drawing out from under the wagon seat a heavy pair of shackles, made them fast around each ankle.

A smothered groan of indignation ran through the whole circle, and Mrs Shelby spoke from the verandah, –

'Mr Haley, I assure you that precaution is entirely unnecessary.'

'Don't know, ma'am; I've lost one five hundred dollars from this yer place, and I can't afford to run no more risks.'

'What else could she spect on him?' said Aunt Chloe, indignantly, while the two boys, who now seemed to comprehend at once their father's destiny, clung to her gown, sobbing and groaning vehemently.

'I'm sorry,' said Tom, 'that Mas'r George happened to be away.'

George had gone to spend two or three days with a companion on a neighboring estate, and having departed early in the morning, before Tom's misfortune had been made public, had left without hearing of it.

'Give my love to Mas'r George,' he said, earnestly.

Haley whipped up the horse, and, with a steady, mournful look, fixed to the last on the old place, Tom was whirled away.

Mr Shelby at this time was not at home. He had sold Tom under the spur of a driving necessity, to get out of the power of a man whom he dreaded, – and his first feeling, after the consummation of the bargain, had been that of relief. But his wife's expostulations awoke his half-slumbering regrets; and Tom's manly disinterestedness increased the unpleasantness of his feelings. It was in vain that he said to himself that he had a *right* to do it, – that everybody did it, – and that some did it without even the excuse of necessity; – he could not satisfy his own feelings; and that he might not witness the unpleasant scenes of the consummation, he had gone on a short business tour up the country, hoping that all would be over before he returned.

Tom and Haley rattled on along the dusty road, whirling past every old familiar spot, until the bounds of the estate were fairly passed, and they found themselves out on the open pike. After they had ridden about a mile, Haley suddenly drew up at the door of a blacksmith's shop, when, taking out with him a pair of handcuffs he stepped into the shop, to have a little alteration in them.

'These yer 's a little too small for his build,' said Haley, showing the fetters, and pointing out to Tom.

'Lor! now, if thar an't Shelby's Tom. He han't sold him, now?' said the smith.

'Yes, he has,' said Haley.

'Now, ye don't! well, reely,' said the smith, 'who'd a thought it! Why, ye needn't go to fetterin' him up this yer way. He's the faithfullest, best crittur –'

'Yes, yes,' said Haley; 'but your good fellers are just the critturs to want ter run off. Them stupid ones, as doesn't care whar they go, and shifless drunken ones, as don't care for nothin', they'll stick by, and like as not be rather pleased to be toted round; but these yer prime fellers, they hates it like sin. No way but to fetter 'em; got legs, – they'll use 'em, – no mistake.'

'Well,' said the smith, feeling among his tools, 'them plantations down thar, stranger, an't jest the place a Kentuck nigger wants to go; they dies thar tol'able fast, don't they?'

'Wal, yes, tol'able fast, ther dying is; what with the 'climating and one thing and another, they dies so as to keep the market up pretty brisk,' said Haley.

'Wal, now, a feller, can't help thinkin' it's a mighty pity to have a nice, quiet, likely feller as good un as Tom is, go down to be fairly ground up on one of them ar sugar plantations.'

'Wal, he's got a fa'r chance. I promised to do well by him. I'll get him in house-servant in some good old family, and then, if he stands the fever and 'climating, he'll have a berth good as any nigger ought ter ask for.'

'He leaves his wife and chil'en up here, s'pose?'

'Yes; but he'll get another thar. Lord, thar's women enough everywhar,' said Haley.

Tom was sitting very mournfully on the outside of the shop while this conversation was going on. Suddenly he heard the quick, short click of a horse's hoof behind him; and, before he could fairly awake from his surprise, young Master George sprang into the wagon, threw his arms tumultuously round his neck, and was sobbing and scolding with energy.

'I declare, it's real mean! I don't care what they say, any of 'em! It's a nasty, mean shame! If I was a man, they shouldn't do it, – they should not, *so!*' said George with a kind of subdued howl.

'O! Mas'r George! this does me good!' said Tom. 'I couldn't bar to go off without seein' ye! It does me real good, ye can't tell!' Here Tom made some movement of his feet, and George's eye fell on the fetters.

'What a shame!' he exclaimed, lifting his hands. 'I'll knock that old fellow down – I will!'

'No you won't, Mas'r George; and you must not talk so loud. It won't help me any, to anger him.'

'Well, I won't, then, for your sake; but only to think of it – isn't it a shame? They never sent for me, nor sent me any word, and, if it hadn't been for Tom Lincon, I shouldn't have heard it. I tell you, I blew 'em up well, all of 'em, at home!'

'That ar wasn't right, I'm 'feard, Mas'r George.'

'Can't help it! I say it's a shame! Look here, Uncle Tom,' said he, turning his back to the shop, and speaking in a mysterious tone, '*I've brought you my dollar!*'

'O! I couldn't think o' takin' on 't, Mas'r George, no ways in the world!' said Tom, quite moved.

'But you *shall* take it!' said George; 'look here – I told Aunt Chloe I'd do it, and she advised me just to make a hole in it, and put a string through, so you could hang it round your neck, and keep it out of sight; else this mean scamp would take it away. I tell ye, Tom, I want to blow him up! it would do me good.'

'No, don't Mas'r George, for it won't do me any good.'

'Well, I won't, for your sake,' said George, busily tying his dollar round Tom's neck; 'but there, now, button your coat tight over it, and keep it, and remember, every time you see it, that I'll come down after you, and bring you back. Aunt Chloe and I have been talking about it. I told her not to fear; I'll see to it, and I'll tease father's life out, if he don't do it.'

'O! Mas'r George, ye mustn't talk so 'bout yer father!'

'Lor, Uncle Tom, I don't mean anything bad.'

'And now, Mas'r George,' said Tom, 'ye must be a good boy; 'member how many hearts is sot on ye. Al'ays keep close to yer mother. Don't be gettin' into any of them foolish ways boys has of gettin' too big to mind their mothers. Tell ye what, Mas'r George, the Lord gives good many things twice over; but he don't give ye a mother but once. Ye'll never see sich another woman, Mas'r George, if ye live to be a hundred years old. So, now, you hold on to her, and grow up, and be a comfort to her, thar's my own good boy, – you will now, won't ye?'

'Yes, I will, Uncle Tom,' said George seriously.

'And be careful of yer speaking, Mas'r George. Young boys, when they comes to your age, is wilful, sometimes – it is natur they should be. But real gentlemen, such as I hopes you'll be, never lets fall on words that isn't 'spectful to thar parents. Ye an't 'fended, Mas'r George?'

'No, indeed, Uncle Tom; you always did give me good advice.'

'I's older, ye know,' said Tom, stroking the boy's fine, curly head with his large, strong hand, but speaking in a voice as tender as a woman's, 'and I sees all that's bound up in you. O, Mas'r George, you has everything, – l'arnin', privileges, readin', writin', – and you'll grow up to be a great, learned, good man and all the people on the place and your mother and father'll be so proud of ye! Be a good Mas'r, like yer father; and be a Christian, like yer mother. 'Member yer Creator in the days o' yer youth, Mas'r George.'

'I'll be *real* good, Uncle Tom, I tell you,' said George. 'I'm going to be a *first-rater*; and don't you be discouraged. I'll have you back to the place, yet. As I told Aunt Chloe this morning, I'll build our house all over, and you shall have a room for a parlor with a carpet on it, when I'm a man. O, you'll have good times yet!'

Haley now came to the door, with the handcuffs in his hands.

'Look here, now, Mister,' said George, with an air of great superiority, as he got out, 'I shall let father and mother know how you treat Uncle Tom!'

'You're welcome,' said the trader.

'I should think you'd be ashamed to spend all your life buying men and women, and chaining them, like cattle! I should think you'd feel mean!' said George.

'So long as your grand folks wants to buy men and women, I'm as good as they is,' said Haley; ''tan't any meaner sellin' on 'em, that 't is buyin'!'

'I'll never do either, when I'm a man,' said George; 'I'm ashamed, this day, that I'm a Kentuckian. I always was proud of it before;' and George sat very straight on his horse, and looked round with an air, as if he expected the state would be impressed with his opinion.

'Well, goodbye, Uncle Tom; keep a stiff upper lip,' said George.

'Goodbye, Mas'r George,' said Tom, looking fondly and admiringly at him. 'God Almighty bless you! Ah! Kentucky han't got many like you!' he said, in the fulness of his heart, as the frank, boyish face was lost to his view. Away he went, and Tom looked, till the clatter of his horse's heels died away, the last sound or sight of his home. But over his heart there seemed to be a warm spot, where those young hands had placed that precious dollar. Tom put up his hand, and held it close to his heart.

'Now, I tell ye what, Tom,' said Haley, as he came up to the wagon, and threw in the hand-cuffs, 'I mean to start fa'r with ye, as I gen'ally do with my niggers; and I'll tell ye now, to begin with, you treat me fa'r, and I'll treat you fa'r; I an't never hard on my niggers. Calculates to do the best for 'em I can. Now, ye see, you'd better jest settle down comfortable, and not be tryin' no tricks; because nigger's tricks of all sorts I'm up to, and it's no use. If niggers is quiet, and don't try to get off, they has good times with me; and if they don't, why, it's thar fault, and not mine.'

Tom assured Haley that he had no present intentions of running off. In fact, the exhortation seemed rather a superfluous one to a man with a great pair of iron fetters on his feet. But Mr Haley had got in the habit of commencing his relations with his stock with little exhortations of this nature, calculated, as he deemed, to inspire cheerfulness and confidence, and prevent the necessity of any unpleasant scenes.

And here, for the present, we take our leave of Tom, to pursue the fortunes of other characters in our story.

CHAPTER ELEVEN

In Which Property Gets into an
Improper State of Mind

It was late in a drizzly afternoon that a traveler alighted at the door of a small country hotel, in the village of N—, in Kentucky. In the bar-room he found assembled quite a miscellaneous company, whom stress of weather had driven to harbor, and the place presented the usual scenery of such reunions. Great, tall, raw-boned Kentuckians, attired in hunting-shirts, and trailing their loose joints over a vast extent of territory, with the easy lounge peculiar to the race, – rifles stacked away in the corner, shot-pouches, game-bags, hunting-dogs, and little negroes, all rolled together in the corners, – were the characteristic features in the picture. At each end of the fireplace sat a long-legged gentleman, with his chair tipped back, his hat on his head, and the heels of his muddy boots reposing sublimely on the mantelpiece, – a position, we will inform our readers, decidedly favorable to the turn of reflection incident to western taverns, where travelers exhibit a decided preference for this particular mode of elevating their understandings.

Mine host, who stood behind the bar, like most of his country men, was great of stature, good-natured, and loose-jointed, with an enormous shock of hair on his head, and a great tall hat on the top of that.

In fact, everybody in the room bore on his head this characteristic emblem of man's sovereignty; whether it were felt hat, palm-leaf, greasy beaver, or fine new chapeau, there it reposed with true republican independence. In truth, it appeared to be the characteristic mark of every individual. Some wore them tipped rakishly to one side – these were your men of humor, jolly, free-and-easy dogs; some had them jammed independently down over their noses – these were your hard characters, thorough men, who, when they wore their hats, *wanted* to wear them, and to wear them just as they had a mind to; there were those who had them set far over back – wide-awake men, who wanted a clear prospect; while careless men, who did not know, or care how their hats sat, had them shaking about in all directions. The various hats, in fact, were quite a Shakespearean study.

Divers negroes, in very free-and-easy pantaloons, and with no redundancy in the shirt line, were scuttling about, hither and thither, without bringing to pass any very particular results, except expressing a generic willingness to turn over everything in creation generally for the benefit of Mas'r and his guests. Add to this picture a jolly, crackling, rollicking fire, going rejoicingly up a great wide chimney, – the outer door and every window being set wide open, and the calico window-curtain flopping and snapping in a good stiff breeze of damp raw air, – and you have an idea of the jollities of a Kentucky tavern.

Your Kentuckian of the present day is a good illustration of the doctrine of transmitted instincts and pecularities. His fathers were mighty hunters, – men who lived in the woods, and slept under the free, open heavens, with the stars to hold their candles; and their descendant to this day always acts as if the house were his camp, – wears his hat at all hours, tumbles himself about, and puts his heels on the tops of chairs or mantelpieces, just as his father rolled on the green sward, and put his upon trees and logs, – keeps all the windows and doors open, winter and summer, that he may get air enough for his great lungs, – calls everybody 'stranger,' with nonchalant bonhommie, and is altogether the frankest, easiest, most jovial creature living.

Into such an assembly of the free and easy our traveler entered. He was a short, thick-set man, carefully dressed, with a round, good-natured countenance, and something rather fussy and particular in his appearance. He was very careful of his valise and umbrella, bringing them in with his own hands, and resisting, pertinaciously, all offers from the various servants to relieve him of them. He looked round the barroom with rather an anxious air, and, retreating with his valuables to the warmest corner, disposed them under his chair, sat down, and looked rather apprehensively up at the worthy whose heels illustrated the end of the mantelpiece, who was spitting from right to left, with a courage and energy rather alarming to gentlemen of weak nerves and particular habits.

'I say, stranger, how are ye?' said the aforesaid gentleman, firing an honorary salute of tobacco-juice in the direction of the new arrival.

'Well, I reckon,' was the reply of the other, as he dodged, with some alarm, the threatening honor.

'Any news?' said the respondent, taking out a strip of tobacco and a large hunting-knife from his pocket.

'Not that I know of,' said the man.

'Chaw?' said the first speaker, handing the old gentleman a bit of his tobacco, with a decidedly brotherly air.

'No, thank ye – it don't agree with me,' said the little man, edging off.

'Don't, eh?' said the other, easily, and stowing away the morsel in his own mouth, in order to keep up the supply of tobacco-juice, for the general benefit of society.

The old gentleman uniformly gave a little start whenever his long-sided brother fired in his direction; and this being observed by his companion, he very good-naturedly turned his artillery to another quarter, and proceeded to storm one of the fire-irons with a degree of military talent fully sufficient to take a city.

'What's that?' said the old gentleman, observing some of the company formed in a group around a large handbill.

'Nigger advertised!' said one of the company, briefly.

Mr Wilson, for that was the old gentleman's name, rose up, and, after carefully adjusting his valise and umbrella, proceeded deliberately to take out his spectacles, and fix them on his nose; and, this operation being performed, read as follows:

'Ran away from the subscriber, my mulatto boy, George. Said George six feet in height, a very light mulatto, brown curly hair; is very intelligent, speaks handsomely, can read and write; will probably try to pass for a white man; is deeply scarred on his back and shoulders; has been branded in his right hand with the letter H.

'I will give four hundred dollars for him alive, and the same sum for satisfactory proof that he has been killed.'

The old gentleman read this advertisement from end to end in a low voice, as if he were studying it.

The long-legged veteran, who had been besieging the fireiron, as before related, now took down his cumbrous length, and rearing aloft his tall form, walked up to the advertisement, and very deliberately spit a full discharge of tobacco-juice on it.

'There's my mind upon that!' said he, briefly, and sat down again.

'Why, now, stranger, what's that for?' said mine host.

'I'd do it all the same to the writer of that ar paper, if he was here,' said the long man, coolly resuming his old employment of cutting tobacco. 'Any man that owns a boy like that, and can't find any better way o' treating on him, *deserves* to lose him. Such papers as these is a shame to Kentucky; that's my mind right out, if anybody wants to know!'

'Well, now, that's a fact,' said mine host, as he made an entry in his book.

'I've got a gang of boys, sir,' said the long man, resuming his attack on the fire-irons, 'and I jest tells 'em – "Boys," says I, – "*run* now! dig! put! jest when ye want to! I never shall come to look after you!" That's the way I keep mine. Let 'em know they are free to run any time, and it jest breaks up their wanting to. More 'n all, I've got free papers for 'em all recorded, in case I gets keeled up any o' these times, and they know it; and I tell ye, stranger, there an't a fellow in our parts gets more out of his niggers than I do. Why, my boys have been to Cincinnati, with five hundred dollars' worth of colts, and brought me back the money, all straight, time and agin. It stands to reason they should. Treat 'em like dogs, and you'll have dogs' works and dogs' actions. Treat 'em like men, and you'll have men's works.' And the honest drover, in his warmth, endorsed this moral sentiment by firing a perfect *feu de joi* at the fireplace.

'I think you're altogether right, friend,' said Mr Wilson; 'and this boy described here *is* a fine fellow – no mistake about that. He worked for me some half-dozen years in my bagging factory, and he was my best hand, sir. He is an ingenious fellow, too: he invented a machine for the cleaning of hemp – a really valuable affair; it's gone into use in several factories. His master holds the patent of it.'

'I'll warrant ye,' said the drover, 'holds it and makes money out of it, and then turns round and brands the boy in his right hand. If I had a fair chance, I'd mark him, I reckon so that he'd carry it *one* while.'

'These yer knowin' boys is allers aggravatin' and sarcy,' said a coarse-looking fellow, from the other side of the room; 'that's why they gets cut up and marked so. If they behaved themselves, they wouldn't.'

'That is to say, the Lord made 'em men, and it's a hard squeeze gettin 'em down into beasts,' said the drover, dryly.

'Bright niggers isn't no kind of 'vantage to their masters,' continued the other, well intrenched, in a coarse, unconscious obtuseness, from the contempt of his opponent; 'what's the use o' talents and them things, if you can't get the use on 'em yourself? Why, all the use they make on 't is to get round you. I've had one or two of these fellers, and I jest sold 'em down river. I knew I'd got to lose 'em, first or last, if I didn't.'

'Better send orders up to the Lord, to make you a set, and leave out their souls entirely,' said the drover.

Here the conversation was interrupted by the approach of a small one-horse buggy to the inn. It had a genteel appearance, and a well-dressed, gentlemanly man sat on the seat, with a colored servant driving.

The whole party examined the new comer with the interest with which a set of loafers in a rainy day usually examine every newcomer. He was very tall, with a dark, Spanish complexion, fine, expressive black eyes, and close-curling hair, also of a glossy blackness. His well-formed aquiline nose, straight thin lips, and the admirable contour of his finely-formed limbs, impressed the whole company instantly with the idea of something uncommon. He walked easily in among the company, and with a nod indicated to his waiter where to place his trunk, bowed to the company, and, with his hat in his hand, walked up leisurely to the bar, and gave in his name as Henry Butler, Oaklands, Shelby County. Turning with an indifferent air, he sauntered up to the advertisement, and read it over.

'Jim,' he said to his man, 'seems to me we met a boy something like this, up at Bernan's, didn't we?'

'Yes, Mas'r,' said Jim, 'only I an't sure about the hand.'

'Well, I didn't look, of course,' said the stranger with a careless yawn. Then walking up to the landlord, he desired him to furnish him with a private apartment, as he had some writing to do immediately.

The landlord was all obsequious, and a relay of about seven negroes, old and young, male and female, little and big, were soon whizzing about, like a covey of partridges, bustling, hurrying, treading on each other's toes, and tumbling over each other, in their zeal to get Mas'r's room ready, while he seated himself easily on a chair in the middle of the room, and entered into conversation with the man who sat next to him.

The manufacturer, Mr Wilson, from the time of the entrance of the stranger, had regarded him with an air of disturbed and uneasy curiosity. He seemed to himself to have met and been acquainted with him somewhere, but he could not recollect. Every few moments, when the man spoke, or moved, or smiled, he would start and fix his eyes on him, and then suddenly withdraw them, as the bright, dark eyes met his with such unconcerned coolness. At last, a sudden recollection seemed to flash upon him, for he stared at the stranger with such an air of blank amazement and alarm, that he walked up to him.

'Mr Wilson, I think,' said he, in a tone of recognition, and extending his hand. 'I beg your pardon, I didn't recollect you before. I see you remember me, – Mr Butler, of Oaklands, Shelby County.'

'Ye – yes – yes, sir,' said Mr Wilson, like one speaking in a dream.

Just then a negro boy entered, and announced that Mas'r's room was ready.

'Jim, see to the trunks,' said the gentleman, negligently; then addressing himself to Mr Wilson, he added – 'I should like to have a few moments' conversation with you on business, in my room, if you please.'

Mr Wilson followed him, as one who walks in his sleep; and they proceeded to a large upper chamber, where a newmade fire was crackling, and various servants flying about, putting finishing touches to the arrangements.

When all was done, and the servants departed, the young man deliberately locked the door, and putting the key in his pocket, faced about, and folding his arms on his bosom, looked Mr Wilson full in the face.

'George!' said Mr Wilson.

'Yes, George,' said the young man.

'I couldn't have thought it!'

'I am pretty well disguised, I fancy,' said the young man, with a smile. ' A little walnut bark has made my yellow skin a genteel brown, and I've dyed my hair black; so you see I don't answer to the advertisement at all.'

'O, George! but this is a dangerous game you are playing. I could not have advised you to it.'

'I can do it on my own responsibility,' said George, with the same proud smile.

We remark, en *passant*, that George was, by his father's side, of white descent. His mother was one of those unfortunates of her race, marked out by personal beauty to be the slave of the passions of her possessor, and the mother of children who may never know a father. From one of the proudest families in Kentucky he had inherited a set of fine European features, and a high, indomitable spirit. From his mother he had received only a slight mulatto tinge, amply compensated by its accompanying rich, dark eye. A slight change in the tint of the skin and the color of his hair had metamorphosed him into the Spanish-looking fellow he then appeared; and as gracefulness of movement and gentlemanly manners had always been perfectly natural to him, he found no difficulty in playing the bold part he had adopted – that of a gentleman travelling with his domestic.

Mr Wilson, a good-natured but extremely fidgety and cautious old gentleman, ambled up and down the room, appearing, as John Bunyan hath it, 'much tumbled up and down in his mind,' and divided between his wish to help George, and a certain confused notion of maintaining law and order: so, as he shambled about, he delivered himself as follows:

'Well, George, I s'pose you're running away – leaving your lawful master, George – (I don't wonder at it) – at the same time, I'm sorry, George, – yes, decidedly – I think I must say that, George – it's my duty to tell you so.'

'Why are you sorry, sir?' said George, calmly.

'Why, to see you, as it were, setting yourself in opposition to the laws of your country.'

'My country!' said George, with a strong and bitter emphasis; 'what country have I, but the grave, – and I wish to God that I was laid there!'

'Why, George, no – no – it won't do; this way of talking is wicked – unscriptural. George, you've got a hard master – in fact, he is – well he conducts himself reprehensibly – I can't pretend to defend him. But you know how the angel commanded Hagar to return to her mistress, and submit herself under the hand; and the apostle sent back Onesimus to his master.'

'Don't quote Bible at me that way, Mr Wilson,' said George, with a flashing eye, 'don't! for my wife is a Christian, and I mean to be, if ever I get to where I can; but to quote Bible to a fellow in my circumstances, is enough to make him give it up altogether. I appeal to God Almighty; – I'm willing to go with the case to Him, and ask Him if I do wrong to seek my freedom.'

'These feelings are quite natural, George,' said the good-natured man, blowing his nose. 'Yes they're natural, but it is my duty not to encourage 'em in you. Yes, my boy, I'm sorry for you, now; it's a bad case – very bad; but the apostle says, "Let everyone abide in the condition in which he is called." We must all submit to the indications of Providence, George, – don't you see?'

George stood with his head drawn back, his arms folded tightly over his broad breast, and a bitter smile curling his lips.

'I wonder, Mr Wilson, if the Indians should come and take you a prisoner away from your wife and children, and want to keep you all your life hoeing corn for them, if you'd think it your duty to abide in the condition in which you were called. I rather think that you'd think the first stray horse you could find an indication of Providence – shouldn't you?'

The little old gentleman stared with both eyes at this illustration of the case; but, though not much of a reasoner, he had the sense in which some logicians on this particular subject do not excel, – that of saying nothing, where nothing could be said. So, as he stood carefully stroking his umbrella, and folding and patting down all the creases in it, he proceeded on with his exhortations in a general way.

'You see, George, you know, now, I always have stood your friend; and whatever I've said, I've said for your good. Now, here, it seems to me, you're running an awful risk. You can't hope to carry it out. If you're taken, it will be worse with you than ever; they'll only abuse you, and half kill you, and sell you down the river.'

'Mr Wilson, I know all this,' said George. 'I *do* run a risk, but –' he threw open his overcoat, and showed two pistols and a bowie-knife. 'There!' he said, 'I'm ready for 'em! Down south I never *will* go. No! if it comes to that, I can earn myself at least six feet of free soil, – the first and last I shall ever own in Kentucky!'

'Why, George, this state of mind is awful; it's getting really desperate, George. I'm concerned. Going to break the laws of your country!'

'My country again! Mr Wilson, *you* have a country; but what country have *I*, or any one like me, born of slave mothers? What laws are there for us? We don't make them, – we don't consent to them, – we have nothing to do with them; all they do for us is to crush us, and keep us down. Haven't I heard your Fourth-of-July speeches? Don't you tell us all, once a year, that governments derive their just power from the consent of the governed? Can't a fellow *think*, that hears such things? Can't he put this and that together, and see what it comes to?'

Mr Wilson's mind was one of those that may not unaptly be represented by a bale of cotton, – downy, soft, benevolently fuzzy and confused. He really pitied George with all his heart, and had a sort of dim and cloudy perception of the style of feeling that agitated him; but he deemed it his duty to go on talking *good* to him, with infinite pertinacity.

'George, this is bad. I must tell you, you know, as a friend, you'd better not be meddling with such notions; they are bad, George, very bad, for boys in your condition, – very;' and Mr Wilson sat down to a table, and began nervously chewing the handle of his umbrella.

'See here, now, Mr Wilson,' said George, coming up and sitting himself determinately down in front of him; 'look at me, now. Don't I sit before you, every way, just as much a man as you are? Look at my face, – look at my hands, – look at my body,' and the young man drew himself up proudly; 'why am I *not* a man, as much as anybody? Well, Mr Wilson, hear what I can tell you. I had a father – one of your Kentucky gentlemen – who didn't think enough of me to keep me from being sold with his dogs and horses, to satisfy the estate, when he died. I saw my mother put up at sheriff's sale, with her seven children. They were sold before her eyes, one by one, all to different masters; and I was the youngest. She came and kneeled down before old Mas'r, and begged him to buy her with me, that she might have at least one child with her; and he kicked her away with his heavy boot. I saw him do it; and the last that I heard was her moans and screams, when I was tied to his horse's neck, to be carried off to his place.'

'Well, then?'

'My master traded with one of the men, and bought my oldest sister. She was a pious, good girl, – a member of the Baptist church, – and as handsome as my poor mother had been. She was well brought up, and had good manners. At first, I was glad she was bought, for I had one friend near me. I was soon sorry for it. Sir, I have stood at the door and heard her whipped, when it seemed as if every blow cut into my naked heart, and I couldn't do anything to help her; and she was whipped, sir, for wanting to live a decent Christian life, such as your laws give no slave girl a right to live; and at last I saw her chained with a trader's gang, to be sent to market in Orleans, – sent there for nothing else but that, – and that's the last I know of her. Well, I grew up, – long years and years, – no father, no mother, no sister, not a living soul that cared for me more than a dog; nothing but whipping, scolding, starving. Why, sir, I've been so hungry that I have been glad to take the bones they threw to their dogs; and yet, when I was a little fellow, and laid awake whole nights and cried, it wasn't the hunger, it wasn't the whipping, I cried for. No, sir, it was for *my mother* and *my sisters*, – it was because I hadn't a friend to love me on earth. I never knew what peace or comfort was. I never had a kind word spoken to me till I came to work in your factory. Mr Wilson, you treated me well; you encouraged me to do well, and to learn to read and write, and to try to make something of myself; and God knows how grateful I am for it. Then, sir, I found my wife; you've seen her, – you know how beautiful she is. When I found she loved me, when I married her, I scarcely could believe I was alive, I was so happy; and, sir, she is as good as she is beautiful. But now what? Why, now comes my master, takes me right away from my work, and my friends, and all I like, and grinds me down into the very dirt! And why? Because, he says, I forgot who I was; he says, to teach me that I am only a nigger! After all, and last of all, he comes between me and my wife, and says I shall give her up, and live with another woman. And all this your laws give him power to do, in spite of God or man. Mr Wilson, look at it! There isn't *one* of all these things, that have broken the hearts of my mother and my sister, and my wife and myself, but your laws allow, and give every man power to do, in Kentucky, and none can say to him nay! Do you call these the laws of *my* country? Sir, I haven't any country, anymore than I have any father. But I'm going to have one. I don't want anything of *your* country, except to be let alone, – to go peaceably out of it; and when I get to Canada, where the laws will own me and protect me, *that* shall be my country, and its laws I will obey. But if any man tries to stop me, let him take care, for I am desperate. I'll fight for my liberty to the last breath I breathe. You say your fathers did it; if it was right for them, it is right for me!'

This speech, delivered partly while sitting at the table, and partly walking up and down the room, – delivered with tears, and flashing eyes, and despairing gestures, – was altogether too much for the good-natured old body to whom it was addressed, who had pulled out a great yellow silk pocket-handkerchief, and was mopping up his face with great energy.

'Blast 'em all!' he suddenly broke out. 'Haven't I always said so – the infernal old cusses! I hope I an't swearing, now. Well! go ahead, George, go ahead; but be careful, my boy; don't shoot anybody, George, unless – well – you'd *better* not shoot, I reckon; at least, I wouldn't *hit* anybody, you know. Where is your wife, George?' he added, as he nervously rose, and began walking the room.

'Gone, sir gone, with her child in her arms, the Lord only knows where; – gone after the north star; and when we ever meet, or whether we meet at all in this world, no creature can tell.'

'It is possible! astonishing! from such a kind family?'

'Kind families get in debt, and the laws of *our* country allow them to sell the child out of its mother's bosom to pay its master's debts,' said George, bitterly.

'Well, well,' said the honest old man, fumbling in his pocket. 'I s'pose, perhaps, I an't following my judgment, – hang it, I *won't* follow my judgment!' he added, suddenly; 'so here, George,' and, taking out a roll of bills from his pocket-book, he offered them to George.

'No, my kind, good sir!' said George, 'you've done a great deal for me, and this might get you into trouble. I have enough, I hope, to take me as far as I need it.'

'No; but you must, George. Money is a great help everywhere; – can't have too much, if you get it honestly. Take it, – *do* take it, *now*, – do, my boy!'

'On condition, sir, that I may repay it at some future time, I will,' said George, taking up the money. 'And now, George how long are you going to travel in this way? – not long or far, I hope. It's well carried on but too bold. And this black fellow, – who is he?'

'A true fellow, who went to Canada more than a year ago. He heard, after he got there, that his master was so angry at him for going off that he had whipped his poor old mother; and he has come all the way back to comfort her, and get a chance to get her away.'

'Has he got her?'

'Not yet; he has been hanging about the place, and found no chance yet. Meanwhile, he is going with me as far as Ohio, to put me among friends that helped him, and then he will come back after her.'

'Dangerous, very dangerous!' said the old man.

George drew himself up, and smiled disdainfully.

The old gentleman eyed him from head to foot, with a sort of innocent wonder.

'George, something has brought you out wonderfully. You hold up your head, and speak and move like another man,' said Mr Wilson.

'Because I'm a *freeman!*' said George, proudly. 'Yes sir; I've said Mas'r for the last time to any man. *I'm free!*'

'Take care! You are not sure, – you may be taken.'

'All men are free and equal *in the grave*, if it comes to that, Mr Wilson,' said George.

'I'm perfectly dumb-founded with your boldness!' said Mr Wilson, – 'to come right here to the nearest tavern!'

'Mr Wilson, it is *so* bold, and this tavern is so near, that they will never think of it; they will look for me on ahead, and you yourself wouldn't know me. Jim's master don't live in this country; he isn't known in these parts. Besides, he is given up; nobody is looking after him, and nobody will take me up from the advertisement, I think.'

'But the mark in your hand?'

George drew off his glove, and showed a newly-healed scar in his hand.

'That is a parting proof of Mr Harris' regard,' he said, scornfully. 'A fortnight ago, he took it into his head to give it to me, because he said he believed I should try to get away one of these days. Looks interesting, doesn't it?' he said, drawing his glove on again.

'I declare, my very blood runs cold when I think of it, – your condition and your risks!' said Mr Wilson.

'Mine has run cold a good many years, Mr Wilson; at present, it's about up to the boiling point,' said George.

'Well, my good sir,' continued George, after a few moments' silence, 'I saw you knew me; I thought I'd just have this talk with you, lest your surprised looks should bring me out. I leave early tomorrow morning, before daylight; by tomorrow night I hope to sleep safe in Ohio. I shall travel by daylight, stop at the best hotels, go to the dinner-tables with the lords of the land. So, good-bye, sir; if you hear that I'm taken, you may know that I'm dead!'

George stood up like a rock, and put out his hand with the air of a prince. The friendly little old man shook it heartily, and after a little shower of caution, he took his umbrella, and fumbled his way out of the room.

George stood thoughtfully looking at the door, as the old man closed it. A thought seemed to flash across his mind. He hastily stepped to it, and opening it, said,

'Mr Wilson, one word more.'

The old gentleman entered again, and George, as before, locked the door, and then stood for a few moments looking on the floor, irresolutely. At last, raising his head with a sudden effort –

'Mr Wilson, you have shown yourself a Christian in your treatment of me, – I want to ask one last deed of Christian kindness of you.'

'Well, George.'

'Well, sir, – what you said was true. I *am* running a dreadful risk. There isn't, on earth, a living soul to care if I die,' he added, drawing his breath hard, and speaking with a great effort, – 'I shall be kicked out and buried like a dog, and nobody'll think of it a day after, – *only my poor wife!* Poor soul! she'll mourn and grieve; and if you'd only contrive, Mr Wilson, to send this little pin to her. She gave it to me for a Christmas present, poor child! Give it to her, and tell her I loved her to the last. Will you? *Will* you?' he added, earnestly.

'Yes, certainly – poor fellow!' said the old gentleman, taking the pin, with watery eyes, and a melancholy quiver in his voice.

'Tell her one thing,' said George; 'it's my last wish, if she *can* get to Canada, to go there. No matter how kind her mistress is, – no matter how much she loves her home; beg her not to go back, – for slavery always ends in misery. Tell her to bring up our boy a free man, and then he won't suffer as I have. Tell her this, Mr Wilson, will you?'

'Yes, George. I'll tell her; but I trust you won't die; take heart, – you're a brave fellow. Trust in the Lord, George. I wish in my heart you were safe through, though, – that's what I do.'

'*Is* there a God to trust in?' said George, in such a tone of bitter despair as arrested the old gentleman's words. 'O, I've seen things all my life that have made me feel that there can't be a God. You Christians don't know how these things look to us. There's a God for you, but is there any for us?'

'O, now, don't – don't, my boy!' said the old man, almost sobbing as he spoke; 'don't feel so! There is – there is; clouds and darkness are around about him, but righteousness and judgment are the habitation of his throne. There's a God, George, – believe it; trust in Him, and I'm sure He'll help you. Everything will be set right, – if not in this life, in another.'

The real piety and benevolence of the simple old man invested him with a temporary dignity and authority, as he spoke. George stopped his distracted walk up and down the room, stood thoughtfully a moment, and then said, quietly,

'Thank you for saying that, my good friend; I'll *think of that.*'

CHAPTER TWELVE

Select Incident of Lawful Trade

'In Ramah there was a voice heard, – weeping, and lamentation, and great mourning; Rachel weeping for her children, and would not be comforted.'

Mr Haley and Tom jogged onward in their wagon, each, for a time, absorbed in his own reflections. Now, the reflections of two men sitting side by side are a curious thing, – seated on the same seat, having the same eyes, ears, hands and organs of all sorts, and having pass before their eyes the same objects, – it is wonderful what a variety we shall find in these reflections!

As, for example, Mr Haley: he thought first of Tom's length, and breadth, and height, and what he would sell for, if he was kept fat and in good case till he got him into market. He thought of how he should make out his gang; he thought of the respective market value of certain supposititious men and women and children who were to compose it, and other kindred topics of the business; then he thought of himself, and how humane he was, that whereas other men chained their 'niggers' hand and foot both, he only put fetters on the feet, and left Tom the use of his hands, as long as he behaved well; and he sighed to think how ungrateful human nature was, so that there was even room to doubt whether Tom appreciated his mercies. He had been taken in so by 'niggers' whom he had favored; but still he was astonished to consider how good-natured he yet remained!

As to Tom, he was thinking over some words of an unfashionable old book, which kept running through his head, again and again, as follows: 'We have here no continuing city, but we seek one to come; wherefore God himself is not ashamed to be called our God; for he hath prepared for us a city.' These words of an ancient volume, got up principally by 'ignorant and unlearned men,' have, through all time, kept up, somehow, a strange sort of power over the minds of poor, simple fellows, like Tom. They stir up the soul from its depths, and rouse, as with trumpet call, courage, energy, and enthusiasm, where before was only the blackness of despair.

Mr Haley pulled out of his pocket sundry newspapers, and began looking over their advertisements, with absorbed interest. He was not a remarkably fluent reader, and was in the habit of reading in a sort of recitative half-aloud, by way of calling in his ears to verify the deductions of his eyes. In this tone he slowly recited the following paragraph:

'EXECUTOR'S SALE, – NEGROES! – *Agreeably to order of court, will be sold, on Tuesday, February 20, before the Court-house door, in the town of Washington, Kentucky, the following negroes: Hagar, aged 60; John, aged 30; Ben, aged 21; Saul, aged 25; Albert, aged 14. Sold for the benefit of the creditors and heirs of the estate of Jesse Blutchford, Esq.*

SAMUEL MORRIS,
THOMAS FLINT,
Executors.'

'This yer I must look at,' said he to Tom, for want of somebody else to talk to.

'Ye see, I'm going to get up a prime gang to take down with ye, Tom; it'll make it sociable and pleasant like, – good company will, ye know. We must drive right to Washington first and foremost, and then I'll clap you into jail, while I does the business.'

Tom received this agreeable intelligence quite meekly; simply wondering, in his own heart, how many of these doomed men had wives and children, and whether they would feel as he did about leaving them. It is to be confessed, too, that the naïve, off-hand information that he was to be thrown into jail by no means produced an agreeable impression on a poor fellow who had always prided himself on a strictly honest and upright course of life. Yes, Tom, we must confess it, was rather proud of his honesty, poor fellow, – not having very much else to be proud of; – if he had belonged to some of the higher walks of society, he, perhaps, would never have been reduced to such straits. However, the day wore on, and the evening saw Haley and Tom comfortably accommodated in Washington, – the one in a tavern, and the other in a jail.

About eleven o'clock the next day, a mixed throng was gathered around the court-house steps, – smoking, chewing, spitting, swearing, and conversing, according to their respective tastes and turns, – waiting for the auction to commence. The men and women to be sold sat in a group apart, talking in a low tone to each other. The woman who had been advertised by the name of Hagar was a regular African in feature and figure. She might have been sixty, but was older than that by hard work and disease, was partially blind, and somewhat crippled with rheumatism. By her side stood her only remaining son, Albert, a bright-looking little fellow of fourteen years. The boy was the only survivor of a large family, who had been successively sold away from her to a southern market. The mother held on to him with both her shaking hands, and eyed with intense trepidation every one who walked up to examine him.

'Don't be feard, Aunt Hagar,' said the oldest of the men, 'I spoke to Mas'r Thomas 'bout it, and he thought he might manage to sell you in a lot both together.'

'Dey needn't call me worn out yet,' said she, lifting her shaking hands. 'I can cook yet, and scrub, and scour, – I'm wuth a buying, if I do come cheap; – tell em dat ar, – you *tell* em,' she added, earnestly.

Haley here forced his way into the group, walked up to the old man, pulled his mouth open and looked in, felt of his teeth, made him stand and straighten himself, bend his back, and perform various evolutions to show his muscles; and then passed on to the next, and put him through the same trial. Walking up last to the boy, he felt of his arms, straightened his hands, and looked at his fingers, and made him jump, to show his agility.

'He an't gwine to be sold widout me!' said the old woman, with passionate eagerness; 'he and I goes in a lot together; I 's rail strong yet, Mas'r and can do heaps o' work, – heaps on it, Mas'r.'

'On plantation?' said Haley, with a contemptuous glance. 'Likely story!' and, as if satisfied with his examination, he walked out and looked, and stood with his hands in his pocket, his cigar in his mouth, and his hat cocked on one side, ready for action.

'What think of 'em?' said a man who had been following Haley's examination, as if to make up his own mind from it.

'Wal,' said Haley, spitting, 'I shall put in, I think, for the youngerly ones and the boy.'

'They want to sell the boy and the old woman together,' said the man.

'Find it a tight pull; – why, she's an old rack o' bones, – not worth her salt.'

'You wouldn't then?' said the man.

'Anybody 'd be a fool 't would. She's half blind, crooked with rheumatis, and foolish to boot.'

'Some buys up these yer old critturs, and ses there's a sight more wear in 'em than a body 'd think,' said the man, reflectively.

'No go, 't all,' said Haley; 'wouldn't take her for a present, – fact, – I've *seen*, now.'

'Wal, 't is kinder pity,now, not to buy her with her son, – her heart seems so sot on him, – s'pose they fling her in cheap.'

'Them that's got money to spend that ar way, it's all well enough. I shall bid off on that ar boy for a plantation-hand; – wouldn't be bothered with her, no way, – not if they'd give her to me,' said Haley.

'She'll take on desp't,' said the man.

'Nat'lly, she will,' said the trader, coolly.

The conversation was here interrupted by a busy hum in the audience; and the auctioneer, a short, bustling, important fellow, elbowed his way into the crowd. The old woman drew in her breath, and caught instinctively at her son.

'Keep close to yer mammy, Albert, – close, – dey'll put us up togedder,' she said.

'O, mammy, I'm feard they won't,' said the boy.

'Dey must, child; I can't live, no ways, if they don't' said the old creature, vehemently.

The stentorian tones of the auctioneer, calling out to clear the way, now announced that the sale was about to commence. A place was cleared, and the bidding began. The different men on the list were soon knocked off at prices which showed a pretty brisk demand in the market; two of them fell to Haley.

'Come, now, young un,' said the auctioneer, giving the boy a touch with his hammer, 'be up and show your springs, now.'

'Put us two up togedder, togedder, – do please, Mas'r,' said the old woman, holding fast to her boy.

'Be off,' said the man, gruffly, pushing her hands away; 'you come last. Now, darkey, spring;' and, with the word, he pushed the boy toward the block, while a deep, heavy groan rose behind him. The boy paused, and looked back; but there was no time to stay, and, dashing the tears from his large, bright eyes, he was up in a moment.

His fine figure, alert limbs, and bright face, raised an instant competition, and half a dozen bids simultaneously met the ear of the auctioneer. Anxious, half-frightened, he looked from side to side, as he heard the clatter of contending bids, – now here, now there, – till the hammer fell. Haley had got him. He was pushed from the block toward his new master, but stopped one moment, and looked back, when his poor old mother, trembling in every limb, held out her shaking hands toward him.

'Buy me too, Mas'r, for de dear Lord's sake! – buy me, – I shall die if you don't!'

'You'll die if I do, that's the kink of it,' said Haley, – 'no!' And he turned on his heel.

The bidding for the poor old creature was summary. The man who had addressed Haley, and who seemed not destitute of compassion, bought her for a trifle, and the spectators began to disperse.

The poor victims of the sale, who had been brought up in one place together for years, gathered round the despairing old mother, whose agony was pitiful to see.

'Couldn't dey leave me one? Mas'r allers said I should have one, – he did,' she repeated over and over, in heart-broken tones.

'Trust in the Lord, Aunt Hagar,' said the oldest of the men, sorrowfully.

'What good will it do?' said she, sobbing passionately.

'Mother, mother, – don't! don't!' said the boy. 'They say you's got a good master.'

'I don't care, – I don't care. O, Albert! oh, my boy! you's my last baby. Lord, how ken I?'

'Come, take her off, can't some of ye?' said Haley, dryly; 'don't do no good for her to go on that ar way.'

The old men of the company, partly by persuasion and partly by force, loosed the poor creature's last despairing hold, and, as they led her off to her new master's wagon, strove to comfort her.

'Now!' said Haley, pushing his three purchases together, and producing a bundle of handcuffs, which he proceeded to put on their wrists; and fastening each handcuff to a long chain, he drove them before him to the jail.

A few days saw Haley, with his possessions, safely deposited on one of the Ohio boats. It was the commencement of his gang, to be augmented, as the boat moved on, by various other merchandise of the same kind, which he, or his agent, had stored for him in various points along shore.

The La Belle Rivière, as brave and beautiful a boat as ever walked the waters of her namesake river, was floating gayly down the stream, under a brilliant sky, the stripes and stars of free America waving and fluttering over head; the guards crowded with well-dressed ladies and gentlemen walking and enjoying the delightful day. All was full of life, buoyant and rejoicing; – all but Haley's gang, who were stored, with other freight, on the lower deck, and who, somehow, did not seem to appreciate their various privileges, as they sat in a knot, talking to each other in low tones.

'Boys,' said Haley, coming up, briskly, 'I hope you keep up good heart, and are cheerful. Now, no sulks, ye see; keep stiff upper lip, boys; do well by me, and I'll do well by you.'

The boys addressed responded the invariable 'Yes, Mas'r,' for ages the watchword of poor Africa; but it's to be owned they did not look particularly cheerful; they had their various little prejudices in favor of wives, mothers, sisters, and children, seen for the last time, – and though 'they that wasted them required of them mirth,' it was not instantly forthcoming.

'I've got a wife,' spoke out the article enumerated as 'John, aged thirty,' and he laid his chained hand on Tom's knee, – 'and she don't know a word about this, poor girl!'

'Where does she live?' said Tom.

'In a tavern a piece down here,' said John; 'I wish, now, I *could* see her once more in this world,' he added.

Poor John! It *was* rather natural; and the tears that fell, as he spoke, came as naturally as if he had been a white man. Tom drew a long breath from a sore heart, and tried, in his poor way, to comfort him.

And over head, in the cabin, sat fathers and mothers, husbands and wives; and merry, dancing children moved round among them, like so many little butterflies, and everything was going on quite easy and comfortable.

'O, mamma,' said a boy, who had just come up from below, 'there's a negro trader on board, and he's brought four or five slaves down there.'

'Poor creatures!' said the mother, in a tone between grief and indignation.

'What's that?' said another lady.

'Some poor slaves below,' said the mother.

'And they've got chains on,' said the boy.

'What a shame to our country that such sights are to be seen!' said another lady.

'O, there's a great deal to be said on both sides of the subject,' said a genteel woman, who sat at her state-room door sewing, while her little girl and boy were playing round her. 'I've been south, and I must say I think the negroes are better off than they would be to be free.'

'In some respects, some of them are well off, I grant,' said the lady to whose remark she had answered. 'The most dreadful part of slavery, to my mind, is its outrages on the feelings and affections, – the separating of families, for example.'

'That *is* a bad thing, certainly,' said the other lady, holding up a baby's dress she had just completed, and looking intently on its trimmings; 'but then, I fancy, it don't occur often.'

'O, it does,' said the first lady, eagerly; 'I've lived many years in Kentucky and Virginia both, and I've seen enough to make any one's heart sick. Suppose, ma'am, your two children, there, should be taken from you, and sold?'

'We can't reason from our feelings to those of this class of persons,' said the other lady, sorting out some worsteds on her lap.

'Indeed, ma'am, you can know nothing of them, if you say so,' answered the first lady, warmly. 'I was born and brought up among them. I know they *do* feel, just as keenly, – even more so, perhaps, – as we do.'

The lady said 'Indeed!' yawned, and looked out the cabin window, and finally repeated, for a finale, the remark with which she had begun, – 'After all, I think they are better off than they would be to be free.'

'It's undoubtedly the intention of Providence that the African race should be servants, – kept in a low condition,' said a grave-looking gentleman in black, a clergyman, seated by the cabin door. '"Cursed be Canaan; a servant of servants shall he be," the scripture says.'

'I say, stranger, is that ar what that text means?' said a tall man, standing by.

'Undoubtedly. It pleased Providence, for some inscrutable reason, to doom the race to bondage, ages ago; and we must not set up our opinion against that.'

'Well, then, we'll all go ahead and buy up niggers,' said the man, 'if that's the way of Providence, – won't we, Squire?' said he, turning to Haley, who had been standing, with his hands in his pockets, by the stove and intently listening to the conversation.

'Yes,' continued the tall man, 'we must all be resigned to the decrees of Providence. Niggers must be sold, and trucked round, and kept under; it's what they's made for. 'Pears like this yer view's quite refreshing, an't it, stranger?' said he to Haley.

'I never thought on 't,' said Haley, 'I couldn't have said as much, myself; I ha'nt no larning. I took up the trade just to make a living; if 'tan't right, I calculated to 'pent on 't in time, ye know.'

'And now you'll save yerself the trouble, won't ye?' said the tall man. 'See what 't is, now, to know scripture. If ye'd only studied yer Bible, like this yer good man, ye might have know'd it before, and saved ye a heap o' trouble. Ye could jist have said, "Cussed be – what's his name? – and 't would all have come right."' And the stranger, who was no other than the honest drover whom we introduced to our readers in the Kentucky tavern, sat down, and began smoking, with a curious smile on his long, dry face.

A tall, slender young man, with a face expressive of great feeling and intelligence, here broke in, and repeated the words, '" All things whatsoever ye would that men should do unto you, do ye even so unto them." I suppose,' he added, 'that is scripture, as much as "Cursed be Canaan."'

'Wal, it seems quite as plain a text, stranger,' said John the drover, 'to poor fellows like us, now;' and John smoked on like a volcano.

The young man paused, looked as if he was going to say more, when suddenly the boat stopped, and the company made the usual steamboat rush, to see where they were landing.

'Both them ar chaps parsons?' said John to one of the men, as they were going out.

The man nodded.

As the boat stopped, a black woman came running wildly up the plank, darted into the crowd, flew up to where the slave gang sat, and threw her arms round that unfortunate piece of merchandise before enumerated – 'John, aged thirty,' and with sobs and tears bemoaned him as her husband.

But what needs tell the story, told too oft, – every day told, – of heart-strings rent and broken, – the weak broken and torn for the profit and convenience of the strong! It needs not to be told; – every day is telling it, – telling it, too, in the ear of One who is not deaf, though he be long silent.

The young man who had spoken for the cause of humanity and God before stood with folded arms, looking on this scene. He turned, and Haley was standing at his side. 'My friend,' he said, speaking with thick utterance, 'how can you, how dare you, carry on a trade like this? Look at those poor creatures! Here I am, rejoicing in my heart that I am going home to my wife and child and the same bell which is a signal to carry me onward towards them will part this poor man and his wife forever. Depend upon it, God will bring you into judgment for this.'

The trader turned away in silence.

'I say, now,' said the drover, touching his elbow, 'there's differences in parsons, an't there? "Cussed be Canaan" don't seem to go down with this 'un, does it?'

Haley gave an uneasy growl.

'And that ar an't the worst on 't,' said John; 'mabbee it won't go down with the Lord, neither, when ye come to settle with Him, one o' these days, as all on us must, I reckon.'

Haley walked reflectively to the other end of the boat.

'If I make pretty handsomely on one or two next gangs,' he thought, 'I reckon I'll stop off this yer; it's really getting dangerous.' And he took out his pocket-book, and began adding over his accounts, – a process which many gentlemen besides Mr Haley have found a specific for an uneasy conscience.

The boat swept proudly away from the shore, and all went on merrily, as before. Men talked, and loafed, and read, and smoked. Women sewed, and children played, and the boat passed on her way.

One day, when she lay to for a while at a small town in Kentucky, Haley went up into the place on a little matter of business.

Tom, whose fetters did not prevent his taking a moderate circuit, had drawn near the side of the boat, and stood listlessly gazing over the railing. After a time, he saw the trader returning, with an alert step, in company with a colored woman, bearing in her arms a young child. She was dressed quite respectably, and a colored man followed her, bringing along a small trunk. The woman came cheerfully onward, talking, as she came, with the man who bore her trunk, and so passed up the plank into the boat. The bell rung, the steamer whizzed, the engine groaned and coughed, and away swept the boat down the river.

The woman walked forward among the boxes and bales of the lower deck, and, sitting down, busied herself with chirruping to her baby.

Haley made a turn or two about the boat, and then, coming up, seated himself near her, and began saying something to her in an indifferent undertone.

Tom soon noticed a heavy cloud passing over the woman's brow; and that she answered rapidly, and with great vehemence.

'I don't believe it, – I won't believe it!' he heard her say. 'You're jist a foolin with me.'

'If you won't believe it, look here!' said the man, drawing out a paper; 'this yer's the bill of sale, and there's your master's name to it; and I paid down good solid cash for it, too, I can tell you, – so now!'

'I don't believe Mas'r would cheat me so; it can't be true!' said the woman, with increasing agitation.

'You can ask any of these men here, that can read writing. Here!' he said, to a man that was passing by, 'jist read this yer, won't you! This yer gal won't believe me, when I tell her what 't is.'

'Why, it's a bill of sale, signed by John Fosdick,' said the man, 'making over to you the girl Lucy and her child. It's all straight enough, for aught I see.'

The woman's passionate exclamations collected a crowd around her, and the trader briefly explained to them the cause of the agitation.

'He told me that I was going down to Louisville, to hire out as cook to the same tavern where my husband works, – that's what Mas'r told me, his own self; and I can't believe he'd lie to me,' said the woman.

'But he has sold you, my poor woman, there's no doubt about it,' said a good-natured looking man, who had been examining the papers; 'he has done it, and no mistake.'

'Then it's no account talking,' said the woman, suddenly growing quite calm; and, clasping her child tighter in her arms, she sat down on her box, turned her back round, and gazed listlessly into the river.

'Going to take it easy, after all!' said the trader. 'Gal's got grit, I see.'

The woman looked calm, as the boat went on; and a beautiful soft summer breeze passed like a compassionate spirit over her head, – the gentle breeze, that never inquires whether the brow is dusky or fair that it fans. And she saw sunshine sparkling on the water, in golden ripples, and heard gay voices, full of ease and pleasure, talking around her everywhere; but her heart lay as if a great stone had fallen on it. Her baby raised himself up against her, and stroked her cheeks with his little hands, and, springing up and down, crowing and chatting, seemed determined to arouse her. She strained him suddenly and tightly in her arms, and slowly one tear after another fell on his wondering, unconscious face; and gradually she seemed, and little by little, to grow calmer, and busied herself with tending and nursing him.

The child, a boy of ten months, was uncommonly large and strong of his age, and very vigorous in his limbs. Never, for a moment, still, he kept his mother constantly busy in holding him, and guarding his springing activity.

'That's a fine chap!' said a man, suddenly stopping opposite to him, with his hands in his pockets. 'How old is he?'

'Ten months and a half,' said the mother.

The man whistled to the boy, and offered him part of a stick of candy, which he eagerly grabbed at, and very soon had it in a baby's general depository, to wit, his mouth.

'Rum fellow!' said the man 'Knows what's what!' and he whistled, and walked on. When he had got to the other side of the boat, he came across Haley, who was smoking on top of a pile of boxes.

The stranger produced a match, and lighted a cigar, saying, as he did so, 'Decentish kind o' wench you've got round there, stranger.'

'Why, I reckon she *is* tol'able fair,' said Haley, blowing the smoke out of his mouth.

'Taking her down south?' said the man.

Haley nodded, and smoked on.

'Plantation hand?' said the man.

'Wal,' said Haley, 'I'm fillin' out an order for a plantation, and I think I shall put her in. They told me she was a good cook; and they can use her for that, or set her at the cotton-picking. She's got the right fingers for that; I looked at 'em. Sell well, either way;' and Haley resumed his cigar.

'They won't want the young 'un on the plantation,' said the man.

'I shall sell him, first chance I find,' said Haley, lighting another cigar.

'S'pose you'd be selling him tol'able cheap,' said the stranger, mounting the pile of boxes, and sitting down comfortably.

'Don't know 'bout that,' said Haley; 'he's a pretty smart young 'un, – straight, fat, strong; flesh as hard as a brick!'

'Very true, but then there's the bother and expense of raisin'.'

'Nonsense!' said Haley; 'they is raised as easy as any kind of critter there is going; they an't a bit more trouble than pups. This yer chap will be running all around, in a month.'

'I've got a good place for raisin', and I thought of takin' in a little more stock,' said the man. 'One cook lost a young 'un last week, – got drowneded in a washtub, while she was a hangin' out the clothes, – and I reckon it would be well enough to set her to raisin' this yer.'

Haley and the stranger smoked a while in silence, neither seeming willing to broach the test question of the interview. At last the man resumed:

'You wouldn't think of wantin' more than ten dollars for that ar chap, seeing you *must* get him off yer hand, any how?'

Haley shook his head, and spit impressively.

'That won't do, no ways,' he said, and began his smoking again.

'Well, stranger, what will you take?'

'Well, now,' said Haley, 'I *could* raise that ar chap myself, or get him raised; he's uncommon likely and healthy, and he'd fetch a hundred dollars, six months hence; and, in a year or two, he'd bring two hundred, if I had him in the right spot; – so I shan't take a cent less nor fifty for him now.'

'O, stranger! that's rediculous, altogether,' said the man.

'Fact!' said Haley, with a decisive nod of his head.

'I'll give thirty for him,' said the stranger, 'but not a cent more.'

'Now, I'll tell ye what I will do,' said Haley, spitting again, with renewed decision. 'I'll split the difference, and say forty-five; and that's the most I will do.'

'Well, agreed!' said the man, after an interval.

'Done!' said Haley. 'Where do you land?'

'At Louisville,' said the man.

'Louisville,' said Haley. 'Very fair, we get there about dusk. Chap will be asleep, – all fair, – get him off quietly, and no screaming, – happens beautiful, – I like to do everything quietly, – I hates all kind of agitation and fluster.' And so, after a transfer of certain bills had passed from the man's pocket-book to the trader's, he resumed his cigar.

It was a bright, tranquil evening when the boat stopped at the wharf at Louisville. The woman had been sitting with her baby in her arms, now wrapped in a heavy sleep. When she heard the name of the place called out, she hastily laid the child down in a little cradle formed by the hollow among the boxes, first carefully spreading under it her cloak; and then she sprung to the side of the boat, in hopes that, among the various hotel-waiters who thronged the wharf, she might see her husband. In this hope, she pressed forward to the front rails, and, stretching far over them, strained her eyes intently on the moving heads on the shore, and the crowd pressed in between her and the child.

'Now's your time,' said Haley, taking the sleeping child up, and handing him to the stranger. 'Don't wake him up, and set him to crying, now; it would make a devil of a fuss with the gal.' The man took the bundle carefully, and was soon lost in the crowd that went up the wharf.

When the boat, creaking, and groaning, and puffing, had loosed from the wharf, and was beginning slowly to strain herself along, the woman returned to her old seat. The trader was sitting there, – the child was gone!

'Why, why, – where?' she began, in bewildered surprise.

'Lucy,' said the trader, 'your child's gone; you may as well know it first as last. You see, I know'd you couldn't take him down south; and I got a chance to sell him to a first-rate family, that'll raise him better than you can.'

The trader had arrived at that stage of Christian and political perfection which has been recommended by some preachers and politicians of the north, lately, in which he had completely overcome very humane weakness and prejudice. His heart was exactly where yours, sir, and mine could be brought, with proper effort and cultivation. The wild look of anguish and utter despair that the woman cast on him might have disturbed one less practised; but he was used to it. He had seen that same look hundreds of times. You can get used to such things, too, my friend; and it is the great object of recent efforts to make our whole northern community used to them, for the glory of the Union. So the trader only regarded the mortal anguish which he saw working in those dark features, those clenched hands, and suffocating breathings, as necessary incidents of the trade, and merely calculated whether she was going to scream, and get up a commotion on the boat; for, like other supporters of our peculiar institution, he decidedly disliked agitation.

But the woman did not scream. The shot had passed too straight and direct through the heart, for cry or tear.

Dizzily she sat down. Her slack hands fell lifeless by her side. Her eyes looked straight forward, but she saw nothing. All the noise and hum of the boat, the groaning of the machinery, mingled dreamily to her bewildered ear; and the poor, dumb-stricken heart had neither cry not tear to show for its utter misery. She was quite calm.

The trader, who, considering his advantages, was almost as humane as some of our politicians, seemed to feel called on to administer such consolation as the case admitted of.

'I know this yer comes kinder hard, at first, Lucy,' said he; 'but such a smart, sensible gal as you are, won't give way to it. You see it's *necessary*, and can't be helped!'

'O! don't, Mas'r, don't!' said the woman, with a voice like one that is smothering.

'You're a smart wench, Lucy,' he persisted; 'I mean to do well by ye, and get ye a nice place down river; and you'll soon get another husband, – such a likely gal as you –'

'O! Mas'r, if you *only* won't talk to me now,' said the woman, in a voice of such quick and living anguish that the trader felt that there was something at present in the case beyond his style of operation. He got up, and the woman turned away, and buried her head in her cloak.

The trader walked up and down for a time, and occasionally stopped and looked at her.

'Takes it hard, rather,' he soliloquized, 'but quiet, tho'; – let her sweat a while; she'll come right, by and by!'

Tom had watched the whole transaction from the first to last, and had a perfect understanding of its results. To him, it looked like something unutterably horrible and cruel, because, poor, ignorant black soul! he had not learned to generalize, and to take enlarged views. If he had only been instructed by certain ministers of Christianity, he might have thought better of it, and seen in it an every-day incident of a lawful trade; a trade which is the vital support of an institution which an American divine tells us has 'no evils but such as are inseparable from any other relations in social and domestic life.' But Tom, as we see, being a poor, ignorant fellow, whose reading had been confined entirely to the New Testament, could not comfort and solace himself with views like these. His very soul bled within him for what seemed to him the *wrongs* of the poor suffering thing that lay like a crushed reed on the boxes; the feeling, living, bleeding, yet immortal *thing*, which American state law coolly classes with the bundles, and bales, and boxes, among which she is lying.

Tom drew near, and tried to say something; but she only groaned. Honestly, and with tears running down his own cheeks, he spoke of a heart of love in the skies, of a pitying Jesus, and an eternal home; but the ear was deaf with anguish, and the palsied heart could not feel.

Night came on, – night calm, unmoved, and glorious, shining down with her innumerable and solemn angel eyes, twinkling, beautiful, but silent. There was no speech nor language, no pitying voice or helping hand, from that distant sky. One after another, the voices of business or pleasure died away; all on the boat were sleeping, and the ripples at the prow were plainly heard. Tom stretched himself out on a box, and there, as he lay, he heard, ever and anon, a smothered sob or cry from the prostrate creature, – 'O! what shall I do? O Lord! O good Lord, do help me!' and so, ever and anon, until the murmur died away in silence.

At midnight, Tom waked, with a sudden start. Something black passed quickly by him to the side of the boat, and he heard a splash in the water. No one else saw or heard anything. He raised his head, – the woman's place was vacant! He got up, and sought about him in vain. The poor bleeding heart was still, at last, and the river rippled and dimpled just as brightly as if it had not closed above it.

Patience! patience! ye whose hearts swell indignant at wrongs like these. Not one throb of anguish, not one tear of the oppressed, is forgotten by the Man of Sorrows, the Lord of Glory. In his patient, generous bosom he bears the anguish of a world. Bear thou, like him, in patience, and labor in love; for sure as he is God, 'the year of his redeemed *shall* come.'

The trader waked up bright and early, and came out to see to his live stock. It was now his turn to look about in perplexity.

'Where alive is that gal?' he said to Tom.

Tom, who had learned the wisdom of keeping counsel, did not feel called upon to state his observations and suspicions, but said he did not know.

'She surely couldn't have got off in the night at any of the landings, for I was awake, and on the look-out, whenever the boat stopped. I never trust these yer things to other folks.'

This speech was addressed to Tom quite confidentially, as if it was something that would be specially interesting to him. Tom made no answer.

The trader searched the boat from stem to stern, among boxes, bales and barrels, around the machinery, by the chimneys, in vain.

'Now, I say, Tom, be fair about this yer,' he said, when, after a fruitless search, he came where Tom was standing. 'You know something about it, now. Don't tell me, – I know you do. I saw the gal stretched out here about ten o'clock, and ag'in at twelve, and ag'in between one and two; and then at four she was gone, and you was a sleeping right there all the time. Now, you know something, – you can't help it.'

'Well, Mas'r,' said Tom, 'towards morning something brushed by me, and I kinder half woke; and then I hearn a great splash, and then I clare woke up, and the gal was gone. That's all I know on 't.'

The trader was not shocked nor amazed; because, as we said before, he was used to a great many things that you are not used to. Even the awful presence of

Death struck no solemn chill upon him. He had seen Death many times, – met him in the way of trade, and got acquainted with him, – and he only thought of him as a hard customer, that embarrassed his property operations very unfairly; and so he only swore that the gal was a baggage, and that he was devilish unlucky, and that, if things went on in this way, he should not make a cent on the trip. In short, he seemed to consider himself an ill-used man, decidedly; but there was no help for it, as the woman had escaped into a state which *never will* give up a fugitive, – not even at the demand of the whole glorious Union. The trader, therefore, sat discontentedly down, with his little account-book, and put down the missing body and soul under the head of *losses!*

'He's a shocking creature, isn't he, – this trader? so unfeeling! It's dreadful, really!'

'O, but nobody thinks anything of these traders! They are universally despised, – never received into any decent society.'

But who, sir, makes the trader? Who is most to blame? The enlightened, cultivated, intelligent man, who supports the system of which the trader is the inevitable result, or the poor trader himself? You make the public statement that calls for his trade, that debauches and depraves him, till he feels no shame in it; and in what are you better than he?

Are you educated and he ignorant, you high and he low, you refined and he coarse, you talented and he simple?

In the day of a future Judgment, these very considerations may make it more tolerable for him than for you.

In concluding these little incidents of lawful trade, we must beg the world not to think that American legislators are entirely destitute of humanity, as might, perhaps, be unfairly inferred from the great efforts made in our national body to protect and perpetuate this species of traffic.

Who does not know how our great men are outdoing themselves, in declaiming against the *foreign* slave-trade. There are a perfect host of Clarksons and Wilberforces risen up among us on that subject, most edifying to hear and behold. Trading negroes from Africa, dear reader, is so horrid! It is not to be thought of! But trading them from Kentucky, – that's quite another thing!

CHAPTER THIRTEEN

The Quaker Settlement

A quiet scene now rises before us. A large, roomy, neatly-painted kitchen, its yellow floor glossy and smooth, and without a particle of dust; a neat, well-blacked cooking-stove; rows of shining tin, suggestive of unmentionable good things to the appetite; glossy green wood chairs, old and firm; a small flag-bottomed rocking-chair, with a patch-work cushion in it, neatly contrived out of small pieces of different colored woollen goods, and a larger sized one, motherly and old, whose wide arms breathed hospitable invitation, seconded by the solicitation of its feather cushions, – a real comfortable, persuasive old chair, and worth, in the way of honest, homely enjoyment, a dozen of your plush or brochetelle drawing-room gentry; and in the chair, gently swaying back and forward, her eyes bent on some fine sewing, sat our fine old friend Eliza. Yes, there she is, paler and thinner than in her Kentucky home, with a world of quiet sorrow lying under the shadow of her long eyelashes, and marking the outline of her gentle mouth! It was plain to see how old and firm the girlish heart was grown under the discipline of heavy sorrow; and when, anon, her large dark eye was raised to follow the gambols of her little Harry, who was sporting, like some tropical butterfly, hither and thither over the floor, she showed a depth of firmness and steady resolve that was never there in her earlier and happier days.

By her side sat a woman with a bright tin pan in her lap, into which she was carefully sorting some dried peaches. She might be fifty-five or sixty; but hers was one of those faces that time seems to touch only to brighten and adorn. The snowy lisse crape cap, made after the strait Quaker pattern, – the plain white muslin handkerchief, lying in placid folds across her bosom, – the drab shawl and dress, – showed at once the community to which she belonged. Her face was round and rosy, with a healthful downy softness, suggestive of a ripe peach. Her hair, partially silvered by age, was parted smoothly back from a high placid forehead, on which time had written no inscription, except peace on earth, good will to men, and beneath shone a large pair of clear, honest, loving brown eyes; you only needed to look straight into them, to feel that you saw to the bottom of a heart as good and true as ever throbbed in woman's bosom. So much has been said and sung of beautiful young girls, why don't somebody wake up to the beauty of old women? If any want to get up an inspiration under this head, we refer them to our good friend Rachel Halliday, just as she sits there in her little rocking-chair. It had a turn for quacking and squeaking, – that chair had, – either from having taken cold in early life, or from some asthmatic affection, or perhaps from nervous derangement; but, as she gently swung backward and forward, the chair kept up a kind of subdued 'creechy crawchy,' that would have been intolerable in any other chair. But old Simeon Halliday often declared it was as good as any music to him, and the children all avowed that they wouldn't miss of hearing mother's chair for anything in the world. For why? for twenty years or more, nothing but loving words, and gentle moralities, and motherly loving kindness, had come from that chair; – headaches and heart-aches innumerable had been cured there, – difficulties spiritual and temporal solved there, – all by one good, loving woman, God bless her!

'And so thee still thinks of going to Canada, Eliza?' she said, as she was quietly looking over her peaches.

'Yes, ma'am,' said Eliza, firmly. 'I must go onward. I dare not stop.'

'And what'll thee do, when thee gets there? Thee must think about that, my daughter.'

'My daughter' came naturally from the lips of Rachel Halliday; for hers was just the face and form that made 'mother' seem the most natural word in the world.

Eliza's hands trembled, and some tears fell on her fine work; but she answered, firmly,

'I shall do – anything I can find. I hope I can find something.'

'Thee knows thee can stay here, as long as thee pleases,' said Rachel.

'O, thank you,' said Eliza, 'but' – she pointed to Harry – 'I can't sleep nights;

I can't rest. Last night I dreamed I saw that man coming into the yard,' she said, shuddering.

'Poor child!' said Rachel, wiping her eyes; 'but thee mustn't feel so. The Lord hath ordered it so that never hath a fugitive been stolen from our village. I trust thine will not be the first.'

The door here opened, and a little short, round, pin-cushiony woman stood at the door, with a cheery, blooming face, like a ripe apple. She was dressed, like Rachel, in sober gray, with the muslin folded neatly across her round, plump little chest.

'Ruth Stedman,' said Rachel, coming joyfully forward; 'how is thee, Ruth?' she said, heartily taking both her hands.

'Nicely,' said Ruth, taking off her little drab bonnet, and dusting it with her handkerchief, displaying, as she did so, a round little head, on which the Quaker cap sat with a sort of jaunty air, despite all the stroking and patting of the small fat hands, which were busily applied to arranging it. Certain stray locks of decidedly curly hair, too, had escaped here and there, and had to be coaxed and cajoled into their place again; and then the new comer, who might have been five-and-twenty, turned from the small looking-glass, before which she had been making these arrangements, and looked well pleased, – as most people who looked at her might have been, – for she was decidedly a wholesome, whole-hearted, chirruping little woman, as ever gladdened man's heart withal.

'Ruth, this friend is Eliza Harris; and this is the little boy I told thee of.'

'I am glad to see thee, Eliza, – very,' said Ruth, shaking hands, as if Eliza were an old friend she had long been expecting; 'and this is thy dear boy, – I brought a cake for him,' she said, holding out a little heart to the boy, who came up, gazing through his curls, and accepted it shyly.

'Where's thy baby, Ruth?' said Rachel.

'O, he's coming; but thy Mary caught him as I came in, and ran off with him to the barn, to show him to the children.'

At this moment, the door opened, and Mary, an honest, rosy-looking girl, with large brown eyes, like her mother's, came in with the baby.

'Ah! ha!' said Rachel, coming up, and taking the great, white, fat fellow in her arms, 'how good he looks, and how he does grow!'

'To be sure, he does,' said little bustling Ruth, as she took the child, and began taking off a little blue silk hood, and various layers and wrappers of outer garments; and having given a twitch here, and a pull there, and variously adjusted and arranged him, and kissed him heartily, she set him on the floor to collect his thoughts. Baby seemed quite used to this mode of proceeding, for he put his thumb in his mouth (as if it were quite a thing of course), and seemed soon absorbed in his own reflections, while the mother seated herself, and taking out a long stocking of mixed blue and white yarn, began to knit with briskness.

'Mary, thee'd better fill the kettle, hadn't thee?' gently suggested the mother.

Mary took the kettle to the well, and soon reappearing, placed it over the stove, where it was soon purring and steaming, a sort of censer of hospitality and good cheer. The peaches, moreover, in obedience to a few gentle whispers from Rachel, were soon deposited, by the same hand, in a stew-pan over the fire.

Rachel now took down a snowy moulding-board, and, tying on an apron, proceeded quietly to making up some biscuits, first saying to Mary, – 'Mary, hadn't thee better tell John to get a chicken ready?' and Mary disappeared accordingly.

'And how is Abigail Peters?' said Rachel, as she went on with her biscuits.

'O, she's better,' said Ruth; 'I was in, this morning; made the bed, tidied up the house. Leah Hills went in, this afternoon, and baked bread and pies enough to last some days; and I engaged to go back to get her up, this evening.'

'I will go in tomorrow, and do any cleaning there may be, and look over the mending,' said Rachel.

'Ah! that is well,' said Ruth. 'I've heard,' she added, 'that Hannah Stanwood is sick. John was up there, last night, – I must go there tomorrow.'

'John can come in here to his meals, if thee needs to stay all day,' suggested Rachel.

'Thank thee, Rachel; will see, tomorrow; but, here comes Simeon.'

Simeon Halliday, a tall, straight, muscular man, in drab coat and pantaloons, and broad-brimmed hat, now entered.

'How is thee, Ruth?' he said, warmly, as he spread his broad open hand for her little fat palm; 'and how is John?'

'O! John is well, and all the rest of our folks,' said Ruth, cheerily.

'Any news, father?' said Rachel, as she was putting her biscuits into the oven.

'Peter Stebbins told me that they should be along tonight, with *friends*,' said Simeon, significantly, as he was washing his hands at a neat sink, in a little back porch.

'Indeed!' said Rachel, looking thoughtfully, and glancing at Eliza.

'Did thee say thy name was Harris?' said Simeon to Eliza, as he re-entered.

Rachel glanced quickly at her husband, as Eliza tremulously answered 'yes;' her fears, ever uppermost, suggesting that possibly there might be advertisements out for her.

'Mother!' said Simeon, standing in the porch, and calling Rachel out.

'What does thee want, father?' said Rachel, rubbing her floury hands, as she went into the porch.

'This child's husband is in the settlement, and will be here tonight,' said Simeon.

'Now, thee doesn't say that, father?' said Rachel, all her face radiant with joy.

'It's really true. Peter was down yesterday, with the wagon, to the other stand, and there he found an old woman and two men; and one said his name was George Harris; and from what he told of his history, I am certain who he is. He is a bright, likely fellow, too.'

'Shall we tell her now?' said Simeon.

'Let's tell Ruth,' said Rachel. 'Here, Ruth, – come here.'

Ruth laid down her knitting-work, and was in the back porch in a moment.

'Ruth, what does thee think?' said Rachel. 'Father says Eliza's husband is in the last company, and will be here tonight.'

A burst of joy from the little Quakeress interrupted the speech. She gave such a bound from the floor, as she clapped her little hands, that two stray curls fell from under her Quaker cap, and lay brightly on her white neckerchief.

'Hush thee, dear!' said Rachel, gently; 'hush, Ruth! Tell us, shall we tell her now?'

'Now! to be sure, – this very minute. Why, now, suppose't was my John, how should I feel? Do tell her, right off.'

'Thee uses thyself only to learn how to love thy neighbor, Ruth,' said Simeon, looking, with a beaming face, on Ruth.

'To be sure. Isn't it what we are made for? If I didn't love John and the baby, I should not know how to feel for her. Come, now do tell her, – do!' and she laid her hands persuasively on Rachel's arm. 'Take her into thy bed-room, there, and let me fry the chicken while thee does it.'

Rachel came out into the kitchen, where Eliza was sewing, and opening the door of a small bed-room, said, gently, 'Come in here with me, my daughter; I have news to tell thee.'

The blood flushed in Eliza's pale face; she rose, trembling with nervous anxiety, and looked towards her boy.

'No, no,' said little Ruth, darting up, and seizing her hands. 'Never thee fear; it's good news, Eliza, – go in, go in!' And she gently pushed her to the door which closed after her; and then, turning round, she caught little Harry in her arms, and began kissing him.

'Thee'll see thy father, little one. Does thee know it? Thy father is coming,' she said, over and over again, as the boy looked wonderingly at her.

Meanwhile, within the door, another scene was going on. Rachel Halliday drew Eliza toward her, and said, 'The Lord hath had mercy on thee, daughter; thy husband hath escaped from the house of bondage.'

The blood flushed to Eliza's cheek in a sudden glow, and went back to her heart with as sudden a rush. She sat down, pale and faint.

'Have courage child,' said Rachel, laying her hand on her head. 'He is among friends, who will bring him here tonight.'

'Tonight!' Eliza repeated, 'tonight!' The words lost all meaning to her; her head was dreamy and confused; all was mist for a moment.

When she awoke, she found herself snugly tucked up on the bed, with a blanket over her, and little Ruth rubbing her hands with camphor. She opened her eyes in a state of dreamy, delicious languor, such as one who has long been bearing a heavy load, and now feels it gone, and would rest. The tension of the nerves, which had never ceased a moment since the first hour of her flight, had given way, and a strange feeling of security and rest came over her; and as she lay, with her large, dark eyes open, she followed, as in a quiet dream, the motions of those about her. She saw the door open into the other room; saw the supper-table, with its snowy cloth; heard the dreamy murmur of the singing tea-kettle; saw Ruth tripping backward and forward, with plates of cake and saucers of preserves, and ever and anon stopping to put a cake into Harry's hand, or pat his head, or twine his long curls round her snowy fingers. She saw the ample, motherly form of Rachel, as she ever and anon came to the bed-side, and smoothed and arranged something about the bed-clothes, and gave a tuck here and there, by way of expressing her good-will; and was conscious of a kind of sunshine beaming down upon her from the large, clear, brown eyes. She saw Ruth's husband come in, – saw her fly up to him, and commence whispering very earnestly, ever and anon, with impressive gesture, pointing her little finger toward the room. She saw her, with the baby in her arms, sitting down to tea; she saw them all at table, and little Harry in a high chair, under the shadow of Rachel's ample wing; there were low murmurs of talk, gentle tinkling of tea-spoons, and musical clatter of cups and saucers, and all mingled in a delightful dream of rest; and Eliza slept, as she had not slept before, since the fearful midnight hour when she had taken her child and fled through the frosty starlight.

She dreamed of a beautiful country, – a land, it seemed to her, of rest, – green shores, pleasant islands, and beautifully glittering water; and there, in a house which kind voices told her was a home, she saw her boy playing, free and happy child. She heard her husband's footsteps; she felt him coming nearer; his arms were around her, his tears falling on her face, and she awoke! It was no dream. The daylight had long faded; her child lay calmly sleeping by her side; a candle was burning dimly on the stand, and her husband was sobbing by her pillow.

The next morning was a cheerful one at the Quaker house. 'Mother' was up betimes, and surrounded by busy girls and boys, whom we had scarce time to introduce to our readers yesterday, and who all moved obediently to Rachel's gentle 'Thee had better,' or more gentle 'Hadn't thee better?' in the work of getting breakfast; for a breakfast in the luxurious valleys of Indiana is a thing complicated and multiform, and, like picking up the rose-leaves and trimming the bushes in Paradise, asking other hands than those of the original mother. While, therefore, John ran to the spring for fresh water, and Simeon the second sifted meal for corn-cakes, and Mary ground coffee, Rachel moved gently, and quietly about, making biscuits, cutting up chicken, and diffusing a sort of sunny radiance over the whole proceeding generally. If there was any danger of friction or collision from the ill-regulated zeal of so many young operators, her gentle 'Come! come!' or 'I wouldn't, now,' was quite sufficient to allay the difficulty. Bards have written of the cestus of Venus, that turned the heads of all the world in successive generations. We had rather, for our part, have the cestus of Rachel Halliday, that kept heads from being turned, and made everything go on harmoniously. We think it is more suited to our modern days, decidedly.

While all other preparations were going on, Simeon the elder stood in his shirt-sleeves before a little looking-glass in the corner, engaged in the anti-patriarchal operation of shaving. Everything went on so sociably, so quietly, so harmoniously, in the great kitchen, – it seemed so pleasant to every one to do just what they were doing, there was such an atmosphere of mutual confidence and good fellowship everywhere, – even the knives and forks had a social clatter as they went on to the table; and the chicken and ham had a cheerful and joyous fizzle in the pan, as if they rather enjoyed being cooked than otherwise; – and when George and Eliza and little Harry came out, they met such a hearty, rejoicing welcome, no wonder it seemed to them like a dream.

At last, they were all seated at breakfast, while Mary stood at the stove, baking griddle-cakes, which, as they gained the true exact golden-brown tint of perfection, were transferred quite handily to the table.

Rachel never looked so truly and benignly happy as at the head of her table. There was so much motherliness and fullheartedness even in the way she passed a plate of cakes or poured a cup of coffee, that it seemed to put a spirit into the food and drink she offered.

It was the first time that ever George had sat down on equal terms at any white man's table; and he sat down, at first, with some constraint and awkwardness; but they all exhaled and went off like fog, in the genial morning rays of this simple, overflowing kindness.

This, indeed, was a home, – home, – a word that George had never yet known a meaning for; and a belief in God, and trust in his providence, began to encircle his heart, as, with a golden cloud of protection and confidence, dark, misanthropic, pining atheistic doubts, and fierce despair, melted away before the light of a living Gospel, breathed in living faces, preached by a thousand unconscious acts of love and good will, which, like the cup of cold water given in the name of a disciple, shall never lose their reward.

'Father, what if thee should get found out again?' said Simeon second, as he buttered his cake.

'I should pay my fine,' said Simeon, quietly.

'But what if they put thee in prison?'

'Couldn't thee and mother manage the farm?' said Simeon, smiling.

'Mother can do almost everything,' said the boy. 'But isn't it a shame to make such laws?'

'Thee mustn't speak evil of thy rulers, Simeon,' said his father, gravely. 'The Lord only gives us our worldly goods that we may do justice and mercy; if our rulers require a price of us for it, we must deliver it up.'

'Well, I hate those old slaveholders!' said the boy, who felt as unchristian as became any modern reformer.

'I am surprised at thee, son,' said Simeon; 'thy mother never taught thee so. I would do even the same for the slaveholder as for the slave, if the Lord brought him to my door in affliction.'

Simeon second blushed scarlet; but his mother only smiled, and said, 'Simeon is my good boy; he will grow older, by and by, and then he will be like his father.'

'I hope, my good sir, that you are not exposed to any difficulty on our account,' said George, anxiously.

'Fear nothing, George, for therefore are we sent into the world. If we would not meet trouble for a good cause, we were not worthy of our name.'

'But, for me,' said George, 'I could not bear it.'

'Fear not, then, friend George; it is not for thee, but for God and man, we do it,' said Simeon. 'And now thou must lie by quietly this day, and tonight, at ten o'clock, Phineas Fletcher will carry thee onward to the next stand, – thee and the rest of thy company. The pursuers are hard after thee; we must not delay.'

'If that is the case, why wait till evening?' said George.

'Thou art safe here by daylight, for every one in the settlement is a Friend, and all are watching. It has been found safer to travel by night.'

CHAPTER FOURTEEN

Evangeline

'A young star! which shone
O'er life – too sweet an image for such glass!
A lovely being, scarcely formed or moulded;
A rose with all its sweetest leaves yet folded.'

The Mississippi! How, as by an enchanted wand, have its scenes been changed, since Chateaubriand wrote his prose-poetic description of it, as a river of mighty, unbroken solitudes, rolling amid undreamed wonders of vegetable and animal existence.

But as in an hour, this river of dreams and wild romance has emerged to a reality scarcely less visionary and splendid. What other river of the world bears on its bosom to the ocean the wealth and enterprise of such another country? – a country whose products embrace all between the tropics and the poles! Those turbid waters, hurrying, foaming, tearing along, an apt resemblance of that headlong tide of business which is poured along its wave by a race more vehement and energetic than any the old world ever saw. Ah! would that they did not also bear along a more fearful freight, – the tears of the oppressed, the sighs of the helpless, the bitter prayers of poor, ignorant hearts to an unknown God – unknown, unseen and silent, but who will yet 'come out of his place to save all the poor of the earth!'

The slanting light of the setting sun quivers on the sea-like expanse of the river; the shivery canes, and the tall, dark cypress, hung with wreaths of dark, funereal moss, glow in the golden ray, as the heavily-laden steamboat marches onward.

Piled with cotton-bales, from many a plantation, up over deck and sides, till she seems in the distance a square, massive block of gray, she moves heavily onward to the nearing mart. We must look some time among its crowded decks before we shall find again our humble friend Tom. High on the upper deck, in a little nook among the everywhere predominant cotton-bales, at last we may find him.

Partly from confidence inspired by Mr Shelby's representations, and partly from the remarkably inoffensive and quiet character of the man, Tom has insensibly won his way far into the confidence even of such a man as Haley.

At first he had watched him narrowly through the day, and never allowed him to sleep at night unfettered; but the uncomplaining patience and apparent contentment of Tom's manner led him gradually to discontinue these restraints, and for some time Tom had enjoyed a sort of parole of honor, being permitted to come and go freely where he pleased on the boat.

Ever quiet and obliging, and more than ready to lend a hand in every emergency which occurred among the workmen below, he had won the good opinion of all the hands, and spent many hours in helping them with as hearty a good will as ever he worked on a Kentucky farm.

When there seemed to be nothing for him to do, he would climb to a nook among the cotton-bales of the upper deck, and busy himself in studying over his Bible, – and it is there we see him now.

For a hundred or more miles above New Orleans, the river is higher than the surrounding country, and rolls its tremendous volume between massive levees twenty feet in height. The traveller from the deck of the steamer, as from some floating castle top, overlooks the whole country for miles and miles around. Tom, therefore, had spread out full before him, in plantation after plantation, a map of the life to which he was approaching.

He saw the distant slaves at their toil; he saw afar their villages of huts gleaming out in long rows on many a plantation, distant from the stately mansions and pleasure-grounds of the master; – and as the moving picture passed on, his poor, foolish heart would be turning backward to the Kentucky farm, with its old shadowy beeches, – to the master's house, with its wide, cool halls, and, near by, the little cabin overgrown with the multiflora and bignonia. There he seemed to see familiar faces of comrades who had grown up with him from infancy; he saw his busy wife, bustling in her preparations for his evening meals; he heard the merry laugh of his boys at their play, and the chirrup of the baby at his knee; and then, with a start, all faded, and he saw again the canebrakes and cypresses and gliding plantations, and heard again the creaking and groaning of the machinery, all telling him too plainly that all that phase of life had gone by forever.

In such a case, you write to your wife, and send messages to your children; but Tom could not write, – the mail for him had no existence, and the gulf of separation was unbridged by even a friendly word or signal.

Is it strange, then, that some tears fall on the pages of his Bible, as he lays it on the cotton-bale, and, with patient finger, threading his slow way from word to word, traces out its promises? Having learned late in life, Tom was but a slow reader, and passed on laboriously from verse to verse. Fortunate for him was it that the book he was intent on was one which slow reading cannot injure, – nay, one whose words, like ingots of gold, seem often to need to be weighed separately, that the mind may take in their priceless value. Let us follow him a moment, as, pointing to each word, and pronouncing each half aloud, he reads,

'Let – not – your – heart – be – troubled. In – my – Father's – house – are – many – mansions. I – go – to – prepare – a – place – for – you.'

Cicero, when he buried his darling and only daughter, had a heart as full of honest grief as poor Tom's, – perhaps no fuller, for both were only men; – but Cicero could pause over no such sublime words of hope, and look to no such future reunion; and if he *had* seen them, ten to one he would not have believed, – he must fill his head first with a thousand questions of authenticity of manuscript, and correctness of translation. But, to poor Tom, there it lay, just what he needed, so evidently true and divine that the possibility of a question never entered his simple head. It must be true; for, if not true, how could he live?

As for Tom's Bible, though it had no annotations and helps in margin from learned commentators, still it had been embellished with certain way-marks and guide-boards of Tom's own invention, and which helped him more than the most learned expositions could have done. It had been his custom to get the Bible read to him by his master's children, in particular by young Master George; and, as they read, he would designate, by bold, strong marks and dashes, with pen and ink, the passages which more particularly gratified his ear or affected his heart. His Bible was thus marked through, from one end to the other, with a variety of styles and designations; so he could in a moment seize upon his favorite passages, without the labor of spelling out what lay between them; – and while it lay there before him, every passage breathing of some old home scene, and recalling some past enjoyment, his Bible seemed to him all of this life that remained, as well as the promise of a future one.

Among the passengers on the boat was a young gentleman of fortune and family, resident in New Orleans, who bore the name of St Clare. He had with him a daughter between five and six years of age, together with a lady who seemed to claim relationship to both, and to have the little one especially under her charge.

Tom had often caught glimpses of this little girl, – for she was one of those busy, tripping creatures, that can be no more contained in one place than a sunbeam or a summer breeze, – nor was she one that, once seen, could be easily forgotten.

Her form was the perfection of childish beauty, without its usual chubbiness and squareness of outline. There was about it an undulating and aerial grace, such as one might dream of for some mythic and allegorical being. Her face was remarkable less for its perfect beauty of feature than for a singular and dreamy earnestness of expression, which made the ideal start when they looked at her, and by which the dullest and most literal were impressed, without exactly knowing why. The shape of her head and the turn of her neck and bust was peculiarly noble, and the long golden-brown hair that floated like a cloud around it, the deep spiritual gravity of her violet blue eyes, shaded by heavy fringes of golden brown, – all marked her out from other children, and made every one turn and look after her, as she glided hither and thither on the boat. Nevertheless, the little one was not what you would have called either a grave child or a sad one. On the contrary, an airy and innocent playfulness seemed to flicker like the shadow of summer leaves over her childish face, and around her buoyant figure. She was always in motion, always with a half smile on her rosy mouth, flying hither and thither, with an undulating and cloud-like tread, singing to herself as she moved as in a happy dream. Her father and female guardian were incessantly busy in pursuit of her, – but, when caught, she melted from them again like a summer cloud; and as no word of chiding or reproof ever fell on her ear for whatever she chose to do, she pursued her own way all over the boat. Always dressed in white, she seemed to move like a shadow through all sorts of places, without contracting spot or stain; and there was not a corner or nook, above or below, where those fairy footsteps had not glided, and that visionary golden head, with its deep blue eyes, fleeted along.

The fireman, as he looked up from his sweaty toil, sometimes found those eyes looking wonderingly into the raging depths of the furnace, and fearfully and pityingly at him, as if she thought him in some dreadful danger. Anon the steersman at the wheel paused and smiled, as the picture-like head gleamed through the window of the round house, and in a moment was gone again. A thousand times a day rough voices blessed her, and smiles of unwonted softness stole over hard faces, as she passed; and when she tripped fearlessly over dangerous places, rough, sooty hands were stretched involuntarily out to save her, and smooth her path.

Tom, who had the soft, impressible nature of his kindly race, ever yearning toward the simple and childlike, watched the little creature with daily increasing interest. To him she seemed something almost divine; and whenever her golden head and deep blue eyes peered out upon him from behind some dusky cottonbale, or looked down upon him over some ridge of packages, he half believed that he saw one of the angels stepped out of his New Testament.

Often and often she walked mournfully round the place where Haley's gang of men and women sat in their chains. She would glide in among them, and look at them with an air of perplexed and sorrowful earnestness; and sometimes she would lift their chains with her slender hands, and then sigh wofully, as she glided away. Several times she appeared suddenly among them, with her hands full of candy, nuts, and oranges, which she would distribute joyfully to them, and then be gone again.

Tom watched the little lady a great deal, before he ventured on any overtures towards acquaintanceship. He knew an abundance of simple acts to propitiate and invite the approaches of the little people, and he resolved to play his part right skilfully. He could cut cunning little baskets out of cherry-stones, could make grotesque faces on hickory-nuts, or odd-jumping figures out of elder-pith, and he was a very Pan in the manufacture of whistles of all sizes and sorts. His pockets were full of miscellaneous articles of attraction, which he had hoarded in days of old for his master's children, and which he now produced, with commendable prudence and economy, one by one, as overtures for acquaintance and friendship.

The little one was shy, for all her busy interest in everything going on, and it was not easy to tame her. For a while, she would perch like a canary-bird on some box or package near Tom, while busy in the little arts afore-named, and take from him, with a kind of grave bashfulness, the little articles he offered. But at last they got on quite confidential terms.

'What's little missy's name?' said Tom, at last, when he thought matters were ripe to push such an inquiry.

'Evangeline St Clare,' said the little one, 'though papa and everybody else call me Eva. Now, what's your name?'

'My name's Tom; the little chil'en used to call me Uncle Tom, way back thar in Kentuck.'

'Then I mean to call you Uncle Tom, because, you see, I like you,' said Eva. 'So, Uncle Tom, where are you going?'

'I don't know, Miss Eva.'

'Don't know?' said Eva.

'No, I am going to be sold to somebody. I don't know who.'

'My papa can buy you,' said Eva, quickly; 'and if he buys you, you will have good times. I mean to ask him, this very day.'

'Thank you, my little lady,' said Tom.

The boat here stopped at a small landing to take in wood, and Eva, hearing her father's voice, bounded nimbly away. Tom rose up, and went forward to offer his service in wooding, and soon was busy among the hands.

Eva and her father were standing together by the railings to see the boat start from the landing-place, the wheel had made two or three revolutions in the water, when, by some sudden movement, the little one suddenly lost her balance and fell sheer over the side of the boat into the water. Her father, scarce knowing what he did, was plunging in after her, but was held back by someone behind him, who saw that more efficient aid had followed his child.

Tom was standing just under her on the lower deck, as she fell. He saw her strike the water, and sink, and was after her in a moment. A broad-chested, strong-armed fellow, it was nothing for him to keep afloat in the water, till, in a moment or two the child rose to the surface, and he caught her in his arms, and, swimming with her to the boat-side, handed her up, all dripping, to the grasp of hundreds of hands, which, as if they had all belonged to one man, were stretched eagerly out to receive her. A few moments more, and her father bore her, dripping and senseless, to the ladies' cabin, where, as is usual in cases of the kind, there ensued a very well-meaning and kind-hearted strife among the female occupants generally, as to who should do the most things to make a disturbance, and to hinder her recovery in every way possible.

It was a sultry, close day, the next day, as the steamer drew near to New Orleans. A general bustle of expectation and preparation was spread through the boat; in the cabin, one and another were gathering their things together, and arranging them, preparatory to going ashore. The steward and chamber-maid, and all, were busily engaged in cleaning, furbishing, and arranging the spendid boat, preparatory to a grand entree.

On the lower deck sat our friend Tom, with his arms folded, and anxiously, from time to time, turning his eyes towards a group on the other side of the boat.

There stood the fair Evangeline, a little paler than the day before, but otherwise exhibiting no traces of the accident which had befallen her. A graceful, elegantly-formed young man stood by her, carelessly leaning one elbow on a bale of cotton, while a large pocket-book lay open before him. It was quite evident, at a glance, that the gentleman was Eva's father. There was the same noble cast of head, the same large blue eyes, the same golden-brown hair; yet the expression was wholly different. In the large, clear blue eyes, though in form and color exactly similar, there was wanting that misty, dreamy depth of expression; all was clear, bold, and bright, but with a light wholly of this world: the beautifully cut mouth had a proud and somewhat sarcastic expression, while an air of free-and-easy superiority sat not ungracefully in every turn and movement of his fine form. He was listening, with a good-humored, negligent air, half comic, half contemptuous, to Haley, who was very volubly expatiating on the quality of the article for which they were bargaining.

'All the moral and Christian virtues bound in black morocco, complete!' he said, when Haley had finished. 'Well, now, my good fellow, what's the damage, as they say in Kentucky; in short, what's to be paid out for this business? How much are you going to cheat me, now? Out with it!'

'Wal,' said Haley, 'if I should say thirteen hundred dollars for that ar fellow, I shouldn't but just save myself; I shouldn't, now, re'ly.'

'Poor fellow!' said the young man, fixing his keen, mocking blue eye on him; 'but I suppose you'd let me have him for that, out of a particular regard for me.'

'Well, the young lady here seems to be sot on him, and nat'lly enough.'

'O! certainly, there's a call on your benevolence, my friend. Now, as a matter of Christian charity, how cheap could you afford to let him go, to oblige a young lady that's particular sot on him?'

'Wal, now, just think on 't,' said the trader; 'just look at them limbs, – broad-chested, strong as a horse. Look at his head; them high forrads allays shows calculatin niggers, that'll do any kind o' thing. I've marked that ar. Now a nigger of that ar heft and build is worth considerable, just as you may say, for his body, supposin he's stupid; but come to put in his calculatin faculties, and them which I can show he has oncommon, why, of course, it makes him come higher. Why, that ar fellow managed his master's whole farm. He has a strornary talent for business.'

'Bad, bad, very bad; knows altogether too much!' said the young man, with the same mocking smile playing about his mouth. 'Never will do, in the world. Your smart fellows are always running off, stealing horses, and raising the devil generally. I think you'll have to take off a couple of hundred for his smartness.'

'Wal, there might be something in that ar, if it warnt for his character; but I can show recommends from his master and others, to prove he is one of your real pious, – the most humble, prayin, pious crittur ye ever did see. Why, he's been called a preacher in them parts he came from.'

'And I might use him for a family chaplain, possibly,' added the young man, dryly. 'That's quite an idea. Religion is a remarkably scarce article at our house.'

'You're joking, now.'

'How do you know I am? Didn't you just warrant him for a preacher? Has he been examined by any synod or council? Come, hand over your papers.'

If the trader had not been sure, by a certain good-humored twinkle in the large eye, that all this banter was sure, in the long run, to turn out a cash concern, he might have been somewhat out of patience; as it was, he laid down a greasy pocket-book on the cotton-bales, and began anxiously studying over certain papers in it, the young man standing by, the while, looking down on him with an air of careless, easy drollery.

'Papa, do buy him! it's no matter what you pay,' whispered Eva, softly, getting up on a package, and putting her arm around her father's neck. 'You have money enough, I know. I want him.'

'What for, pussy? Are you going to use him for a rattle-box, or a rocking-horse, or what?'

'I want to make him happy.'

'An original reason, certainly.'

Here the trader handed up a certificate, signed by Mr Shelby, which the young man took with the tips of his long fingers, and glanced over carelessly.

'A gentlemanly hand,' he said, 'and well spelt, too. Well, now, but I'm not sure, after all, about this religion,' said he, the old wicked expression returning to his eye; 'the country is almost ruined with pious white people; such pious politicians as we have just before elections, – such pious goings on in all departments of church and state, that a fellow does not know who'll cheat him next. I don't know, either, about religion's being up in the market, just now. I have not looked in the papers lately, to see how it sells. How many hundred dollars, now, do you put on for this religion?'

'You like to be jokin, now,' said the trader; 'but, then, there's *sense* under all that ar. I know there's differences in religion. Some kinds is mis'rable: there's your meetin pious; there's your singin, roarin pious; them ar an't no account, in black or white; – but these rayly is; and I've seen it in niggers as often as any, your rail softly, quiet, stiddy, honest, pious, that the hull world couldn't tempt 'em to do nothing that they thinks is wrong; and ye see in this letter what

Tom's old master says about him.'

'Now,' said the young man, stooping gravely over his book of bills, 'if you can assure me that I really can buy *this* kind of pious, and that it will be set down to my account in the book up above, as something belonging to me, I wouldn't care if I did go a little extra for it. How d'ye say?'

'Wal, raily, I can't do that,' said the trader. 'I'm a thinkin that every man'll have to hang on his own hook, in them ar quarters.'

'Rather hard on a fellow that pays extra on religion, and can't trade with it in the state where he wants it most, an't it, now?' said the young man, who had been making out a roll of bills while he was speaking. 'There, count your money, old boy!' he added, as he handed the roll to the trader.

'All right,' said Haley, his face beaming with delight; and pulling out an old inkhorn, he proceeded to fill out a bill of sale, which, in a few moments, he handed to the young man.

'I wonder, now, if I was divided up and inventoried,' said the latter as he ran over the paper, 'how much I might bring. Say so much for the shape of my head, so much for a high forehead, so much for arms, and hands, and legs, and then so much for education, learning, talent, honesty, religion! Bless me! there would be small charge on that last, I'm thinking. But come, Eva,' he said; and taking the hand of his daughter, he stepped across the boat, and carelessly putting the tip of his finger under Tom's chin, said, good-humoredly, 'Look-up, Tom, and see how you like your new master.'

Tom looked up. It was not in nature to look into that gay, young, handsome face, without a feeling of pleasure; and Tom felt the tears start in his eyes as he said, heartily, 'God bless you, Mas'r!'

'Well, I hope he will. What's your name? Tom? Quite as likely to do it for your asking as mine, from all accounts. Can you drive horses, Tom?'

'I've been allays used to horses,' said Tom. 'Mas'r Shelby raised heaps of 'em.'

'Well, I think I shall put you in coachy, on condition that you won't be drunk more than once a week, unless in cases of emergency, Tom.'

Tom looked surprised, and rather hurt, and said, 'I never drink, Mas'r.'

'I've heard that story before, Tom; but then we'll see. It will be a special accommodation to all concerned, if you don't. Never mind, my boy,' he added, good-humoredly, seeing Tom still looked grave; 'I don't doubt you mean to do well.'

'I sartin do, Mas'r,' said Tom.

'And you shall have good times,' said Eva. 'Papa is very good to everybody, only he always will laugh at them.'

'Papa is much obliged to you for his recommendation,' said St Clare, laughing, as he turned on his heel and walked away.

CHAPTER FIFTEEN

Of Tom's New Master, and Various Other Matters

Since the thread of our humble hero's life has now become interwoven with that of higher ones, it is necessary to give some brief introduction to them.

Augustine St Clare was the son of a wealthy planter of Louisiana. The family had its origin in Canada. Of two brothers, very similar in temperament and character, one had settled on a flourishing farm in Vermont, and the other became an opulent planter in Louisiana. The mother of Augustine was a Huguenot French lady, whose family had emigrated to Louisiana during the days of its early settlement. Augustine and another brother were the only children of their parents. Having inherited from his mother an exceeding delicacy of constitution, he was, at the instance of physicians, during many years of his boyhood, sent to the care of his uncle in Vermont, in order that his constitution might be strengthened by the cold of a more bracing climate.

In childhood, he was remarkable for an extreme and marked sensitiveness of character, more akin to the softness of woman than the ordinary hardness of his own sex. Time, however, overgrew this softness with the rough bark of manhood, and but few knew how living and fresh it still lay at the core. His talents were of the very first order, although his mind showed a preference always for the ideal and the aesthetic, and there was about him that repugnance to the actual business of life which is the common result of this balance of the faculties. Soon after the completion of his college course, his whole nature was kindled into one intense and passionate effervescence of romantic passion. His hour came, – the hour that comes only once; his star rose in the horizon, – that star that rises, so often in vain, to be remembered only as a thing of dreams; and it rose for him in vain. To drop the figure, – he saw and won the love of a high-minded and beautiful woman, in one of the northern states, and they were affianced. He returned south to make arrangements for their marriage, when, most unexpectedly, his letters were returned to him by mail, with a short note from her guardian, stating to him that ere this reached him the lady would be the wife of another. Stung to madness, he vainly hoped, as many another has done, to fling the whole thing from his heart by one desperate effort. Too proud to supplicate or seek explanation, he threw himself at once into a whirl of fashionable society, and in a fortnight from the time of the fatal letter was the accepted lover of the reigning belle of the season; and as soon as arrangements could be made, he became the husband of a fine figure, a pair of bright dark eyes, and a hundred thousand dollars; and, of course, everybody thought him a happy fellow.

The married couple were enjoying their honeymoon, and entertaining a brilliant circle of friends in their splendid villa, near Lake Pontchartrain, when, one day, a letter was brought to him in *that* well-remembered writing. It was handed to him while he was in full tide of gay and successful conversation, in a whole room-full of company. He turned deadly pale when he saw the writing, but still preserved his composure, and finished the playful warfare of badinage which he was at the moment carrying on with a lady opposite; and, a short time after, was missed from the circle. In his room, alone, he opened and read the letter, now worse than idle and useless to be read. It was from her, giving a long account of a persecution to which she had been exposed by her guardian's family, to lead her to unite herself with their son: and she related how, for a long time, his letters had ceased to arrive; how she had written time and again, till she became weary and doubtful; how her health had failed under her anxieties, and how, at last, she had discovered the whole fraud which had been practised on them both. The letter ended with expressions of hope and thankfulness, and professions of undying affection, which were more bitter than death to the unhappy young man. He wrote to her immediately:

'I have received yours, – but too late. I believed all I heard. I was desperate. *I am married*, and all is over. Only forget, – it is all that remains for either of us.'

And thus ended the whole romance and ideal of life for Augustine St Clare. But the *real* remained, – the *real*, like the flat, bare, oozy tide-mud, when the blue sparkling wave, with all its company of gliding boats and white-winged ships, it music of oars and chiming waters, has gone down, and there it lies, flat, slimy, bare, – exceedingly real.

Of course, in a novel, people's hearts break, and they die, and that is the end of it; and in a story this is very convenient. But in real life we do not die when all that makes life bright dies to us. There is a most busy and important round of eating, drinking, dressing, walking, visiting, buying, selling, talking, reading, and all that makes up what is commonly called *living*, yet to be gone through; and this yet remained to Augustine. Had his wife been a whole woman, she might yet have done something – as woman can – to mend the broken threads of life, and weave again into a tissue of brightness. But Marie St Clare could not even see that they had been broken. As before stated, she consisted of a fine figure, a pair of splendid eyes, and a hundred thousand dollars; and none of these items were precisely the ones to minister to a mind diseased.

When Augustine, pale as death, was found lying on the sofa, and pleaded sudden sick-headache as the cause of his distress, she recommended to him to smell of hartshorn; and when the paleness and headache came on week after week, she only said that she never thought Mr St Clare was sickly; but it seems he was very liable to sick-headaches, and that it was a very unfortunate thing for her, because he didn't enjoy going into company with her, and it seemed odd to go so much alone, when they were just married. Augustine was glad in his heart that he had married so undiscerning a woman; but as the glosses and civilities of the honeymoon wore away, he discovered that a beautiful young woman, who has lived all her life to be caressed and waited on, might prove quite a hard mistress in domestic life. Marie never had possessed much capability of affection, or much sensibility, and the little that she had, had been merged into a most intense and unconscious selfishness; a selfishness the more hopeless, from its quiet obtuseness, its utter ignorance of any claims but her own. From her infancy, she had been surrounded with servants, who lived only to study her caprices; the idea that they had either feelings or rights had never dawned upon her, even in distant perspective. Her father, whose only child she had been, had never denied her anything that lay within the compass of human possibility; and when she entered life, beautiful, accomplished, and an heiress, she had, of course, all the eligibles and non-eligibles of the other sex sighing at her feet, and she had no doubt that Augustine was a most fortunate man in having obtained her. It is a great mistake to suppose that a woman with no heart will be an easy creditor in the exchange of affection. There is not on earth a more merciless exactor of love from others than a thoroughly selfish woman; and the more unlovely she grows, the more jealously and scrupulously she exacts love, to the uttermost farthing. When, therefore, St Clare began to drop off those gallantries and small attentions which flowed at first through the habitude of courtship, he found his sultana no way ready to resign her slave; there were abundance of tears, poutings, and small tempests, there were discontents, pinings, upbraidings. St Clare was good-natured and self-indulgent, and sought to buy off with presents and flatteries; and when Marie became mother to a beautiful daughter, he really felt awakened, for a time, to something like tenderness.

St Clare's mother had been a woman of uncommon elevation and purity of character, and he gave to his child his mother's name, fondly fancying that she would prove a reproduction of her image. The thing had been remarked with petulant jealousy by his wife, and she regarded her husband's absorbing devotion to the child with suspicion and dislike; all that was given to her seemed so much taken from herself. From the time of the birth of this child, her health gradually sunk. A life of constant inaction, bodily and mental, – the friction of ceaseless ennui and discontent, united to the ordinary weakness which attended the period of maternity, – in course of a few years changed the blooming young belle into a yellow faded, sickly woman, whose time was divided among a variety of fanciful deseases, and who considered herself, in every sense, the most ill-used and suffering person in existence.

There was no end of her various complaints; but her principal forte appeared to lie in sick-headache, which sometimes would confine her to her room three days out of six. As, of course, all family arrangements fell into the hands of servants, St Clare found his menage anything but comfortable. His only daughter was exceedingly delicate, and he feared that, with no one to look after her and attend to her, her health and life might yet fall a sacrifice to her mother's inefficiency. He had taken her with him on a tour to Vermont, and had persuaded his cousin, Miss Ophelia St Clare, to return with him to his southern residence; and they are now returning on this boat, where we have introduced them to our readers.

And now, while the distant domes and spires of New Orleans rise to our view, there is yet time for an introduction to Miss Ophelia.

Whoever has travelled in the New England States will remember, in some cool village, the large farmhouse, with its clean-swept grassy yard, shaded by the dense and massive foliage of the sugar maple; and remember the air of order and stillness, of perpetuity and unchanging repose, that seemed to breathe over the whole place. Nothing lost, or out of order; not a picket loose in the fence, not a particle of litter in the turfy yard, with its clumps of lilac bushes growing up under the windows. Within, he will remember wide, clean rooms, where nothing ever seems to be doing or going to be done, where everything is once and forever rigidly in place, and where all household arrangements move with the punctual exactness of the old clock in the corner. In the family 'keeping-room,' as it is termed, he will remember the staid, respectable old book-case, with its glass doors, where Rollin's History, Milton's Paradise Lost, Bunyan's Pilgrim's Progress, and Scott's Family Bible, stand side by side in decorous order, with multitudes of other books, equally solemn and respectable. There are no servants in the house, but the lady in the snowy cap, with the spectacles, who sits sewing every afternoon among her daughters, as if nothing ever had been done, or were to be done, – she and her girls, in some long-forgotten fore part of the day, '*did up the work,*' and for the rest of the time, probably, at all hours when you would see them, it is '*done up.*' The old kitchen floor never seems stained or spotted; the tables, the chairs, and the various cooking utensils, never seem deranged or disordered; though three and sometimes four meals a day are got there, though the family washing and ironing is there performed, and though pounds of butter and cheese are in some silent and mysterious manner there brought into existence.

On such a farm, in such a house and family, Miss Ophelia had spent a quiet existence of some forty-five years, when her cousin invited her to visit his southern mansion. The eldest of a large family, she was still considered by her father and mother as one of 'the children,' and the proposal that she should go to *Orleans* was a most momentous one to the family circle. The old gray-headed father took down Morse's Atlas out of the book-case, and looked out the exact latitude and longitude; and read Flint's Travels in the South and West, to make up his own mind as to the nature of the country.

The good mother inquired, anxiously, 'if Orleans wasn't an awful wicked place,' saying, 'that it seemed to her most equal to going to the Sandwich Islands, or anywhere among the heathen.'

It was known at the minister's and at the doctor's and at Miss Peabody's milliner shop, that Ophlia St Clare was 'talking about' going away down to Orleans with her cousin; and of course the whole village could do no less than help this very important process of *talking about* the matter. The minister, who inclined strongly to abolitionist views, was quite doubtful whether such a step might not tend somewhat to encourage the southerners in holding on to their slaves; while the doctor, who was a stanch colonizationist, inclined to the opinion that Miss Ophelia ought to go, to show the Orleans people that we don't think hardly of them, after all. He was of opinion, in fact, that southern people needed encouraging. When however, the fact that she had resolved to go was fully before the public mind, she was solemnly invited out to tea by all her friends and neighbors for the space of a fortnight, and her prospects and plans duly canvassed and inquired into. Miss Moseley, who came into the house to help to do the dress-making, acquired daily accessions of importance from the developments with regard to Miss Ophelia's wardrobe which she had been enabled to make. It was credibly ascertained that Squire Sinclare, as his name was commonly contracted in the neighborhood, had counted out fifty dollars, and given them to Miss Ophelia, and told her to buy any clothes she thought best; and that two new silk dresses, and a bonnet, had been sent for from Boston. As to the propriety of this extraordinary outlay, the public mind was divided, – some affirming that it was well enough, all things considered, for once in one's life, and others stoutly affirming that the money had better have been sent to the missionaries; but all parties agreed that there had been no such parasol seen in those parts as had been sent on from New York, and that she had one silk dress that might fairly be trusted to stand alone, whatever might be said of its mistress. There were credible rumors, also, of a hemstitched pocket-handkerchief; and report even went so far as to state that Miss Ophelia had one pocket-handkerchief with lace all around it – it was even added that it was worked in the corners; but this latter point was never satisfactorily ascertained, and remains, in face, unsettled to this day.

Miss Ophelia, as you now behold her, stands before you, in a very shining brown linen travelling-dress, tall, square-formed, and angular. Her face was thin, and rather sharp in its outlines; the lips compressed, like those of a person who is in the habit of making up her mind definitely on all subjects; while the keen, dark eyes had a peculiarly searching, advised movement, and travelled over everything, as if they were looking for something to take care of.

All her movements were sharp, decided, and energetic; and, though she was never much of a talker, her words were remarkably direct, and to the purpose, when she did speak.

In her habits, she was a living impersonation of order, method, and exactness. In punctuality, she was as inevitable as a clock, and as inexorable as a railroad engine; and she held in most decided contempt and abomination anything of a contrary character.

The great sin of sins, in her eyes, – the sum of all evils, – was expressed by one very common and important word in her vocabulary – 'shiftlessness.' Her finale and ultimatum of contempt consisted in a very emphatic pronunciation of the word 'shiftless;' and by this she characterized all modes of procedure which had not a direct and inevitable relation to accomplishment of some purpose then definitely had in mind. People who did nothing, or who did not know exactly what they were going to do, or who did not take the most direct way to accomplish what they set their hands to, were objects of her entire contempt, – a contempt shown less frequently by anything she said, than by a kind of stony grimness, as if she scorned to say anything about the matter.

As to mental cultivation, – she had a clear, strong, active mind, was well and thoroughly read in history and the older English classics, and thought with great strength within certain narrow limits. Her theological tenets were all made up, labelled in most positive and distinct forms, and put by, like the bundles in her patch trunk; there were just so many of them, and there were never to be any more. So, also, were her ideas with regard to most matters of practical life, – such as house-keeping in all its branches and the various political relations of her native village. And, underlying all, deeper than anything else, higher and broader, lay the strongest principle of her being – conscientiousness. No where is conscience so dominant and all-absorbing as with New England women. It is the granite formation, which lies deepest, and rises out, even to the tops of the highest mountains.

Miss Ophelia was the absolute bond-slave of the 'ought.' Once make her certain that the 'path of duty,' as she commonly phrased it, lay in any given direction, and fire and water could not keep her from it. She would walk straight down into a well, or up to a loaded cannon's mouth, if she were only quite sure that there the path lay. Her standard of right was so high, so all-embracing, so minute, and making so few concessions to human frailty, that, though she strove with heroic ardor to reach it, she never actually did so, and of course was burdened with a constant and often harassing sense of deficiency; – this gave a severe and somewhat gloomy cast to her religious character.

But, how in the world can Miss Ophelia get along with Augustine St Clare, – gay, easy, unpunctual, unpractical, sceptical, – in short, – walking with impudent and nonchalant freedom over every one of her most cherished habits and opinions?

To tell the truth, then, Miss Ophelia loved him. When a boy, it had been hers to teach him his catechism, mend his clothes, comb his hair, and bring him up generally in the way he should go; and her heart having a warm side to it, Augustine had, as he usually did with most people, monopolized a large share of it for himself, and therefore it was that he succeeded very easily in persuading her that the 'path of duty' lay in the direction of New Orleans, and that she must go with him to take care of Eva, and keep everything from going to wreck and ruin during the frequent illnesses of his wife. The idea of a house without anybody to take care of it went to her heart; then she loved the lovely little girl, as few could help doing; and though she regarded Augustine as very much of a heathen, yet she loved him, laughed at his jokes, and forbore with his failings, to an extent which those who knew him thought perfectly incredible. But what more or other is to be known of Miss Ophelia our reader must discover by a personal acquaintance.

There she is, sitting now in her state-room, surrounded by a mixed multitude of little and big carpet-bags, boxes, baskets, each containing some separate responsibility which she is tying, binding up, packing, or fastening, with a face of great earnestness.

'Now, Eva, have you kept count of your things? Of course you haven't, – children never do: there's the spotted carpet-bag and the little blue band-box with your best bonnet, – that's two; then the India rubber satchel is three; and my tape and needle box is four; and my band-box, five; and my collar-box; and that little hair trunk, seven. What have you done with your sunshade? Give it to me, and let me put a paper round it, and tie it to my umbrella with my shade; – there, now.'

'Why, aunty, we are only going up home; – what is the use?'

'To keep it nice, child; people must take care of their things, if they ever mean to have anything; and now, Eva, is your thimble put up?'

'Really, aunty, I don't know.'

'Well, never mind; I'll look your box over, – thimble, wax, two spools, scissors, knife, tape-needle; all right, – put it in here. What did you ever do, child, when you were coming on with only your papa. I should have thought you'd a lost everything you had.'

'Well, aunty, I did lose a great many; and then, when we stopped anywhere, papa would buy some more of whatever it was.'

'Mercy on us, child, – what a way!'

'It was a very easy way, aunty,' said Eva.

'It's a dreadful shiftless one,' said aunty.

'Why, aunty, what'll you do now?' said Eva; 'that trunk is too full to be shut down.'

'It *must* shut down,' said aunty, with the air of a general, as she squeezed the things in, and sprung upon the lid; – still a little gap remained about the mouth of the trunk.

'Get up here, Eva!' said Miss Ophelia, courageously; 'what has been done can be done again. This trunk has *got to be* shut and locked – there are no two ways about it.'

And the trunk, intimidated, doubtless, by this resolute statement, gave in. The hasp snapped sharply in its hole, and Miss Ophelia turned the key, and pocketed it in triumph.

'Now we're ready. Where's your papa? I think it time this baggage was set out. Do look out, Eva, and see if you see your papa.'

'O, yes, he's down the other end of the gentlemen's cabin, eating an orange.'

'He can't know how near we are coming,' said aunty; 'hadn't you better run and speak to him?'

'Papa never is in a hurry about anything,' said Eva, 'and we haven't come to the landing. Do step on the guards, aunty. Look! there's our house, up that street!'

The boat now began, with heavy groans, like some vast, tired monster, to prepare to push up among the multiplied steamers at the levee. Eva joyously pointed out the various spires, domes, and way-marks, by which she recognized her native city.

'Yes, yes, dear; very fine,' said Miss Ophelia. 'But mercy on us! the boat has stopped! where is your father?'

And now ensued the usual turmoil of landing – waiters running twenty ways at once – men tugging trunks, carpet-bags, boxes – women anxiously calling to their children, and everybody crowding in a dense mass to the plank towards the landing.

Miss Ophelia seated herself resolutely on the lately vanquished trunk, and marshalling all her goods and chattels in fine military order, seemed resolved to defend them to the last.

'Shall I take your trunk, ma'am?' 'Shall I take your baggage?' 'Let me 'tend to your baggage, Missis?' 'Shan't I carry out these yer, Missis?' rained down upon her unheeded. She sat with grim determination, upright as a darning-needle stuck in a board, holding onto her bundle of umbrella and parasols, and replying with a determination that was enough to strike dismay even into a hackman, wondering to Eva, in each interval, 'what upon earth her papa could be thinking of; he couldn't have fallen over, now, – but something must have happened;' – and just as she had begun to work herself into a real distress, he came up, with his usually careless motion, and giving Eva a quarter of the orange he was eating, said,

'Well, Cousin Vermont, I suppose you are all ready.'

'I've been ready, waiting, nearly an hour,' said Miss Ophelia; 'I began to be really concerned about you.'

'That's a clever fellow, now,' said he. 'Well, the carriage is waiting, and the crowd are now off, so that one can walk out in a decent and Christian manner, and not be pushed and shoved. Here,' he added to a driver who stood behind him, 'take these things.'

'I'll go and see to his putting them in,' said Miss Ophelia.

'O, pshaw, cousin, what's the use?' said St Clare.

'Well, at any rate, I'll carry this, and this, and this,' said Miss Ophelia, singling out three boxes and a small carpet-bag.

'My dear Miss Vermont, positively you mustn't come the Green Mountains over us that way. You must adopt at least a piece of southern principle, and not walk out under all that load. They'll take you for a waiting-maid; give them to this fellow; he'll put them down as if they were eggs, now.'

Miss Ophelia looked despairingly, as her cousin took all her treasures from her, and rejoiced to find herself once more in the carriage with them, in a state of preservation.

'Where's Tom?' said Eva.

'O, he's on the outside, Pussy. I'm going to take Tom up to mother for a peace-offering, to make up for that drunken fellow that upset the carriage.'

'O, Tom will make a splendid driver, I know,' said Eva; 'he'll never get drunk.'

The carriage stopped in front of an ancient mansion, built in that odd mixture of Spanish and French style, of which there are specimens in some parts of New Orleans. It was built in the Moorish fashion, – a square building enclosing a court-yard, into which the carriage drove through an arched gateway. The court, in the inside, had evidently been arranged to gratify a picturesque and voluptuous ideality. Wide galleries ran all around the four sides, whose Moorish arches, slender pillars, and arabesque ornaments, carried the mind back, as in a dream, to the reign of oriental romance in Spain. In the middle of the court, a fountain threw high its silvery water, falling in a never-ceasing spray into a marble basin, fringed with a deep border of fragrant violets. The water in the fountain, pellucid as crystal, was alive with myriads of gold and silver fishes, twinkling and darting through it like so many living jewels. Around the fountain ran a walk, paved with a mosaic of pebbles, laid in various fanciful patterns; and this, again, was surrounded by turf, smooth as green velvet, while a carriage-drive enclosed the whole. Two large orange-trees, now fragrant with blossoms, threw a delicious shade; and, ranged in a circle round upon the turf, were marble vases of arabesque sculpture, containing the choicest flowering plants of the tropics. Huge pomegranate trees, with their glossy leaves and flame-colored flowers, dark-leaved Arabian jessamines, with their silvery stars, geraniums, luxuriant roses bending beneath their heavy abundance of flowers, golden jessamines, lemon-scented verbenum, all united their bloom and fragrance, while here and there a mystic old aloe, with its strange, massive leaves, sat looking like some old enchanter, sitting in weird grandeur among the more perishable bloom and fragrance around it.

The galleries that surrounded the court were festooned with a curtain of some kind of Moorish stuff, and could be drawn down at pleasure, to exclude the beams of the sun. On the whole, the appearance of the place was luxurious and romantic.

As the carriage drove in, Eva seemed like a bird ready to burst from a cage, with the wild eagerness of her delight.

'O, isn't it beautiful, lovely! my own dear, darling home!' she said to Miss Ophelia. 'Isn't it beautiful?'

''T is a pretty place,' said Miss Ophelia, as she alighted; 'though it looks rather old and heathenish to me.'

Tom got down from the carriage, and looked about with an air of calm, still enjoyment. The negro, it must be remembered, is an exotic of the most gorgeous and superb countries of the world, and he has, deep in his heart, a passion for all that is splendid, rich, and fanciful; a passion which, rudely indulged by an untrained taste, draws on them the ridicule of the colder and more correct white race.

St Clare, who was in heart a poetical voluptuary, smiled as Miss Ophelia made her remark on his premises and, turning to Tom, who was standing looking round, his beaming black face perfectly radiant with admiration, he said,

'Tom, my boy, this seems to suit you.'

'Yes, Mas'r, it looks about the right thing,' said Tom.

All this passed in a moment, while trunks were being hustled off, hackman paid, and while a crowd, of all ages and sizes, – men, women, and children, – came running through the galleries, both above and below to see Mas'r come in. Foremost among them was a highly-dressed young mulatto man, evidently a very *distingué* personage, attired in the ultra extreme of the mode, and gracefully waving a scented cambric handkerchief in his hand.

This personage had been exerting himself, with great alacrity, in driving all the flock of domestics to the other end of the verandah.

'Back! all of you. I am ashamed of you,' he said, in a tone of authority. 'Would you intrude on Master's domestic relations, in the first hour of his return?'

All looked abashed at this elegant speech, delivered with quite an air, and stood huddled together at a respectful distance, except two stout porters, who came up and began conveying away the baggage.

Owing to Mr Adolph's systematic arrangements, when St Clare turned round from paying the hackman, there was nobody in view but Mr Adolph himself, conspicuous in satin vest, gold guard-chain, and white pants, and bowing with inexpressible grace and suavity.

'Ah, Adolph, is it you?' said his master, offering his hand to him; 'how are you, boy?' while Adolph poured forth, with great fluency, an extemporary speech, which he had been preparing, with great care, for a fortnight before.

'Well, well,' said St Clare, passing on, with his usual air of negligent drollery, 'that's very well got up, Adolph. See that the baggage is well bestowed. I'll come to the people in a minute;' and, so saying, he led Miss Ophelia to a large parlor that opened on the verandah.

While this had been passing, Eva had flown like a bird, through the porch and parlor, to a little boudoir opening likewise on the verandah.

A tall, dark-eyed, sallow woman, half rose from a couch on which she was reclining.

'Mamma!' said Eva, in a sort of a rapture, throwing herself on her neck, and embracing her over and over again.

'That'll do, – take care, child, – don't, you make my head ache,' said the mother, after she had languidly kissed her.

St Clare came in, embraced his wife in true, orthodox, husbandly fashion, and then presented to her his cousin. Marie lifted her large eyes on her cousin with an air of some curiosity, and received her with languid politeness. A crowd of servants now pressed to the entry door, and among them a middle-aged mulatto woman, of very respectable appearance, stood foremost, in a tremor of expectation and joy, at the door.

'O, there's Mammy!' said Eva, as she flew across the room; and, throwing herself into her arms, she kissed her repeatedly.

This woman did not tell her that she made her head ache, but, on the contrary, she hugged her, and laughed, and cried, till her sanity was a thing to be doubted of; and when released from her, Eva flew from one to another, shaking hands and kissing, in a way that Miss Ophelia afterwards declared fairly turned her stomach.

'Well!' said Miss Ophelia, 'you southern children can do something that *I* couldn't.'

'What, now, pray?' said St Clare.

'Well, I want to be kind to everybody, and I wouldn't have anything hurt;

but as to kissing –'

'Niggers,' said St Clare, 'that you're not up to, – hey?'

'Yes, that's it. How can she?'

St Clare laughed, as he went into the passage. 'Halloa, here, what's to pay out here? Here, you all – Mammy, Jimmy, Polly, Sukey – glad to see Mas'r?' he said, as he went shaking hands from one to another. 'Look out for the babies!' he added, as he stumbled over a sooty little urchin, who was crawling upon all fours. 'If I step upon anybody, let 'em mention it.'

There was an abundance of laughing and blessing Mas'r, as St Clare distributed small pieces of change among them.

'Come, now, take yourselves off, like good boys and girls,' he said; and the whole assemblage, dark and light, disappeared through a door into a large verandah, followed by Eva, who carried a large satchel, which she had been filling with apples, nuts, candy, ribbons, laces, and toys of every description, during her whole homeward journey.

As St Clare turned to go back his eye fell upon Tom, who was standing uneasily, shifting from one foot to the other, while Adolph stood negligently leaning against the banisters, examining Tom through an opera-glass, with an air that would have done credit to any dandy living.

'Puh! you puppy,' said his master, striking down the opera glass; 'is that the way you treat your company? Seems to me, Dolph,' he added, laying his finger on the elegant figured satin vest that Adolph was sporting, 'seems to me that's my vest.'

'O! Master, this vest all stained with wine; of course, a gentleman in Master's standing never wears a vest like this. I understood I was to take it. It does for a poor nigger-fellow, like me.'

And Adolph tossed his head, and passed his fingers through his scented hair, with a grace.

'So, that's it, is it?' said St Clare, carelessly. 'Well, here, I'm going to show this Tom to his mistress, and then you take him to the kitchen; and mind you don't put on any of your airs to him. He's worth two such puppies as you.'

'Master always will have his joke,' said Adolph, laughing. 'I'm delighted to see Master in such spirits.'

'Here, Tom,' said St Clare, beckoning.

Tom entered the room. He looked wistfully on the velvet carpets, and the before unimagined splendors of mirrors, pictures, statues, and curtains, and, like the Queen of Sheba before Solomon, there was no more spirit in him. He looked afraid even to set his feet down.

'See here, Marie,' said St Clare to his wife, 'I've bought you a coachman, at last, to order. I tell you, he's a regular hearse for blackness and sobriety, and will drive you like a funeral, if you want. Open your eyes, now, and look at him. Now, don't say I never think about you when I'm gone.'

Marie opened her eyes, and fixed them on Tom, without rising.

'I know he'll get drunk,' she said.

'No, he's warranted a pious and sober article.'

'Well, I hope he may turn out well,' said the lady; 'it's more than I expect, though.'

'Dolph,' said St Clare, 'show Tom down stairs; and, mind yourself,' he added; 'remember what I told you.'

Adolph tripped gracefully forward, and Tom, with lumbering tread, went after.

'He's a perfect behemoth!' said Marie.

'Come, now, Marie,' said St Clare, seating himself on a stool beside her sofa, 'be gracious, and say something pretty to a fellow.'

'You've been gone a fortnight beyond the time,' said the lady, pouting.

'Well, you know I wrote you the reason.'

'Such a short, cold letter!' said the lady.

'Dear me! the mail was just going, and it had to be that or nothing.'

'That's just the way, always,' said the lady; 'always something to make your journeys long, and letters short.'

'See here, now,' he added, drawing an elegant velvet case out of his pocket, and opening it, 'here's a present I got for you in New York.'

It was a daguerreotype, clear and soft as an engraving, representing Eva and her father sitting hand in hand.

Marie looked at it with a dissatisfied air.

'What made you sit in such an awkward position?' she said.

'Well, the position may be a matter of opinion; but what do you think of the likeness?'

'If you don't think anything of my opinion in one case, I suppose you wouldn't in another,' said the lady, shutting the daguerreotype.

'Hang the woman!' said St Clare, mentally; but aloud he added, 'Come, now, Marie, what do you think of the likeness? Don't be nonsensical, now.'

'It's very inconsiderate of you, St Clare,' said the lady, 'to insist on my talking and looking at things. You know I've been lying all day with the sick-headache; and there's been such a tumult made ever since you came, I'm half dead.'

'You're subject to the sick-headache, ma'am!' said Miss Ophelia, suddenly rising from the depths of the large arm-chair, where she had sat quietly, taking an inventory of the furniture, and calculating its expense.

'Yes, I'm a perfect martyr to it,' said the lady.

'Juniper-berry tea is good for sick-headache,' said Miss Ophelia; 'at least, Auguste, Deacon Abraham Perry's wife, used to say so; and she was a great nurse.'

'I'll have the first juniper-berries that get ripe in our garden by the lake brought in for that special purpose,' said St Clare, gravely pulling the bell as he did so; 'meanwhile, cousin, you must be wanting to retire to your apartment, and refresh yourself a little, after your journey. Dolph,' he added, 'tell Mammy to come here.' The decent mulatto woman whom Eva had caressed so rapturously soon entered; she was dressed neatly, with a high red and yellow turban on her head, the recent gift of Eva, and which the child had been arranging on her head. 'Mammy,' said St Clare, 'I put this lady under your care; she is tired, and wants rest; take her to her chamber, and be sure she is made comfortable,' and Miss Ophelia disappeared in the rear of Mammy.